Praise for
The Road to Jerusalem

"A great book. . . . Beautifully constructed. . . . Despite the intricate plot, *The Road to Jerusalem* is a surprisingly understated book overall. Skillfully written and translated, it's detailed but sparingly so. . . . [Guillou] has a remarkable grasp of the mindset of the period."　　　　　—Diana Gabaldon, *Washington Post*

"Destined to become a classic, *The Road to Jerusalem* is a brilliant, dramatic re-creation of the medieval world, offering suspense, intrigue, a touching love story, and an extremely appealing young hero. I cannot recommend this book highly enough."

> —Sharon Kay Penman, *New York Times* bestselling author of
> *Devil's Brood*

"It is thrilling and inspiring, bloody and romantic, utterly of the time it is set in, and utterly of the modern. A thoroughly stirring achievement."

> —Tom Holland, author of *Rubicon: The Triumph and
> Tragedy of the Roman Republic*

"A resolutely medieval world—bleak, hidebound, saturated with religious faith, full of both miracles and almost untraceably complex political intrigue—but one shaped with enough compassion and skill to appeal to contemporary readers, who will be eagerly awaiting the next volume of the saga."

> —*Kirkus Reviews*

"The translation is seamless. One never senses a falter or a misstep. *The Road to Jerusalem* tells the story of a young Swedish nobleman who ends up conscripted into the Knights Templar. But this is a thick and engaging novel; I've taken a very short route to tell the story. Guillou's path is much less direct and far more exciting. . . . Fans of historical fiction—particularly those with an interest in Crusades-era material—simply must read *The Road to Jerusalem*."   —JanuaryMagazine.com

"Guillou tells a magnificent story while the reader is swept along in the slow rhythm, the kind of literary adagios, of the text. The setting is superbly depicted, and the novels portray the great seductive ability of the Scandinavian universe."
                              —*El Periodico* (Barcelona)

"This book tells of a Shakespearian quest for power that becomes a metaphor for what is happening in our day and age."
                              —*Corriere della Sera* (Milan)

"This is passionate writing, packed with an incredibly rich historical and political contents."   —*LDC L'Hebdo* (France)

"One of the greatest historical novels to come out of Scandinavia in recent years. Far from being just a costume drama, Jan Guillou's narrative is a spiritual journey, a study of society, and above all the story of his protagonist."
                              —C. Ahl, *Le Monde des Livres* (Paris)

© Ulla Montan

About the Author

Swedish-born journalist JAN GUILLOU is the creator of the two most successful Swedish works of fiction of all time—the Hamilton series and the Crusades Trilogy. His books have been translated into more than twenty languages.

THE ROAD TO
JERUSALEM

THE ROAD TO
JERUSALEM

BOOK ONE OF THE
Crusades Trilogy

JAN GUILLOU

TRANSLATED FROM THE SWEDISH
BY STEVEN T. MURRAY

HARPER

NEW YORK • LONDON • TORONTO • SYDNEY

HARPER

A hardcover edition of this book was published in 2009 by HarperCollins
Publishers.

THE ROAD TO JERUSALEM. Copyright © 1998 by Jan Guillou. English translation
© 2009 by Steven T. Murray. All rights reserved. Printed in the United States
of America. No part of this book may be used or reproduced in any manner
whatsoever without written permission except in the case of brief quotations
embodied in critical articles and reviews. For information address Harper-
Collins Publishers, 10 East 53rd Street, New York, NY 10022.

HarperCollins books may be purchased for educational, business, or sales
promotional use. For information please write: Special Markets Department,
HarperCollins Publishers, 10 East 53rd Street, New York, NY 10022.

FIRST HARPER PAPERBACK PUBLISHED 2010.

The Library of Congress has catalogued the hardcover edition as follows:

Guillou, Jan, 1944–
    [Vägen till Jerusalem / Jan Guillou; translated from the Swedish by
Steven T. Murray. — 1st ed.
        p. cm. — (The Crusades trilogy; bk. 1)
    ISBN 978-0-06-168853-9 (Hardcover)
    ISBN 978-0-06-183286-4 (International Edition)
    1. Västergötland (Sweden)—History—Fiction. I. Murray, Steven T.
II. Title.
PT9876.17.U38V3413 2009
839.73'74--dc22   2008049212

ISBN 978-0-06-168854-6

    12 13 14 OV/RRD 10 9 8 7

The road to hell is paved with good intentions.

—GEORGE HERBERT, *Jacula Prudentum*, NO. 170, 1651

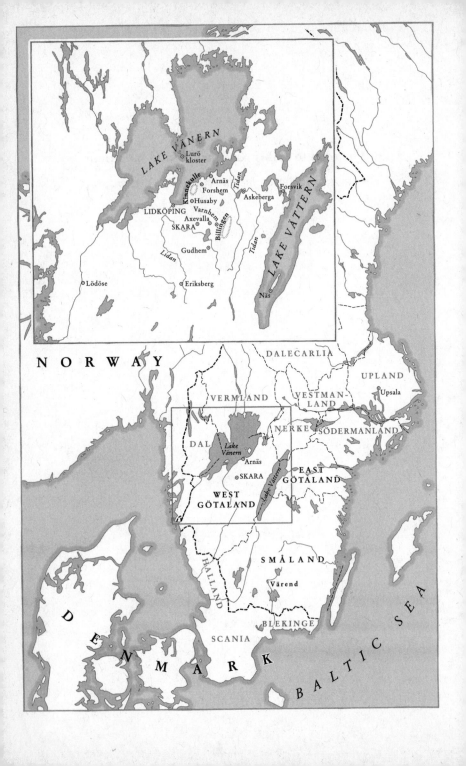

NORWAY

DALECARLIA

UPLAND

VERMLAND

VESTMAN-
LAND

Upsala

DAL

Lake
Vänern

NERKE

SÖDERMANLAND

Arnäs

SKARA

EAST
GÖTALAND

Lake Vättern

WEST
GÖTALAND

SMÅLAND

HALLAND

DENMARK

Värend

BLEKINGE

SCANIA

BALTIC SEA

LAKE VÄNERN

Lurö
kloster

Arnäs

Forshem

Husaby

LIDKÖPING

Varnhem

Axevalla

SKARA

Billingen

Gudhem

Lidan

Lödöse

Eriksberg

Askeberga

Forsvik

LAKE VÄTTERN

Tidan

Tidan

Näs

Kinnekulle

Cast of Primary Characters

THE FOLKUNG CLAN (INCLUDING THE BJÄLBO BRANCH)

Magnus Folkesson, master of Arnäs

Fru Sigrid, first wife of Magnus Folkesson and mother of Eskil and Arn

Erika Joarsdotter, second wife of Magnus Folkesson

Eskil Magnusson, first son of Magnus Folkesson

Arn Magnusson, second son of Magnus Folkesson

Birger Brosa, younger brother of Magnus Folkesson

THE ERIK CLAN

King Erik Jedvardsson, king of Svealand

Joar Jedvardsson, brother of Erik Jedvardsson

Kristina Jedvardsson, wife of Erik Jedvardsson (and kinswoman to Fru Sigrid)

King Knut Eriksson, son of Erik Jedvardsson

THE SVERKER CLAN

King Sverker, king of Eastern Götaland

Queen Ulvhild, first wife of King Sverker

King Karl Sverkersson, son of King Sverker and Ulvhild

Rikissa, second wife of King Sverker

Knut Magnusson, son from Rikissa's first marriage, later king of Denmark

Emund Ulvbane (aka "Emund One-Hand")

Boleslav and Kol, half brothers of King Karl Sverkersson

THE PÅL CLAN

Algot Pålsson, steward of Husaby
Katarina Algotsdotter, older daughter of Algot
Cecilia Algotsdotter, younger daughter of Algot

THE CLERGY (CISTERCIANS FROM FRANCE)

Father Henri de Clairvaux, prior of Varnhem
Brother Guilbert de Beaune, the weapons smith
Brother Lucien de Clairvaux, the gardener
Brother Guy le Breton, the fisherman
Brother Ludwig de Bêtecourt, the music master
Brother Rugiero de Nîmes, the chef
Archbishop Stéphan

THE DANES

King Sven Grate of Denmark
Magnus Henriksen, the king-slayer

Chapter 1

In the year of Grace 1150, when the ungodly Saracens, the scum of the earth and the vanguard of the Antichrist, inflicted many defeats on our forces in the Holy Land, the Holy Spirit descended upon Fru Sigrid and gave her a vision which changed her life.

Perhaps it could also be said that this vision had the effect of shortening her life. What is certain is that she was never the same again. Less certain is what the monk Thibaud wrote much later, that at the very moment the Holy Spirit revealed itself to Sigrid of Arnäs, a new realm was actually created up in the North, which at the end of the era would come to be known as Sweden.

It was at the Feast of St. Tiburtius, the day regarded as the first day of summer, when the ice melts in Western Götaland. Never before had so many people gathered in Skara, since it was no ordinary mass that was now to be celebrated. The new cathedral was going to be consecrated.

The ceremonies were already into their second hour. The procession had made its three circuits around the church, moving with infinite slowness because Bishop Ödgrim was a very old man, shuffling along as if it were his last journey. He also seemed a bit confused, because he had read the first prayer inside the blessed church in the vernacular instead of in Latin:

God, Thou who invisibly preserveth everything
but maketh Thy power visible for the salvation
  of humanity,
take Thy house and rule in this temple,
so that all who gather here to pray
might share in Thy solace and aid.

And God did indeed make His power visible, though whether for the salvation of humanity or for other reasons is unknown. It was a pageant like none ever seen before in all of Western Götaland: there were dazzling colors from the vestments of the bishops in light-blue and dark-red silk with gold thread, there were overpowering fragrances from the censers which the canons swung as they walked about, and there was a music so heavenly that no ear in Western Götaland could ever have heard its like before. And if you raised your eyes it was like looking up into Heaven itself, but under a roof. It was inconceivable that even the Burgundian and English stonemasons could have created such a high vault that would not come crashing down, if for no other reason than that God might be angry at the vanity of attempting to build an edifice that could reach up to Him.

Fru Sigrid was a practical woman. Because of this some people said that she was a hard woman. She had absolutely not wanted to set off on the difficult journey to Skara, since spring had come early and the roads had softened to a sea of mud. She was uneasy at the thought of sitting in a wagon that jolted and bounced and careened back and forth, in her blessed condition. More than anything else in this earthly life, she feared the coming birth of her second child. And she knew very well that if a cathedral was being consecrated, it would mean standing on the hard stone floor for several hours and falling to her knees repeatedly in prayer. She was well versed in the many rules of church life, surely far better than most of the noblemen and their daughters surrounding her just now, but she had not acquired this knowledge through faith or free will. When she was sixteen years old her father, with good reason, took it into his head that she was paying too much attention to a kinsman from Norway of far too low birth, which might have led to something that belonged only within the sacrament of marriage, as her father gruffly summed up the problem. So she had been sent away for five years to a convent in Norway. She probably never would have been released if she hadn't come into an inheritance from a childless uncle in Eastern Götaland; thus she became a woman to be married off instead of languishing in a convent.

So she knew when to stand and when to kneel, when to rattle off the Pater Nosters and Ave Marias which some of the bishops at the altar were intoning, and when to say her own prayers. Each time she had to say her own prayer, she prayed for her life.

God had given her a son three years before. It had taken two days and nights to give birth to him; twice the sun had gone up and gone down again while she was bathed in sweat, anguish, and pain. She knew she was going to die, and in the end all the good women helping her knew it too. They had sent for the priest in Forshem, and he had given her extreme unction and forgiveness for her sins.

Never again, she had hoped. Never again such pain, such terror of death, she now prayed. It was a selfish thing to ask, she knew that. It was common for women to die in childbed, and a human being is born in pain. But she had made the mistake of praying to the Holy Virgin to spare her, and she had tried to fulfill her marital duties in such a way that they would not lead to another childbed. Their son, Eskil, had lived after all.

The Holy Virgin had punished her, of course. New torments now awaited her, that was certain. And yet she prayed over and over to come through it easily.

To lighten the lesser but irksome nuisance of standing and kneeling, standing up and then kneeling down again, for hours on end, she'd had her thrall woman Sot baptized so that she could come along into God's house. She had Sot stand next to her, and she leaned on the thrall when she had to get up and down. Sot's big black eyes were open wide like terrified horse's eyes, staring at everything she now observed. If she wasn't a real Christian before then she ought to have become one by now.

Three man-lengths in front of Sigrid stood King Sverker and Queen Ulvhild. The two of them, both weighed down by age, were having more and more trouble standing up and kneeling down without too much puffing. Yet it was for their sake and not for God's that Sigrid was in the cathedral. King Sverker held neither her Norwegian and Western Götaland kinsmen nor her husband's Norwegian and Folkung lineage in high esteem. But now, at his advanced age, the king had grown both suspicious and anxious about his life after this earthly one. Missing the king's great and blessed church dedication might have caused a misunderstanding. If a man or woman offended God in some way, that matter might be taken up with God Himself. Sigrid considered it worse to be on the wrong side of the king.

But during the third hour Sigrid's head began to swim, and she was having more and more trouble kneeling down and getting up again. The child inside her kicked and stirred all the more, as if in protest. She had the feeling that the pale-yellow, polished marble floor was undulating beneath her. She thought she saw it begin to crack, as if it might suddenly open up and swallow her whole. Then she did something quite outrageous. She walked resolutely, silk skirts rustling, over to a little empty bench off to the side and sat down. Everyone saw it, the king too.

Just as she sank with relief onto the stone bench next to the church wall in the middle of the side aisle, the monks from the island of Lurö came filing in. Sigrid wiped her brow and face with a small linen handkerchief and gave her son, standing next to Sot, an encouraging wave.

Then the monks began to sing. Silently and with bowed heads they walked up the entire length of the center aisle and took their places by the altar, where the bishops and their acolytes now drew aside. At first it sounded like a muffled, soft murmur, but then the high voices of the boys joined in. Some of the Lurö monks had brown cowls, not white, and were quite clearly young boys. Their voices rose like ethereal birds up to the huge vaults of the ceiling. When their singing had risen so high that it filled the entire enormous space, the low voices of the monks themselves joined in, singing the same melody and yet not the same. Sigrid had heard psalms sung in both two and three voices, but this had at least eight different parts. It was like a miracle, something that could not happen, since even a three-part psalm was difficult to master.

Exhausted, Sigrid stared wide-eyed in the direction of the miracle, listening with her entire being, her entire body. She began to tremble with excitement. Blackness fell over her eyes, and she no longer saw but only heard, as if her eyes too had to lend their powers to her hearing. She seemed to vanish, as if she were transmuted into tones, into a part of the holy music, more beautiful than any music ever heard in this earthly life.

A while later she came to her senses when someone took her by the hand, and when she looked up she discovered King Sverker himself.

He patted her gently on the hand and thanked her with a wry

smile because he, as an old man, was in need of a woman with child who would be the first to sit down. If a blessed woman could do so, then so too could the king, he said. It would not have looked proper for him to go first.

Sigrid firmly suppressed the idea of telling him that the Holy Spirit had just spoken to her. It seemed to her that such an admission would merely seem as if she were boasting, and kings saw more than enough of that, at least until someone chopped off their heads. Instead she quickly whispered an idea that had come to her.

As the king no doubt already knew, there was a dispute over her inheritance of Varnhem. Her kinswoman Kristina, who had recently married that upstart Erik Jedvardsson, was laying claim to half the property. But the monks on the island of Lurö needed to live in a region with less severe winters. Much of their farming had been in vain out there, and everyone knew it; not to disparage King Sverker's great generosity in donating Lurö to them. But if she, Sigrid, now donated Varnhem to the Cistercian monks, the king could bless the gift and declare it legal, and the whole problem would be resolved. Everyone would gain.

She had been speaking quickly, in a low voice, and a little breathlessly, her heart still pounding after what she had witnessed in the heavenly music after the darkness turned to light.

The king seemed a bit taken aback at first; he was hardly used to people near him speaking so directly, without courtly circumlocutions. Especially women.

"You are a blessed woman in more than one respect, my dear Sigrid," he said at last, taking her hand again. "Tomorrow when we have slept our fill in the royal palace after today's feast, I shall summon Father Henri, and we will take care of this entire matter. Tomorrow, not now. It's not proper for us to sit here together for very long, whispering."

With the wave of a hand she had now given away her inheritance, Varnhem. No man could break his word to the king, nor any woman either, just as the king may never break his word. What she had done could not be undone.

But it was also practical, she realized when she had recovered a bit. The Holy Spirit could indeed be practical, and the ways of the Lord were not always inscrutable.

Varnhem and Arnäs lay a good two days' ride from each other. Varnhem was outside Skara, not far from the bishop's estate near Billingen Mountain. Arnäs was up in the north of the region, on the eastern shore of Lake Vänern, where the forest Sunnanskog ended and the woods of Tiveden began, near Kinnekulle Mountain. The Varnhem estate was newer and in much better condition, which is why she wanted to spend the coldest part of the year there, especially as the dreaded childbed approached. Magnus, her husband, wanted them to take his ancestral estate Arnäs as their abode, while she preferred Varnhem, and they had not been able to agree. At times they could not even discuss the subject in a friendly, patient manner as befitted a husband and wife.

Arnäs needed to be repaired and rebuilt. But it lay in the unclaimed borderlands along the edge of the forest; there was a great deal of common land and royal land that could be acquired by trade or purchase. Much could be improved, especially if she moved all her thralls and livestock from Varnhem.

This was not precisely the way the Holy Spirit had expressed the matter when He revealed Himself to her. She had seen a vision that was not altogether clear: a herd of beautiful horses shimmering in many colors like mother-of-pearl. The horses had come running toward her in a meadow covered with flowers. Their manes were white and pure, their tails were raised haughtily, and they moved as playfully and lithely as cats. They were graceful in all their movements, not wild but not free either, since these horses belonged to her. And somewhere behind the gamboling, frisky, unsaddled horses came a young man riding on a silver stallion. It too had a white mane and raised tail. She knew the young man and yet did not. He carried a shield but wore no helmet. She didn't recognize the coat of arms from any of her own kinsmen or her husband's; the shield was completely white with a large blood-red cross, nothing more.

The young man reined in his horse right next to her and spoke to her. She heard all the words and understood them, and yet did not grasp their import. But she knew what they meant—she should give God the gift that was now needed most of all in the country where King Sverker ruled: a good place for the monks of Lurö to live. And Varnhem was a very good place.

✠

When she came out onto the steps of the cathedral her head cleared with the cold, fresh air. She understood with sudden insight, almost as if the Holy Spirit was still upon her, how she would tell all this to her husband, who was coming toward her in the crowd carrying their cloaks over his arm. She regarded him with a cautious smile, utterly confident. She was fond of him because he was a gentle husband and a considerate father, although not a man to be respected or admired. It was hard to believe he was actually the grandson of a man who was his direct opposite, the powerful jarl Folke the Stout. Magnus was a slender man, and if he hadn't been wearing foreign clothes he might be taken for anyone in the crowd.

When he came up to Sigrid he bowed and asked her to hold her own cloak while he first swung his large, sky-blue cloak lined with marten fur around him and fastened it under his chin with the silver clasp from Norway. Then he helped her with her cloak and tentatively caressed her brow with his soft hands, which were not the hands of a warrior. He asked her how she had managed to stand for such a long praise-song to the Lord in her blessed state. She replied that it hadn't been any trouble, because she had brought Sot along to serve as support, and because the Holy Spirit had granted her a revelation. She spoke in the way she did when she wasn't being serious. He smiled, thinking it was one of her usual jokes, and then looked around for his man who was bringing his sword from the church entryway.

When Magnus swept his sword in under his cloak and began fastening its scabbard, both his elbows jutted out, making him look broad and mighty in a way that she knew he was not. Then he offered Sigrid his arm and they made their way carefully through the crowd, where the most distinguished churchgoers now mixed with the common folk and thralls. In the middle of the marketplace Frankish acrobats were performing, along with a man who spit fire; pipes and fiddles were being played, and muffled drums could be heard over by one of the large ale tents. After a while Sigrid took a deep breath and bluntly told him everything at once.

"Magnus, my dear husband, I hope you'll take it with manly calm and dignity when you hear what I've just done," she began, taking another deep breath and continuing quickly before he could reply. "I have given my word to King Sverker that I will donate Varnhem to the Cistercian monks of Lurö. I can't take back my word to a king, it's irreversible. We're going to meet him tomorrow at the royal estate to have the promise written out and sealed."

As she expected, he stopped short to give her a searching glance, looking for the smile she always wore when she was teasing him in her own special way. But he soon realized that she was completely serious, and then anger overcame him with such force that he probably would have struck her for the first time if they hadn't been standing in the midst of kinsmen and enemies and all the common folk.

"Have you lost your wits, woman? If you hadn't inherited Varnhem you'd still be withering away in the convent. It was only because of Varnhem that we were married at all."

He managed to control himself and speak in a low voice, but with his teeth firmly clenched.

"Yes, all that is true, my dear husband," she replied with her eyes lowered chastely. "If I hadn't inherited Varnhem, your parents would have chosen another wife for you. I would have been a nun by now in that case. But Eskil and the new life I'm carrying under my heart would not have existed without Varnhem."

Magnus did not reply. Just then Sot approached them with Eskil, who ran to his mother at once and took her hand, chattering excitedly about everything he had seen inside the cathedral.

Magnus lifted his son in his arms and stroked his hair lovingly as he regarded his lawful wife with something other than affection. But then he put the boy down and barked at Sot to take Eskil with her to watch the players; they would join her again soon. Sot took the boy by the hand and led him off whining and protesting.

"But as you also know, my dear husband," Sigrid resumed quickly, "I wanted Varnhem to be my bridal morning gift, and I had that gift deeded to me under seal, along with little more than the cloak on my back and some gold for my adornment."

"Yes, that is also true," replied Magnus sullenly. "But even so, Varnhem is one-third of our common property, a third that you have now taken from Eskil. What I can't understand is why you would do something like this, even though it is within your right."

"Let's stroll over toward the players and not stand here looking as if we might be quarreling with each other, and I'll explain everything." She offered him her arm.

Magnus looked around self-consciously, forced a smile, and took her by the arm.

"All right," she said hesitantly. "Let's begin with earthly matters, which seem to be filling your head the most right now. I will take all the livestock and thralls with me up to Arnäs, of course. Varnhem does have better buildings, but Arnäs is something we can rebuild from the ground up, especially now that we'll have so many more hands to put to work. This way we'll have a better place to live, particularly in the wintertime. More livestock means more barrels of salted meat and more hides that we can send to Lödöse by boat. You want so much to trade with Lödöse, and we can easily do so from Arnäs in both summer and winter, but it would be difficult from Varnhem."

Leaning forward, he walked silently by her side, but she could see that he had calmed down and was starting to listen with interest. She knew that they wouldn't have to argue now. She saw everything as clearly before her as if she had spent a long time planning it all out, although the whole idea was less than an hour old.

More leather hides and barrels of salted meat for Lödöse meant more silver, and more silver meant they could buy more seed. More seed meant that more thralls could earn their freedom by breaking new ground, borrowing seed, and paying them back twofold in rye that could be sent to Lödöse and exchanged for more silver. And then they could repair the fortifications that Magnus was always worrying about, since Arnäs was difficult to defend, especially in the frost of winter. By gathering all their forces at Arnäs instead of dividing their efforts between two places, they would soon grow richer and own even more land with all the newly broken ground. They would have a warmer, safer house, and leave a larger inheritance to Eskil than they could have otherwise.

When they had made their way to the front of the crowd, Magnus stood silent and pensive for a long time. Out of breath, Sot appeared with little Eskil in her arms; she held him up in front of her so that people could see from his clothing that she had the right to push through the crowd. Then the boy jumped down and stood in front of his mother, who gently laid her hands on his shoulders, stroked his cheek, and straightened his cap.

The players in front of them were busy building a high tower composed of nothing but people, with a little boy, perhaps only a couple of years older than Eskil, climbing alone to the very top. The people shouted in fear and amazement. Eskil pointed eagerly and said he wanted to be a performer too, which made his father break out in surprisingly hearty laughter. Sigrid glanced at him cautiously and thought that with that laughter the danger had passed.

He noticed her sneaking a glance at him and kept laughing as he bent forward and kissed her on the cheek.

"You are truly a remarkable woman, Sigrid," he whispered with no anger in his voice. "I've thought over what you said, and you're right about everything. If we gather all our forces at Arnäs we *will* grow richer. How could any merchant have a better, more faithful wife than you?"

With downcast eyes she replied at once, softly, that no wife could ever have a kinder, more understanding husband than she did. But then she raised her glance, gazed at him gravely, and admitted that she'd had a vision in the church; all her ideas must have come from the Holy Spirit Himself, even the clever part that had to do with business.

Magnus looked a little cross, as if he didn't really believe her, almost as if she were making fun of the Holy Spirit. He was much more devout than she was, and they both knew it. Her years in the convent had not softened her in the least.

When the players finished their performance they went off to the ale tent to collect their free ale and the well-turned piece of roast they had earned. Magnus picked up his son and walked with Sigrid at his side, with Sot ten respectful paces behind, and headed for the town gate; on the other side of the fence their wagons and retainers were waiting. On the way Sigrid told him about the vision that she'd had. She also offered her interpretation of the holy message.

It was well known that a difficult childbirth was often followed by another difficult one, and soon it would be time again. But by donating Varnhem she was ensured many prayers of intercession, and by men who were particularly knowledgeable about such prayers. She and the new child would be allowed to live.

More important, of course, was that their united lineages would now grow stronger as the power and wealth of the Arnäs estate increased. The only thing she was unsure of was who the young man might be on the silver horse with the thick white mane, its long white tail raised boldly in the air. Probably not the Holy Bridegroom, at any rate. He wouldn't be likely to appear riding on a frisky stallion and carrying a shield on his arm.

Magnus was intrigued by the conundrum and pondered it a while; he began interrogating her about the size of the horses and the way they moved. Then he protested that such horses probably did not exist, and he wondered what she meant by saying that the shield had a cross of blood on it. In that case it would indeed be a red cross, but how could she know it was blood and not merely red paint?

She replied that she simply knew. The cross was red, and of blood. The shield was all white. She hadn't seen much of the young man's clothing because his shield concealed his breast, but he was wearing white garments. White, just like the Cistercians, but he was definitely no monk because he bore the shield of a warrior.

With interest Magnus asked about the shape and size of the shield, but when he found out it was heart-shaped and only big enough to protect the chest, he shook his head in disbelief and explained that he had never seen a shield like that. Shields were either big and round, like those once used when venturing out on Viking raids, or they were long and triangular so that warriors could move easily when gathered in a phalanx. A shield as small as the one she had seen in the vision would be more trouble than protection if anyone tried to use it in battle.

But no ordinary person could expect to understand everything in a revelation. And in the evening they would pray together, grateful that the Mother of God had showed them her kindness and wisdom.

Sigrid sighed, feeling great relief and serenity. Now the worst was over, and all that was left was to cajole the old king so that he wouldn't pass off her gift as his own. Since the king had grown old, people had begun to worry about the number of daily prayers of intercession offered on his behalf; he had already founded two cloisters to ensure this would be done for him. Everyone knew about this, his friends as well as his enemies.

King Sverker had a ferocious hangover and was in a rage when Sigrid and Magnus entered the great hall of the royal palace. The king now had to settle a good day's worth of decisions about everything, from how the thieves caught at the market the day before were to be executed—whether they should just be hanged or tortured first—to questions regarding disputes about land and inheritance that could not be resolved at a regular *ting*, the assembly of noblemen.

What made him more cross than the hangover was the day's news about his next youngest son, the scoundrel, who had deceived him in a deplorable way. His son Johan had left on a plundering raid to the province of Halland in Denmark; that in itself was probably not so dangerous. Young men were liable to do such things if they wanted to gamble with their lives instead of just playing at dice. But Johan had lied about the two women he had abducted and brought home to thralldom, claiming they were foreign women he had kidnapped at random. But now a letter had arrived from the Danish king, unfortunately claiming something quite different, which no one doubted. The two women were the wife of the Danish king's jarl in Halland and her sister. It was an affront and an outrage, and anyone who was not the son of a king would have been executed at once for such a crime. The king had reprimanded him, of course. But it wasn't enough to send back the women as blithely as they had been stolen. It was going to cost a great deal of silver, no matter what; in the worst case they might have a war on their hands.

King Sverker and his closest advisers had become embroiled in such a quarrel that everyone in the hall was soon aware of the whole story. The only thing that was certain was that the women had to be returned. But agreement ended there. Some thought it would be a sign of weakness to make payments in silver; it might give the Danish king, Sven Grate, the incentive to invade, plunder, and seize land. Others thought that even a great deal of silver would be less costly than being invaded and plundered, no matter who the victor might be in such a war.

After a long, exhaustive argument the king suddenly gave a weary sigh and turned to Father Henri de Clairvaux, who sat waiting at the far end of the hall for the Lurö case to be presented.

The priest's head was bowed as if in prayer, with his white cowl drawn over his face so no one could see whether he was praying or sleeping, although the latter was more likely. In any case, Father Henri hadn't been able to follow the heated discussion, and when he replied to the king's summons it sounded like Latin. As there was no other clergyman present, no one understood. The king looked angrily around the hall; red in the face, he roared, "Bring me some devil who can understand this snooty cleric language!"

Sigrid instantly saw her opportunity. She stood up and walked forward in the hall with her head bowed, curtseying deferentially first to King Sverker and then to Father Henri.

"My king, I am at your service," she said and stood waiting for his decision.

"If there is no man here who speaks that language, then so be it," the king sighed wearily again. "By the way, how is it that you speak it, Sigrid, my dear?" he added more kindly.

"I'm afraid I must admit that the only thing I really learned during my banishment to the cloister was Latin," replied Sigrid demurely. Magnus was the only man in the hall who noticed her mocking smile; she often spoke in this manner, saying one thing but meaning another.

The king promptly asked Sigrid to sit down next to Father Henri, explain the situation to him, and then ask for his view of the matter. She obeyed at once, and while she and Father Henri began a hushed conversation in the language which they alone understood among all the people in the hall, a mood of embarrassment began to spread. The men looked querulously at one another, some shrugged their shoulders, some demonstratively folded their hands and raised their eyes to heaven. A woman in the king's court among all these good men? But so be it. What was already done could not be undone.

After a while Sigrid stood up. To quiet the muttering in the hall, she explained in a loud voice that Father Henri had considered the matter and now believed that the wisest thing to do would be to force the blackguard to marry the sister of the jarl's wife. But the jarl's wife must be sent home with gifts and fine clothing, with banners and fanfare. King Sverker and his scoundrel son would thus have to refuse a dowry, so the question of silver was solved. No consideration could be given to what the knave himself thought; if he and the sister of the jarl's wife could be married, the blood bond would prevent a war. But the rascal would have to do something to pay for his roguish behavior. War would still be the most costly solution.

When Sigrid fell silent and sat down, it was quiet at first while those assembled considered the implications of the monk's proposal. But gradually a murmur of approval spread. Someone unsheathed his sword and slammed the broadside hard on the heavy tabletop that ran along both sides of the hall. Others followed his example and soon the hall was booming with the clamor of weapons. And so the matter was decided for the time being.

King Sverker now decided to deal with the question of Varnhem at once. He waved over a scribe, who began to read aloud the document the king had ordered drawn up to confirm the matter before the law. According to the text, however, it sounded as if the gift came from the king alone.

Sigrid asked to see the document so that she could translate it for Father Henri, but she also suggested cautiously that perhaps Herr Magnus should take part in the ensuing discussion. "Certainly, certainly," said the king with a wave of dismissal, and he gestured to Magnus to step forward in the hall and take a seat next to his wife.

Sigrid quickly translated the document for Father Henri, who leaned his head back and tried to follow along in the text as Sigrid pointed. When she was ready she added hastily, so it looked as if she were still translating, that the gift was from her and not from the king, but that according to the law she needed the king's approval. Father Henri gave her a brief glance and a smile resembling her own, then nodded pensively.

"Well," said the king impatiently, as if he wanted to dispose of the matter quickly, "does the Reverend Father Henri have anything to say or suggest in this matter?"

Sigrid translated the question, looking the monk straight in the eye, and he had no trouble understanding her intentions.

"Hmm," he began cautiously, "it is a blessed deed to give to the most assiduous workers in His garden. But before God as before the law, a gift may be accepted only when one is quite certain who is the donor and who is the recipient. Is this His Majesty's own property which we will now so generously share?"

He waved his hand in a little circle as a sign to Sigrid to translate. She reeled off the translation in a monotone.

The king was clearly embarrassed and gave Father Henri a dark look, while Father Henri gazed at the king in a friendly manner, as if he assumed everything was in order. Sigrid said not a word, waiting.

"Yes, perhaps . . . perhaps," muttered the king self-consciously. "One might say that for the sake of the law the gift must come from the king, so that no one will be able to complain about the matter. But the gift also comes from Fru Sigrid who is here among us."

While the king hesitated, Sigrid translated what he had just said, in the same formal, monotonous voice as before. Father Henri's face brightened as if in friendly surprise when he now heard what he already knew. Then he shook his head slowly with a smile and explained, in quite simple words but with all the serpentine courtliness required when admonishing a king, that before God it would probably be more suitable to cleave to the whole truth even in formal documents. So if this letter were now drawn up again with the name of the actual donor, and with His Majesty's approval and confirmation of the gift, then the matter would be settled and prayers of intercession could be duly vouchsafed to His Majesty as well as to the donor herself.

And so the matter was decided in just this way, precisely as Sigrid had wished. Nothing else was possible for King Sverker;

he quickly made the decision, adding that the letter should be drafted in both the vernacular and Latin; he would affix his seal to it that very day. And perhaps now they could cheer themselves up a bit by returning to the question of how and when the executions were to take place.

In Father Henri and Fru Sigrid, two souls had found each other. Or two human beings on earth with quite similar outlooks and intelligence.

The question of Varnhem was thus decided, at least for now.

✠

Around the Feast of Filippus and Jakob, the day when the grass should be green and lush enough to let out the livestock to graze and when the fences had to be inspected, Sigrid was gripped by fright as if a cold hand had seized her heart. She felt that her time had come. But the pain vanished so quickly that it must have been her imagination.

She had been walking with little Eskil, holding his hand, heading down to the stream where the monks and their lay brothers were busy raising a huge mill wheel into position, using block and tackle and many draft animals.

Sigrid had spent a great deal of time at the building sites. Father Henri had patiently walked her through all of the plans. And she had taken two of her best thralls with her, Svarte, who was Sot's fecundator, and Gur, who had left his wife and brood up in Arnäs. Sigrid carefully translated into their language what Father Henri had described.

Magnus had complained that she still didn't have any employment for the best thralls, at least not the male ones, down at Varnhem. They should have been busy on the construction work up at Arnäs. But Sigrid had stood firm, explaining that there were many useful things to be learned from the Burgundian lay brothers and the English stonemasons Father Henri had engaged. As so often before, she had pushed her will through, although it was difficult to explain to a man from Western Götaland that the foreigners were much better builders than local workers.

In only a few months Varnhem had been transformed into a huge construction site, with the echo of hammer blows, the noise of saws, and the creaking and rattling of the big sandstone grinding wheels. There was life and movement everywhere. At first glance it might look frenzied and chaotic, like looking down into an anthill in the spring, when the ants seem to be running amok. But there were precise plans behind everything that was being done. The steward was an enormous monk named Guilbert de Beaune. He was the only monk who joined in the work himself; otherwise the brown-robed lay brothers took care of all the manual labor. It might be said that Brother Lucien de Clairvaux also broke this rule. He was the cloister's head gardener, and he refused to entrust the sensitive planting to anyone else. It was a bit late in the year to be planting and difficult to do it successfully without the right touch or the right eye for the task.

The other monks, who had taken over the longhouse for the time being as both residence and chapel, busied themselves primarily with spiritual matters or with writing.

After some time Sigrid had volunteered both Svarte and Gur to help the lay brothers; her thought was that the two should initially become apprentices rather than offer any particular help. Some of the lay brothers had come to Father Henri and complained that the boorish and untrained thralls were too clumsy at their tasks. But Father Henri waved aside such complaints because he understood full well Sigrid's intentions for these apprentices. In fact, he had spoken in private with Brother Guilbert about the matter. To the vexation of many lay brothers, just as Svarte and Gur began to learn enough to be helpful at one work site, they would be sent on to the next, where the fumbling and foolish incompetence would begin anew. Cutting and polishing stone, shaping red-hot iron, fashioning waterwheels from oak pieces, lining a well or canal with stone, weeding garden plots, chopping down oak and beech trees and shaping the logs for various purposes: soon the two burly thralls had learned the basics of most tasks. Sigrid queried them about their progress and made plans for how they might be used in the future. She envisioned that they would both be able to work their way to freedom; only someone who knew how to do something of value could support himself as a freedman. Their faith and salvation interested her less, in fact. She had not coerced any of her thralls except Sot to be baptized, and that was only because of her special need for support on the church floor when the cathedral was being consecrated.

It had been a peaceful time. As mistress of a household Sigrid hadn't had as much to do as she would have had as Varnhem's owner, or if she had to be responsible for all the farm work up at Arnäs. She tried to think as little as possible about the inevitable, what would come to her as surely as death came to everyone, thralls and people alike. Since the longhouse was not consecrated as a cloister, she could participate whenever she liked in any of the five daily prayers held by the monks. The more time passed, the more assiduously she had taken part in the prayer hours. She always prayed for the same things: her life and that of her child, and that she might receive strength and courage from the Holy Virgin and be spared the pain she had endured the last time.

Now she walked with cold sweat on her brow, softly and gingerly as if she might call forth the pain with movements that were too strenuous. She was headed away from the construction noise, up toward the manor. She called Sot over to her and did not have to tell her what was wrong. Sot nodded, grunting in her laconic language, and hurried off toward the cookhouse where she and the other thrall women began preparing for dinner. They quickly carried out everything that had to do with baking bread and cooking meat, swept and mopped the floor clean, and then brought in straw beds and fur rugs from the little house where Sigrid stored all her own supplies. When all was ready and Sigrid was about to lie down inside, she felt a second wave of pain, which was so much worse than the first that she went white in the face and collapsed. She had to be led to the bed in the middle of the floor. The thrall women had blown more life into the flames, and in great haste they cleaned tripod kettles, which they filled with water and set over the fire.

When the pain subsided, Sigrid asked Sot to fetch Father Henri and then see to it that Eskil was kept with the other children a good distance away, so that he would not have to hear his mother's screams, if it should come to that. But someone would also have to watch the children so they wouldn't come too close to the perilous mill wheel, which more than anything else seemed to arouse their curiosity. The children should not be left unattended.

She lay alone for a while and looked out through the smoke vent in the roof and the large open window in one wall. Outside the birds were singing—the finches that sang in the daytime before the thrushes took over and made all the other birds fall silent in shame.

Her brow was sweating, but she was shivering with cold. One of her thrall women shyly approached and stroked her forehead with a moist linen cloth but didn't dare look her in the eye.

Magnus had admonished her to send for good women from Skara when her time was nearing, and not to give birth among thrall women. But he was just a man, after all. He wouldn't understand that the thrall women, who were accustomed to breeding more often than others, had a good knowledge of what needed to be done. They didn't have white skin, elegant speech,

or courtly manners, like the women Magnus would have preferred, who would have filled the room with their chatter and
flighty bustling. The thrall women were knowledgeable enough
to suffice, if indeed mortal help alone would be enough. The
Holy Virgin Mary would either help or not help, regardless of
the souls that were in the room.

The thrall women did have souls like other people; Father
Henri had told her as much in strong and convincing terms. And
in the Kingdom of Heaven there were no freedmen or slaves,
wealthy or lowborn, only the souls who had proved themselves
worthy through acts of goodness. Sigrid thought that this might
well be true.

When Father Henri came into the room she saw that he had
his prayer vestments with him. He had understood what kind
of help she now sought. But at first he didn't let on, nor did he
bother to chase out the thrall women who were rushing around
sweeping, or who came running in with fresh buckets of water,
and linen and swaddling clothes.

"Greetings, honorable Mistress Sigrid, I understand that now
we are nearing an hour of joy here at Varnhem," said Father
Henri, his expression calmer and more kindly than his voice.

"Or an hour of woe, Father, we won't know until it's over,"
whimpered Sigrid, staring at him with eyes full of terror as she
felt more pain on its way. But she was just imagining it; none
came.

Father Henri pulled over a little three-legged stool to her
bedside and reached out a hand to her. He held her hand and
stroked it.

"You're a clever woman," he said, "the only one I've met in
this temporal world who has the wit to speak Latin, and you also
understand many other things, like teaching the thralls what we
know how to do. So tell me, why should what awaits you be so
unusual, when all other women go through it? Highborn women

like yourself, thralls and wretched women, thousands upon thousands of others. Just think, at this very moment you are not alone on this earth. As we speak, at this moment, you are together with ten thousand women the world over. So tell me, why should *you* have anything to fear, more than all the others?"

He had spoken well, using a sermon-like tone, and Sigrid thought he had probably been thinking about this for days—the first words he would say to her when the hour of dread approached. She couldn't help smiling when she looked at him, and he saw by her smile that she had seen through him.

"You speak well, Father Henri," she said in a weak voice. "But of those ten thousand women you speak of, almost half will be dead tomorrow, and I could be one of them."

"Then I would have a hard time understanding Our Sàvior," said Father Henri calmly, still smiling with his eyes, which remained fixed on hers.

"There is something Our Savior does that you still don't understand, Father?" she whispered as she braced herself in anticipation of the next contraction.

"That's true, of course," nodded Father Henri. "There are even things that our founder, Holy Saint Bernard de Clairvaux, doesn't understand. Such as the terrible defeats our knights are now suffering in the Holy Land. He wants more than anyone for us to send more men; he wants nothing more than victory for our righteous cause against the infidels. And yet we were beaten badly, despite our strong faith, despite our good cause, despite the fact that we are fighting against evil. So of course it's true that we human beings cannot always understand Our Savior."

"I want to have time to confess," she whispered.

Father Henri chased out the thrall women, pulled on his prayer vestments, and blessed her. Then he was ready to hear her confession.

"Father forgive me, for I have sinned," she gasped with fear

shining in her eyes. She had to take a few deep breaths and collect herself before continuing.

"I've had ungodly thoughts, worldly thoughts. I gave Varnhem to you and yours not only because the Holy Spirit told me
that it was a right and just cause. I also hoped that with this gift I
would be able to appease the Mother of God because in foolishness and selfishness I had asked her to spare me from more child-
beds, even though I know it's our duty to populate the earth."

She had been talking low and fast, waiting for the next jab of
pain, which struck just as she finished speaking. Her face con-
torted and she bit her lip to keep from screaming.

Father Henri got up and fetched a linen cloth, dipping it in
cold water in a pail by the door. He went to her, raised her head,
and began bathing her face and brow.

"It is true, my child," he whispered, leaning forward to her
cheek and feeling her fiery fear, "that God's grace cannot be
bought for money, that it's a great sin both to sell and buy what
only God can bestow. It's also true that you in your mortal
weakness have felt fear and have asked the Mother of God for
aid and consolation. But that is no sin. And as far as the gift of
Varnhem is concerned, it was prompted by the Holy Spirit descending upon you and giving you a vision which you were ready
to accept. Nothing in your will can be stronger than His will,
which you have obeyed. I forgive you in the name of the Father,
the Son, and the Holy Spirit. You are now without sin and I will
leave you so, for I must go and pray."

He carefully laid her head back down and could see that
somewhere deep inside her pain she seemed relieved. Then he
left quickly and brusquely ordered the women back into the
house; they rushed in like a flock of black birds.

But Sot stayed where she was and tugged cautiously on his
robe, saying something that he didn't understand at first, since
neither of them was fluent in the common Swedish speech. She

renewed her effort, speaking very slowly, and supplementing her words with gestures. It then dawned on him that she had a secret potion made of forbidden herbs that could alleviate pain; the thralls used to give it to their own who were about to be whipped, maimed, or gelded.

He looked down at the diminutive woman's dark face as he pondered. He knew quite well that she was baptized, so he must talk to her as if she were one of his flock. He also knew that what she told him might be true: Lucien de Clairvaux, who took care of all the garden cultivation, had many recipes that could achieve the same effect. But there was a risk that the potion the thrall woman spoke of had been created using sorcery and evil powers.

"Listen to me, woman," he said slowly and as clearly as he could. "I'm going to ask a man who knows. If I come back, then give drink. No come back, no give drink. Swear before God to obey me!"

Sot swore obediently before her new God, and Father Henri hurried off to converse with Brother Lucien first, before he gathered all the brothers to pray for their benefactress.

A short time later he spoke to Brother Lucien, who vehemently rejected the idea in fright. Such potions were very strong; they could be used for those who were wounded, dying, or for medicinal purposes when an arm or foot had to be amputated. But on pain of death one must not give such a potion to a woman giving birth, for then one would be giving it to the child as well, who might be born forever lame or confused. As soon as the child was born, of course, it would be permitted. Although by that time it was usually no longer necessary. But it could be interesting to hear what that painkilling potion was composed of; perhaps one might gain some new ideas.

Father Henri nodded shamefully. He should have known all this, even though he specialized in writing, theology, and music, not medicine or horticulture. He hurriedly gathered the brothers to begin a very long hour of prayer.

For the time being, Sot had decided to obey the monk, even though she thought it was a shame not to lighten her mistress's suffering. She now took charge of the other women in the room, and they pulled Sigrid out of bed, let down her hair so it flowed free: long, shiny, and almost as black as Sot's own hair. They washed her as she shivered with cold, and then pulled a new linen shift over her head and made her walk about the room, to hasten the birth.

Through a fog of fear, Sigrid staggered around the floor between two of her thrall women. She felt ashamed, like a cow being led about at market. She heard the bell chime from the longhouse but was unsure if it was only her imagination.

The next wave of pain hit; it started deeper inside her body, and she could feel that it would last longer this time. Then she screamed, more from terror than pain, and sank down on the bed. One of the thrall women held Sigrid under the arms from behind and lifted her body upward, while they all shrieked at once that she had to help, she had to push. But she didn't dare push. She must have fainted.

When the twilight turned to night and the thrushes fell silent, a stillness seemed to come over Sigrid. The pains that had come so often in the last few hours seemed to have stopped.

Sot and all the others knew this was an ominous sign. Something had to be done. Sot took one of the others with her and they padded out into the night, sneaking past the longhouse where the murmuring and singing of the monks could be heard faintly through the thick walls, and on to the barn. They brought out a young ram with a leather rope around its neck and led it away in the falling darkness toward the forbidden grove. There they bound the rope around one rear hoof and slung the other end over one of the huge oak branches in the grove. As Sot pulled on the rope so that the ram hung with one hind leg in the air, the other thrall woman fell upon the animal. She grabbed it around the shoulders, and forced the animal toward the ground with all her weight, as she drew out a knife and slit its throat. They both hoisted up the struggling, screeching ram, as blood sprayed in all directions. After they tied the rope to a root of the tree, they stripped off their shifts and stood naked beneath the shower of blood and smeared it into their hair, over their breasts, and between their legs as they prayed to Frey.

When the morning dawned, Sigrid awoke from her torpor with the fires of hell burning in her anew, and she prayed desperately to the dear blessed Virgin Mary to save her from the pain, to take her now, if that was how it was to end, but at least to spare her from the pain.

The thrall women, who had been dozing around her, came quickly to life and started running their hands over her body and speaking rapidly to one another in their own unintelligible tongue. Then they began to laugh, smiling and nodding eagerly to her and to Sot, whose hair was so soaked that it hung straight down, dripping cold water as she bent over Sigrid, telling her that now was the time, now her son would soon come, but for the last time she must try to help. And the women took her under the arms and raised her halfway up in a sitting position, and Sigrid screamed wild prayers until she realized she might wake her little Eskil and frighten him. So she bit her wounded lip again and it began to bleed anew, and her mouth was filled with the taste of blood. But softly, in the midst of all that was unbearable, she found more and more hope, as if the Mother of God were now actually standing at her side, speaking gently to her and encouraging her to do as her clever and loyal thralls instructed. And Sigrid bore down and bit her lip again to keep from screaming. Now the monks' voices could be heard out in the dawn, very loud, like a praise-song or a psalm meant to drown out the terror.

Suddenly it was over. She saw through her sweat and tears a bloody bundle down below. The women in the room bustled about with water and linen cloths. She sensed them washing and chattering, she heard some slaps and a cry, a tiny, tremulous, bright sound that could be only one thing.

"It's a fine healthy boy," said Sot, beaming with joy. "Mistress has borne a well-formed boy with all the fingers and toes he should have. And he was born with a caul!"

They lay him, washed and swaddled, next to her aching, distended breasts, and she gazed into his tiny wrinkled face and was amazed he was so small. She touched him gently and he got an arm free and waved it in the air until she stuck out a finger, which he instantly grabbed and held tight.

"What will the boy be named?" asked Sot with a flushed, excited face.

"He shall be called Arn, after Arnäs," whispered Sigrid, exhausted. "Arnäs and not Varnhem will be his home, but he will be baptized here by Father Henri when the time comes."

Chapter 2

King Sverker's son Johan died as he deserved. King Sverker had of course followed the advice he had been given by Father Henri, to see to it that the Danish jarl took his wife back to Halland at once. But both King Sven Grate and his jarl scornfully rejected the subsequent part of Father Henri's plan, to arrange a marriage between the royal but roguish son and the other violated Danish woman, so that war could thus be avoided with a blood bond.

The fault lay perhaps not so much in Father Henri's plan as in the fact that King Sven Grate wanted war. The more proposals for mediation came from King Sverker, the more King Sven Grate wanted war. He thought, possibly correctly, that the king of the Goths was exhibiting weakness when he offered first one thing and then another to avoid going into battle.

As a last resort, King Sverker had prevailed upon the Pope's Cardinal Nicolaus Breakspear to pay a visit to Sven Grate on his way to Rome and speak of reason and peace.

The cardinal failed at this task, just as he had recently failed to ordain an archbishop over a unified Götaland and Svealand.

The papal commission to name an archbishop had failed because the Swedes and Goths were unable to agree on the location of the archbishop's cathedral, and thus where the archbishop should have his see. The cardinal's peace-making assignment failed for the simple reason that the Danish king was convinced of his coming victory. His newly conquered realms would then be subject to Archbishop Eskil in Lund, so Sven Grate could see no Christian reason for refraining from war.

King Sverker had made no preparations for the defense of the realm, since he was too wrapped up in mourning his queen, Ulvhild, and preparing for a wedding with yet another twice-widowed woman, Rikissa. Perhaps he also thought that all the intercessions he had secured for himself at the cloister would save both him and the country.

His oafish son Johan harbored no such belief in salvation by intercession. And if the Danes should emerge from the coming battle victorious, for his part all hope would be lost. So he, and not his father the king, called a *ting* at the royal manor in Vreta to decide how to plan the defense against the Danes.

He had no idea how hated he was as an outcast. If his father had not been both old and weak of flesh, he would have condemned his son to death for committing two heinous deeds as well as perjury. Everyone understood that except possibly Johan himself. No man of honor wanted to prolong the war and risk losing his life for the sake of an outcast—the worst sort of violator of women.

On the other hand, many men came to the *ting* at Vreta filled with anticipation, but for entirely different reasons than those Johan imagined.

They had come to kill him. And they did. His own retainers didn't lift a finger to protect him. Johan's corpse was chopped into pieces of the proper size and flung to the swine in the back yards of Skara so that no royal funeral could take place.

✠

In the year of Grace 1154 winter came early, and when the ice had settled in, King Sven Grate led his army up from Skåne and into the Finn Woods in Småland. The army burned and pillaged wherever they went, of course, but the advance was slowed by all the snow that year. Horses and oxen had a hard time making headway.

In addition, the peasants in Värend took defensive measures. They had decided at their *ting* that if they had to die, it was better to die like men in accordance with their forefathers' ancient beliefs. Dying like a servant or thrall without offering resistance was to die in vain. Besides, nothing was certain when it came to war except for one thing: He who did not fight, or who stood alone against a foreign army, would surely die if the army passed his way. Everything else was in the hands of the gods.

And King Sven Grate truly had a difficult time of it. The residents of Värend defended themselves one stretch of land at a time, from behind logjams, which they dragged onto the forest roads. It took a great deal of force and time to deal with these barricades, and victory was elusive. If the momentum seemed in their favor in the evening when the battle had to be broken off for supper, prayer, and sleep, by morning the defenders of the barricade would be gone. By then they would have regrouped in a village a bit farther on, with new people who had their own homes to defend, and then it would start all over again.

At night the soldiers in the Danish army deserted in large groups and began walking home. Those who were professional fighters knew that too much of the winter had already passed. Even though they might finally manage to get through these damned peasant defenders, they would end up mired in the spring mud on the plains of Western Götaland. Besides, the peasants of Värend had a nasty way of defending themselves. At night they would sneak up in small groups, overtake the guards, and then stab as many horses and oxen in the belly as they could before reinforcements arrived. Then they would flee into the dark forest.

A horse that has been stabbed in the belly dies quite rapidly. Oxen are a bit more resilient, but even oxen die if a pitchfork or lance point has penetrated their underbelly. Naturally, the Danish army ended up with plenty of beef to roast, but it was cold comfort, since they were forced to consume their only hope of victory.

When at last Sven Grate had to accept the fact that the war could not be won, at least not this year, he decided that the army should be divided for the retreat. He would proceed home through Skåne to the islands of Denmark. His jarl would take the other half of the remaining army home with him to Halland and his own manor. Sven Grate also had messengers sent home to announce that when they returned, the war would be over.

But in Värend there was plenty to avenge. And the story was long told of the woman Blenda, who sent out messages to the other women, and together they met the jarl and his men near the Nissa River with bread and salt pork. Quite a lot of salt pork, as it turned out. They provided an extraordinary feast, and oddly enough, there was plenty of ale to go with the salt pork.

The jarl and his men finally staggered off to a barn to sleep while the soldiers, just as drunk as the noblemen, had to make do as best they could underneath ox and sheep hides out in the snow. It was then that Blenda and the other women made their preparations. They tarred big torches and summoned their men, who were hiding in the forest.

When silence had fallen over the army's encampment and only

snoring could be heard, they carefully barred the door of the barn and then set fire to all four corners simultaneously. Then they attacked the sleeping soldiers.

The next morning, with joyous laughter, they drowned the last of the captives beneath the ice on the Nissa River, where they had chopped two big holes so that they could drag the prisoners down under the ice as if on a long fishing line.

King Sverker had won the war with the Danes without lifting a finger or sending out a single man.

No doubt he believed that this was due both to his prayers of intercession and to God's providence. Yet he was man enough to have Blenda and her kinsmen brought before him. And he proclaimed that the women of Värend, who had shown themselves so manly in the defense of the country, should henceforth inherit just as men did. And as an eternal emblem of war they would wear a red sash with an embroidered cross of gold, an insignia that would be granted to them alone.

If King Sverker had lived longer, his decrees would surely have had greater legal effect than they did. But King Sverker's days were numbered. He would soon be murdered.

⛨

No fortress can be built to be impregnable. If strong enough motivation exists, any man's home can be pillaged and burned. But the question then is whether it is worth the price. How many besiegers had been shot to death with arrows, how many had been crushed by stones, how many had lost their will and health during the siege?

Herr Magnus knew all this, and he was greatly troubled as the construction progressed. Because what he couldn't know, what no one at that time could know, was what would happen after the death of old King Sverker. And that time was fast approaching.

Anything was possible. Sverker's eldest son Karl might win the king's power, and then nothing in particular would change. If nothing else, Sigrid had seen to improving her husband's relationship to King Sverker by donating Varnhem almost as if in his name.

But it was difficult to know much about what was happening up in Svealand, and which of the Swedes was now preparing for the battle to become king. Perhaps it was some Western Goth? Perhaps someone in their own lineage or in a friendly clan or in a hostile clan. As they waited for the decision to be made, there was nothing to do but keep building.

Arnäs was located at the tip of a peninsula that jutted out into Lake Vänern, and so had a natural water defense on three sides. Next to the old longhouse a stone tower was now being erected that was as tall as seven men. The walls around the tower were still not finished, but the area was mainly protected by palisades of tightly packed, pointed oak logs. Here there was still plenty to do.

Magnus stood for a long time up in the tower on his property, trying out shots with a longbow, aiming at a bale of hay on the other side of the two wall moats. It was truly remarkable how far an arrow from a longbow could reach if he fired down from an elevated position. And after very little practice he was learning to calculate the angle so that he hit the target almost perfectly, at most an arm's length to one side or the other. Even in its present unfinished state, Arnäs would be difficult to take, at least for a group of soldiers returning from some war or other who might need provisions on the way home. And eventually it would become even more fortified, although everything had its season, and Sigrid mostly wanted something different from Magnus.

He was well aware that she often got her way when they disagreed. By now he was even aware of how she behaved to make it look as if she weren't actually driving him before her, but rather was obediently following the will of her husband and lord—as she had done with the matter of the high seat of his Norwegian forefathers.

In the old longhouse the high seat and the walls around the end of the hall had been decorated with oak carvings from Norway, in which the dragon ship plowed through the sea, and a great serpent whose name he had forgotten encircled the entire scene. The runic inscription was ancient and difficult to decipher.

Sigrid had first proposed that they burn all these old ungodly images now that they were building afresh. The walls should be covered instead with the tapestries of the new era, in which Christian men defended the Holy City of Jerusalem, where churches were erected and heathens baptized.

Magnus had had a hard time agreeing to the idea of burning all his forefathers' skillfully made carvings. Such things were no longer created nowadays; in any case their like could not be found anywhere in Western Götaland. But he'd also had difficulty arguing with her words about ungodliness and heathen art. In that sense she was right. And yet the forefathers who had carved those writhing dragons and runes had known no other way of carving; now the lovely work of their hands was all that remained of them.

At the same time as they were quarreling about the dragon patterns and the runes, they were also addressing the question of who knew how to build walls. Should the stonemasons' talents be used first for the outer defenses, or should they build the gable of the new longhouse first?

In the old longhouse, the fireplace had stretched the whole length of the building, down the middle of the floor, so that the heat was distributed more or less evenly. In the far end of the longhouse were kept the thralls and the animals, while the master of the estate and his people and their guests lived in the part where

the high seat was placed. During hard winters, heat was best con-
served in this manner.

But now Sigrid had come up with new ideas, which of course
she had learned from the monks down in Varnhem. Magnus still
remembered his amazement and his skepticism when she drew
it all in the sand before him. Everything was new, nothing was
as before.

Her longhouse was divided into two halves, with a big door in
the middle that led into an anteroom, and from there you entered
either the master's half or the half with the thralls and animals.
In addition, the half with the thralls and animals was divided
into two floors. The upper floor served as a barn for fodder, and
the lower floor as stall for the livestock. In this half of the house
there was no fireplace; on the contrary, fire was something that
would be forbidden on pain of severe punishment.

In the other half of the longhouse, which would be their own,
with a high seat as before, the far gable would be built entirely of
stone. In front of it large, flat slabs would be mortared to a fireplace almost as wide as the house, and above the fireplace a huge
chimney to conduct the smoke would be built into the stone.

He'd offered many objections, and she had answers to all of
them. The lack of fire along the floor was not a problem; the
stone walls at the end would hold the heat inside the building,
keeping it warm even through the night. No, the old vents were
not necessary, as the smoke would go straight up the stone chimney above the hearth. And there was no need to worry about
winds blowing through the stacked logs, as the cracks would be
sealed with flax and tar.

As to his concern that the thralls and animals would have
no fire in their part of the house, she patiently explained that
by dividing their living quarters into two floors, the heat from
the animals would remain downstairs, while upstairs the thralls
(and the men) could make comfortable beds of hay.

But then, in response to one of his questions, Sigrid happened to invoke the Norwegian stave churches, which certainly had no lack of dragon patterns, and she seemed to reconsider. On closer reflection she thought she could yield on the matter of the ancestral high seats and their less than Christian ornamentation. And then, quite exhilarated and relieved, Magnus agreed at once that first they had to finish the masonry work on the new longhouse. Since now he had indeed achieved what he wanted.

Of course he had seen through her, and he understood how she managed to push through her will on almost every matter. Sometimes he felt a brief wave of anger flow through his limbs and head at the thought that his wife was acting as though she and not he was the master of Arnäs.

But now, as he unstrung his longbow and shouted at one of the thralls down in the moat to gather up the arrows and return them to their place in the armory, what he saw was not merely a beautiful sight. It was a very convincing sight.

Below him in the stronghold area, the new longhouse stood with its tarred walls gleaming and its turf roof a luxuriant green. They had converted all the thatched roofs on the buildings to turf roofs with grass, even though reeds could be easily harvested nearby. This was not only for the sake of warmth, but also because a single flaming arrow could transform thatched roofs into huge torches.

At the other end of the courtyard in the stronghold area, under protection of the high section of wall that had been completed, stood a long livestock house. Below him in the tower were stored grain and weapons. Even in its present state, he would now be able to organize the defense of Arnäs in half a day.

If he looked inland, a whole village was cropping up on the other side of the moat. There stood the tannery, stinking along the lakefront beyond the other buildings where ox-hides and skins of marten and ermine were prepared, which brought in so many silver coins in Lödöse. Up toward the fortress the other buildings stood in two rows, livestock stalls and thrall dwellings, stonecutter workshops and smithies, food storehouses, cookhouses, cooperages, and flax-houses. Now there were twice as many thralls and animals as there were only a few years ago.

The latter turn of events was like a miracle and just as hard to understand. He had learned from his father, who had learned from his forefathers as far back as anyone could remember, exactly how many thralls and animals a field could support in relation to its size, so that the estate owner would not be eaten out of house and home.

Now there was a whole swarm down there, twice as many as he should have had by his own reckoning, and yet Arnäs had grown richer and bigger with each month that passed. The forest that had once come right up to the northern moat had now been cut as far away as ten shots with the longbow, which was as far as the eye could clearly see. The forest had become timber, which had been used to construct all the new buildings down there. New fields and pastures now covered the land that had once been forest.

And no matter how many silver coins he had spent on things that could not be made at Arnäs, or those that could only be purchased for silver, such as salt or the services of the woodcarver from Bjälbo who was working on the gates, the quantity of his silver coins still kept growing, as if the coins were able to propagate like animals and thralls inside their oaken chests in the vaults and chambers of the tower.

When King Sverker had started minting coins down in Lödöse two winters ago, he was the only king who had endorsed coinage as legal tender since farther back than anyone could remember, ever since the heathen time. Most tradesmen had been skeptical of the newfangled money and preferred to stay with the old ways, bartering for salt and iron, hides, butter, and furs measured in bushels.

But Sigrid had urged Magnus to adopt the new method right from the start, and to be the first to accept silver for everything. She had argued that in this way he would be helping King Sverker establish a difficult new custom that others were reluctant to accept, and thus the king would remain favorably disposed toward Arnäs.

So at first he had received ten times as much silver for an item as he could get now that everyone else had begun to follow the new ways. By being the first, Magnus had doubled his fortune in a few short years.

When he realized this for the first time, what power now resided in his money cached in the tower—without understanding why—he had felt an urge to chastise her, let her feel the rod, make her know her place as wife. But his anger had quickly abated. Instead, when he saw a whole district teeming with all the life that had been created around Arnäs, he turned to God with a prayer of thanksgiving that God had granted him the wisest wife in the entire land of the Goths. Sigrid was a gift from God, that much was certain and true. And when he was alone under the roof of heaven where only God could hear his thoughts, Magnus acknowledged this without bitterness. After all, it was just he and God—yes, and Sigrid herself, of course—who knew. No man knew of this. They all thought that the flourishing region around Arnäs and the two villages that belonged to Arnäs down toward Forshem were his work and none other's. They all believed that he was a great man, a man to reckon with, a man who knew how to create wealth.

Presumably, although he wasn't sure, Sigrid too believed that he was floating along on that conceited delusion. He resolved never to let her see that he understood quite well that she was behind it all.

And besides, he consoled himself, he and Sigrid were as one, since whatsoever God has joined together, no man can put asunder. Everything that thrived around Arnäs was the result of their common efforts, in the same way that their sons Eskil and Arn were half himself and half Sigrid.

When viewed this way, which was after all the only Christian way to look at it, he was indeed a great man, through God's providence. And in what other way except through God's providence could it have happened?

Winter was the time of feasts in Western Götaland. But this winter, especially, when King Sverker's days were waning, there was an unusual number of feasts. Sleighs crisscrossed the countryside, and it was not only for the sake of the roast meat and ale. It was a cold time of uncertainty for some people, and a hot time for hammering out plans at the forge of intrigue for others.

Erik Jedvardsson had announced that he intended to visit Arnäs just before midwinter, and the reason he gave, other than the prospect of getting to know each other better since Sigrid and his wife Kristina were kin, was that there was much for them to discuss. Besides, they might be able to have done with the dispute about Varnhem.

Only one part of the message—that there was much to discuss—bothered Magnus. Everyone knew that Erik Jedvardsson was a man with high-flying plans for his own benefit. In the worst case he had his eye on the king's throne. And that meant in turn that he now sought to establish who was his enemy and who would be his friend in this struggle.

Magnus wrestled inwardly and at length with this question. He knew what he wanted to do with his own life. That was to build Arnäs into a strong and rich estate and leave a good inheritance to Eskil and perhaps something to Arn. But anyone who allowed himself to be drawn into the struggle for the king's crown might gain much, but just as easily could lose everything. So far the choice was not difficult for Magnus, since his means of achievement in his life had been staked out all the way until his death, which would come at an advanced age, he hoped. He would continue to build, continue his trading, and continue to break new ground. That was his sure path to profit and a good life.

On the other hand, what made the matter truly worrisome was the fact that whoever did not aid the victor in the struggle for the crown could expect trouble when the victor next came to visit and asked why he had received no support until it was no longer needed. Magnus knew enough about Erik Jedvardsson to realize that he was sure to enter the fray, and he was also known to be a man who was loath to forgive his enemies. No matter how Magnus positioned himself, he risked losing.

Secretly Magnus did not consider himself to be a man of war. Certainly he could handle a sword and shield, lance and bow; what else had he done as a young man but learn such skills? His retainers numbered a dozen men, distant kinsmen and mostly young, who had no hope of inheritance but who knew no other work than that involving weapons. Lazy ne'er-do-wells mostly, Magnus thought. Nevertheless, he would be able to provide a dozen retainers. And if necessary he could arm eight dozen of his peasants in the two villages near Forshem. This wasn't a warrior force that could tip the balance in a struggle for the crown. Crucial to his future would be which side he had taken in the struggle, for or against the victor. And whether half of his clan, who lived as he did in Western Götaland, backed Erik Jedvardsson or not would probably depend on what position the other half of his kinsmen took, the ones from Bjälbo in Eastern Götaland.

Magnus had sent for his younger brother Birger, who although he was not the eldest or most prominent, still acted as spokesman for the Bjälbo family in many difficult matters. Birger was regarded as both shrewd and forthright in negotiations. Many had predicted that, despite the down on his cheeks, he would one day hold a high position in the realm, no matter who controlled the kingdom, for the Bjälbo lineage was very strong, as reckoned in lands and retainers.

Birger came riding up like a whirlwind in the snow one evening before the other guests had arrived. With loud shouts he drove his sleigh into the courtyard in front of the longhouse and with an abrupt skid made snow spray from the runners. He leapt down briskly from the sleigh and left it in the care of stable thralls who came rushing over. He also tossed a dead wolf onto the ground so that it could be carried away at once to the tannery to be flayed. Many of the thralls thought that it was unlucky to let a dead wolf come too close to where people lived.

Then he heaved the knapsack with his good clothes onto his back and was already on his way into the longhouse as Magnus came stumbling out to welcome him. When Birger entered the longhouse and met Sigrid, whom he greeted with caution and chivalry, he was at once full of praise for their construction. Led by Sigrid, with Magnus traipsing along behind, he walked through the hall and felt the heat radiating from the stone gable wall with the log fires, rubbing his hands in delight. He quickly selected a place to sleep, dropped off his change of clothes, and pulled the woolen blanket over his sleeping place. Then he promptly went over to the bench near the fire, and began to tell them about his journey across the ice of Lake Vättern. He recounted how he had discovered a pack of wolves and how the horse managed to catch up with them on the ice covered with a thin layer of snow and how he shot a wolf, but the fallen wolf unfortunately got caught up in the sleigh's runners and the other wolves were able to flee.

Then he stretched out his hand in a practiced gesture and was handed a tankard of ale without so much as casting a glance at the house thrall who brought it. He drank a toast to his hosts and heaved a great sigh of satisfaction.

Magnus felt almost dumbfounded by his lively young brother, for whom nothing ever seemed difficult or impossible. Who would even think of venturing out alone on a sleigh ride across unstable ice in bad weather, traveling all the way from Bjälbo to Arnäs in a single day without the least trepidation? It made Magnus wonder how much having the same father actually meant since he and his half brother had different mothers.

It took a long time before they had sufficiently discussed all their kinsmen at the two estates, and Magnus almost timidly was able to turn the conversation to the difficult questions awaiting them the next day.

But none of this seemed difficult for Birger, either. He disposed of the whole problem in a few sentences.

"It is true and certain," he said as he reached out his arm to take another tankard of ale, "that this Erik Jedvardsson is a man who will either end up as king or be a head shorter, or both. We all know this. But as things now stand, he can't get us involved in any strife. He can't turn Eastern Götaland against Western Götaland or vice versa. He could possibly win over the Swedes to his cause, with or without a heathen sacrifice. If he does that, we'll have to consider then what position to take. Then the game will have changed. But enough of these minor matters, when do we eat?"

✠

The arrival of Erik Jedvardsson at Arnäs on the following day was an event not missed by anyone. He came in four sleighs and had twelve retainers with him, as though he were already king, or at least the jarl, the second in line to power. Moreover, he arrived four hours before he was expected, due to the fact that he had left his home estate of Ladås the day before, stopping halfway and staying overnight with King Sverker's man at the king's Husaby estate, although he was reticent about what had transpired during such a brief visit.

The meat being tended by the roast-turners was still half raw; the turnips were still being carried into the cookhouses, and Sigrid had scarcely managed to sweep the hall and hang the tapestries; so after a brief welcome for form's sake, when they tested the ale and shared some of the white bread that was the pride of Arnäs, they divided up the company in the most opportune way so as to make the time pass without boredom. Magnus asked his eldest retainer to take care of his warrior brothers from Ladås, get them settled in, and assuage their thirst. Sigrid took Kristina on a tour of the house and around all the new buildings on the estate, and Magnus took Erik Jedvardsson to see the work on the fortifications.

Erik Jedvardsson was not impressed. He thought that the walls were too low and too fragile, that the double moat might be an ingenious idea, but that it didn't do much good to have deep moats if they had to defend themselves in the winter when the water turned to ice. And he went on like that, boasting the whole time about his own structures and comparing them, especially the church building in Eriksberg, which was now nearly completed. Naturally he used English stonemasons, whom he had requisitioned from his father's clan; these Englishmen, he proposed, might be hired out to Magnus when the spring came instead of returning home.

Magnus let him talk. If the walls at Arnäs were too low and fragile, then he meant they were too low and fragile for a king.

If there was a king to capture in the fortress, then the besiegers would be both more numerous and more stubborn than if there were only a tradesman inside. It wasn't difficult to see that Erik Jedvardsson was already dreaming of being king.

But Magnus did not feel comfortable in his company. The other man was taller and heavier, which made him speak and behave as though he were the host and not the guest.

This made the surprise so much the better for Magnus when they left the fortifications and began to inspect the stables and the longhouse. This was indeed a whole new method of building—the long pine logs stacked on top of each other—and the stonework gable of the longhouse, with its three big chimneys on the roof ridge, was also entirely new to Erik Jedvardsson. At his home they were still building with vertical logs that were sealed with straw and clay.

Magnus was immediately in a better mood as he began to describe his construction ideas. And when Erik Jedvardsson was invited into the hall and the heat from the stone gable near the high seat radiated toward him, he became voluble in his praise. He ran his hand over the logs and their sealed seams to confirm that there wasn't the slightest cold draft. As ale was brought out for the guest, Magnus modestly told him that up here where the Sunnan Forest met the Nördan Forest there was so much good timber—tall, straight pines—that it provided building possibilities completely different from, for example, the land down by the Lidan River, with its mostly deciduous forest.

The ale warmed them and Magnus's mood continued to improve.

✠

Sigrid had not been looking forward to showing her kinswoman Kristina around the grounds. The mood between them could not be other than coldly polite, given the claim Kristina had made to the priests and the king that Varnhem was at least partially hers, and that she had no intention of giving away any of her inheritance to some monks.

But that was not a suitable topic to take up now, without the presence of their husbands. If anything was to be said on this matter, it would be best to do so when all those who had a right to discuss the problem were gathered in the same room.

Kristina couldn't help being impressed by all the various workshops that had sprung up around the estate, however. They didn't go all the way down to the tannery because of the smell, but they visited the cookhouses, the stonecutters' workshops, the smithies, the cooperages, and the linen-makers before they took a turn through the storehouses and one of the thrall's huts, where they surprised a couple fornicating, which didn't bother the two women in the least. It did prompt Kristina to joke that at home she had at least every other male thrall gelded, because those brutes otherwise had the ability to create too many new mouths to feed.

Sigrid explained that she had given up that custom. Not for the sake of the thralls, but because one could never have too many thralls.

Kristina couldn't understand this reasoning. More thralls meant more mouths to feed, more animals to slaughter, and more grain to the mill—wasn't that as clear as water?

Sigrid tried to explain the method of moving them out, breaking new ground, and freeing them at the same rate as the thralls propagated, and how that in turn produced income in the form of extra barrels of grain from the new plantings each year. The thralls also ate less food if they had to pay for it themselves.

Kristina merely laughed at these foolish ideas; it was like letting the cattle out onto a green pasture to milk, slaughter, and finally roast themselves. Sigrid soon gave up all attempts to explain and at last took Kristina to the bathhouse, where a group of house thralls was busy washing up for the evening.

The steam billowed out in big clouds when they opened the door and the midwinter cold met the moist heat inside. When they closed the door behind them and their vision cleared, Kristina was so astonished that for the first time she couldn't hide her surprise. The room was filled with naked thralls running about with pails of hot water which they dumped into big oaken tubs, while others sat in the tubs of steaming water. Sigrid went over and grabbed a female house thrall and let Kristina feel her flesh. They certainly were healthy and well-fed, weren't they?

Yes indeed, they looked splendid. But what was the idea of letting thralls use up wood and have their own building as if they were fine folk? She couldn't understand it.

Sigrid explained that they were house thralls, of course. They had to turn the roasts and serve them and pour the ale and carry out the scraps all night. But wasn't it more pleasant to have clean house thralls that didn't stink? And they would all be dressed in clean linen after the bath; at Arnäs they produced much more linen at present than they could sell.

Kristina shook her head. She couldn't hide how absurd she found this method for treating thralls. It might give them ideas, she said. They already *had* ideas, Sigrid replied, with a smile that Kristina had a hard time understanding.

But when the feast commenced that evening it was a lovely sight when all the clean-scrubbed house thralls entered the hall in procession, clad in their white linen clothing, and carrying the first round of meat, turnips, white bread, and a soup made from leeks, beans, and something that Sigrid called red roots.

In the Norwegian high seat adorned with the winding dragon arabesques sat Magnus and Erik Jedvardsson. To the left of

Magnus sat his brother Birger, his sons Eskil and little Arn, and beside them Erik Jedvardsson's son Knut, who was the same age as Eskil. To the right of the high seat sat Kristina and Sigrid. Along the walls the tar torches burned in their iron sconces. At the long table where the twenty-four retainers sat arranged by age, expensive wax candles burned as though in church, and from the stone wall behind the high seat the heat radiated, although it was less warm farther down in the hall. The youngest retainers at the end soon pulled their cloaks around them.

The spit-turners had begun to serve the tenderest morsels from the roasting house, succulent piglets to awaken the palate. After that would come heavier meats—veal, lamb, and young wild boar—and also the old-fashioned coarse rye bread for those who didn't like the newfangled white bread. Ale was brought to the table in large quantities, either unspiced strong ale or the kind that was given to women and children, spiced with honey and juniper berries.

In the beginning everyone behaved well at the feast, conversing easily about insignificant things, and Birger, smiling as ever, had another chance to tell the story about his journey the day before when he shot a wolf.

Erik Jedvardsson and his men drank a toast to their host. Magnus and his men drank to their guests, and everyone was in a good mood and without rancorous thoughts or harsh words.

Erik Jedvardsson praised the beauty of the hall once again— the new method of building with horizontal logs, the beautiful dragon designs looping around the high seat, and above all the beds, arranged in a row of compartments along one wall, stacked on top of each other with plenty of quilts and pelts so that several people could fit in the same bed without it being too crowded or too warm. This might be something to think about when he built his own new house. Magnus modestly explained that this method of arranging the beds was customary in Norway; every Norwegian knew that it was easier to escape the cold if the bed was up off the floor.

But as Erik Jedvardsson quaffed more ale his tongue began to grow sharp, though at first it was hardly noticeable. He joked about King Sverker, the only king in the North who could win a war by being a coward; he joked even more about monks and how troublesome they were. He then returned to the cowardly King Sverker and made fun of the old man for marrying an old crone like Rikissa, who had been the wife of a Rus, Volodar or whatever his name was, on the other side of the Eastern Sea.

"But my dear guest, by doing so he saved the country once again from war and devastation, haven't you thought about that?" Sigrid put in with a merry expression on her face, as if the ale had also gone to her head and she could therefore loosen her tongue with less responsibility than otherwise. Magnus gave her a stern look that she pretended not to see.

"What! What do you mean? What great deeds for the country can that old man perform in bed with a woman twice widowed?" replied Erik Jedvardsson in a loud voice, more to his own men farther down the table than to Sigrid. His retainers found instant humor in his words.

"Because Rikissa's son is Knut Magnusson from her first marriage, and because Knut Magnusson has now become the new king of Denmark and would find it difficult to attack the country in which his mother is queen," Sigrid replied sharply as soon as the guffaws of the retainers had subsided. But she said it with good humor. And when Erik Jedvardsson's expression clouded over she feigned even greater merriment, adding during the embarrassed silence that this was how an old man who could do nothing manly in bed was still able to use his bed to prevent war. So even a limp cock could do some good, and that didn't happen every day.

The last joke about the king's limp cock made all the retainers burst out in even louder laughter and greater applause than after Erik Jedvardsson's joke.

Sigrid lowered her eyes as if abashed and seemed to blush at her own boldness. But Magnus suspected mischief. Nobody knew better than he what a honeyed, sharp tongue his wife possessed. And nobody knew better than he that if this feast ended up being about who won when they crossed words in the air like sword blades, then Sigrid would conquer them all, except possibly Birger. And that must not happen; it would only end in misery.

For the time being he saved the situation by launching into a long and somewhat convoluted explanation of the importance of all the knowledge that the monks had brought with them to this country. Naturally it was hard for a guest to interrupt his host, but when Magnus began to repeat himself and for the third time mentioned the importance of silver coinage in trade, Erik Jedvardsson made a show of getting up to go outside and piss. Then Magnus fell silent and shot his brother Birger an uneasy glance. But Birger smiled as usual and didn't look the slightest bit concerned as he leaned over toward Magnus and whispered that perhaps now he would go out and piss too, because soon it would be time for what the guest had come for.

Besides, a break would be good. Half the retainers followed the honored guest's example, and soon almost all the men were standing outside in a row, talking together happily as they relieved themselves into the fir branches spread outside. In the wintertime a courtyard would look unclean after a good feast unless they laid out fir branches, which the thralls had to hasten to replace at regular intervals.

When Erik Jedvardsson again took his place next to Magnus in the high seat and was served fresh ale, he held up his hand to signal that he wished to speak undisturbed. With a little smile Birger gave Magnus a look and nodded in affirmation.

"Before all this fine hospitality goes too much to our heads and we start talking about what terrific fellows we are," he began, smiling and waiting for the polite laughter that came mostly from his own men, "it is now time to discuss a serious matter. King Sverker's days are numbered. I would not be exaggerating too much to say that soon he will no longer be with us in this earthly life. Karl Sverkersson is sitting over in Linköping thinking that the king's crown will fall into his lap. There are many of us in Western Götaland who refuse to accept such a misfortune, and I am one of them. With God's help I shall therefore win the king's crown. And now I ask you all, kinsmen and friends, do I have your support, or must I leave this beautiful house as your enemy?"

There was total silence in the hall. Even the three small boys next to Birger stared with big-eyed astonishment at Erik Jedvardsson, who had now declared that he wanted to be king. And at the same time threatened them with enmity.

Magnus gave Birger a desperate glance, but his brother merely smiled and nodded that he would take responsibility for the rest.

"Sir Erik, you speak with such power and determination that I do not for a moment doubt that you could become king of us all," Birger began in a loud voice so that everyone would hear that it was he, the younger brother below the high seat, and not Magnus who was speaking. Then he lowered his voice.

"Allow me to answer you first. I speak for the entire Bjälbo lineage, since I have been entrusted to do so. My brother Magnus will have his say after me, but you must know that our two clans are connected by many blood ties and can hardly go against each other. No doubt you can sense the trust. We are not your enemies, but neither are we your friends in this particular matter at this particular time. If you wish to be king, you will have to start at a different end of the country from ours. You must get the Swedes to elect you as king at Mora Stones. If you succeed in this task, then half will already be won. However, if you try to become king in Western Götaland against the will of the Eastern Goths, you will only bring war down upon yourself, and no one knows who would emerge the victor from that calamity. The same will happen if you go the other way. So you must win over the Swedes first. And when you have done that, then you can undoubtedly count on our support. Tell me, brother Magnus, am I not right?"

Magnus realized that everyone was staring at him. The silence was much like the moment when the bow is drawn taut and the arrow will momentarily be loosed at its target. All he could manage was to nod slowly and pensively as if he were a wise old man. A murmur of discontent arose from Erik Jedvardsson's men at the far end of the hall.

"You, Birger, are nothing but a young rascal," Erik Jedvardsson yelled, red in the face. "I could slay you here and now for your impudent words. Who are you to teach a full-grown warrior his course of action?"

Erik Jedvardsson made a move toward the place where he thought his sword should be, as if he had forgotten that it was no longer the custom for men to attend a feast with their swords at their sides. All the weapons were in the stable out in the connecting building with the spit-turners.

Birger was not about to be cowed by the feigned move toward the empty scabbard, and his smile did not flinch even for an instant when he replied.

"You may well think that I am a rascal, Erik Jedvardsson," he began calmly, but now in a somewhat louder voice so that no one in the hall could avoid hearing his words. "This does not please me, but it still has nothing to do with the larger matter, for if you draw your sword on me, at the same moment you will draw misfortune upon yourself no matter how things may turn out."

"You scamp, do you think for a moment that you could stand against me with a sword?" shrieked Erik Jedvardsson, even more red in the face, turning so that everyone in the hall now feared the worst. A female thrall rushed up and carried off the three small boys sitting next to Birger.

Birger rose slowly, but his smile did not falter as he replied.

"Now I really must beg you as our guest to stop and think, Erik Jedvardsson," he said. "If you and I were to exchange sword blows, it would go badly for you. If you die here and now, you will never be king. If you kill me, the rest of your life will be one long journey with the whole Bjälbo clan chasing you from one *ting* to the next, and if that does no good they will kill you in the end. Stop and think! You have a kingdom within an arm's length, that I don't doubt. Don't squander it because you think that the spokesman for the Bjälbo clan is too young and too impudent! First win over the Swedes, then us. For the second time, this is my advice."

Birger calmly sat down and reached for a fresh tankard of ale from one of the female thralls, who was scared out of her wits. Yet he behaved as if nothing special had happened.

Erik Jedvardsson sat glumly for a long time before he answered. He had realized that young Birger from Bjälbo had spoken rightly, with words clear as water. He now had to admit that he had been rebuked and flustered by a quick-witted youth. What everyone had heard could not be unsaid.

"So be it," he said at last. "I had already thought of going to Mora Stones to win over the Swedes, so in that matter we seem to agree. But for these words of yours I will still have a goose to pluck with you when I return as your king."

"I don't doubt that at all, my future lord and king," said Birger with a broad and almost exaggerated smile. He paused playfully before he went on. "But since you do seem to accept my advice, I would suggest that you make me your jarl rather than pluck me like a goose!"

His bold manner of saying this straight to Erik Jedvardsson's angry face had a remarkable effect. At first Erik Jedvardsson stared at him with dark eyes, but Birger merely smiled back, until Erik Jedvardsson's face suddenly broke into a broad grin. And then he began to laugh. The next moment his retainers started laughing, and then Magnus's men laughed, then the women, and finally the thralls and the three small boys who were now allowed to return to their seats. By then the hall was booming with laughter and the storm had passed.

Erik Jedvardsson now knew that all further discussion about his path to the king's crown had better wait until another time. He clapped his hands and called for the Norwegian bard whom he'd brought along in the rear sleigh. He demanded stories from the time when people in the North had energy and the courage that one saw all too infrequently these days.

The bard rose from his miserable seat among the youngest retainers and began walking to the front of the hall to stand by the fire at the end, where he would tell stories and sing. In the meantime the house thralls quickly cleaned up the scraps and brought more ale, wiping up piss and vomit by the door. An expectant silence spread as the bard paused dramatically with his head bowed to let the excitement rise to the bursting point before he began.

He started in a faint but beautiful, melodious voice, telling of Sigurd Jorsalafar's eight great victories on the road to Jerusalem, how he had plundered in Galicia, how off the coast of Särkland, where the infidels lived, he first encountered ships full of Saracen heathens who came rowing toward him with a huge fleet of galleys, but how he then attacked without hesitation and soon vanquished the heathens, who clearly had never encountered a Nordic fleet before and had no understanding of such a battle that could end in only one way:

The poor heathens
attacked the king.
The mighty prince
killed them all.
The army cleared out eight ships
in the terrible battle.
The much befriended prince
brought booty on board.
The raven flew off to fresh wounds.

Here the bard took a break and asked for more ale so he could resume his tales, and all the men pounded their fists on the long table as a sign that they wanted to hear more.

The two youngest boys, Arn and Knut, had listened with mouths agape and eyes wide during the story, but the somewhat older Eskil began to fret and yawn. Sigrid motioned to her house thralls to put the boys to bed. She had already made up beds for them in one of the cookhouses.

Eskil followed along obediently, yawning again; he believed that a warm bed would be preferable to an old man telling the ancient sagas in a language that was difficult to understand. Arn and Knut kicked, whined, and protested, begging to hear more and promising to sit still, but it did no good.

Soon all three boys were tucked in under thick pelts in a cookhouse with three of the biggest iron pots filled with glowing charcoal. Eskil quickly turned over and fell asleep, snuffling, while Arn and Knut lay wide awake, indignant that the eldest of them was the one who had ruined their fun. Whispering, they agreed to get dressed and slip out into the dark. Like little elves they passed two men who stood puking outside the door. They sneaked nimbly into the hall and sat down near the door in the dark where no one would see them; Arn found a big pelt, which he carefully pulled over them both, revealing only their blond bangs and wide eyes. They sat there quiet as mice, with all their attention focused on Sigurd Jorsalafar's heroic deeds.

✠

Despite the fact that a dozen men stumbled past Arn and Knut, and some even tripped over them on their way out or in, nobody discovered the boys hiding like grouse chicks in the forest at night. They listened, rapt and wide-eyed, as the bard sang of Sigurd Jorsalafar's triumph at Sidon, repeating the verses that the men, whose applause was growing increasingly thunderous, demanded.

> Sigurd won
> at Sidon, men remember this.
> Weapons were wielded fiercely
> in the heated battle.
> With might the warriors crushed
> the stubborn army's fortress.
> Beautiful swords were colored with
> blood when the prince prevailed.

The applause from the hall went on and on, followed by the buzz of voices as everyone began talking at once, about the great deeds in olden times, and the kings of their own time who were like Sverker Limp-Cock and not Sigurd Jorsalafar. Magnus attempted a witty joke that it was different with Norsemen, since he himself was of Norwegian lineage. But nobody thought it was a good joke, least of all Erik Jedvardsson, who now stood up holding the old drinking horn they had placed before him—a Norwegian drinking horn at that, although he was probably unaware of it. And he drank with manly vigor, draining it to the bottom without taking the horn from his lips. Then he explained that he had just seen before him, as if in a vision, the new coat of arms that would be his and that of the whole realm. There would be three golden crowns: one crown for Svealand, one for Eastern Götaland, and one for Western Götaland. The three crowns would be set against a field the color of the sky. This, he now swore, would become in the future the new coat of arms for him and the entire kingdom.

The hall seethed with excited applause. But Erik Jedvardsson wanted to say more. At the same time he had to piss, and since he wanted to do both equally urgently, he announced in a loud, slurred voice on the way out the door that each and every one who followed him in the future would be assured of reaping honor during the crusade. Perhaps going only so far as to the Finns on the other side of the Eastern Sea on the first venture, but then, after the Finns were converted, perhaps our men needed to gain a foothold in the Holy Land as well.

When he reached the door he didn't bother to go outside across the high threshold; staggering, he leaned against the doorjamb for support and relieved himself right where he stood.

He never noticed that he was pissing on Arn and his own son Knut. And they in turn could do nothing but huddle together and suffer in silence. Neither of the boys would ever forget it.

Especially since they had now been pissed on by a man who would become a saint as well as king.

Chapter 3

The winter held Arnäs in an iron grip. All roads to the south had been impassable since the eighth day of Christmas, and even though the ice on Lake Vänern was thick enough to cross, at least with wide-runnered sleighs, right now there was no great reason to take the trouble. What Magnus wanted to sell over there, toward Lödöse, would bring double the price toward the end of winter when supplies began running low in many storehouses. At Arnäs the work went on as usual in the cooperages, the slaughterhouses, and the salting houses, as it did in the women's workshops where they prepared wool and linen and wove both thick cloth and tapestries to the delight of both man and God.

For the boys Eskil and Arn, the hard winter was a wonderful time. Their teacher and lay brother Erlend from Varnhem had returned to the monastery just before Christmastime, and although Paulsmas was rapidly approaching on January 25th, he had still not been able to make his way back through the snow to Arnäs. The days that the boys should have spent sitting with their noses in the Latin text about the philosopher Saint Bernard had now become free, and they spent the time in lively winter games and boys' mischief. What was most fun was to catch mice down in the grain stores and then release them among the thrall women in the cookhouses. Shrieking with laughter, the boys would run off as shrill screams and loud banging and clattering spoke of what was happening to the mice.

Once they sneaked into the armory and took two old-fashioned round shields out to the long slope in front of the barn near the longhouse where the hay was brought in late in the summer. They sat down on the shields and slid like small otters down the whole slope. Their loud, happy laughter attracted attention, and when their father came and saw what they were doing with the equipment of grown men, he flew into a rage and gave them a thrashing that made them run wailing to their mother in the weaving house. But that little trouble soon passed. The thrall Svarte, who had seen the boys' inventiveness, went to the carpenters' workshop, found some suitable boards, and fashioned them with dowels into a toboggan. Then he steamed one end of the board and bent it slowly upward like the front end of sleigh runners, and ran a leather cord through it as reins for the toboggan, and soon the boys were sliding full speed down the snowy slopes with shrieks and laughter once more.

At first Magnus was out of sorts at seeing his sons tumbling about in the snow in happy games with the thralls' children. He didn't think it was seemly. Eskil and Arn were going to grow up to be the owners of thralls, not their playmates. In Sigrid's opinion, however, children were children, and the vagaries of adult life probably wouldn't elude any of them when they got a little older, be they thrall or son of the lord. Besides, now the boys got out of studying Latin.

She smiled in her ambiguous way as she said that. The fact

that the boys had to learn Latin was just as obvious to her as it was incomprehensible to Magnus. She believed that it was the language of the future. He thought that only monks and priests needed such knowledge; in Lödöse he could trade with people from afar in everyday language, even if he had to muddle through and repeat things sometimes. Anyway, as soon as the lay brother managed to get through the snow from Varnhem to resume studying with the boys, the games with the thralls would be over.

But the winter refused to release its grip on Arnäs, and Eskil and Arn had never spent a winter that was more fun, since they were able to play even more games with the thrall children. They built a fort in the snow, and took turns defending it while the others attempted to take the fort, each side with the same number of thrall children. Eskil and Arn had little wooden swords in their hands, while the others had to make do with snowballs, since they were thralls and not allowed to bear arms. The result was a few tears and some black-and-blue marks.

They also helped Kol, Svarte's boy who was their own age, to catch live mice for Svarte to use as bait in his ermine traps. Ermine pelts were very valuable; four of them would buy a thrall. When the wolves began to come near Arnäs, Svarte put scraps from the slaughterhouses by an opening in one of the most distant hay-barns, to keep watch for the wolves when the night was moonlit, calm, and quiet.

Foolishly Eskil now claimed, and Arn nodded eagerly in agreement, that their father had said they were allowed to join Svarte during the watch, as long as they kept quiet as mice. Svarte had his doubts, but he didn't dare ask Herr Magnus if it was really true that the master's children would have tried to trick him. When the weather was good, Eskil and Arn took to sneaking out at night with thick sheepskins under their arms to meet Svarte, who had two crossbows loaded. Since Svarte had said too much at home, Kol came out as well. Three boys with sparkling eyes and impatiently pounding hearts sat next to Svarte and waited, trying not to rustle in the hay, as they kept an eye on the white snowfield and the offal heap that was visited every night by foxes.

Finally one night when the moon had already waned to half, but the weather was clear and calm and very cold, the wolves came. Svarte and the boys could hear their cautious steps on the crust of snow long before they could spy them with their eyes. Svarte made excited gestures for the boys to keep absolutely still. In his fervor he drew a hand across his throat to emphasize the serious punishment that would befall them otherwise, and saw at once Eskil and Arn open their eyes wide in surprise. They had never in their lives been threatened by a thrall, not even in jest. But they nodded eagerly and held up their small index and middle fingers pressed together in a sign that they swore not to make the slightest sound.

Svarte moved unbearably slowly as he drew both crossbows without the least rustle, click, or creak. Then he laid one at the ready and cautiously raised the other into position, poised to shoot.

But the wolves were wary. Now they looked like black shadows out there on the snow. It took a while before they came closer, and Svarte had to lower his crossbow so his arms wouldn't tire. Finally the first wolf came forward, nibbled a little meat, and quickly vanished out of shooting range, pursued by the other wolves. Out of sight they could be heard snarling as they fought over the food. Then they calmed down and came forward one by one, and soon they stood there eating, gulping down the meat with growls and muffled gurgling sounds. The boys found the tension almost intolerable and couldn't understand why Svarte was taking so long.

He again motioned them to sit absolutely still, more polite

in his gestures this time; then he raised one crossbow and took careful aim. The instant he loosed the shot he reached for the second crossbow, slung it into position, aimed hastily, and shot again. Down in the snow a pitiful whimpering was heard.

As soon as the boys heard Svarte move, they dared to shout with joy, and then they pushed forward, scrambling to get the best view. Below them lay a wolf kicking in the snow. Svarte gazed in silence over their heads. Then he told them that now it wasn't safe for small boys; one of the wolves had limped off, injured. They either had to go home or else stay up here in safety while he went down to check on what had happened. They promised at once to stay where they were.

When Svarte reached the scene of the shooting, he stopped, leaning forward to examine the snow a short distance away. He wasn't worried about the wolf that had now stopped kicking and lay dead. Then he discovered the trail of blood and began heavily trudging off through the deep snow.

The boys sat for a long time listening in silence; they were starting to feel very cold. Finally a howl that turned their marrow to ice was heard in the dark, followed by gurgling growls that sounded like when the wolves were devouring the meat. Eskil, Arn, and Kol now sat pale and quiet and scared, waiting. But then they pricked up their ears and heard, first faintly and then more clearly, Svarte's heavy, plodding footsteps and panting.

"Father is carrying the second wolf on his back, that's why he's walking so heavily," Kol explained with poorly feigned confidence. Eskil and Arn nodded in awe.

✠

By Paulsmas, the winter was half gone, the bear had turned in its den, and just as much snow would fall afterward as before. Magnus had ordered the road cleared down to Forshem church so that he and his immediate family could attend mass for the first time in far too long.

The weather was pleasant, with sunshine and no wind, and the temperature was just warm enough for a few drips to fall from the roof, so the sleigh ride was comfortable on the newly blazed path. Magnus could hear how the boys, well ensconced in their grandfather's huge wolf-skin pelt, were shouting and laughing in the back of the sleigh as it lurched in the tracks. He urged on his two powerful sorrel horses to run faster, because he enjoyed hearing happy little boys squeal. He also allowed himself this diversion because he had a sense of foreboding, although he couldn't say why. But he had left half his retainers back home, something that the men grumbled about because after the long winter months in isolation at Arnäs they would have liked the chance to swagger a bit for whoever was on the church green. It was there their hearts lay, rather than inside the church listening to God's word like Christian folk.

When the sleigh party from Arnäs drove up onto the church green, what Magnus saw reinforced his premonitions. People were standing about in small groups, talking in low voices, and they hadn't mixed together as was the custom; each group stood near their own clan, and many of the men were wearing chain mail underneath their cloaks, garb that was worn only in uneasy times. The church would be full, because all the neighbors from the south and all those from the west and Husaby had come. But from the east there were no other neighbors beside his own stewards, and they stood off by themselves, huddling together as if they had not yet learned how to behave like free men. Normally Magnus would have sought them out and spoken with them about the weather in a loud voice, but now was not the time for such solicitude. When Sigrid and the boys climbed down from the sleigh he left all care of the horses to his house thralls and strode with his family over to the most favorably disposed neighbors, the Pål clan from Husaby, to find out what had happened.

King Sverker had been assassinated on his way to the morning service on Christmas Day at Tollstad church, and he had already been buried next to his wife Ulvhild in Alvastra. The outlaw who did it was known, King Sverker's own steward and stable-man from Husaby. The fellow had already fled, presumably to Denmark.

But the big question was not who had wielded the sword, but who had stood behind it. Some thought that it must be Erik Jed-vardsson, who was now up in Östra Aros with the Swedes, and who according to rumor had already been elected king of the Swedes at Mora Stones. Others thought that the instigator had to be sought in Denmark, that it was Magnus Henriksen who was now laying claim to the royal crown.

In Linköping, Karl Sverkersson had proclaimed himself king and called a *landsting* to confirm the fact. So now the question was who would be elected king of Western Götaland: Karl Sverkersson or Erik Jedvardsson. But the matter would not likely be resolved quietly or peacefully.

When the church bells rang for mass, all gossip ceased and the people streamed into God's house to quell their unrest, console themselves with the Gospel, or cool their excitement with holy song. But some, like Magnus, stood lost in other thoughts, unable to cleanse themselves of all worldly things, as was the intention. Yet it was conceivable that most men of noble lineage and armorial bearings secretly shared Magnus's worry: that this might be the last time they stood as friends beneath the same church roof. Only God could know what the future would bring and which clans would be set against each other. Not since King Sverker took the royal crown, back when Magnus was only a boy, had the Goths been forced to make war against one an-other. But now that time was not far off.

When the mass was over, Magnus was so deeply lost in thought that he didn't notice it was time to go until Sigrid gave him a light poke in the side. But by then he had decided precisely what he should and should not say.

Lengthy discussions followed amongst the men, while the women and children grew more and more impatient as they waited in the sleighs, freezing. And Magnus chose his words well. He admitted that Erik Jedvardsson had visited Arnäs just before the murder, but he pointed out that Erik's wife Kristina had stirred up a lot of trouble with her dispute over Varnhem. So his clan was both for and against Erik Jedvardsson.

He also admitted that Sigrid had been very close to King Sverker, but that the king did not look upon his own Norwegian mother's clan with tender eyes. So his lineage was both for and against the Sverker clan.

Others took a clearer position, most of them in favor of the Sverker clan, as it turned out, but Magnus did not want to bind himself or point to any of those present as his future enemy. That would be unwise no matter what happened. The enemies that God would give to a man would have to be faced sooner or later with the sword, regardless of what a man said on the spur of the moment in front of the church.

But his expression was dark and gloomy on the way home, and as they were nearing Arnäs he gazed about restlessly, as if he already expected the estate to be under siege, although the snow still protected Arnäs from any assaults by soldiers from the north and east.

When they arrived home Magnus called for more wood to be brought to the forges and he had them fired up. He summoned all the smithy thralls and set them to work at the bellows and anvil to forge arrowheads and spear points, as many as they could make. They had plenty of raw iron at Arnäs, but it was unsuited for making swords.

The very next day Magnus outfitted two heavy sleighs to travel to Lödöse and acquire the provisions that would be necessary for the coming war.

✠

But the winter only slowly loosened its grip over Arnäs, and no news was heard of armies being mobilized in either Eastern Götaland or in Svealand. Magnus fell into a better humor and converted the work in the smithies and carpenters' shops to more everyday purposes. Sigrid had also calmed him with the idea that Arnäs would hardly be the first place the war would strike. If Erik Jedvardsson was now declared king of the Swedes, and Karl Sverkersson king of Eastern Götaland, then those two ought to fight it out amongst themselves. Here in Western Götaland the most important thing was to swear allegiance to the victor afterward.

Magnus half agreed with her. But he thought it equally likely that one of them would turn first to Western Götaland to acquire yet another of the three crowns that Erik Jedvardsson said he wanted to possess. And then a decision would have to be made. Would Erik Jedvardsson be the first to make such a demand? Or would it be Karl Sverkersson? Both possibilities were wide open.

Sigrid believed that in any case they could not affect the situation by sitting at Arnäs and speculating as they drank ale late into the night. Sooner or later everything would be made clear. Then, and only then, would it be time to decide. Magnus was content with that plan for the time being.

But when the icicles had been dripping from the roofs for a week and the ice on the lake had begun to thaw, a misfortune befell Arnäs that was considerably greater than the one that would have occurred if either of the two kings had come to visit and demanded an oath of allegiance.

Eskil and Arn were now more subdued and disciplined since lay brother Erlend had returned to Arnäs just after Blasiusmas on February 3rd. From dawn to dusk they were kept in a corner of the hall in the longhouse, close to the fireplaces, where lay brother Erlend hammered knowledge into their reluctant little minds. Both boys found their work tedious, because the texts Erlend had brought back from Varnhem were few in number and dealt with things that held no interest for little boys or even grown men in Western Götaland. They contained mostly various philosophical dissertations on the elements and physics. Yet the work was not intended merely to teach them philosophy, for they were far too young for that; it was meant to torment them with Latin grammar. Without grammar there was no learning at all; without grammar the world would be closed to all understanding, as Erlend constantly repeated. And with a sigh the boys would once again obediently bend their heads over the texts.

Now it's true that lay brother Erlend did not complain. But he too could have imagined a more important demonstration of his calling from God, or at least a more pleasant task, than trying to pound knowledge into the reluctant minds of small boys. But he would never dream of questioning the orders of Father Henri. And, as he sometimes told himself gloomily, perhaps this assignment was merely a difficult test that he had to endure, or a continued punishment for the sins he had committed in his earthly life before he had heard the call.

But the day of rest was sanctified, even for boys who worked only with Latin. And on the Sabbath the two dashed out after morning prayers and vanished from sight like soaped squirrels. Magnus and Sigrid had agreed to leave them alone, and they preferred not to know what the boys did outside the quiet and meditation that the day of rest required in accordance with God's commandment.

The thrall boy Kol had a tame jackdaw that he carried around on his shoulder wherever he went, and he had promised Eskil and Arn that together they would catch new baby jackdaws as soon as this year's brood was big enough in early summer to pluck baby birds from their nests up in the tower.

Now they had snuck up to see how many nests there were, and if there were already eggs. There were no eggs yet, but they saw that the jackdaws had begun to weave their nests for the year, and that was promising.

Eskil had asked to borrow the jackdaw from Kol and let it sit on his shoulder, and Kol of course agreed, although he pointed out that the bird might be a bit more standoffish with strangers than it was with him.

And just as Kol feared, the jackdaw suddenly left Eskil's shoulder and flew off to perch far out on the parapet. Eskil didn't dare do anything about the matter, because he was afraid of heights. Kol didn't dare do anything because he was afraid of scaring the bird into flying off somewhere between heaven and earth. But Arn crawled cautiously along the parapet to catch hold of the string that was tied around one of the bird's legs. He couldn't reach it and had to climb up into the icy arrow slit, stand on tiptoe, and stretch out his hand as far as he could. When he reached the string and gingerly grabbed it, the jackdaw lifted off with a shriek, and Arn was dragged along as the bird plummeted. To the other terrified boys it seemed an eternity before they heard a dull thump down below as Arn struck the ground.

Soon Arnäs was resounding with shouts and wails as Arn, unconscious, was carefully carried off on a stretcher to the cookhouse. By the time they laid him down, they saw that all hope was gone. Arn lay completely pale and still and he wasn't breathing.

When Sigrid came running from the longhouse, she was at

first beside herself, as any mother would have been at the news that a son had fallen and been knocked senseless. But when she saw that it was Arn lying there, she stopped short and fell silent, and her face was filled with doubt. She thought that what she was seeing couldn't be true. Arn couldn't possibly die so young; she had been convinced of that ever since the moment he was born, with the caul of victory.

But lifeless he lay, pale, not breathing.

When Magnus a moment later sank to his knees beside her, he already knew that all hope was gone. In despair he waved everyone out of the room except for lay brother Erlend, since he didn't want to show his tears to thralls and housefolk.

To pray any longer for Arn's life seemed meaningless; rather, Magnus admonished them to pray for forgiveness of the sins that had unquestionably drawn God's punishment upon them. Erlend did not dare venture an opinion in the matter.

With tears streaming down her face, Sigrid appealed to them both not to give up hope but to pray for a miracle. And they silently acquiesced, since miracles could happen, and nothing was certain until they had at least tried to pray for it.

Magnus suggested that they direct their prayers to Our Lady, since she had clearly had the most to do with the birth of the boys.

But Sigrid felt inside that Our Lady, the Mother of God, had probably lost patience with her by now, and she feverishly pondered for a moment before it struck her that the saint who stood closest to Arn had to be the holy Saint Bernard. He was a brand-new saint; no one really knew anything about his powers in the North.

Lay brother Erlend agreed at once with her suggestion and recited one prayer after another before the kneeling parents. When darkness fell, Arn had still shown no sign of life. But they didn't give up, even though Magnus on one occasion mumbled that all hope was gone and that now it was more a matter of accepting God's punishment with sorrow, dignity, and regret.

But Sigrid swore before Saint Bernard and God that if Arn were saved, the boy would be given to do God's holy work among human beings here on earth. And she repeated her promise and made Magnus repeat it for a third time along with her.

Just as Sigrid felt that the last spark of hope was about to be extinguished in her heart as well, the miracle occurred.

Arn raised himself up on one elbow and looked about in confusion as if he had just awakened from a night's sleep instead of returning from the realm of the dead. He whimpered something about having such a pain in his other arm that he couldn't lean on it. But the three adults did not hear him because they were immersed in prayers of thanksgiving, which were no doubt the purest and most sincere prayers they had ever offered to God.

Arn was able to walk, with his mother at his left side, into the warmth of the longhouse, where he was put to bed near the fireplaces by the gable wall. But since he still had pain in his right arm, Sot was summoned and they told her to use only her purest skills and not besmirch the Lord's miracle with any sorcery or impure healing arts. Sot carefully squeezed Arn's arm and examined the places that made him squeal the most, which was not easy because Arn wanted to show how brave he was and not admit to the pain while so many people were watching him, his father among them.

But he didn't fool Sot. She fetched dried nettles and cooked a gruel that she smeared around his arm and wrapped with linen. Then she spoke with Svarte, who went to the carpenters' shop. He worked for a while and came back with two slightly concave pieces of fir that he measured before vanishing again to finish the work as Sot had directed.

When Svarte was done, Sot bound the two splints around Arn's arm with more linen bandages and warned him and Sigrid to keep the arm still, because it was badly sprained. Then she gave the boy a decoction of new dried leaves and the roots of meadow-sweet so that he would sleep without a fever.

Soon Arn was sleeping with a calm expression on his face, as if no misfortune had befallen him and no miracle had occurred. Sigrid and Magnus sat for a long time gazing at their slumbering son, both filled with awe that the Lord God had allowed one of his miracles to occur at their estate.

Their second son Arn had been resurrected from the dead. No one could doubt that. But the question was whether it was because the Lord wanted to show his benevolence toward those who prayed to Him with the same tears as all fathers and mothers would have shed at this most difficult of times. Or whether it was really true, as Sigrid was convinced in her soul, that the Lord had prepared a special task for Arn when he became a man.

No one could know for certain, however, since the Lord's ways often surpass the understanding of human beings. They could only take the miracle at Arnäs to heart and pray with renewed gratitude.

Lay brother Erlend had long felt compelled by his sacred task. He had to record the account of the miracle at Arnäs with great care and include every small detail. Since the death of holy Saint Bernard had occurred only a few years in the past, this might be the first miracle that could be associated with him in Western Götaland, and so it was of great importance. Erlend also thought that he would undoubtedly make Father Henri very happy with this story, and that his industriousness and exactitude in carrying out this task might also shorten his wait to be admitted as a full brother in the Cistercian order. In any case, it couldn't hurt to be the bearer of such marvelous news.

Parchment was not made at Arnäs, but there was thin calfskin which was rubbed smooth on one side and which Herr Magnus sold for the making of clothing. Erlend had been allowed to use remnants of this material for his writing practice with the boys and now there was much more writing and printing and reading going on in the study corner of the hall. Both boys were adept with a writing quill and ink. Mostly they were asked to copy onto calfskin remnants the text that Erlend wrote out in Latin. Then they had to try translating it into rune text on the line below. Herr Magnus had said sternly that if the boys had to print in church language, they might as well learn their forefathers' script at the same time. For future merchants it was not at all a useless art.

During their first writing exercises Erlend had noticed that little Arn, whose right arm was still unusable, wrote, printed, and drew pictures just as well with his left hand. Because the boy was injured Erlend had not worried about this; otherwise it was not a good sign if someone favored using the unclean hand. But when Arn's right hand healed, it turned out that he used it just as much as his left. It was as though it made no difference to him. It seemed to be a matter of mood that dictated which hand he used to pick up the goose quill.

Once Erlend, after much travail, rewriting, and prayers, considered his account to be finished, he was eager to make a trip to Varnhem as soon as possible. He justified his departure by saying that he had obligations at the cloister, something about certain saints requiring the presence of all the lay brothers, and that his absence might provoke a rebuke. Filled with anticipation, he was allowed to ride down to Varnhem on Annunciation Day, the day that the cranes returned to Western Götaland.

The boys did not mourn his leaving. When spring came and

the farmyards, the courtyard of the fortress, and other large areas surrounding the buildings of Arnäs were free of snow, the time of play arrived for all the children. A special game at Arnäs was to swipe a thin band from the cooperage and then run along rolling the hoop and steering it, using a stick to give it more speed. The game had developed into a contest with the children trying to take the hoops from each other, using only the sticks. They would drive the hoops before them between the walls of the fortress courtyard. When someone managed to make the hoop strike the fortress wall, he won the game. This was no easy task, because all the others who didn't have a hoop under their own stick did everything they could to interfere.

Arn, of course, was not one of the oldest boys, but he soon proved to be the one who won this game most often, small as he was. He was as quick as a ferret, and he could also do something that the others couldn't do, and that was to switch back and forth between his hands, changing the direction of the rolling hoop so that all the other boys would suddenly run the wrong way. He could be stopped only if they tripped him or pulled on his kirtle or physically held him back. The older boys grew eager to employ such methods, but Arn's agility also increased. Finally Eskil, who was the only one who would have dared, began stopping him by slapping him in the face if he came close.

Then Arn got tired of the game and went off to sulk by himself.

Magnus found a way to console him. He had a bow and arrows made in the proper size, and then he took Arn aside and began to teach him to shoot. It wasn't long before Eskil came trudging over to them, wanting to shoot too. But to his dismay he found that his younger brother always shot better than he did, and soon another quarrel erupted between the brothers. Magnus of course intervened and decided that if they were going to squabble like this, the boys could shoot only when he was present. In this way their games were suddenly transformed into studies, almost like sitting and printing words or reading incomprehensible texts about the elements and categories of philosophy. And so the pleasure was lost, at least for Eskil, who was always defeated by both his father and little brother.

But what Magnus had witnessed of his sons made him think. Eskil was like all other boys in the way he moved and shot a bow and arrow, just as Magnus had been when he was a boy. But Arn had something inside him that other boys didn't have, an ability that had to be God-given. What might come of it no one could say for sure, but the boy's talent was remarkable.

Magnus spoke with Sigrid about this on several light spring nights, after the boys had gone to bed. It was taken for granted that Eskil would inherit Arnäs; that was God's will since Eskil was the firstborn son. Eskil would manage the estate and their trade. But what did God have in mind for Arn?

Sigrid agreed that it looked as though God intended a warrior's training for Arn, but she was not entirely sure that she liked that explanation, no matter how obvious it might seem. And inside she felt guilt nagging at her because she had promised God—in a moment when tears were streaming down and her mind was racked with despair, to be sure—but she had still promised Him that Arn's life would be dedicated to God's work on earth.

She hadn't spoken with Magnus about this matter; it seemed as though the promise was something that Magnus had wiped from his memory, although he must remember it as well as Sigrid did. And he was a man who prided himself on always keeping his word. But right now Magnus envisioned his son's future as a mighty warrior in the foremost phalanx of the clan, and that image certainly gave him more joy than the thought of Arn as a bishop in Skara or the prior of some cloister. That's how men thought. This did not surprise Sigrid.

But soon God sent a severe reminder of His will. It began as a slightly annoying cut on Sigrid's hand, which as far as she could recall came from a splinter of wood in one of the livestock buildings when an unruly heifer shoved her and she had to grab hold of the wall so as not to fall into the muck. The wound would not heal; it swelled and began to grow more and more foul.

And one morning Magnus noticed something odd on her face. When she went to a tub of water and looked at her reflection, she saw a new sore like the one she had on her hand, and when she touched it she found that it was full of pus and mucus.

After that her illness quickly grew worse. The sore on her face spread, and soon she could no longer see out of the eye closest to it. The spot began to itch fiercely and she often had to rub it. She began hiding her face, and she offered up fervent prayers every dawn, midday, and evening. But nothing seemed to help. Her husband and the boys began looking at her with alarm.

When lay brother Erlend came riding back from Varnhem he was full of news both good and bad. The good news, which he related first, was that the report about the miracle at Arnäs had been welcomed so heartily at Varnhem that it had now been printed on real parchment in manuscript lettering in the cloister's diary.

The bad news concerned Erik Jedvardsson's wife Kristina. She had been staying at one of her slaughtering farms in the vicinity with a mighty retainer provided to her by her husband, the Swedish king. Yes, it was true after all, Erik Jedvardsson was the king of Svealand.

Kristina had instigated one devilish trick after another and incited her peasants against the brothers. She had even persuaded the occasional priest to take her side. She claimed that the cloister was built on unlawfully captured land, that a large portion of the land rightfully belonged to her, and if they didn't want to yield willingly according to her wishes, things would not be pleasant when King Erik arrived in Western Götaland.

On one occasion in the middle of a mass, a crowd of women had forced their way into the cloister clad only in their shifts and danced and sang indecent songs in this immodest garb. Then they had sat down in the midst of the cloister, thus defiling it. It had been a hard task for the brothers to clean and bless the cloister anew.

Sigrid now understood God's reminder. And she took her husband and Erlend aside in the hall, told all the house thralls to leave, and revealed her deformed face to Erlend, who turned pale, frightened by what he saw. Then she said what had to be said.

"Magnus, my dear lord and husband. Surely you recall just as well as I what we promised Saint Bernard and the Lord God just before the Lord recalled Arn to life. We promised to dedicate him to God's holy work on earth if he was allowed to live. But then we never spoke of the matter again. Now God is telling us what He thinks of our neglect. We must repent and do penance, don't you understand that?"

Magnus wrung his hands and admitted that he actually did remember the promise very well, but it was a promise made at a very difficult moment, and surely God would understand that, wouldn't He?

Sigrid now turned to Erlend, who was much more familiar with all things holy than were she and Magnus. Erlend could do nothing but agree. It looked like leprosy, he had to say straight out. And that plague did not exist at Arnäs or anywhere else in Western Götaland, so it couldn't have come from anywhere but from the Lord Himself. And the fact that Sigrid's most pleasing deed before God, her donation of the land to the Varnhem cloister, was now in jeopardy, must also be viewed as a clear warning.

God demanded they make good on their promise. And He
was punishing Sigrid for her ambivalence in that matter. What
had happened could not be interpreted any other way.

The next day, sorrow hung heavy over Arnäs. In the farmyards and the castle courtyard, no laughter or squabbling was
heard from playing children. The house thralls moved like silent
forest beasts in the hall, and several of them had a hard time
hiding their tears.

Magnus was at a loss as to how he would present the weighty
news to his youngest son. But while Sigrid was busy packing
for the journey, he took Arn up to the tower where they could
be alone. Arn, who still did not understand what was going to
happen to him, looked more pensively curious than afraid.

Magnus lifted him up onto one of the arrow slits so he could
look at his son face to face. Then it occurred to him that Arn
might be afraid of this high ledge from which he had plummeted
all the way into the realm of the dead.

But Arn showed no fear. Instead he leaned out over the parapet so he could look straight down at where he had fallen, since
his father seemed to be lost in his own thoughts.

Magnus carefully pulled Arn back and embraced him, and
then began his difficult explanation. He pointed out over the district, where as far as the eye could see work was being done on
the spring planting. Then he said that all this would be Eskil's
realm one day when he was no longer alive, but that Arn's inheritance would be an even greater kingdom—the kingdom of God
here on earth.

Arn didn't seem to understand his words. Perhaps to the
young boy's ears it sounded like the usual church talk when
people wanted to sound solemn and said things that meant nothing for a while before they ventured to say something that really
did have meaning. Magnus had to start over.

He talked about the difficult time when Arn was not with

them among the living, and how he and Sigrid in their despair had promised God to give their son to God's work on earth if only he would be allowed to come back to life. Then they had hesitated in fulfilling their promise, but now God had punished them harshly for this disobedience, so the promise had to be honored at once.

Arn slowly began to sense that something unpleasant was coming. And his father immediately confirmed this when he revealed what was going to happen. Arn must now travel to Varnhem with his mother and Erlend. There he would enter the cloister as an oblate, which is what children were called who entered the service of God. God would assuredly watch over him, just as his patron saint, Saint Bernard, always did, for God most certainly had great plans for him.

Now Arn began to understand. His parents were going to offer him to God. Not like in the olden days, not like in the sagas from the heathen times, but they would still offer him to God. And he could do nothing at all about it, since children always had to obey their father and their mother. He started to cry, and no matter how ashamed he was to cry in front of his father, he could not stop.

Magnus took him in his arms and tried awkwardly to console him with words about God's good will and protection, about Saint Bernard who would watch over him, and anything else he could think of. But the boy's little body shook with sobs in his embrace, and Magnus felt that he too, God forbid, would eventually show his sorrow.

Then the wagons came driving up and the retainers reined in the horses as they waited in the courtyard before the door to the longhouse. Sigrid came out first with her face covered and went over to the lead wagon. Then Erlend emerged, looked about shyly, and slipped into the second wagon.

Last came Magnus with the two small boys, who were

holding each other and crying, clinging to each other as if the strength of their little child-arms might prevent what was going to happen. Magnus separated them gently but firmly, lifted up Arn and carried him over to Sigrid's wagon and set him down next to his mother. Then he took a deep breath and slapped the horses so that the wagon started with an abrupt lurch while he turned around and walked back toward the door, making a vain attempt to catch Eskil, who managed to escape.

Magnus went inside and closed the door behind him without turning around. Eskil ran behind the wagons for a while, crying, until he fell and helplessly watched his brother vanish in the dust from the road.

Arn cried bitterly as he knelt in the wagon and looked back toward Arnäs, which grew smaller and smaller in the distance. He understood that he would never see his home again, and it was impossible for Sigrid to console him.

Sigrid's visit came at an inopportune time for Father Henri. His old friend and colleague from Clairvaux, Father Stéphan, who was now the prior in Alvastra, was visiting so that they could discuss the difficult situation that had arisen with Queen Kristina, who was stirring up trouble and inciting the people against the monks at Varnhem. Naturally Stéphan was the one with whom Father Henri most wanted to discuss complicated questions. They had been together ever since their youth, and they were part of the first group that had received the terrible orders from holy Saint Bernard himself, that they should depart for the cold, barbaric North to start a daughter cloister. It had been a long journey, horrendously cold and gloomy.

Father Stéphan had already read the account of the miracle from Arnäs and was familiar with Sigrid's problem. To be sure,

both at Alvastra and Varnhem, as well as in the mother cloister in Burgundy, they had stopped accepting oblates, and the
thought behind the change was logical and easy to understand.
The free will of a human being to choose either God's way or the
path of perdition was eliminated if they accepted small children
and raised them in the cloister. Such children would already be
molded into monks by the age of twelve, since they knew no
other life than that of the cloister. Such an upbringing might rob
the children of their free will, and therefore it was a wise decision no longer to accept oblates.

On the other hand, the miracle at Arnäs could not be ignored,
because it was definitely no small event. If the parents had promised their child to God at the most critical moment, and they did
so clearly and openly, and God had then let the miracle happen,
the parents' promise had to be construed as so sanctified that it
would be impossible to break.

But what if they, God's servants, now made the promise
impossible to fulfill by refusing to accept the boy because the
custom of oblates had been abolished?

Then the parents might be released from their promise. But
in that case, the monks at the same time would be placing themselves, knowingly and willingly, above the clearly manifested
will of God. That could not happen. So they had to accept the
boy.

And how should they respond to Fru Sigrid? It seemed that
God had punished her severely for her ambivalence, and now
she was here wanting to do penance. There was also the much
bigger question of whether the monks might simply have to
abandon Varnhem, return home to Clairvaux, and from there
seek to have Kristina and even her husband excommunicated so
that they could be rid of the problem and start over again. Fac-
toring in travel time and everything else, that process might take
a couple of years.

The two men sat inside in the shade of the covered arcade that connected the church to the monks' quarters. Before them out in the sunshine, Brother Lucien's garden was blazing with color. Father Henri had sent Brother Lucien, who had a knowledge of medicinal herbs, up to the guesthouse of the old farm, where Sigrid and her son were staying. Right now their grave and difficult conversation was interrupted as Brother Lucien returned with a worried look on his face.

"Well," he said with a sigh, sinking down on the stone bench next to them. "I don't know quite what to believe. I don't think it's leprosy; it's much too watery and ulcerous. I think it's some variant of swine pox, something that comes from the uncleanness of the animals. But it looks bad, I have to admit."

"If it is only some sort of swine pox, what can you do for her, dear Brother Lucien?" asked Father Henri with interest.

"Well now . . . do you really think, Father, that I should try to do something for it?" wondered Brother Lucien dubiously.

"How do you mean?" asked the other two at the same time, both equally astonished.

"I mean . . . if the Lord Himself has visited this illness upon her, who am I to revoke the Lord's will?"

"Look here, Brother Lucien, don't make a fool of yourself now!" snorted Father Henri in irritation. "You are the Lord's instrument, and if you do the best you can and He finds your work good, then it will help. Otherwise nothing at all will help and nothing will make any difference. So what had you thought to do about the matter?"

The monk explained that as far as he understood it was a question of cleaning and drying out the sores. Boiled and consecrated water for washing, then clean air and sunshine, should dry out the abscesses in about a week. Her hand looked more dire, and in the worst case it might turn out to be something other than harmless swine pox.

Father Henri nodded in agreement, showing great interest. As usual when Brother Lucien described his initial medical diagnosis, he sounded quite convincing. What Father Henri especially admired was the monk's ability to stay calm when confronting problems and not rush off at once to slap on all sorts of herbs in the hope that one of them might do some good. According to Brother Lucien, such ill-considered conduct could easily cause an illness to go from bad to worse.

When Brother Lucien had gone, Father Stéphan again took up his previous train of thought and said that it was rather obvious that the Lord God wanted something special with that boy. If he was to be just one more monk among all the other monks, then it seemed a bit extreme to resort to both a miracle and a case of leprosy, didn't it? People became monks for lesser reasons than that.

Father Henri burst out laughing at his colleague's outrageous but humorous logic. Still, there was no real counterargument. So they should take in the boy, but treat him carefully, like one of Brother Lucien's sensitive plants, and make sure that his free will was not broken. Some time in the future, perhaps, they would have a better idea of the Lord's intentions for the boy. So the boy was allowed to become an oblate. And if they had to move out of Varnhem, he would have to come along with them. But that was a matter for a later time.

The question of Fru Sigrid remained. Naturally the simplest approach would be to start by letting her confess and ask for her own opinion. Father Stéphan went into the scriptorium to reread, perhaps a bit more attentively than before, the account of the miracle from Arnäs. With a concerned expression Father Henri walked up toward the old guesthouse outside the cloister walls to hear Sigrid's confession.

He found mother and son in a pitiful state. There was only one bed in the room, and there lay Sigrid, panting with fever with her eyes closed. At her side sat a little fellow, his face red from crying, clutching her healthy hand. The house hadn't been cleaned; it was filled with all sorts of rubbish and there was a cold draft. While it hadn't been used in many years, it hadn't been torn down because there were more pressing things to do, or possibly because the wooden walls were old and rotten and the lumber couldn't be reused.

He draped the prayer stole over his shoulders and went over to Arn, cautiously stroking the boy's head. But Arn seemed not to notice, or else he was pretending he didn't.

Father Henri then gently asked the boy to leave for a moment while his mother made confession, but the boy just shook his head without looking up and squeezed his mother's hand all the harder.

Sigrid now awoke, and Arn left the room reluctantly, slamming the drafty door behind him. Sigrid seemed indignant at his behavior, but with a smile Father Henri put his right index finger to his lips and shushed her, indicating that she shouldn't worry. Then he asked if she was ready to confess.

"Yes, Father," she replied, her mouth dry. "Forgive me, Father, for I have sinned. With the help of holy Saint Bernard, my lord and husband and I, together with lay brother Erlend, managed through sincere prayers to ask the Lord to return Arn to live among us. But just before this miracle occurred I made a solemn and sacred promise to the Lord to give the boy to God's holy work among the people here on earth if He saw fit to save my son."

"I know all this; it's exactly as it was written by lay brother Erlend. Your Latin is as fluid as water, by the way. Have you been practicing lately? Well, never mind that, now back to your confession, my child."

"Well, I have studied with the boys . . ." she murmured wearily, but took a deep breath and thought intently before she went on. "I betrayed my sacred promise to the Lord God; I ignored it, and therefore He has afflicted me with leprosy as you can see. I want to do penance, if it is possible to do penance for such a grave sin. My idea is that I should live here in this house as the wife of no one and eat only scraps from the monks' table as long as I live."

"I can see, my dear Sigrid, that you who have done so much for those of us who toil here in the garden of the Lord at Varnhem, to you it may seem that the Lord has been harsh toward you," said Father Henri pensively. "But one cannot ignore the fact that it is a grave sin to break a sacred promise to the Lord God, even if one makes this promise in a difficult moment. For is it not in our greatest difficulties that we give the Lord our greatest promises? We shall take good care of your son as both the Lord and you yourself, although in different ways, have asked us to do. The boy's name is Arn, is it not? I should know, since I was the one who baptized him. And we will also tend to your affliction and you may stay here to eat, ahem, well, as you say, the scraps from our table. But I can't give you absolution for your sins just now, and I beg you not to be unduly frightened because of this. I don't yet know what the Lord will tell us. Perhaps He merely wanted to give you a little reminder. You must say twenty Pater Nosters and twenty Ave Marias, then go to sleep and know that you are in safe and tender hands. I'll send Brother Lucien to you to take care of your sores with the utmost care, and if it then turns out, as I sense but do not know, that the Lord will make you whole again, then you will soon be without sin. Rest now. I'll take the boy with me down to the cloister."

Father Henri got up slowly and studied Sigrid's deformed face. One eye was so sealed shut by pus that it couldn't be seen: the other eye was only half open. He leaned forward and sniffed cautiously at the sores, then nodded thoughtfully and left the room as he stuffed the prayer stole in his pocket.

Outside the boy sat on a rock looking at the ground and didn't even turn around when Father Henri came out.

He stood for a moment looking at Arn, until the boy couldn't help glancing up at him. Then Father Henri gave him a kindly smile, but received only a sob in response before the boy again looked away.

"Look here, *mon fils*, come along with me like a good boy," said Father Henri as gently as he could, and accustomed as he was to always being obeyed, he stepped forward to pull on Arn's arm.

"Can't you even speak Swedish, you old devil?" Arn spat, kicking and struggling as Father Henri, who was quite a big and heavy man, dragged him along toward the cloister with the same ease as if he were carrying a basket of herbs from Brother Lucien's gardens.

When they reached the arcade by the cloister garden, Father Henri found his colleague from Alvastra sitting in the same place where they had held their discussion earlier.

Father Stéphan's face lit up at once when he caught sight of the unruly and sullen little Arn.

"Aha!" he exclaimed. "Here we have . . . er, our *jeune oblat. Enfin* . . . not particularly filled with gratitude *de Dieu* at the moment, eh?"

Father Henri shook his head in agreement with a smile and promptly lifted Arn onto the lap of his colleague, who easily warded off a bold fist from the little boy.

"Hold him as long as you can, dear brother. I must have a little chat with Brother Lucien first," said Father Henri and left the garden to find his fellow monk in charge of medicinal matters.

"There there, don't *strug-gél*," Father Stéphan hushed Arn in amusement.

"It's *struggle*, not *strug-gél*!" Arn fumed, trying to get loose, but he soon discovered that he was trapped by strong arms and gave up.

"So, if you think that my Nordic language sounds bad to your little ears, maybe we should speak something that suits me better," whispered Father Stéphan to him in Latin, without actually expecting an answer.

"It probably suits both of us better since you can't speak our language, you old monk," replied Arn in the same language.

Father Stéphan beamed, happily surprised.

"In truth I believe that we're going to get along just fine, you and I and Father Henri, much better and faster than you think, young man," the monk whispered in Arn's ear as if conveying a great secret to him.

"I don't want to sit like a slave poring over all those tedious old books all day long," Arn muttered, although less angry than a moment earlier.

"And what would you rather do?" asked Father Stéphan.

"I want to go home. I don't want to be your captive and slave," said Arn, no longer able to keep up his impudent front. He burst into tears again, but leaned against Father Stéphan's chest as the monk quietly stroked and patted his slender young back.

✠

As so often was the case, Brother Lucien was correct with his first diagnosis. The sores on Sigrid's face had nothing to do with leprosy, and he made rapid progress with his treatment.

First he had sent some of the lay brethren up to the guesthouse to scour it clean and seal and whitewash the walls, even though Sigrid protested against the improvements, believing that in her misery she didn't deserve either cleanliness or adornments.

Brother Lucien had attempted to explain that it was not a matter of esthetics but of medicine, but they didn't seem to really understand each other on this topic.

However, Sigrid's face was soon restored with precisely the remedies Brother Lucien had prescribed in the beginning: clean, sanctified water, sunshine, and fresh air. On the other hand, he hadn't any success with the sores, which spread from her hand and up her arm, causing a nasty swelling that was tinged blue. He had tried a number of preparations that were very strong, sometimes downright dangerous, but without success. In the end he realized that there could be only one cure for this toxicity in the blood. One sure sign was that he hadn't been able to allay her fever.

But he didn't want to tell this to Sigrid herself; instead he explained to Father Henri what had to be done. They would have to cut away all the diseased flesh—take her arm from her. Otherwise the evil from the arm would soon spread to her heart. If it had been one of the brothers themselves, all they'd have to do would be to call on Brother Guilbert with his big axe, but they undoubtedly could not act in the same way toward Fru Sigrid, their benefactor.

Father Henri agreed. He would try to present the matter as best he could to Fru Sigrid, although at the moment he had other things to tend to. Then Brother Lucien rebuked him, cautiously and probably for the first time ever. Because they did not have much time; it was a matter of life or death.

And yet Father Henri postponed the difficult matter, because Fru Kristina was on her way to the cloister along with an entire retinue of armed men.

When Kristina arrived at Varnhem she was riding at the vanguard of her retainers as if she were a male commander, and she was dressed in ceremonial garb. To display her nobility she wore a queen's crown on her head.

Father Henri and five of his closest brothers met her outside the cloister gate, which they demonstratively had locked behind them.

Kristina did not dismount, for she preferred to talk down to the monks; she now announced that one of the buildings had to be torn down, and promptly, namely Father Henri's scriptorium. A good portion of that particular building was apparently situated on the land that was rightfully hers.

Kristina knew quite well where to deliver the lance blow. Her intention was to make Father Henri lose his patience once and for all, and preferably his composure as well. She now found that she had succeeded with the first, at least. Father Henri spent most of his time among the books in the scriptorium; these were his brightest hours in the murky barbarity of the North. It was the part of the cloister that more than any other was his own.

He resolutely declared that he had no intention of tearing down the scriptorium.

Kristina replied that if the building was not demolished within a week, she would return, not only with her retainers, but with thralls who under the whips of the retainers would do the work rapidly. Perhaps the thralls would be less careful than the brothers would be if they saw fit to carry out her orders themselves. The choice was theirs.

Father Henri was now so angry that he could hardly control himself, and he told her that instead he intended to leave Varnhem. The journey would end with an audience with the Holy Father in Rome with the intention of excommunicating her, and her husband if he was an accomplice, if she dared to do the unthinkable and challenge God's servants on earth and His Holy Roman Church. Didn't she understand that she was about to bring eternal misfortune down upon both herself and Erik Jedvardsson?

What Father Henri threatened was true. But Kristina seemed

not to comprehend what he said, just as she did not understand the threat she was posing to her own husband's ambitious plans. A king who was excommunicated would have little to hope for in the Christian world.

But she merely tossed her head reproachfully, and wheeled her horse around in a wide turn, forcing the monks to dive for cover so as not to be trampled. As she rode away she called over her shoulder that in a week her thralls would arrive, her heathen thralls for that matter, to carry out their official duties.

✠

Arn had been treated leniently and was not forced to read more than four hours of Latin grammaticus per day. The first step was to make his Latin flawless; then they could move on to the next language. First a tool for the knowledge, then the knowledge itself.

But to assuage the boy's heavy heart, Father Henri had also seen to it that he was allowed to spend almost an equal amount of time with the mighty Brother Guilbert de Beaune, who would teach him arts altogether different from Latin and singing.

Brother Guilbert's main occupation at Varnhem was in the smithies, particularly the weapons smithy, which was the largest and best equipped of them all. The weapons smithy was run as a business and nothing else, because the swords that Brother Guilbert forged were so clearly superior to any others made in this barbaric part of the world. The fame of the monk's swords had spread rapidly and brought in goodly sums of silver to the convent.

Precisely according to intention, Arn was cajoled by watching and even occasionally helping Brother Guilbert, who took the boy in with the same gravity and precision as if he had been assigned to teach him to be a smith, showing him everything from the simple basics to the finer arts.

But when Arn after a time became less sulky and more open-minded, he also grew bolder when it came to asking about matters other than those pertaining to the work itself. Such as whether Brother Guilbert had ever shot a bow and arrow, and if so, whether he would like to have a contest.

To Arn's dismay, Brother Guilbert found this so amusing that he burst out laughing. He laughed so hard that he lost track of what he was working on and tossed a glowing piece of metal into a bucket of water. Then he sat down to finish laughing, his eyes wet with tears.

Finally, after he had composed himself and cheerfully wiped his eyes, he admitted that he may indeed have handled a bow and arrow, and that the two of them might soon make time for such games. Then he added that of course he feared meeting a young warrior as bold as Arn de Gothia. And then he broke out laughing anew.

It would be a long time before Arn was made aware of what was so funny. Right now he merely felt indignant. He snorted that perhaps Brother Guilbert was afraid. And provoked another salvo of laughter from Guilbert de Beaune.

✠

Faced with the decision between death or having her arm cut off and perhaps being able to cope with life as a cripple, Sigrid chose death. She felt that she could not understand the Lord's will in any other way. With sorrow in her heart she allowed Father Henri to hear her confession one last time, forgive her all her sins, and give her Holy Communion and extreme unction.

At Persmas, when the summer reached its apex and the time for hay-making had arrived, Sigrid died quietly up in the guest-house.

It was also time for the departure of Father Henri and the

seven brothers who would accompany him on his journey to the south. Sigrid was buried inside the cloister church, beneath the floor close to the altar, and the place was marked with only tiny secret signs, for Father Henri was very distrustful of Fru Kristina and her husband. Two brothers were sent to Arnäs with the news of her death, and the invitation to visit Sigrid's grave at any time.

During the four-hour-long funeral mass, Arn stood straight and still, the lone boy among all the monks. It was only the heavenly singing that now and then made his heart break so that he could no longer hold back the tears. But he was not ashamed of this, because he had noticed that he was not the only one weeping.

The next day the long journey to the south began, heading first for Denmark. Arn was now certain that his life belonged to God and that no human being, good or evil, strong or weak, would be able to do a thing to alter that fact.

He never looked back.

Chapter 4

So often things turn out much differently than people had imagined. What the poor in spirit call small coincidences, what the faithful call God's will, can sometimes alter an event to such an extent that no one could have predicted the result. That applies to powerful men who are convinced that they are the instigators of their own fortune, men like Erik Jedvardsson. But it also applies to such men who stand much closer to God than others and should be better able to understand His ways, men such as Henri of Clairvaux. For both these men the ways of the Lord had truly seemed inscrutable in recent years.

When Father Henri and his seven companions and a boy arrived in Roskilde on their way south through Denmark, he was firmly resolved to continue all the way to the general capital of the Cistercian order in Cîteaux in order to present his case for the excommunication of Erik Jedvardsson and his wife Kristina. It was an extremely grave matter of principle. For the first time the Cistercians had been forced to close down a monastery because of the whim of some king or king's wife. It was a question that was of crucial significance to the whole Christian world: Who controlled the Church? The Church itself or the sovereign power of the king? The strife over this had raged for a long time, but it took a Nordic barbarian queen such as Kristina to be ignorant of the matter.

Varnhem had to be regained at all costs. No compromise was acceptable in this matter.

And had Father Henri and his company come to Roskilde several years earlier, or several years later, everything would have gone as planned. There is no doubt about that.

But Father Henri and his company arrived just at the moment when a violent, ten-year-long civil war had ended and a new mighty lineage had ascended to power. The new king was named Valdemar, and he would be known in due course as Valdemar the Great.

He had finally succeeded in killing both his rivals, Knut and Svend, and before the decisive battle he had vowed that if God granted him victory he would establish a Cistercian monastery. Archbishop Eskil in Lund was well aware of this promise, having been forced to bless the war before the decisive battle. Archbishop Eskil was an old personal friend of no less than Holy Saint Bernard himself. It was when visiting Saint Bernard in Clairvaux that he had also become friends with Father Henri.

When the two now met in Roskilde, just as the Danish church convened for a synod, they were overjoyed to see each other again. But beyond that they were also taken by how wisely God could steer people's paths down to the smallest detail.

All the pieces fit together with miraculous precision. Here came a Cistercian prior just at the moment when the new king was about to honor, or forget, his promise to God to build a new monastery. Instead of entering into a correspondence for many years with Cîteaux, everything could be arranged at once, since both an archbishop and a prior were present.

King Valdemar himself could also clearly feel the power of God's will when his archbishop informed him that his sacred vow to God could actually be fulfilled immediately, since God had arranged it so.

King Valdemar set aside a portion of his inherited property, a peninsula named Vitskøl on the shores of the Limfjord in Jutland, as the site of the new monastery. The synod, which handily enough had already been convened at Roskilde, blessed the matter, and Father Henri could then resume his journey at once, as if he had merely stopped to rest in Roskilde. But he was now heading toward a completely different destination from his two home monasteries of Clairvaux and Cîteaux.

With regard to the question of Varnhem and the excommunication of Kristina and Erik Jedvardsson, what had occurred did not involve any change of principle, of course. Rather, it entailed a practical change, since the matter now had to be handled by correspondence and would therefore require somewhat more time. This meant that Father Henri had a number of important letters to write before setting off on the journey to Vitskøl, but it was quickly done. He wrote to Varnhem and instructed twenty-two of his monks to pack up plenty of the monastery's possessions, in particular all the books, and take them along to the new monastery in Vitskøl. However, five men should stay behind in Varnhem with the ominous task of trying to protect the buildings against pillaging and destruction. At the same time they were to tell one and all about the coming excommunication of Fru Kristina and Erik Jedvardsson, to whatever effect that might have.

Next, Father Henri addressed two letters to the general chapter of the Cistercians and to the Holy Father Hadrianus IV, in which he described the immoral and drunken Erik Jedvardsson, who wanted to call himself king despite the fact that he had allowed his wife to desecrate a monastery. Then he was ready to leave for Vitskøl, which was where the Lord without a doubt was now leading his steps.

And where the Lord led Father Henri, there too he led Arn.

✠

Erik Jedvardsson was soon to feel the power of the church. Now that he had captured one of the three royal crowns he had been striving for, he sent negotiators to the lawspeakers in both Western and Eastern Götaland. But the replies he received were disheartening. In those regions Varnhem had functioned as a smoldering and smoking pit of rumors, and the smoke had spread over both landscapes: Erik Jedvardsson and his wife Kristina were going to be excommunicated. Nobody wanted an excommunicated king.

Fortunately the Swedes didn't know what was being said, or else they didn't understand what excommunication meant. Erik was still sitting securely as the king of the Swedes.

Two things had to be done, one easy and one difficult. The easy task was to send a group of negotiators to that French monk who was now staying somewhere in Denmark. The king would have to humble himself in writing, rescind his demands, and beg the monks to come back to Varnhem, assuring them of the king's support. He would ask to be allowed to have Varnhem as the burial place for his lineage, and vouchsafe that the monks would be given more land for Varnhem, and whatever else he could think of to offer. His bishop Henrik, who was a practical man of God, assured him that the alternative would be far worse. For then it would become necessary to walk on foot to Rome, dressed in sackcloth and ashes for the last bit of the journey. Barefoot, he would have to prostrate himself at the feet of the Holy Father. This would not only be difficult and time-consuming; there was no guarantee that such tactics would placate the Pope. And wouldn't it be exceedingly vexing to have made all those efforts in vain?

So much easier to placate the monks, since it could be done with a few letters, a few pleasant words, and some land that was only a very small part of the king's vast holdings. This was the easy task.

The difficult task had to do with washing away the widespread gossip about the ungodly king. Erik's old idea about a crusade to Finland was reconsidered, and Bishop Henrik found it appealing. A king who was also God's own warrior for the good faith would come to be honored by all. The path to the two remaining crowns therefore must pass through Finland.

The Swedes, who were a warlike people and who had not been able to demonstrate that quality to themselves or others for a long time, gladly joined in the new king's plans for a plundering campaign against Finland. There were wrongs to avenge, besides everything else, since the Finns and the Estonians had conducted vicious raids along the coasts of Svealand.

The war went well for two years. The Swedes took rich booty. The raven flew to fresh wounds.

Of course the first Finns they encountered were already Christian, but making them choose between the sword and being baptized anew by a Swedish bishop could never hurt. But occasional heathens were found farther inland, in the second year of the war.

One day when Erik's soldiers left the army's column to find peasants they could plunder for food they encountered an old witch. The strange thing about the woman was that she spoke almost the same language as in Svealand, and she was not all afraid when she was taken captive. Instead she pluckily asked to be taken to the commander, since she had a suggestion to make which he would be hard pressed to refuse. If the soldiers did not obey her she would cast a spell that would bring them eternal misfortune.

The soldiers did as she said, more out of curiosity at what the witch might suggest to Erik Jedvardsson that he could not refuse than out of fear of her sorcery.

When Erik Jedvardsson heard about what had happened, he thought it might provide an amusing interlude that night, and so he let the witch accompany him until they made camp toward evening.

Then he had his executioner called to the royal tent, with his block and axe prepared. His closest men in the army gathered expectantly for the amusing game, and then they brought in the witch and forced her to her knees before the king.

"So, foul witch! You had a suggestion for me that I as king would not dare refuse. Let's hear it!" shouted Erik to the filthy woman who was bound and kneeling before him. And he smiled cheerfully at his men, reaping much merriment.

"Well yes," the woman wheezed hoarsely, because a soldier was holding her around the neck, "I have a suggestion that a wise king would not wish to refuse."

"I'm sure everyone would like to hear it, but you understand that the executioner isn't standing here for nothing, so what if I say no?" replied Erik, still just as cheerful.

"Release me and let me stand up so that I may speak. If you say no to my proposal I'll go straight to your executioner," replied the woman, strong and confident.

Erik gestured to the men to release her and then, just as cheerful as before, showed that he was prepared to listen. The men all around him were extremely amused by what was going on.

The woman straightened her hair with dignity and cleared her throat before she spoke.

"My proposal is as follows, King Erik. Let me read your palm and say who you are and what your future holds. If you find that I speak falsely about you, or if you don't believe what I say about what is to come, then you may send me at once to your executioner. If you believe what I have to say, I need a horse and wagon to take me back to where I was abducted."

Erik immediately turned pensive, and the men's laughter quieted to a murmur. They all realized that a woman who was so sure of her soothsaying that she would wager her head on its truthfulness perhaps really could see into the future after all. But not everyone wanted to know their future, because it could turn bad the very next day: an arrow flying out of the woods where no one saw the archer, a lance cast in error at the end of a battle when there was no longer anything at stake. And if a pox would strike one's family, would a man really want to know something like that in advance? It took courage to look into the future.

Erik assessed the matter in this way: he would be seen as showing cowardice if he merely sent the babbling witch off to the executioner. On the other hand, if he listened to her first and then had her beheaded, he would make a much better impression.

"Very well," said Erik Jedvardsson. "I shall listen to your words. If I find them true, you have my word as king that you shall return home with a horse and wagon. If I think ill of your words, I shall let the executioner take care of you here and now. So let's hear what you have to say!"

"Well." The witch shilly-shallied. "We must go into your tent so that you and only you hear my words."

A murmur of astonishment spread among the men. To be

alone with a witch might not be wise. Erik saw their fear, and he was just as enraged by it as by the witch's impudence.

"And if I now say no to your proposal, if I tell you to give me your prophecy here and now!" he boomed in the gruff voice he used for giving commands.

"Then you shall not know who you are or where you are bound, for your future belongs to you alone, and perhaps you would find it unwise for it to belong to everyone. Afterward you can always decide what you choose to tell of what you alone have heard," replied the woman with confidence, as if she knew that Erik would agree to her proposal.

And he did. The woman was searched by the hands of un-abashed soldiers to ensure that she had no sharp weapon on her. Erik turned and went into his tent, and the woman was shoved in roughly after him.

Inside the tent she fell at once to her knees before the king and asked to be allowed to read one of his palms. She was given the royal hand and studied it in silence.

"I see England . . ." she began hesitantly. "Someone in your lineage . . . your father came from England. I see Rome and the man called Pope . . . no, that line is broken here. You were on your way to Rome . . . barefoot . . . how can that be? Well, noth-ing will come of that journey . . . hmm, your future is indeed interesting."

Erik Jedvardsson had turned quite cold inside when he heard the reference to his English origins and how he had almost trav-eled to see the Pope. He was now convinced.

"So, woman! I know who I am, now tell me my future without more ado!" he ordered without his voice quavering too much.

"I see . . . I see three royal crowns. A new realm with three crowns as the coat of arms, and these armorial bearings will still endure after a thousand years, everywhere in your kingdom. Generation after generation, king after king for all eternity, and your mark will remain. The three crowns mean three countries will be united into a mighty kingdom, and in a thousand years these your crowns will still be the emblem of the realm, everywhere, on all seals, on all documents."

"And what will happen to that pope?" Erik Jedvardsson was so shaken that he almost whispered.

"I see your picture everywhere . . ." the woman muttered low. "Everywhere pictures of you . . . as a saint, your head wreathed in gold against a blue sky. You began by doing evil against your god . . . there was that interrupted path to Rome . . . then you did good and thus your name shall live forever."

"What do you have to say about my death?" asked Erik Jedvardsson, now reverently.

"Your death . . . your death. Do you really want to know that? Few men do."

"Yes, say something!"

"I can't see very clearly . . ." muttered the woman, who suddenly seemed a bit afraid to say what she had seen with utter clarity. But then she mustered her courage and once again her voice sounded confident.

"Your name will live on forever. No man born of woman in Svealand or the two lands of the Goths will be able to kill or even injure you," she said hastily, standing up.

Erik Jedvardsson, who now was filled with the certainty that all his dreams would come true, and that not one of his foreseeable enemies would ever be able to kill him, strode out of the tent and in a mighty voice gave the order for a horse and wagon to be brought forth for the woman. No one was to touch her or speak to her indecorously; she was granted the protection of the king.

Erik Jedvardsson returned home to Östra Aros, his mind alight with the glorious future he now felt would be his. For he had nothing to fear from any man in Svealand or Western Götaland or Eastern Götaland.

Magnus Henriksen, however, was not a man born of woman in Svealand, Western Götaland, or Eastern Götaland. He was Danish.

He was one of the many great men of Denmark that the winds of war had blown like chaff out across the world after Valdemar finally won the long Danish war of succession. Fleeing Denmark, Magnus sailed up the Eastern Sea, stopped for a time in Linköping, and had private discussions with King Karl Sverkersson. He then continued up the coast, into Lake Mälaren and up the Fyris River.

He took King Erik Jedvardsson by surprise, and he was the one who personally chopped off the head that according to the witch in Finland would become the eternal symbol of the future kingdom.

Magnus had himself proclaimed the new king, since he had killed the old one. In those days that was the most common way to become king in the North, and on his mother's side he was in a direct line of descent from King Inge the Old.

Magnus Henriksen lived for a year. Erik Jedvardsson lived forever.

✠

Reading is the basis of all knowledge. It was Father Henri's firm conviction that even men such as himself, whose main occupation was text, either writing or copying it, had to spend at least two hours a day reading, which was a means of cultivating the soul, a sort of permissible enjoyment.

The rules for reading text at Vitskøl were therefore quite strict. The brothers who had the work of their hands as their primary duty, such as the cooks from Provence, the lay brothers who busied themselves with masonry work or stone polishing, Brother Guilbert and his smith apprentices, and Brother Lucien and his garden apprentices—they all had to learn something each day that was not related to their usual work.

But this obligation took on a different aspect when it came to the little boy Arn. The first four or five years of his studies had not been designed for any practical purpose other than to hone his linguistic instrument. For the same reason he was always required to speak Latin with Father Henri, French with Brother Guilbert, and Norse with the Nordic lay brothers. The text he worked with in the first years had been mostly the psalms, since he had to learn them anyway. He had a very passable soprano voice, and when he sang the lead his voice lent extra beauty to the early morning and evening mass, in particular.

It was now Arn's fifth year, and the cloister church in Vitskøl was finally ready. It would be consecrated by Archbishop Eskil, who was coming all the way from Lund. When the church was consecrated, the monastery would also be given its name; all Cistercian monasteries had their own name. For Vitskøl's part Father Henri had long ago decided that the name would be Vitae Schola, the School of Life.

Arn certainly had something to do with that choice of name. Even though it was still impossible to say why God had placed this child with the Cistercian brothers, it was easy to see how the name Vitae Schola applied to Arn quite literally. Everything of any importance that he would learn in life would presumably be learned here.

And now that the boy was beginning to master his linguistic instrument, Father Henri had released him into the great sea of literature. Arn had to work on his obligatory reading every day, just like everyone else.

Father Henri was convinced that worldly literature was almost as important as theological literature to the formation of a young man's mind. But it required a certain attentiveness on Father Henri's part, since Arn at first darted in and out of the scriptorium at will, and sometimes discovered books that were unsuitable for boys.

The purpose of reading Ovid, for example, was naturally to concentrate on the *Metamorphoses*, around two hundred tales about magical transformations, texts that taught their reader much about legends and cultures that had been part of the Roman empire. On the other hand, it was less fortunate when the boy grabbed *Ars amatoria*, *The Art of Love*. Father Henri had discovered Arn with that very book in a corner of the kitchen. Arn had also appeared to be unduly excited in a manner that human nature could not conceal.

Naturally Father Henri had then administered suitable punishment, cold rubdowns and a certain number of prayers and the like, but he had not taken such a stern view of the matter as he outwardly professed. On the contrary, he had merrily related the whole incident to Brother Guilbert, who had a good laugh at the boy's naïve sin.

The more unsuitable texts by Ovid, however, were taken away to Father Henri's own sleeping cell, and thereafter the choice of literature for Arn's elective reading was selected with more precision and caution.

Reading was the basis of all knowledge and all pure and wise thoughts. Of course everyone would agree with that; it was obvious. But Father Henri may possibly have differed slightly from many of his colleagues in his belief that even little boys should be given these texts in time, before they became mired too much in theological scholarship. On the other hand, it was not possible to neglect Arn's theological training. At Vitae Schola there were only two copies of the guide to reading the Bible, *Glossa Ordinaria*, which all the brothers were constantly consulting. But Father Henri saw to it that Arn was given as much access to that text as possible.

And in order to avoid new embarrassments such as the incident with the unsuitable text by Ovid, Arn was now required to fetch all his books directly from Father Henri's possession. In addition, at least one working hour each day was devoted to teaching the boy what was easy and what was hard to understand in the Holy Scriptures.

Father Henri was secretly rather happy at the eagerness with which Arn came running to get his new reading instructions, or to be quizzed on the previous day's Bible text. The plan was for the boy to be trained half in physical labors and half in spiritual matters. Since God's intentions for him had not yet been revealed, this method could not be called faulty, at least.

It was possible to imagine, and without thinking especially ill of him for that matter, that the time spent with Brother Guilbert was more pleasant than the time spent in the scriptorium; that his time with the lay brothers who were building the walls, where Arn was asked to carry mortar to places where it was difficult for a grown man to squeeze through, was more pleasant than the time he had to spend in the kitchen; that his time down at the harbor and out on the fjord with the fishermen was more pleasant than the time spent practicing a complicated vocal part for the next big mass.

But with little Arn, Father Henri noticed nothing of the sort; it was as though Arn attended with the same eagerness to everything actually implied by the cloister's chosen name: Vitae Schola.

This boy might become any sort of man. He might end his days as the prior of a monastery, as far as Father Henri could see. He might also become something that was the complete opposite, about which Brother Guilbert spoke in secret, and which they ought not mention aloud, according to Father Henri. With regard to God's intentions for Arn, they had no certainty as yet.

So it was a matter of continuing as they had so far, to give both the spirit and the hand their due.

Father Henri had moved his daily lesson books to one of the arcades leading to the garden, and it was here that he sat deeply engrossed one morning when Arn came darting in. His feet were wet because he had come directly from the lavatorium; it was against the rules to pass from work of the hands to work of the spirit without first cleaning oneself. He had spent the past two hours on the last of the masonry work up in the tower of the cloister church. There had been more to do at the end than they had thought when they finally decided on the date for the conse-cration. The scaffolding should really be removed before Arch-bishop Eskil arrived to bless the church.

But when they began tearing down the scaffolding they also had a better view. Brother Guilbert and Brother Richard stood on the ground and discovered first one and then another crack that had to be patched, or joints that were not properly done. Arn was sent up to the top to climb about like a little marten to carry out all their demands for final improvements. Since he was so small compared to all the others, Arn was the only one who could climb without fear or difficulty after the wooden scaffolds had been removed. The height didn't bother him at all, since he was firmly convinced that God would not easily visit misfortune on someone who was just a child. Besides, he was laboring to complete a work in His honor. At least that was how Arn ex-plained it when one of the brothers tentatively asked whether he was afraid of heights.

His reply was perhaps not entirely true. Not that he was lying. At Vitae Schola no one lied; such behavior would be a gross breach of the rules of the monastery. But Arn also held a conviction, which he had no doubt imbibed with his mother's milk, that God had a definite plan for his life and that this plan could hardly be that Arn should lay stones for some brief years of his childhood and then lose his footing and fall to his death or knock himself senseless, as two lay brothers had done during the construction. That was why he felt no fear.

But giving such an answer, if anyone had asked him, would have been to demonstrate pride, to express a belief that he was superior to others. And it would also have been a great sin, perhaps even greater than lying.

Once he had fallen from a high tower. He didn't remember much about it, but he had read the account in a copy of the book of memory up at Varnhem, and Father Henri had talked with him about how he should understand it all. God had wanted to save his life for a future task, a great task. That was the most important part of the interpretation of the account, and anyone could see that.

About a year earlier, the reading lessons had become more and more directed toward that very purpose: how one should interpret text, and above all the Holy Scriptures. It was to such a lesson that Arn had now come running, a bit late and out of breath with his feet bare but newly washed, slipping on the polished limestone tiles in the arcade where he found Father Henri.

But Father Henri did not chide him; he seemed to be in a very good mood. He sat there with a pleased smile, as if lost in thought, and simply stroked the boy's little shaved head for a moment before he said anything.

Arn, who had sat down next to Father Henri on the stone bench, saw that *Glossa Ordinaria* lay open before him. Even though the boy was sitting too far away to read the text, he could guess quite well which section of the book the monk was reading.

"Well," said Father Henri presently, as he slowly left his world of thought. "If we begin with the text that you will sing solo toward the end of the singing mass . . . how are we to understand . . . by the way, sing me the first lines!"

The Lord is my shepherd; I shall not want.
He maketh me to lie down in green pastures: he leadeth
  me beside the still waters.
He restoreth my soul: he leadeth me in the paths of righ-
  teousness for his name's sake.

Arn sang in his clear soprano, so that the brothers in the garden stood up from their work, leaned on their tools, and listened with gentle smiles. They all loved the boy's singing.

"Excellent, excellent, we can stop there," said Father Henri. "And now we have to understand this text. Shall we interpret it morally or literally? No, of course not, but how then?"

"It's obviously an allegorical text," said Arn, panting; he needed more air since he had sung when he was still slightly out of breath.

"So you mean that we're not actually sheep, my son? Well, that's obvious, but why use this simile?"

"It's clear, it's easy to understand," Arn surmised with a little frown. "Everyone has seen sheep and shepherds, and just as the sheep need their shepherd for protection and care, we need God. Even though we're human beings and not sheep, God becomes *like* our shepherd."

"Hmm," said Father Henri. "So far it's not difficult. But what does 'He restoreth my soul: he leadeth me in the paths of righteousness' mean? Do sheep have souls?"

"No," said Arn thoughtfully. He sensed one of Father Henri's traps of logic, but he had already declared that the text should be interpreted allegorically. "Since the allegory from the beginning is obvious . . . that of the sheep representing us, so . . . the text following it should be interpreted literally. The Lord really does restore our souls."

"Yes, that's probably true," muttered Father Henri with a sly little smile. "But what about what follows: 'he leadeth me in the paths of righteousness'? What paths are we talking about? Literal meaning or allegorical?"

"I don't know," said Arn. "Can't it be both?"

"Can that be so? A text that should be read both literally and allegorically? Now you're going to have to explain yourself, my son."

"In the line before it says that God restores our souls, so it's literally about us and not about some sheep," Arn began, to win a little time while he thought as incisively as he could. "But of course God can lead us on the right paths in the literal sense; paths on the ground, visible paths, the sort of paths that horses and oxcarts and people walk on. If He wants to, He can lead us on the path to Rome, for example, don't you think?"

"Hmm," said Father Henri, looking a little stern. "It probably hasn't escaped you that this part about paths here and there is one of the most common metaphors in the Holy Scriptures. If the Lord's ways are inscrutable, then we're not talking about any livestock paths, are we?"

"No, that's obvious, the paths of righteousness refer to things like the path away from sin, the path to salvation, and so on. Allegorical, that is."

"Good. Where were we? How does the next verse go? No, don't sing it, or the brothers in the garden will just idle about. Well?"

"'Yea, though I walk through the valley of the shadow of death, I will fear no evil: for Thou art with me,'" Arn rattled off. "The meaning must be general, I think. If I find myself in great difficulties, if I'm in the presence of death, such as climbing high up in the tower carrying mortar, for example, then I need fear nothing because God is with me. The phrase 'shadow of death' must be allegorical; death doesn't literally cast its shadow anywhere, and there is no special valley where I could walk beneath that shadow. And even if there were . . . purely theoretically, then it would not be the only place where I would feel solace. Not even in the darkest valley, that is, in dark moments, in sorrow or in danger, do I need to despair. Is that about right?"

On the day that Arn outgrew his old bow and arrow, that small pleasure came to an end for the time being. He had his practice area just outside the smithy and could run out now and then during the natural pauses in the work to shoot while the iron cooled down or new forges were fired up. But one day Brother Guilbert came out and saw how the boy, without hesitation but also without seeming especially interested in the task, shot twelve arrows in a row into the moving target, a wad of linen rags tied up with thongs and dangling back and forth on a thin rope.

It was time once again to start on something new. For even though Brother Guilbert thought it important that the instruments he put into Arn's hands be adapted to his size and strength, it was equally important that the boy always practice with full concentration. If it became too easy, the practice would be blunted and have a negative effect. Brother Guilbert found this difficult to explain, even to grown men. To Arn he did not explain much, nor was it necessary, since obedience was one of the most important rules at the monastery.

They found yew trees as material for the new bow and ash for the arrows. Because when the bow was changed, new arrows were also needed, since everything had to be in the right proportion to function together, just as the movement of the hand and the power of thought must be in balance.

It took a long time, from the cold springtime when only the

snowdrops ventured forth until the early summer when the tulips stretched in long red rows along the arcades, to fabricate the new bow and its arrows. Arn had to be present to learn from every task, how the wood was supposed to dry in a dark and sufficiently cool place, how to cut laminates from various parts of the wood and polish them to an even shape, how to join them together with fish glue and lay them in a press, and then polish them anew. With the arrows it was simpler, of course. Arrow points belonged to the simple forging tasks that Arn could manage entirely on his own.

When it was finally time to begin testing the new working instruments, Brother Guilbert also changed the distance to the target from eighteen long paces to twenty-five. It was hard and strenuous to draw the new bow, and the effort affected the aim of the arrows so that sometimes Arn missed completely. When he then showed annoyance, Brother Guilbert was upon him at once, scolding him for indolence and insufficient confidence, the one sin as serious as the other. And Arn had to pray a number of Pater Nosters on his knees before the bow and arrows as punishment before he was called back to practice.

At such moments Brother Guilbert was tempted to explain to the boy how well he shot, without a doubt better than most of the adult, well-trained archers. But Arn had never been able to compare himself with anyone but Brother Guilbert himself. Brother Guilbert had always kept quiet about his earlier life and what it was that had made him renounce that life for constant penance at a Cistercian monastery. Father Henri had forbidden him from telling his story to Arn.

One day a group of soldiers on their way home from the Danish island of Fyn, all of them in good humor because some war was over and they would soon see their loved ones, stopped outside the cloister at the very place where Arn was practicing.

At first they had found it comical to see a little lay brother with a shaved head, brown monk's cowl, and fluttering locks around his ears holding a bow and arrow in his hands. The image seemed entirely implausible. They uttered some coarse humor but then stopped to watch the little boy, expecting to fling about some more jokes. Brother Guilbert, who was standing next to Arn and instructing him, pretended not to understand the Nordic language or at least not to hear the remarks.

But the soldiers soon fell silent, because they could not believe their eyes. The little lay brother stood at eighteen paces and put one arrow after another into the target in the space of half a palm's breadth. When he missed by a thumb's breadth he seemed annoyed and apologized to his teacher, sharpening his concentration for the next shot. The soldiers moved off in silence. A short distance away they began arguing about something.

Brother Guilbert understood quite well the soldiers' embarrassment. None of them, any more than Brother Guilbert himself, had ever seen a boy with such talent. But neither then nor later did Arn comprehend this, because for him there were only two archers: himself and Brother Guilbert, and compared with the smith he was the worst archer in the world.

Father Henri had often shown himself unwilling to discuss the topic. He thought that Arn was diligent in reading and as intelligent as one could expect of a boy whose voice had not yet begun to break—woe the day that happened—but neither more nor less. Father Henri didn't consider himself to have been particularly bright as a child, yet he was reminded of himself when he looked at Arn. The most important thing was the zeal with which both he and now Arn studied. He also recalled with a smile how as a very young boy he had also discovered books that were not intended for small boys; he had been caught in the act, and was punished in much the same way he now punished Arn for the same thing. But most important was the inspiration to read, the diligence to learn, and perseverance. God gave everyone nearly equal intelligence, and it was the responsibility of each and every one to fill his mind with content, to make the most of one's talents.

To counter that logic, however, Brother Guilbert had a simple objection. Because in that case, God must have also given everyone the ability to handle a bow or a sword equally, yet some got markedly less from the instrument and others got much more. Little Arn had been given more of such gifts than any man, young or old, that Brother Guilbert had ever encountered in his life, he claimed.

That statement made Father Henri hesitant, because hardly any living man had encountered so many other men with weapons in hand as had Brother Guilbert; that much was certain. On the other hand, Brother Guilbert could not possibly lie to his own prior.

But Father Henri had felt uncomfortable with this topic of discussion, and had come to an agreement with Brother Guilbert—that is, he had forbidden him to put any whims into the boy's head. And that was why Arn never understood when he was doing well with the bow or sword, but only knew or was brusquely reminded of when he did something wrong.

Arn had not yet been allowed to use a real sword in any of his practice sessions. Nor was it necessary, for Brother Guilbert could see what would happen later when the boy's arms grew stronger and he made the transition from wooden sticks to steel.

When it came to handling a sword, the quickness of the mind and the eye, the balance of the foot, and the feeling in the hand were much more important than the strength of the arm. Brother Guilbert had seen little of the way that Nordic men handled swords, yet he could tell that these barbarians' technique was based almost entirely on strength. Their swords were short, because they never fought on horseback; they believed that horses were unsuited to war, oddly enough. And they stood in ranks close to each other, almost like the ancient Romans and Greeks a thousand years before, although they didn't call their formation a phalanx but a *fylking*. This technique required them almost exclusively to hack at an angle from above, either from the left or the right. Each man, using at least a semblance of a shield and with at least a minimum of self-preservation, could parry every such blow without having to think or move. And so they would keep at it until one of the opponents tired and the other more or less by accident landed a blow on his opponent's skull. Under these circumstances it was a matter of course that the one with the strongest arms would win in the end.

For the first three or four years Arn had been given his early training with swaddled wooden sticks, and Brother Guilbert methodically drummed into the boy's head the three-count rhythm so that it would stick and remain there forever. High blow from the left, low blow from the right, and then a lunge straight ahead or a new blow from the side. Thousands and thousands of times.

The first thing Arn learned in this way was the rhythm and the movement. The second thing he learned was to control his anger, for Brother Guilbert always struck him with the third blow, every time during the first two years. Not until the third year had Arn learned to control his feet, his movements, and his rhythm sufficiently that he could sometimes parry the third, painful thrust.

In the fourth year Brother Guilbert made fairly heavy wooden swords, which he weighted precisely with an inserted metal rod. It was important that the wooden sword in Arn's hand have the same weight in relation to his small arms that a real sword would have later in life, the same way that the bows gradually had to be made more difficult to draw. So Brother Guilbert had to experiment a good deal with the fabrication until it seemed right.

It was during practice with the sword that Brother Guilbert discovered that the boy, just as in the smithy, could use his left hand as well as his right. In every other context in the cloister, Arn's teachers, just as they hounded him in the scriptorium, tried to wean him from using the unclean hand. But for Brother Guilbert the matter appeared in a different light. He consulted his conscience and he consulted God. He didn't want to involve Father Henri in this dilemma.

Soon he realized that it wasn't a case of normal lefthandedness, because such men did exist and on occasion in his former life Brother Guilbert had faced such a man with sword in hand. And it was not easy, he knew that. It was as if everything one had learned was suddenly backwards.

So from the beginning he had trained Arn to use both hands, to shift from day to day or from week to week. But he had never seen any appreciable difference in his technique, except that the boy's left arm seemed to be somewhat stronger than his right. But that also meant that it was possible from the very first to build a secret skill into the boy's technique; he could suddenly toss the sword from one hand to the other and then begin to circle clockwise instead of counterclockwise around his opponent. If the opponent was dressed in heavy gear and his fighting fundamentals were unsure, the sudden change in tactics would have a devastating effect.

Brother Guilbert was well aware that such a line of thinking might possibly be sinful. He had also confessed them to Father Henri, but explained that as long as his task was merely to teach the boy, he had to do it as best he could. Since God had still not expressed His wish for the boy's calling in life, there was probably no difference for the time being in reading Ovid in secret with red cheeks or holding the sword in his left hand, was there?

When Father Henri consulted God, he received the answer that as long as the boy showed the same zeal in his studies as in Brother Guilbert's warlike games, then all was as it should be. But not so if he should begin to prefer arrows and sword to *Glossa Ordinaria*. Fortunately Arn showed no such tendencies in that direction.

And while Father Henri always preached diligence and discipline, cleanliness and prayer, Brother Guilbert always preached agility and agility, agility and diligence. It was important, just as in musical rhythm, to learn to feel when the arrow would fly toward a spot ahead of the moving target so that arrow and target would meet there. But it was equally important always to keep moving his feet, never to stand still waiting for the opponent's blow; he had to be somewhere else when the blow came so that he could strike back the very next instant.

Diligence and discipline. Cleanliness and prayer. Agility and agility, agility and diligence. Arn followed all these rules with the same ease as he followed the rules about obeying and loving all the brothers, the two most important rules at the monastery, always to speak the truth, the third rule; and then all the other less important ones, which sometimes barely made sense, such as the rules about eating at the dinner table and going to bed.

But it was no trick at all for him to follow this divine order of things. On the contrary, it was a joy. Sometimes he wondered how other children behaved out there in the base world; he did have faint memories of tobogganing, rolling hoops, and other childish games. He may have missed some of that, just as every night at the last prayer hour he prayed for his mother's soul and then missed her breath, her voice, and her hands; just as he prayed for his brother Eskil and remembered how they had been torn from each other in tears. But he understood, at any rate he felt that he understood, that the greatest happiness for a boy must be to be able to divide his time between all the wonders that books held and all the hard work in sweat and sometimes tears of pain that Brother Guilbert offered.

✠

Magnus Folkesson had made a promise to God that he would mourn Sigrid for five years before he would remarry. Within his family this decision had aroused astonishment, since it was not usual for a man who was still fit, and who had only one legitimate son as heir, to refrain for so long from begetting new sons to strengthen the clan.

Magnus had consoled himself somewhat with a thrall, Suom, and had a love child with her. But Arnäs had become a gloomy fortress where not much happened or ever changed. After Sigrid's death Magnus had felt empty in his head and could no longer find new ideas for his trade and businesses. Everything ran in the same old ruts.

He had built some things; he had finished the walls and about six miles of road up toward Tiveden. Building a road was a deed pleasing to God, and he had promised this construction when he visited Sigrid's grave the first time and prayed for her at Varnhem and purchased prayers of intercession for her.

It couldn't hurt to combine what was pleasing to God with what would be good for future business. The day there was a road all the way through Tiveden wood he would be able to trade to the north with the Swedes. They were simple men who understood little, but they had good iron and offered a fine trade in pelts that could bring plenty of silver if there were passable roads.

Contributing to the gloominess at Arnäs was the fact that his mother, Tora Guttormsdotter, had come from her farms in Norway to tend to everything that a wife would usually oversee, for as long as he remained unmarried. But she was hard on

the thralls and wanted to run everything according to old Norwegian customs, and Magnus, like many men, had a hard time
putting his own mother in her place. The fact that he ought to
be a better lord of his own house was a strong reason to find a
new wife soon. In Magnus's view it would be wise to join forces
with the Pål clan in Husaby, since his own lands bordered theirs.
In that case any of the Pål daughters would bring to the estate a
suitable dowry of oak forests covering the slopes of the mountain Kinnekulle. Of course, the unmarried daughters were still
scarcely more than children, but youth was something that soon
passed.

Eskil was both a joy and a secret sorrow to Magnus. Eskil
was like himself, and also much like his mother Sigrid, whose
intelligence he seemed to have inherited. Eskil wanted most of
all to take part in trading expeditions, to meet foreign merchants
and learn from their wares and prices how best to calculate the
value of two casks of bacon in terms of wheat or hides and how
to trade raw iron for silver. In this Eskil was indeed his father's
son.

Yet as an almost full-grown man he was still unable to throw
a lance or handle a sword the way a man of a clan with a coat of
arms should be able to do. But it was true that Magnus himself
resembled his eldest son in this.

Only once had Magnus as the lord of Arnäs been forced to
set out for war. That was when Henriksen the Dane proclaimed
himself king over the Swedes after he had ignominiously hacked
off the head of Erik Jedvardsson up in Östra Aros. There were
two versions of the event: some held that it occurred just after
the high mass in the Trinity Church, and that Erik Jedvardsson
died courageously facing great odds, and a spring emerged from
the spot where his head struck the ground.

According to Erik Jedvardsson's enemies, and to King Karl

Sverkersson, Erik Jedvardsson died unnecessarily because he had been too full of ale to defend himself like a man.

And yet it made little difference how King Erik had been murdered; there would have to be war in any case. The fact that the Swedes felt indignant that a Dane had come and murdered their king was easy to understand. At once they sent off a message all the way to Helsingland and the darkest forests of Svealand, and soon had gathered a great army heading for Östra Aros. But the question was how people would react in Western Götaland and in Eastern Götaland. Should they let the Swedes settle accounts with the Danish slayer of their king on their own, or should they take part in the war?

For King Karl Sverkersson and his men in Linköping, this was not a difficult decision. He had to choose between going off to war against the Danish king-slayer with as many forces as he could muster, and thus winning the crown of the Swedes for himself, or allowing them to win on their own and then elect a new king, who could be anyone at all among the Swedish chieftains or lawspeakers. For King Karl Sverkersson the choice was simple.

When the Folkungs gathered for the clan *ting* in Bjälbo in Eastern Götaland, they soon found that there wasn't much choice. Magnus's own brother Birger, who was now called Brosa, the Smiling One, had quickly convinced the clan *ting*. One war was unavoidable for all in Eastern Götaland, Birger Brosa had declared, and that was the war against the Danish murderer of the king. For the Eastern Goths the only right thing was to support King Karl in this matter. But after the victory he would probably become king of Svealand as well. Because victorious they would be; the army raised in Sweden was itself large enough to win the victory on its own. The days of the Dane, Magnus Henriksen, on earth were numbered. Now they had to look beyond his death.

For the Folkungs it was crucial that they not be split apart and end up on different sides in a war. If King Karl now won the royal crown in Svealand, he would soon demand recognition in Western Götaland as well—then all the Folkungs would be set against one another, the east against the west.

Better then to combine all the problems into a single war, so that both Western Goths and Eastern Goths would rally around King Karl in his war. If they did not do so, the same thing would happen later anyway, but at the cost of much spilled blood and in the worst case with brother set against brother.

No one at the clan meeting could contradict Birger Brosa on this. And from then on Birger Brosa usually got what he wanted.

Magnus took part in the war with his retainers in the way he found best. He and his men did not enter into the dispute until it was already won, which then mostly involved executing the last of the Danes and taking captive those who could pay ransom. He was able to return to Arnäs as a victor who had not lost a single man in the conflict but became 50 marks richer in silver, and for this he was popular with the women, though the men did not think highly of him.

He had left Eskil at Arnäs when he went off to war, despite the boy's nagging and whining. Eskil was not yet a man; besides, as the eldest son and heir, he could not be replaced like some fallen retainer.

Magnus had tried to forget his second son whom God had taken alive from him. But since he knew that Arn was the son that Sigrid had loved best, he could not forget as easily as he should for the peace of his soul. Nor could he forget Sigrid during the five years of mourning he had assigned himself. In secret he told himself that she was still the one person above all others whom he valued most highly, more than any man, even a man such as his brother Birger Brosa.

But this was something he had to keep to himself. If he said such a thing out loud he would be disdained, or regarded as crazy. Not even to Eskil could he admit these thoughts about a woman who was after all Eskil's mother.

While the ice on the lakes still held, there now came a summons to another clan *ting* in Bjälbo. Magnus set off with a small retinue and Eskil. For the first time his son would be allowed to take part in the men's council and therefore he admonished him not to interfere, drink too much, or say anything, but to listen and learn.

Birger Brosa received his brother and nephew with great warmth and from the start offered them more hospitality than other kinsmen. Magnus could not tell whether this had to do with brotherly love or with Birger Brosa's plans concerning the matters they would soon be disputing. But he enjoyed being treated as a worthy man, even though the gathering now included several men who were great warriors with scars from many battles. In those days such things were valued much more highly than silver. The fattest bishop could own great quantities of silver, but that did not make him a great man.

The first days were devoted only to the pleasures of hospitality, and they all spoke freely about what there might be to discuss with regard to kinsmen who were unable to attend; for example, the Norwegian kinsmen, who at the moment were at war, as usual. In this way they could also wait for those who arrived somewhat later because a winter road was impassable or the ice too dark and unreliable. Hence no one would come too late for discussions that had already been decided while they were far away swearing and groaning, struggling with a broken or overturned sleigh.

But once they all had gathered, deliberations began in the largest hall in the tower. What was surprising to many, including Magnus and Eskil, was that they gathered for the council immediately after the midday prayers were held in the tower's lower chapel, and this without eating. The roasts had just begun to be turned and would not be ready for many hours.

Birger Brosa, who had introduced this new arrangement, believed that their forefathers' custom of eating, drinking, and holding council simultaneously undoubtedly had its merits. Ale loosened the bonds of the tongue and no one felt timid when discussing things that affected them all. But sometimes the ale could loosen the tongue so much that nothing sensible was decided, or no one remembered the next day what had been decided. And sometimes kinsmen parted on bad terms.

Instead this council began in a cold hall where they had to sit with their cloaks wrapped around them, with only a few braziers that had been brought in.

The big question was the clan's allegiance to Karl Sverkersson. No one considered him a powerful king; no one thought that he could protect the kingdom if the Danes or plunderers from across the Eastern Sea fell upon the country—even less if the Norwegians came, but they were usually fully occupied killing one another. Yet was the time truly ripe for their own clan to enter the fray over the royal crowns?

Birger Brosa said that while he was convinced the time would come, it was not yet upon them. The clan stood stronger in Eastern Götaland than in Western Götaland, but Eastern Götaland was also the country where King Karl stood strongest and had the most kinsmen, especially in Linköping and the surrounding regions. In order to prevail, the Western Goths would need to turn out to a man to wage a battle over some king's crown, though most of them cared not a whit about it. That would never happen.

So it was wisest to keep their own counsel for now, to support King Karl and let no one know that their support could cease like a bolt from the blue if the conditions proved right.

Instead they would patiently continue to reinforce the clan the way they had always done, through wise marriages. And an excellent opportunity now presented itself since Birger Brosa could no longer evade that obligation, no matter how pleasant it might be for him to live as a young lord without the responsibilities that God placed upon all men sooner or later.

Birger Brosa went on, and now everyone listened attentively with no bellowing, snoring, or loud shouts for ale to disturb their thoughts: Through his brother Magnus, the clan had a bond with the Norwegian king, Magnus Sigurdsen. However, King Magnus had been defeated by Harald Gille, and the king's power would pass to Harald's sons, as things now stood. This was the opinion of everyone who had any understanding of the Norsemen's doings. Although when it came to the Norwegians, one could never be absolutely sure, since everything could change with a single blow of the sword, turning a kinsman of the king into a kinsman in exile.

Now, however, Birger Brosa volunteered to go on a courting expedition to Norway in order to become betrothed to one of Harald Gille's daughters, either Solveig or Brigida, whichever would be deemed most suitable. That would strengthen the clan's bond with Norway, no matter how long the Norsemen continued killing each other. Birger would then be married into Harald Gille's clan, and his brother Magnus into Magnus Sigurdsen's clan.

The men turned and twisted the problem in their minds for a while. Another possibility, of course, would be for Birger to marry into Karl Sverkersson's clan. But that might prove foolhardy instead of a lucky stroke, because what use would it be to become a kinsman if one day the king's crown was passed to Karl's son, if he had one. No, reinforcing the bond with Norway would be a safer and with time probably a wiser move. The matter was thus concluded, and no more needed to be said about this marriage.

Then came the question of whom Magnus ought to court. His period of mourning for Sigrid had expired, and he was a good prospect, with plenty of land and great wealth, which always made things easier. But the question was who would be the wisest choice.

First Magnus had to tell them his own thoughts on the matter. Not entirely sure of his voice, or of how he should choose his words, he took the floor. If he married into the Pål clan in Husaby, another strong clan in Western Götaland would be bound together with Bjälbo. Besides, it was advantageous that his own land and that of the Pål clan adjoined each other; a marriage would thus mean that a large portion of the shore of Lake Vänern would end up legally bound together. This meant that they would acquire a stronger grip over trade in all of Western Götaland, since Lake Vänern for the greater part of the year was the most important link to Lödöse, as well as to Denmark and Norway. There were two daughters at Husaby, and both were fair but rather young.

When Magnus sat down he could hear from the muttering and whispering of his kinsmen that they thought he had spoken well, but were not completely convinced. He surmised that someone might have other plans for him, and in that case it was not difficult to reckon who would wax eloquent.

Quite rightly Birger Brosa demanded the floor, first speaking in words of praise for his older brother, his profits and shrewdness in business, and his willingness to make a good marriage in order to strengthen the clan and please his kinsmen.

But soon his tone turned curt and harsh as he described how more audacious and more important bonds were needed for the sake of all their kinsmen. The clan of Erik had in no way given up its struggle for the crown, although they had made exacting inquiries. In Norway Erik Jedvardsson's greedy widow was plotting revenge and raising her sons to be future contenders for the throne. The clan of Erik was strong south of Skara and also had offshoots in Svealand. It was a clan that they would be wise to count a friend rather than a foe.

Erik Jedvardsson's brother Joar was the owner of one of the farms outside Eriksberg, and he had a daughter, his eldest and not very fair, but for whom he would no doubt gladly hold a betrothal ale even for a man less wealthy than Magnus.

Magnus sighed when he heard his younger brother present this proposal. He already knew how it would turn out. His own blood would be used to bind the clan to a future important enemy or a future important ally. About this matter he could say nothing but that it sounded wise. So be it.

Eskil, who was having a hard time seeing the logic in choosing kinsmen among those who killed instead of those who had the right sort of wealth, gave his father a distressed look. He knew how it would turn out. He would soon have a new stepmother, about whom he knew nothing except that she was evidently not very fair.

Never had Arn seen Brother Guilbert as happy as the day the new horses arrived. There was a stallion, two mares, and a colt, and they were led in at once to their own pasture so that they wouldn't mix with the Nordic horses. They seemed to be in fine condition. Their journey had not been arduous in such a good season with plenty of grazing and water along the way. They had returned with Father Henri from one of his constant journeys to the general chapter in Cîteaux. Since Father Henri and the brothers who accompanied him had traveled most of the way on foot, as usual, and since the two heavy wagons with traveling goods had been pulled by donkeys, the horses seemed to be thoroughly rested.

It was always a big event at the monastery when Father Henri returned from the general chapter. All the monks faithfully obeyed and for the most part honestly applied the rule of charity, but they were also eager for everything else he brought: the news, the letters, the new books, the knowledge of what was happening out in the secular world as well as in the ecclesiastical circles, as well as all the kernels, seeds, and cuttings that Brother Lucien cast himself upon with the enthusiasm of a child. Finally the monks were also eager to receive the cheeses and casks of wine that at least the Burgundian brothers had a hard time living without, just as the Provençal cooks had a hard time imagining cloister life without a new supply of certain herbs that Brother Lucien had not managed to grow in the harsh Danish climate.

Many of the brothers had difficulty observing the discipline and dignity that such a homecoming demanded, although they first had to celebrate mass to mark Father Henri's return. And it was always longer than usual because the choir had learned some new songs, or old songs were presented in new voicings for this occasion, with prayers of thanksgiving for the father's return. Arn, who still retained his lovely soprano voice, had a particularly difficult time at such masses.

But afterward the brothers would stream out of the church chattering happily like small boys in anticipation of the ceremonies, led by Father Henri, which would begin as they unpacked the heaps of baggage. Father Henri read through his list, checking off each item and distributing God's gifts. Some brothers then went off whispering and giggling with glee with a long-awaited volume in their hands, while others praised the Lord with more dignity. The same was true of those who received new items for the garden or the kitchen.

But this time Brother Guilbert slipped away with Arn, taking him by the arm to show him the finest gift of all, though none of the other monks had any understanding of such matters: the new horses.

When they reached the pasture Arn tried hard to understand what was making the otherwise restrained Brother Guilbert so visibly excited. To Arn's eye these horses did indeed differ a great deal from ordinary horses. They were leaner and livelier, they moved all the time as if they were nervous at being cooped up, they ran back and forth with catlike soft movements with their tails held high. Their faces looked a little wider and more triangular than those of Nordic horses, and their eyes were very big and intelligent. Their color was different. One of the mares was reddish-brown like many other horses, but had a big gray spot down her left shoulder, while her half-grown foal was almost white with gray shading. The stallion and the other mare were dapple gray in color.

More than this Arn was unable to judge, even though he had worked a long time in the second most important of Brother Guilbert's workshops, the horseshoe smithy. Arn could shoe a horse so that neither Brother Guilbert nor any of the lay brothers had to redo his work.

Brother Guilbert stood silently leaning over the fence of the enclosure with tears in his eyes as he looked at the horses, as if he were far away in his thoughts. Arn waited expectantly.

To the boy's surprise, Brother Guilbert suddenly began talking to the stallion in a language Arn had never heard before; he didn't understand a word of it. But the stallion seemed to pay attention at once. He stopped and pricked up his ears toward Brother Guilbert, and after a brief hesitation calmly approached him. Brother

Guilbert then rubbed his face against the horse's muzzle in an unbecoming way and again spoke the strange language.

"Come, my boy, we're going to go riding, you and I. You can take the colt," said Brother Guilbert, swinging in under the fence and pulling Arn with him.

"But the colt . . . that won't work, will it? He isn't broken yet, is he?" Arn objected with obvious hesitation in his voice.

"Come here and I'll show you, it's not necessary!" said Brother Guilbert, calling the little colt, who came trotting over.

What happened then seemed to Arn like a miracle. Brother Guilbert stroked the colt over his muzzle and cheeks and neck, again speaking the foreign language, which the horses seemed to understand better than French or Latin. After a moment he simply lifted Arn up with one arm like a mitten so that Arn ended up astride the horse. The boy automatically grabbed hold of the colt's mane so he could hold on tight when the bucking started; he had helped break horses before, but never from the very first day.

The next moment Brother Guilbert swung himself up onto the stallion in one fluid movement; he seemed to fly up, and the stallion instantly set off on a wild gallop around the pasture. There sat Brother Guilbert bareback, holding lightly onto the stallion's mane with one hand, leaning daringly into the sharpest curves, yelling one thing after another to the horse in that odd language.

Arn's young colt was soon infected by the glee and began running around too, although at a jerky, more infantile gait. But soon the two of them were galloping faster and faster. In his delight Arn began mimicking Brother Guilbert's foreign language, as if intoxicated by the speed and the wind.

With a little shame Arn felt that he was now experiencing true and pure joy, and this was something he should not forget to bring up with Father Henri at his next confession. It was as if the horse's life and power were flowing through him, even though the colt was so young and so far from being an accomplished steed. And if he hadn't been broken for riding, which he certainly could not have been since he was so young, and if he had never had a rider on his back, then this in truth was a miracle.

"You see, my young chevalier, the horse is in truth man's best friend," said Brother Guilbert much later, when the nightingales had begun their evening song and it would soon be time for vespers, as they sat in the grass in the garden simply enjoying watching the new horses. "But these new horses are not like others, as you have already seen. They are the most noble, intelligent, fast, and tolerant horses that exist. Praise God for this gift, because they are horses from the Holy Land, Outremer."

Brother Guilbert was red in the face with excitement, and he was still breathing hard after his wild exhibition of the stallion's great power.

Arn had already begun to understand what distinguished these horses from others, not only in their appearance and their bearing and movements, but also in how they could be used. Yet he still asked and then received the answer he was expecting.

These horses were horses of war. What was true of swords was also true of horses: agility, agility, and more agility.

Since the men up here in the barbaric North had not yet adopted the art of fighting on horseback, Brother Guilbert went on, Nordic men needed strong, slow horses that could carry a heavy load to the battlefield. There the Nordic men would dismount, tether their horses, and then enter the fray on foot. If the Christians had attempted to meet the accursed Saracens in that manner, Jerusalem never would have been liberated.

But in the rest of the world, men fought on horseback; it was only the barbaric North that had not seized upon that strategy. And that's why Brother Guilbert had a clear, simple idea for using these horses, whose bloodlines he could now spread throughout Denmark. He would introduce the techniques associated with the new horses, and thus bring in a great deal of silver to the cloister. Almost the same way they did so by forging better swords for the men of the North. The one method ought to be as logical and profitable as the other.

Still sensing the wind in his hair and the speed on the horse, Arn now asked eagerly and without the proper courtesy to be taught the art of fighting on horseback, as the Christians did out in the great civilized world.

Brother Guilbert laughed silently to himself, grabbed Arn playfully by the tonsure, and explained that he had been doing that all along. From the beginning. Everything that Arn had learned about horses since the day he had been put to work was directed toward that goal.

What was of foremost importance was balance, above all balance. When Arn had practiced with his wooden swords, sometimes with one in each hand, he had stood on a pole with leather sacks full of sand swinging back and forth above him, always threatening to knock him to the ground. In the same way he had practiced riding horses from the beginning, always riding bareback without a saddle. All this was for the sake of balance, so that he would be able to sit his horse no matter which way it moved.

Now his task was to break the colt, at first without a saddle, and get to know the horse, talk to him, stroke him, and always take care of him. And his name had to be a secret name, not secret from God but otherwise just between the two of them. The colt would be called Khamsiin, which was the name of a desert wind, a wind that could blow for fifty days and never grow weary. The two mares would be called Aisha and Khadiya, and the stallion Nasir. Brother Guilbert did not explain the names, saying only that each name came from the secret language of the horses. It was not something that concerned other monks in the cloister, but only the two who were chevaliers.

A saddle would be made as soon as Khamsiin was grown, but until then it was the fundamentals that were important: trust, love, and balance.

The bell rang for vespers and they had to run to the lavatorium. As they dashed off, Arn asked whether it would be possible for him to learn the secret language of the horses too. If he spoke three languages already, surely he could speak four? Brother Guilbert smiled to himself and muttered something to the effect that the day would no doubt come. But that was all he said.

Arn had always been obedient. He loved the brothers as much as he loved books. He loved hard work as much as the easier tasks. He had set stones up in the tower of the cloister church, he had caught fish in the fjord. He loved the work with sword and bow as much as the work of following the path of faith in the Holy Scriptures, verse by verse and with the help of the *Glossa Ordinaria*. He may have loved Aristotle somewhat less and Ovid somewhat more, although in secret he occasionally composed imitations of the unchaste verses he had managed to read before they were taken away and locked up. Naturally he confessed afterward and took his punishment for the sin, but it was worth it. What were a few extra Pater Nosters compared with the hot rushing sensation in his body at the thought of Ovid?

Father Henri had no difficulty tolerating Arn's flagging interest in the philosopher and his somewhat overheated interest in writings that were inappropriate for boys. As far as Ovid was concerned, more than one God-fearing man of his acquaintance had put more emphasis on these studies than was suitable, both as a youth and as a man. It was nothing to cause alarm; he belonged to that category himself, at least when he looked back on his time as a novice. These were the normal fluctuations of life, nothing more. God in his wisdom had created life so that there was constant variation. If the boy did not find the philosopher very interesting—he sometimes made little impertinent objections, especially to the logical arguments—it was no wonder that, if this was a sin, it would be a sin that the boy shared with Brother Lucien, for example. Brother Lucien was devoted to the art of better enriching the world, in God's name, with plants that could be grown for the table, or to cure the ills of humankind, or perhaps merely to bring beauty into people's lives. But he was not very interested in reading Aristotle. Yet Father Henri would never dream of thinking of Brother Lucien as any less worthy because of that, or a brother to love less than the other brothers.

On the other hand, if someone in jest was to argue the logic the way the philosopher would have done, it might seem that the boy belonged to those who were also devoted to Brother Lucien's teaching. It was very exacting and meticulous but important work that lay behind the monastery's demonstration of the beauty that God could create on earth with the help of faithful brothers. The white snowdrops were the first flowers, pushing up through winter's still hard and inhospitable shell; then with the warmth came the Easter lilies, the white narcissus, and the tulips, all of them new to the barbaric North. Visitors who came at the right time would gasp in enchantment at the blossoms on the fruit trees, all of them unknown to the barbarians, fruits such as apples, pears, and cherries. The sales of these fruits had gone wonderfully in recent years, and Arn was also the one who helped Brother Lucien fetch the wares and translate into the Nordic tongue.

Arn had maintained a balance with everything that he'd learned, and there was nothing to worry about in that respect. As long as one didn't believe, like some of the more rigid brothers, that sword and lance had nothing to do with God's work on earth. But brothers who thought this way had not sufficiently studied the father of them all, Saint Bernard, who had been the leading creator of the Knights Templar, more than the Pope or any other man of the cloth.

And yet. There was now a problem with the boy. Since the new horses had arrived he seemed to have gone a bit crazy. It seemed fair to say that he had acquired a vice or an urge, an interest that overshadowed all other interests. And the question then became, in a higher and strategic perspective, whether God truly wanted this or whether God wanted to see his chosen lad reprimanded. And in a more tactical perspective, how should a wise prior go about handling such a rebuke?

Father Henri had summoned Brother Guilbert on more than one occasion in order to discuss the problem. But it seemed as though the good Guilbert wanted to defuse the matter with clichés such as "boys will be boys" and "what would you have done or thought at that age?" He also said they needed to understand the delight of novelty, and mentioned that it was all part of the general education he was giving Arn.

Perhaps that was true. And yet the boy's infatuation was so strong that it obviously risked overshadowing, at least temporarily, even his interest in books. As Arn's confessor, Father Henri knew much more about this than Brother Guilbert. Arn was no more capable than anyone else of lying when he made confession to his prior.

Arn saw the problem simply as a matter of confessing and admitting his sinful disposition and then doing penance. He had no idea that it was something that actually worried Father Henri; that would have made him feel both sad and ashamed. For now it led only to the minor punishments of extra prayers and maybe a few days on bread and water.

When Khamsiin had grown so much that he was no longer a

colt but a real horse, the love between Arn and the young stallion grew. One night when the summer was in full bloom, so that the nights were light and mild in Jutland, Arn got up after only a few hours of sleep following the midnight mass. He sneaked out to the stable, took down the saddle and bridle, and whispered some words into the darkness of night. Khamsiin came to him at once, bending his head down and accepting the boy's hot kisses and caresses on his soft muzzle.

Then Arn mounted the horse, and cautiously they moved off toward the fence, which Khamsiin gently jumped over in almost feline silence. They walked slowly for a while, finally increasing speed so much that they must have been the fastest horse and rider ever to cross Danish soil. They stormed along like the horsemen of the apocalypse through the soft, rolling landscape and the sparse beech woods. Some nights they went all the way out to the sea, knowing that they risked having to keep up the same pace on the way back to be able to arrive in time for morning mass.

Rumors soon spread in the region about a ghost rider, an omen, a bad sign, a spirit who rode as no mortal man could ride even in dreams, a dwarf with evil sharp teeth and a glittering sword of fire.

The sword, however, was made of wood with an iron core inside for the sake of weight. But in his fantasies Arn rode with a sword that could well have been of fire. He swung it back and forth with his left hand, switched the sword and reins at full gallop and then brandished the weapon in his right hand. But the sword was not the most important thing. It was more as if he were placating his guilty conscience by doing a little work while he was out riding for pleasure instead of sleeping the sleep of the just, which was recommended by God.

It was the speed that captivated him. As young as he was, Khamsiin had a power in his legs that no other horse Arn had ridden could ever match. Arn imagined that Khamsiin was being carried forward by a supernatural power, as if this speed was something that only God could have created, and as if on Khamsiin he was flying closer to God than at any other time.

It was a sinful thought, of course. Arn knew that. He said the prayers and denied himself what he must to seek forgiveness.

But what speed! he thought. Shamefully enough, even during his most remorseful prayers.

Chapter 5

On Christmas Day in the year of Grace 1144, the Christians in the Kingdom of Jerusalem suffered their greatest defeat since they conquered the Holy Land. In Christian Europe there were many people who realized that the fall of the city of Odessa was a catastrophe. But nobody could imagine that what had happened was the beginning of the end of the Christian occupation.

At that time, a half century after the victory that had cost the Christians more than 100,000 lives, the Kingdom of Jerusalem consisted of a cohesive coastal region that stretched from Gaza in southern Palestine through Jerusalem and Haifa to the coast of Lebanon and up to Antioch. But north of Antioch, there was a large Christian enclave around the city of Odessa, which together with Antioch on the coast controlled all the roads between the Christian Eastern Roman Empire in Constantinople and the three cities of Baghdad, Jerusalem, and Damascus. Second only to Jerusalem itself, Odessa had been the Christians' most important fortress.

But now the city had been conquered, plundered, and relegated to the oblivion of history by a commander whose name hardly anyone in Europe knew. He was called Unadeddin Zinki. The conquest ended in a bloodbath in which 5,000 Franks and 6,000 Armenians and other local Christians were massacred after the walls fell. In their stead Zinki let 300 Jews move into the city in an attempt to bring Odessa back to life. The Jews were much closer to the Muslims than to the Christians, since the Christians had the peculiar custom of murdering all the Jews they encountered.

Zinki was a powerful, ambitious, and ruthless commander. He made no secret of the fact that he wanted to take Damascus, the next most important city after Jerusalem, and from there draw the noose tighter around the Christians.

The Muslim inhabitants of Damascus, however, felt not the slightest enthusiasm at the thought of having this unpredictable and cruel ruler inside their high city walls. And when Zinki was on his way to Damascus, he was forced to stop and lay siege to the town of Baalbek. He grew angry that it was taking so long, so when Baalbek finally capitulated after the garrison had been given the usual assurances of safe conduct, he had all the defenders beheaded and the commander flayed alive.

Perhaps he thought that such actions would strike terror into the inhabitants of Damascus and encourage them to offer less resistance. But the effect was the direct opposite. Damascus formed an alliance with the Christian king of Jerusalem, because both cities, regardless of religion, had just as much to fear from a conqueror such as Zinki.

When his troops understood that the war was over for the time being, and that they would never succeed in conquering and plundering Damascus itself, they headed for home well loaded with booty and satisfied for now. Zinki's army melted away. At this time, he came upon his Christian eunuch secretly drinking wine out of his personal goblet. He contented himself with hurling threats about what the punishment would be for such a display of insolence, but decided first to sleep on the matter. The eunuch decided it was better to stick his dagger into him while he slept.

This too might have looked like a favorable matter for the Christians, for now Zinki's conquests would be divided up among his sons, and that would take time and possibly lead to minor wars among themselves. The second avenging crusade could hardly wish for a more advantageous situation.

But Allah had something else in mind. Of Zinki's sons, the one who now pulled the ring, the sign of the ruler, from his dead father's hand was Mahmud; he would soon be given the surname Nur ed-Din, the Light of Religion.

Nur ed-Din soon created a revival movement. But he was careful not to try to take Damascus before the time was ripe, and instead made Aleppo his capital.

With Nur ed-Din and above all the one who would come after him, Salah ed-Din, the Christian presence in the Holy Land was doomed to destruction. It was now only a matter of time before Jerusalem would fall. But only someone who writes with the wisdom of hindsight and who knows the true sequence of events can tell this story.

When the news of the fall of Odessa spread through Europe, it aroused as much gloom as consternation. If Christendom did not strike back soon and hard, the unbelievers might decide to attack Jerusalem itself; that was the purely military conclusion even men of faith could understand.

Pope Eugenius III began working at once to promote a second crusade that would secure Christian access to the Holy Sepulchre and all the other destinations for pilgrims.

He did the only right thing in this awkward situation. He called in Bernard de Clairvaux under the holy banners.

Bernard de Clairvaux was at this time the most influential man within the spiritual world, and probably the best speaker in the secular world. When it became known that Bernard was going to speak in the cathedral in Vézelay in March 1146, such huge crowds came that it was obvious that the cathedral would not be able to hold them all. Instead a wooden platform was constructed outside the town. Bernard had not been speaking long before the ten thousand or more gathered there began shouting for crosses.

A great number of cloth crosses had been readied, and Bernard now began to pass them out, first to the king and his vassals—not even the reluctant counts and barons would have been able to resist the wave of enthusiasm and conviction that now swept forward—and then to all the others. Finally Bernard began tearing strips from his own clothes to give new recruits a cross of cloth to wear as a sign that they had now sworn themselves to the Holy War; it also indicated that after a brief campaign they would obtain eternal forgiveness for all their sins.

Not without some pride Bernard was able to write to the Pope about his efforts:

You gave the order. I obeyed. And the Power that gave the order made my obedience bear fruit. I opened my mouth. I spoke and instantly the number of Crusaders had multiplied beyond counting. Entire villages and towns are now deserted. There is hardly one man for every seven women, and everywhere one sees widows whose husbands are still alive.

The Christian revival in Europe now spread with the same force as Nur ed-Din's revival spread around Aleppo. Bernard de Clairvaux had to venture out on long journeys and day after day repeat what he had said, first to Burgundy, then to Lorraine and Flanders.

But since the revival had spread to Germany the usual problems arose, the same as those during the First Crusade. The Archbishop of Cologne had to hurriedly summon Bernard because a Cistercian monk by the name of Peter the Venerable was going around Germany with a message that was Bernard's when it reached the Holy Land but a quite different one when it reached the Jews of Europe.

As a result of his preaching, pogroms broke out in Cologne, Mainz, Worms, Spies, and Strassburg. The Jews were murdered, in some places down to the very last one.

On his arrival Bernard quickly imposed a penance on Peter the Venerable to take a vow of silence for a year, to repent, and at once to return to his cloister in Cluny and never again get involved in something he didn't understand.

After that Bernard had to replicate his whole French tour in Germany, where, despite the fact that he had to work through an interpreter, he won the same reception for the Holy War. But now he also had to make a monumental effort to put a stop to the persecution of the Jews, repeating over and over that "whosoever attacks a Jew to take his life, it will be as though he had struck Jesus Christ Himself."

With that, the focus of the aroused masses could once again be directed toward what was important, and the Second Crusade became a reality. The German king Konrad made a pact with King Louis VII, and soon an army of countless soldiers plundered its way through Europe on its way to the Holy War. By the time they arrived in Christian Constantinople the French and German armies had created great internal discord, mostly due to quarrels about who had the first right to plunder and who would plunder second. From Constantinople they decided to take different routes toward Jerusalem. Konrad would proceed through the interior of Asia Minor while Louis would take the coastal route, and they would meet up in Antioch. King Konrad of Germany, who had chosen the interior but more dangerous road through Asia Minor in the belief that there would be more to plunder than along the safer coast road, became brutally familiar with what could happen when a heavily armored European army of knights faced the superior light Oriental cavalry. He was attacked by Turkish forces at Dorylaeum and lost nine-tenths of his army.

When the two European armies met at Antioch, the French considerably less decimated than the German, they were received in princely style by the local ruler, Count Raymond. King Baldwin of Jerusalem also joined them, and it was then time for feasting, of course, but later for careful planning.

The newly arrived warriors in God's army probably had no idea who Zinki was, much less that he was dead, and that now they would face a considerably more dangerous enemy in his son, Nur ed-Din.

The local Frankish Christians naturally had a clearer sense of the situation. Either they should now go straight to Odessa and retake the city, since it was the fall of Odessa that had triggered the whole crusade, and such a victory would be of great psychological importance, for both sides.

Or else they should head for Aleppo and the main enemy Nur ed-Din, joining the battle that must come sooner or later, and preferably now when they were at their strongest.

But King Louis and King Konrad, who no doubt understood little about conditions in the part of the world where they now found themselves, decided to strike at Damascus instead. If they could conquer the second most important city after Jerusalem then, they agreed, they would be starting the crusade with a great victory that would resound throughout the world. In addition, although they might or might not have said as much out loud, Damascus would be a most magnificent prize to plunder. If nothing else, they would rapidly recoup all their expenses.

The local Franks tried in vain to explain what a mistake it would be to attack Damascus, but they were voted down by the two kings, who were in agreement and also possessed the two largest armies.

So the entire Christian host marched on Damascus, which was sheer madness in more than one sense.

Damascus was not only the most important Muslim city in the region, it was also the only Muslim city that was allied with Jerusalem. If that pact was now broken, it would prove that a Christian's word was not to be trusted. This was something that especially worried the Knights Templar, who did indeed make up the backbone of all Western cavalry.

Worst of all was the fact that they were playing right into Nur ed-Din's hands—soon the carrier pigeons began flying in every direction, and all of Nur ed-Din's brothers and other allies set off with large armies from the north, from the south, and from the east.

After laying siege to Damascus for only four days, the Christians were surrounded by an army many times larger. They had also chosen to make camp in the least favorable place, on the south side of the city where there was no protection, and where the Damascenes had filled in all the wells in good time. The commander of the Knights Templar could see that this tactical positioning was so obviously idiotic that the only possible explanation was bribery—either King Louis or King Konrad must have been paid to lose.

The Christian positions soon proved indefensible. It was not a question of even setting up any siege engines; it was a matter of fleeing for their lives.

When the Christian army broke camp and began their retreat to the south, they were attacked by the light Arab cavalry which, always out of reach, rained arrows down on the fleeing troops. The losses were unimaginable, and the stench of death lay heavy over large parts of the Holy Land for several months.

And so the Second Crusade ended.

King Konrad of Germany, as usual in extreme disagreement with King Louis, took the land route home, proceeding cautiously along the safer Mediterranean coast of Asia Minor.

King Louis no longer had a large army, so he chose to take the sea route from Antioch toward Sicily. On the way his fleet was plundered by the Byzantine navy. After that both King Louis and King Konrad remained forever uninterested in new crusades.

King Louis quite rightly received derision from his wife when he returned home. The Second Crusade was a calamitous fiasco. Nur ed-Din would soon take Damascus without raising a sword or firing a single arrow.

Logically, the Christian empire should have been doomed. There was nothing more to hope for from Europe. None of Europe's big countries would send a new expedition after the disaster they had just witnessed, no matter how eloquently Bernard de Clairvaux and others spoke of salvation and the forgiveness of all sins for anyone who joined the Holy War. And yet it would be a long time before Jerusalem was liberated by the faithful. And it would not be granted to Nur ed-Din to cleanse the holy city of the barbaric and bloodthirsty European occupiers.

That would depend on an order of monks. The Knights Templar shared the same religious origin with the Cistercian order; it was Bernard de Clairvaux himself who had written the cloister rules for the Templar knights. From the beginning this order was conceived primarily as a sort of religious police force to protect Christian pilgrims, above all on the roads between Jerusalem and the River Jordan. Arabic robber bands had found this constant stream of pilgrims on the way to bathe in the Jordan both easy and profitable to rob. But the idea of warrior monks, at first something that must have seemed like a paradox, quickly spread far beyond the Holy Land, and many of the best knights in Europe heeded the call. But few were chosen. Only the best of the best, and the most serious in their faith, had a chance of being accepted as brothers in the order. The Knights Templar created the best force of knights that ever rode with lance and sword in the Holy Land. Or, for that matter, in any land.

The Arabs in general had no great respect for Western warriors. Often they were too heavily armored, rode poorly, and had a hard time coping with the heat and staying sober. But there was one kind of European knight they avoided, unless they had a superiority of ten to one. Sometimes even then, because victory could be very costly. The Knights Templar never surrendered. And unlike other knights, weaker in their faith, they did not fear death. They were unshakably convinced that their war was holy and that the instant they died in battle they would enter into Paradise.

These knights wearing the white mantle with a red cross and carrying the white shields with the same red cross were now the only hope of the Kingdom of Jerusalem.

✠

On the day when Arn's voice had changed so much that he could no longer sing, and everyone noticed, he was convinced that God was punishing him severely and yet the cause was incomprehensible. He had obviously committed a great sin deserving of such harsh punishment. But how could he commit a great sin without knowing what it was? He had obeyed, he had loved all the brothers, he hadn't lied, he had tried hard to be truthful in his confessions with Father Henri, even about the things he was most ashamed of. Without grumbling or cheating in any way he had performed the penance that Father Henri had imposed on him for self-defilement. But each time Arn had received forgiveness for his sins. Why would God punish him so sternly?

He prayed to God for forgiveness for even asking such a question, which might be interpreted as suspecting that God's punishment was unjust. Then he added that he would like to know what his sin had been so that he might improve his ways. But God did not answer.

Yet the music master at Vitae Schola, Brother Ludwig de Bêtecourt, took a surprisingly sanguine view of the matter. He consoled Arn by explaining that what had happened was part of God's natural order, that all boys sooner or later lost their soprano voice and for a time croaked like a raven. It was no more strange than the fact that boys grew up to be men, or that Arn was growing taller and stronger. But when Brother Ludwig could not guarantee that Arn's voice after this metamorphosis would ever be good for singing again, even at a lower register, the boy refused to be consoled.

Singing had been his most important task at Vitae Schola, to such an extent that it was through his singing during mass that he felt he was doing the most good, and that his efforts had some meaning. Naturally he had been useful when the church tower was being built, but it was through singing that he accomplished something that others could not. In everything else he was only a little boy who had to learn from all the others. His other work was such that it provided sheer joy for either body or soul, like the horse or the books or Brother Guilbert's exercises, but he felt it was of more use to himself than to the brothers. And since he

loved the brothers as the rules prescribed, he longed to be able
to reciprocate by making himself deserving of the brothers' love.
Singing had been the most effective way of accomplishing that,
or so he thought.

Now he could no longer sing, even though the song was still
inside his head and he could imagine each note correctly voiced
before his lips released it so falsely. It was like suddenly losing his
sense of balance and being unable to walk or run or ride. Brother
Ludwig had explained that he was no longer needed at mass, and
Arn deemed this harsh punishment for his failure.

Father Henri felt a certain impatience that something so
natural should be so difficult to explain to the boy. It obviously
wasn't enough, as he first believed, simply to explain that his
voice breaking was something that happened to all men. It surprised him that not even the simple and, as he thought, easily
observable fact that men sounded different from boys seemed to
have any effect on Arn's reason. What troubled Father Henri was
that Arn's apparently unwarranted worries might actually be ex-
pressing something else, a great loneliness. If he had been able
to grow up with other boys, either inside or outside the cloister
walls, he might have had an easier time seeing himself as what he
was: a boy and perhaps a future brother, but not yet a brother.

The fact that Arn could not accept the fact that a breaking
voice existed somewhere between birth and death, and with the
same inevitability, was a warning sign of his immaturity. On the
one hand, the boy was more educated than any grown man, at
least up here in the barbaric North. Presumably he could also
handle weapons better than anyone outside the walls.

On the other hand, he was completely innocent when it came
to the base world. He wouldn't be able to sit at table with his
countrymen without feeling disgust. He couldn't stay out there
even for a day without seeing that people lied, and that most of

the seven deadly sins, which Arn apparently understood as some sort of theoretical moral example in a cautionary tale, were committed daily by each and every person in the outside world.

In all probability Arn did not understand what *pride* was, unless he took examples from the Holy Scriptures. What *gluttony* was he could presumably not even imagine; what *greed* was he no doubt didn't understand at all; *wrath* he knew only as God's wrath, which would stir up the concept of sin quite literally for him. *Envy*, as far as Father Henri could see, was something altogether foreign to Arn, who felt only admiration for the brothers who could do more than he could, and boundless gratitude that he was allowed to learn. And *sloth*; how foreign would that concept seem to a boy who always jumped with eagerness to be allowed to dash on to the next of the day's tasks or lessons?

Only *lust* possibly remained, although Arn seemed to possess both a somewhat exaggerated concept of young boys' sinfulness when it came to self-defilement, as well as immunity to admonitions in that regard. Father Henri suddenly recalled with a certain irony how Arn in one of his remorseful moments had associated his breaking voice, or "God's punishment," as he viewed it, with terrible sins, which in his case were quite mundane. The boy had prayed to be allowed to keep his voice if he did much penance; at the same time he prayed to be free of the itch that made it so hard to refrain from sin.

Father Henri, as usual rather amused behind his stern mask, had then let his words get ahead of his thoughts. Suddenly, to his own astonishment, he found himself bantering about the problem by assuring the boy that there was indeed a simple method that would both secure his high voice and do away with that itch, though this means of penance was not to be recommended.

Arn had not understood what he was getting at, and then Father Henri sat there embarrassed at his own thoughtlessness, and tried to explain that for a number of reasons they did not castrate boys in monasteries, even though their voices were enchanting. And consequently and finally, Arn's breaking voice was not a sin but part of God's natural order.

Yet Father Henri was convinced that God really did have a definite plan for young Arn. And until God made His intention clear, it was Father Henri's duty to prepare Arn for the calling that would be his one day. He had tried to do his best, he could honestly say that without boasting, but now it seemed that all his efforts were still not enough. Sooner or later Arn had to learn what God's less beautiful world, the one outside the cloister walls, actually looked like. Otherwise he would remain as innocent as a child, even when he became a man, and such a man would more often than not become a foolish man. And that could not be God's will.

✠

When the autumn storms began to pound the west coast of Jutland it was time to go salvaging. People in the fishing villages on the long sandy coast had always reckoned that salvaging from shipwrecks was their ancient right, but King Valdemar had now forbidden anyone from seizing salvaged goods except the monks from Vitskøl. The monks were in a much better position than anyone else to know what to salvage and then see to it that what they found was put to good use. This would appear to be a wise new order from the king.

But not everyone along the coast found it fair or right to give up customs they had followed since ancient times. There were those who said that the monks behaved like a swarm of Egyptian locusts over every wreck they found, leaving not even the tiniest scrap visible at the site. There was truth in such claims, but also envy. For the monks at Vitskøl usually did not hurry with their work, except when haste was dictated by the forces of weather.

The monks carried home everything they found to their Vitae Schola, chopping up the timbers for wood, and using whole deck planking and masts as building material for their own boat-building. They found wool for their own spinning mills, seed for their fields, or rye and wheat to sell. They salvaged skins and leather for their tanneries, iron rods for the smithies, tackle and lines for scaffolding, and jewels and valuables to be sent to Rome—they could find a use for everything. But they also did something that the old scavengers on the coast never would have bothered to do. All the dead they found were given a Christian burial.

A salvage expedition like this from Vitskøl might take up to ten days. Most things were transported on heavy oxcarts, and the great loads usually made the trip back take twice as long as the journey out. Brother Guilbert always went along on these forays, not only because his great strength often came in handy, but also because on horseback, together with Arn, he could cover great stretches of the beaches in a short time. When the entourage from Vitae Schola arrived at the sandy beaches on the coast, they set up camp and then Arn and Brother Guilbert rode in opposite directions to scout which way they should go the next day. Brother Guy le Breton also came along, of course, because nobody at Vitae Schola knew as much about the sea, its dangers, its fruits, and its weather as he did. Otherwise the brothers had to take turns according to a schedule drawn up by Father Henri. Almost all the brothers were eager to take part in these expeditions to the sea, because it was a completely differ-ent sort of work and because the water was so beautiful. It was exciting to see what God with one hand took from the seafarers to give with the other hand to those who toiled most assiduously in the garden.

Arn was doubly grateful that he was always allowed to come along. He had a chance to ride as fast as he liked on Khamsiin along the endless sandy beaches, preferably just above where the waves broke. There the sand was hard-packed and smooth so that Khamsiin had a good foothold and a clear view and could fly along in a straight line, giving Arn a chance to do what he loved best.

During Arn's second year as a scout on the salvage trips, something unheard of happened. In the sparse pine forest about a mile from the sea the column from Vitae Schola was attacked on its way home by drunken robbers. They were probably no highwaymen, but frustrated wreck-plunderers who had been sitting in one of the nearby villages, drinking too much ale and working themselves up over the fact that fat monks were now stealing what rightfully belonged to the people who made their living from the sea. But they were armed with lances and swords, and one of them, riding a short and stout Nordic horse, made threatening swings with an old-fashioned battle-axe in his hands.

The heavy oak wagons with steel-rimmed wheels stopped with a screech. The monks made no move to flee but lowered their heads in prayer. The man with the battle-axe clumsily maneuvered his horse toward Brother Guilbert, who was riding at the head of the column with Arn behind him and off to one side. Arn at once did as Brother Guilbert did, sweeping off the hood of his cloak and lowering his head in prayer, although he wasn't sure what he should pray for. But suddenly the man with the battle-axe yelled at Brother Guilbert for everyone to move away from the wagons, because here came those who rightfully owned the harvest of the sea. Brother Guilbert did not reply, since he was still praying. This made the man with the battle-axe both uncertain and angry, prompting him to say in very coarse language that no prayers were going to help here, because now the goods had to be unloaded from the wagons, and double-quick.

Then Brother Guilbert replied calmly that naturally he was not praying for something as simple as salvaged goods. He was praying for the souls of these misguided men now that they were about to make themselves unhappy for the rest of their earthly days. At first the man with the battle-axe was surprised, but then he became even angrier, and he spurred his horse forward to aim a mighty blow at Brother Guilbert.

Arn, who was sitting on Khamsiin only a few yards away, now knew instinctively what Brother Guilbert was going to do, and at least in the first moment Arn was right. The drunken wreck-plunderer raised his battle-axe, gripping it with both hands and directing the blow at a downward angle, a blow that would have killed if it struck home. But Brother Guilbert made two almost imperceptible adjustments with his legs that made Nasir move quick as a snake, taking one step to the side and one step back. The man with the battle-axe struck into thin air and was dragged from his saddle by his own momentum, flipping a half turn in the air before he thumped to the ground on his back.

If this had been an exercise session with Brother Guilbert and Arn had been crawling there on the ground, at the next instant he would have felt Brother Guilbert's foot land on his sword hand, his weapon would have been taken from him, and then he would have been roundly rebuked.

But now Brother Guilbert sat with his hands clasped before him, holding Nasir's reins in a light grip between his little fingers.

The humiliated robber crawled to his feet. Swearing, he grabbed his battle-axe again and now attacked on foot, which ended the same way. He ran at Brother Guilbert, aimed a mighty blow, and then found himself again striking at the air. He fell to the ground from his own weight. His fellow criminals couldn't help laughing, which made him even more furious.

When he gripped his battle-axe a third time Brother Guilbert held up his palm to stop him and explained that no one would prevent the robbery if that was the only reason for the attack.

But he wanted to warn the man one last time against repeating his attempts at assault.

"You have a choice," he explained calmly. "All of you steal what you came here to steal. We neither can nor will stop you by force. But think on this, that then all of you will have sold your souls to the Devil and become criminals who can expect a severe punishment from the king. Or else you can repent and go home. Then we will forgive you and pray for you."

But the man with the battle-axe didn't want to hear any such talk. Like a fool he repeated that the salvage goods since ancient times had belonged to the people on the coast. The men behind him shook their lances, pitchforks, and a few swords in agitation, and one of them suddenly threw a lance straight at Brother Guilbert.

It was a heavy, slow lance with an old-fashioned broad-bladed point, so Arn had plenty of time to picture what would happen. Brother Guilbert leaned lightly to the side in his saddle, grabbed the lance in the air, and then pointed it at the mob, as if for a brief instant he considered attacking. Arn saw the robbers' eyes widen and gleam with fear. But then Brother Guilbert quickly turned the lance over his knee and broke it in two as if he were snapping a little twig. Contemptuously he flung the bits to the ground.

"We are the Lord's servants, we cannot fight with you and you know it!" he shouted. "But if you absolutely want to make yourselves miserable for the rest of your wretched earthly lives, then steal what you want to steal. We can't stop you from such foolishness."

The mob deliberated for a moment. The man with the battle-axe staggered back to his followers and a vehement argument ensued. Brother Guilbert gathered his brothers and Arn around himself and said that if it came to violence, each of them should save himself by running from this place. There was nothing else to do. Arn was sharply admonished to stay at a safe distance from all the robbers and, should things turn violent, ride home at once to tell everyone what had happened.

The robbers' problem was that they thought they could certainly steal whatever they wanted from the heavy load. But they wouldn't be able to kill all the witnesses, as they before had killed all the unfortunate seamen who survived a shipwreck to wash ashore, thinking they were saved, only to discover at the last moment of their lives that they had been rescued by wreckplunderers. But here the robbers would never be able to kill the two monks on horseback. They decided to take what they wanted anyway in the hope that, since no one was killed, no royal revenge would befall them just because there was a little less weight in the fat monks' heavily loaded wagons.

That's how the matter was settled. The robbers took what they could carry and anything that seemed valuable, while the monks stood back and prayed for their lost souls. When the robbers had finished plundering the wagons and, loudly bellowing, left the scene, the monks repacked their loads and continued home to Vitae Schola.

When they arrived, Father Henri wrote a letter of complaint to King Valdemar, whose royal command had been flouted. Shortly thereafter soldiers were sent out to arrest the guilty parties, which proved a simple matter. Most of the goods that were stolen were returned to Vitae Schola with the soldiers. The robbers were all hanged.

The event had made a big impression on Arn, giving him much to think about. He felt sorry for the robbers, who were affected with the deadly sin of greed, which had led them so rapidly into perdition where they were now suffering eternal torment. He could understand that they felt their rights had been subverted. It was true that plundering shipwrecks had been their ancient right as coastal dwellers, and it must feel wrong for foreign monks to take that income away. And besides, the men had been drunk. Even though Arn didn't know much about intoxication, a couple of brothers sometimes drank too much wine, hence proving quiet clearly that where wine went in, wits went out. Afterwards they had to do penance for months on bread and water. So Arn thought he grasped that a person who was drunk didn't really fully understand his responsibilities.

But Arn could not comprehend why Brother Guilbert had acted the way he did. The men who attacked them were fishermen, after all, who knew nothing about the weapons they were holding in their hands; at least that's what Arn believed. Brother Guilbert could have taken their weapons from them and sent them fleeing. Then the theft would never have taken place, and the royal soldiers wouldn't have had to track the men down and hang them. Didn't love for one's fellow man mean trying to ameliorate his stupidity if one could?

Arn had hesitated to discuss the matter with Brother Guilbert. Since the monk had acted as he did and had not saved the lost men from their own stupidity, he must be convinced that he had done the right thing.

But Arn did take up the problem with Father Henri, admitting that he was still praying for the souls of the hanged robbers.

Father Henri had no objection to Arn praying for the souls of those wretches. He viewed such a response as a demonstration of the boy's strong empathy with the example set by Jesus Christ for the way life should be lived on earth. He saw only good in it.

But it was more disturbing that Arn obviously did not understand why it was impossible for Brother Guilbert to use violence. *Thou shalt not kill* was a commandment that was utterly without compromise.

Arn argued that the Holy Scriptures were full of commandments that were unreasonable. Take the fact that Brother Guy le Breton had so far failed to get the Danes to eat mussels. Out in

the fjord the mussel beds had rapidly grown as soon as Brother
Guy had come to Vitae Schola. But so far it had led only to the
brothers themselves feasting on mussels prepared in one peculiar
way after another, because the Danes around Limfjord believed
that "whatever does not have fins and scales you shall not eat; it
is unclean for you." According to Deuteronomy 14:8 or whatever
it was.

Deuteronomy 14:10, Father Henri corrected him. 14:8 pro-
hibited the eating of pigs and rabbits. Which basically illustrated
the same problem, or at least the reverse of the problem, since
the Danes certainly had nothing against eating pigs or rabbits.
Nevertheless, and Arn ought to know by now that there was a
big difference between various small prohibitions of that sort
and more serious prohibitions. If one searched for small prohibitions in the Holy Scriptures one could find many that were
downright ridiculous—for instance, the hair should not be shorn
in a certain way when in mourning—as well as things that were
unreasonable and un-Christian in their severity, such as: he who
contradicts his mother or father shall be stoned to death.

But once again the important thing was how one learned to
understand the Holy Scriptures, and the guiding principle in
that respect was of course the Lord Jesus himself. Through his
example he had shown how the text should be understood. In
short, killing was among the most forbidden of actions.

But Arn refused to yield. He now claimed, using the logic in
argumentation that Father Henri had personally pounded into
his head for most of his life, that a letter could kill as easily as
a sword. By writing to King Valdemar, Father Henri had sealed
the fate of the unfortunate and unsuccessful robbers, since the
outcome was never in any doubt the moment the king received
the letter from Vitae Schola.

In the same way one could kill through omission, by *not* using
force. If Brother Guilbert had knocked two or three of the un-

successful robbers to the ground, wouldn't he have committed only a comparatively *little* sin?

Arn was astonished that Father Henri did not interrupt him or scold him, but instead moved his hand in a gentle circle as a sign for Arn to continue his argument.

So, if Brother Guilbert committed a *little* sin, for which he easily would have been able to do penance for a month, by giving a couple of robbers a beating and thus scaring off the others, the result could have been good. The robbers wouldn't have turned into robbers but merely drunkards out on a foolish foray. They would have been prevented from committing theft, they would not have been hanged, their children would not have been fatherless, and their wives would not now be widows. Weighing the pros and cons in this equation, one would probably find that Brother Guilbert, by employing violence without anger, would have served a good purpose. And so he probably wouldn't have done anything evil, would he? After all, this was a theme that Saint Bernard himself often repeated.

Arn fell silent. He was so astonished by the priest's silence that he could not go on with his argument: Father Henri sat deep in thought with his brow furrowed in a way that usually meant he didn't want to be disturbed, because he was trying to crack a hard nut.

Arn waited patiently for a long time, since he had not been dismissed. Finally Father Henri looked up at Arn and gave him an encouraging smile, patting him lightly on the hand and nodding in agreement as he prepared to give an explanation, preceded by much clearing of his throat, as usual. Arn waited tensely.

"Young man, you surprise me by showing such acuity in an area which was perhaps not one of your best," he began. "You have touched on two problems, although they are related. Your argument that a little sin from Brother Guilbert could have obviated something worse than a little sin is formally correct. And yet it is false. When Brother Guilbert had to choose between using violence, the worst sin he of all people could commit, or acting as he did, if he had known at that moment what the result would be, *then* but only then would your reasoning be valid. Without being unkind to you, however, I must point out that the formal way in which you have set up the argument, although Aristotle himself would have approved it, still presupposes that Brother Guilbert is not the man he is—a mortally sinful person—but rather that he is God and can see the truth and all that is to come. But it's an uplifting example, because it so clearly shows how clumsy we humans can be even when with a clear conscience we try to act justly. A very uplifting example, indeed."

"Not especially uplifting for the poor devils who were led further into sin, were hanged, and now must suffer eternal torment in hell," Arn muttered crossly and was instantly given a sharp rebuke to pray ten Pater Nosters for his impertinence.

Arn obediently said his prayers, and Father Henri was grateful for the respite, which he spent thinking further, and not without a certain amount of guilt. He found to his shock that he was no longer sure of his counterargument.

Wouldn't it be exaggerating to say that Brother Guilbert would have had to be God to foresee that measured violence, without anger, could in that situation have done a greater good than the usual peaceful response enjoined by Christ?

Wasn't it true instead that Brother Guilbert had once lived a life in which, with God on his side, he could smite anyone who attacked him when he was protecting the church's property? But afterwards he had imposed on himself such strict penance for sins he'd committed in the Holy War that he had to refrain from violence in any situation. Wasn't it simply that Brother Guilbert was now closed off, or had closed himself off, from any sort of intellectual examination in such a context and blindly followed his self-imposed penance?

In that case Brother Guilbert was certainly pure and without sin with regard to the way he had acted. But little Arn had also for the first time shown proof of theological acumen and, what was even better, a genuine insight into the faith.

However, it was the larger problem that Arn had touched on that would be easier to take up just now. They would come back to the other issue a week later when Father Henri had had time to collect his thoughts and read up on it.

"Now let's take up your second problem," Father Henri said, displaying great friendliness to Arn after he had rattled off his ten Pater Nosters. "Saint Bernard pointed out quite rightly that whatsoever is done with good intent—you know what I mean, let's skip the definitions—whatsoever is done with *good* intent cannot lead to evil. In what context does this assurance have the greatest practical significance?"

"When it applies to the crusades, obviously," replied Arn obediently.

"Correct! But a crusade involves killing large numbers of Saracens, doesn't it? So, doesn't the commandment against killing apply here? And if not, why not?"

"It doesn't apply because it is done, always done, with the blessing of the Holy Father in Rome," Arn replied cautiously.

"Yes, but that's a circular argument, my son. I asked *why*?"

"Because we have to imagine that the good is very good, that the good in preserving the Holy Sepulchre for believers is so much greater than the evil of killing Saracens," Arn ventured hesitantly.

"Yes, you're on the right track," Father Henri assured him with a thoughtful nod. "But even when the Lord Jesus drove the moneylenders out of the temple he was never close to killing them, was he?"

"No, but that could be because, through his Father's wrath, which naturally is much different from our human wrath, he

used only as much force as was necessary. He actually did drive
the moneylenders out of the temple. He didn't need to kill them;
it's as if Brother Guilbert had—"

"All right! Let's get back to the question at hand," Father
Henri interrupted him brusquely. But behind his stern mask he
was secretly smiling at how Arn had suddenly and as if by chance
managed to find an almost devastating argument that would
strengthen his earlier position that Brother Guilbert should have
used limited force. He should have simply acted as did the Lord
Jesus himself in the temple.

"Did the Lord Jesus repudiate the soldiers, did he ever condemn them for being soldiers?" asked Father Henri in a deliberately subdued tone of voice.

"No, not that I know of . . ." Arn pondered. "Like that part
about the coin, render unto Caesar what is Caesar's and unto
God what . . . something like that. And then of course we have
almost the same thing in the gospel of Luke, 3:14, I think . . .
'Then some soldiers asked him, "And what should we do?" He
replied, "Don't extort money and don't accuse people falsely—be
content with your pay."' If the soldiers behave like honest men
when they're not soldiers . . . then it's not wrong to be a soldier?"

"Correct! And what do soldiers do?"

"They kill people. Like the ones who came in response to your
letter to the king, Father. But soldiers and kings out there in the
base world, what do they have to do with us?"

"Your question is very interesting, my son. Because you're
simply asking the following: Is there a situation when such as
you or I would be able to kill? I see that you are doubtful, and
before you say anything foolish that you might regret I will
answer you. There is indeed an exception. The Lord Jesus in his
ineffable kindness of course meant that we should not kill other

children of God, not even Roman soldiers, or Danish ones for that matter. But there is a people not included in the Lord's prohibition, and I think you can guess who they are, can't you?"

"The Saracens!" Arn said at once.

"Right again! Because the Saracens are the most nefarious race that the Devil has put on our earth. They are not human beings, they are devils in human form. They do not hesitate to impale Christian babies on their spears and roast them over fires and then eat their fill. They are known for their dissolute lives, their excessive drinking, and their constant habit of sodomy and fornication with animals. They are the scum of the earth, and every dead Saracen is a pleasing sight for Our Lord, and whoever kills Saracens has committed a holy act and is therefore assured of a place in Paradise!"

Father Henri had gradually grown more agitated as he enumerated the heinous ways of the Saracens, and Arn's eyes had grown wider and wider as he listened to these comments. What Arn had heard surpassed his understanding. His mind refused even to picture such a scene with these detestable creatures eating roasted Christian babies from their spear points. He couldn't conceive how such devils could take the form of human beings.

But he could easily understand that it would be a pleasing deed to God, even for brothers within walls, to kill such evil. He also drew the conclusion that there was a vast distance between the Danish riffraff that had so unfortunately turned to the path of robbery and the Saracens. In that one case the commandment *Thou shalt not kill* was valid without exception. In the second case it was the direct opposite.

Although such a simple and clear conclusion had little practical importance up here in the North.

✠

During the years Arn had not been able to sing, he had changed, just as his work had changed. The time that he previously would have spent with Brother Ludwig and the choir brothers, several hours each day, had now become time spent with Brother Guy down by the shore. Brother Guy soon taught him the methods from his home district for knotting nets, catching fish, and maneuvering small boats. For safety's sake Brother Guy had also seen to it that Arn learned how to dive and swim.

With Brother Guilbert he had now become both a worker and a pupil. He was given all the heavier tasks in the smithies, and his arms grew in bulk almost as fast as his body shot up in height. He mastered most of the everyday smithing activities so that he could make good and marketable items. Only when it came to forging swords did he still lag far behind Brother Guilbert.

The two mares, Khadiya and Aisha, had now given birth to three foals, and Khamsiin had grown into a stallion as powerful as Nasir. It was Arn's job to take care of all the horses from Outremer, to break the new foals, and make sure that Nasir and Khamsiin were each kept isolated in a fenced pasture so that they wouldn't mate with Nordic mares in an order other than what Brother Guilbert had determined after precise studies.

Yet Brother Guilbert's great hope that these horses from Outremer would bring in much silver was fulfilled only slowly. The Danish magnates who came to visit primarily to buy new swords for themselves and herbs for their women regarded the foreign horses with suspicion. They thought that these animals were too spindly and didn't look like they could do very much. At first Brother Guilbert had a hard time taking such objections seriously and actually suspected that the Danes were joking with him. Then he realized that the barbarians were quite serious, sometimes even leading in their own animals to show him proudly how a real horse should look. Brother Guilbert grew dejected.

Finally circumstances led him to devise a trick that did indeed work well, but which made him feel guilty and contrite. One of these Danes led in his chubby, unruly Nordic horse to compare its advantages to those of the "skinny" ones. The man extolled both his steed's strength and his speed, which far surpassed anything foreign. Brother Guilbert at once had a bright idea. He suggested that the honorable Danish knight should race down to the shore and back to the cloister, and that only a little cloister boy would ride one of the new horses. And if the honorable Danish gentleman won the race, he wouldn't have to pay anything for the sword he had just purchased.

To his wide-eyed surprise Arn was told that he was to ride Khamsiin, and race a fat old man on a horse that looked very similar to the man. Arn had a hard time believing his ears, but he had to obey. When the two riders were ready outside the cloister walls, Arn asked Brother Guilbert, speaking in Latin out of sheer nervousness although the two of them always spoke French together, whether he was supposed to ride full tilt or take it easy so that the sausage-looking horse could keep up. Oddly enough, Brother Guilbert gave him strict orders to ride at full speed. He obeyed, as always.

Arn was already back at the cloister when the Danish knight had made it only halfway and was down by the shore turning around.

Then some rich men from Ringsted, who enjoyed racing horses and betting money on them, now found that the skinny horses from Vitskøl were at least good for one thing. The rumor then spread to Roskilde, and soon horses from Vitae Schola were commanding large sums of money. But that was not what Brother Guilbert had had in mind.

The exercises Brother Guilbert was now asking Arn to try on horseback were no longer simply about balance and speed, but had to do with matters of considerably greater finesse. They spent about an hour each day in one of the stallion's pastures, riding around each other in specific patterns, backing, rearing and turning in the air, moving sideways or sideways and forward or back at the same time, teaching the horses which signals meant strike with the forehooves and jump forward at the same time, or backward kick with both legs followed by a jump to the side. It was an art that Arn liked when everything went as planned, but he could find it somewhat monotonous. At least during the obligatory practices. It was more exciting with the completely free exercises when they practiced with wooden swords or lances against each other.

The practice on foot had become much more difficult, and was mainly about striking and parrying with swords; for a long time now, Arn had been using a real steel sword. He was still humbly convinced that he was a wretched swordsman. Yet he didn't give up; he persevered with this work in this Lord's vineyard as well. Lack of faith would have been a great sin.

His work with Brother Guy down at the beach was quite another story. Brother Guy had finally given up the apparently impossible task of enticing the Danes around Limfjord to eat mussels. The mussel beds had been reduced to a fraction of their original ambitious size and now yielded only enough to meet the demand of the Provençal cooks at Vitae Schola.

Brother Guy's task was not to bring in income to Vitae Schola but to spread the blessings of civilization, and he was going to do that by setting a good example. The intentions behind his work were much the same as those for the brothers who worked in farming: not to focus on selling the produce, primarily, but to inform. In that respect he had begun by failing miserably in introducing the populace to the blessings of mussels.

But things went better with fishing gear and boat-building. When he saw the Limfjordings' fish-spears with straight tips, he went to Brother Guilbert and asked him to make some fish-spears with barbed tips, which he later distributed to the fishermen. When he discovered that the Limfjordings fished only with stationary equipment inside the fjord, he began to make movable nets and bottom seines. The difference between his nets and the nets of the Limfjordings was primarily the suppleness that came from the larger mesh and thinner material that he used.

It took Arn about a year to learn the art of tying nets well enough that Brother Guy pronounced his nets to be as good as those made by a boy from home. For Arn the work was not hard, but tedious.

Soon enough everything began functioning the way Brother Guy had intended. The Limfjordings started coming from the villages around Vitae Schola to study with curiosity, and at first with some suspicion, how to use movable nets. Brother Guy, with Arn as his interpreter, naturally offered to share his knowledge in a Christian spirit.

This meant that now and then Brother Guy would leave Arn alone at the boathouse on the shore while he took Danish fishermen out in the boats to show them how to place nets from a moving boat. But those who came to learn how to tie the new nets were all women, young and old, since net-tying was women's work around the Limfjord.

And that was how Arn, whose only experience of women was what resembled a mirage in his evening prayers when he prayed for his mother's soul, now suddenly found himself almost daily surrounded by women. At first all the women, young and old, made merry at the expense of the gangly young man with the strong arms who, blushing and stammering, kept his eyes fixed on the ground so that he always showed his shaved pate instead of his blue eyes.

Arn knew in theory how a teacher should behave, since he had had so many. But what he thought he knew about the art of teaching did not match what he now experienced, since his pupils did not behave with the obedience and dignity that befitted pupils. They joked and giggled, and the older women sometimes even unchastely stroked his head.

But Arn gritted his teeth, because he had a task to carry out responsibly. After a while he dared raised his eyes somewhat. And then he raised his eyes unavoidably to their breasts under thin summer shifts and their happy, coquettish smiles and their curious eyes.

Her name was Birgite and she had thick copper-red hair gathered in a single braid down her back; she was the same age as he was, and she often wanted him to show her something over again even though he was sure she had already learned it. When he sat down next to her he could feel the warmth of her thigh, and when she pretended to fumble he took her hands to show her one more time how to knot and crochet the net.

He didn't know that now he was a sinner, so it took a while before Father Henri realized what was happening. But by then it was too late.

She was the most beautiful creature Arn had ever seen in his life, with the possible exception of Khamsiin. And he began dreaming of her at night, so that he awoke self-defiled without having consciously done it. He began dreaming of her in the daytime too, when he was supposed to be busy with other things. When Brother Guilbert once gave him a box on the ear because he wasn't paying attention during practice, he hardly knew what had happened.

When Birgite shyly asked him to bring some of the herbs that they had in the cloister, the ones that smelled like a dream, he assumed that she must mean lemon balm or lavender. A brief furtive question to Brother Lucien quickly decided the choice;

all women were crazy about lavender, muttered Brother Lucien absentmindedly, having no idea what a fire he had just ignited.

At first Arn smuggled out a twig or two now and then. But when she kissed him on the forehead, quickly so that no one would see, he lost his wits completely. The next time he brought her a whole armful, which Birgite, chirping with glee, at once carried off home. He watched her nimble bare feet moving so swiftly that the sand sprayed around them.

It was in that state, pining with an absent look and gaping mouth, that Brother Guy found his young apprentice. And with that there was a brusque stop to the infatuation, because at the same time Brother Lucien, to his perplexity, had found big, mysterious holes in his supply of lavender.

Arn was punished with two weeks on bread and water and isolation for meditation and prayer during the first week. Since he didn't have his own cell but shared one with several lay brothers, he now had to do his penance in a free cell inside the closed section of the monastery. With him he took the Holy Scriptures, the oldest and most worn-out copy, and nothing else.

Of his two great sins he could understand one of them, but the other one he could not. No matter how much he honestly tried, no matter how much he prayed for the Holy Virgin's forgiveness.

He had stolen lavender; that was something concrete and understandable. Lavender was a desirable product outside the cloister, and Brother Lucien sold it with much success. Arn had simply mistaken something that was *gratia*, such as teaching the method for knotting nets, with something that existed for income, such as Brother Guilbert's sword-forging or Brother Lucien's plants—although not all the plants, by any means. Some of them, like chamomile, were *gratia* as well.

Father Henri had also noticed this. Even though theft was theft, and thus an abominable breach of the cloister's rules, this was something that, to say the least, had occurred out of youthful ignorance. Father Henri had carefully listened to Brother Guy's view of what had happened. Yet this led to Brother Guy also receiving a reprimand since he had not taken Arn's errors very seriously, and had even slipped in an explanation that if Father Henri had seen the girl himself then the whole matter would not have seemed so mysterious.

Arn's second and worse sin was that he had felt lust. Had he been a brother admitted to the order, he would have been punished with half a year of bread and water, and he would have been allowed to work only with the kitchen garbage and the latrines.

In his isolation Arn now had to repent for his sin of stealing the lavender, a sin that he easily could regret sincerely. But it was impossible for him to understand why it was worse than theft to long for and dream about Birgite. He couldn't stop himself. His hair shirt didn't help, the cold of night in his cell didn't help, nor did the hard wooden bed without a lambskin or blanket. When he lay awake he saw her before him. If he managed to fall asleep he dreamed about her freckled face and brown eyes or her naked feet running quick as little kid-goats through the sand. And his body behaved shamefully as soon as he fell asleep. In the morning one of the brothers, without saying a word, would put a bucket of ice-cold water in Arn's cell. The first thing he did was to shove his shameful member into the water to cool off the all-too-obvious sin.

And when he had to compose himself so he could devote himself to the Holy Scriptures, it was as if the Devil himself were leading him to the very passages that he shouldn't read. He could find his way around in the Holy Scriptures so well that he tried looking up verses at random with his eyes closed. And yet he found verses such as:

*Love is strong as death; jealousy is cruel as the grave: the
coals thereof are coals of fire, which hath a most vehement flame.*
*Many waters cannot quench love, neither can the floods
drown it: if a man would give all the substance of his
house for love, it would utterly be contemned.*

No matter how Arn tried to use his knowledge of how God's
word should be read and interpreted, he could not view love as
a sin. This power, which God the Father called a blessing to humanity, which was so strong that an ocean could not drown it,
and no man, no matter how rich, could buy it for himself for
coins of silver, this power that was as impossible to subdue as
death itself, how could that be a sin?

During Arn's second week of penance on bread and water,
when he was allowed to speak, Father Henri sternly brought up
the subject, since they had soon agreed about the theft of the lavender. He wanted to try to get the overheated young man to understand what love was. Hadn't Saint Bernard himself described
it all as clearly as water?

A human being begins by loving himself for his own sake.
The next stage in development is that humans learn to love God,
but still for their own sake and not for God's sake. Then humanity does learn to love God, and no longer for their own sake but
for God's sake. Finally, humanity learns to love humanity, but
only for God's sake.

What happened in that process of development was that
cupiditas, or desire, which lies at the heart of all human appetite, ended up in control and was converted into *caritas,* so that
all base desire was cleansed away and love became pure. All this
was elementary, wasn't it?

Arn reluctantly agreed that it was indeed elementary; like

almost everyone else at Vitae Schola he was quite familiar with all the texts of Bernard de Clairvaux. But as Arn understood it, there must be two types of love. It was true that he loved Father Henri, Brother Guilbert, Brother Lucien, Brother Guy, Brother Ludwig, and all the other monks. Without hesitation he could fix his blue eyes on Father Henri's brown eyes and confirm this, and he knew that Father Henri could see straight into his soul.

But that couldn't be the whole truth . . . and so he suddenly, without being able to stop, began citing long passages from the Song of Songs.

What was God's intention with this? And what had Ovid been talking about in those texts that Arn had read by mistake as a boy? Wasn't Ovid's text suspiciously similar to God's Word in certain respects?

After his uncontrollable outburst Arn bowed his head in shame. He had never before uttered such an insubordinate polemic to Father Henri. He wouldn't have found it unfair to receive another two weeks on bread and water as punishment, since he had shown himself to be unrepentant.

But Father Henri's reaction was not what he expected. He almost seemed glad about what he'd heard, although naturally he couldn't share Arn's view.

"Your will is strong, your mind is still free and at times intractable, like something in those horses you break. I have certainly watched you do it, let me tell you," said Father Henri thoughtfully. "This is good, because more than anything I was afraid that I'd broken your will so that you would not understand God the day He calls you. So much for that. Now to why you are wrong."

Father Henri explained the whole thing calmly and quietly. It was true that God had given human beings a *libido* which was not shameful, and it was this that the Song of Songs, for example, talked about. The divine order behind this, of course, was that humankind had the task of replenishing the earth, and that goal was better served by the fact that the special activity required to fulfill this duty was pleasant. And in a bond sanctified by God, within the sanctity of marriage, with the purpose of begetting children, this desire was pleasing to God and not at all a sin.

From this explanation Arn immediately drew the completely absurd conclusion that a man and a woman should wait until they found someone they loved and then have their *libido* blessed by marriage. Father Henri was much amused by this bizarre idea.

But Arn did not yield, encouraged by Father Henri's unexpectedly tempered disposition. Because, Arn went on, if love in itself, that is, the form of love talked about in the Song of Songs, was not something evil but quite the opposite, under certain given premises, something pleasing to God—why was all such activity forbidden for those who toiled in God's garden? In short, how could love be a gross sin punishable by bread and water and a hair shirt if one was enticed by it, and yet at the same time be a blessing for humanity?

"Well," said Father Henri, clearly amused by the question. "To begin with, one must of course distinguish between the higher world and the lower. Plato, you know. We belong to the higher world, that is the basic theoretical starting point, but I presume you want more meat on the bones than that, because you do know your Plato. Imagine then all the greening fields around Vitae Schola, think of all of Brother Lucien's herbs and fruits and the knowledge he spreads to our neighbors, think of Brother Guilbert's forging art and horse training, or Brother Guy's fishery. Observe now that I'm not speaking in metaphors but keeping to the practical plane. When you think about all this, what does it mean?"

"We do good for our neighbors. Just as the Lord is always our shepherd, we can at least be the shepherds of humanity. We give people a better life through our knowledge and our work, is that what you mean, father?"

"Yes, my son, that's exactly what I mean. We are like God's knowledge-bearers going out into the unknown—who said that, by the way?"

"Holy Saint Bernard, of course."

"Yes, that's right. We test the unknown, we tame nature, we bend the steel in new ways, we find a remedy for evil, and we make the bread last longer. That is what we do in a purely practical sense. Added to that is the knowledge we disseminate, in the same way as we sow wheat, about the Word of God and how it is to be understood. Are you with me so far?"

"Yes, of course, but how can that . . ." Arn began, but he was much too filled with the argumentative spirit and had to restrain himself and start over. "Forgive me, father, but let me ask the question anew and from a purely concrete perspective. Forgive me if I'm impertinent, I understand all that you say about our good work. But why can't the brothers in the order ever enjoy the pleasures of love? If love is good, why do we have to refrain from it?"

"That can be explained on two levels," said Father Henri, seemingly still equally untroubled and amused by his pupil's brooding. "Our high calling, our work as God's most assiduous servants on earth, has a price. And that price is that we must devote both our soul and our body to the service of God. Otherwise we could never accomplish anything lasting. Imagine if the brothers here had women and children in every nook and cranny! At least half our time would be spent on things other than what we now are able to achieve. And we would start looking around anxiously for property, since our children would need an inheritance from us—and that's only one thing! Our vow of poverty thus has much the same function as our vow of chastity. We own nothing, and when we die the Church owns everything we have used and created."

Arn fell silent. He saw the logic in what Father Henri had said; he was also grateful that Father Henri had chosen to explain using base earthly examples instead of casting himself into the teachings of Plato and Saint Bernard's theories about different human souls at different stages. But he was still not satisfied; it felt as though something was missing in the logic. If nothing else, one might ask why self-defilement should be so terrible. Was it like a sort of gluttony of the soul, perhaps? Or merely something that drew one's thoughts away from God? Actually it was impossible, he admitted with a blush, to think about God at the same time he was doing that.

When Father Henri saw that Arn seemed to have understood and at least largely accepted the simple explanations he had received, Father Henri, clearly in high spirits, decided that the rest of Arn's week of penance should take place in the cookhouses with the Provençal brothers. Still on a diet of bread and water, however, which could be a very difficult test in a cookhouse, but strengthening for the will of the soul.

The cookhouses were the most intense workplaces in all of Vitae Schola. The brothers who worked in the fields went home to vespers, the brothers who worked in the smithies and carpentry shops, those who did stonecutting or spinning, those who worked in the farrieries, the brickworks, or the barns, the monks in charge of sheep tending or beekeeping or the herb gardens or the vegetable field—all had their nightly pauses from work, and they all had time for their reading without getting behind in their daily tasks.

Yet in the cookhouses there were only two quiet hours in the day, after midnight mass when the fires were banked and all was silent and shining clean. Long before dawn the work began again, first with the bread-baking for the day. Gradually the cookhouses were filled with more and more monks and lay brothers. The hours before the big midday meal were the most intense, with ten monks and lay brothers working simultaneously and in a great rush. Each day there were between fifty and sixty mouths to feed, depending on how many brothers happened to be away and how many guests they had. In the cookhouses Brother Rugiero de Nîmes ruled with absolute power, and serving under him were his own brothers Catalan and Luis. They however had not yet been accepted as members of the order, possibly because they never had enough time left over for their studies.

The morning that Arn showed up for service, the midday meal was going to be lamb. So Arn's first task was go down to the shepherds and fetch two young lambs, then lead them back up to the slaughterhouse next to the cookhouses. These particular animals were not the ones to be served that day. Two lambs had been slaughtered ten days earlier and were then hung up and cured for the day's meal. They were now to be replaced in the cooling room next to the big cookhouse with two freshly slaughtered animals, which in turn would be served in ten days. Only barbarians ate uncured meat.

Arn didn't enjoy leading the two unsuspecting lambs up to the cookhouses. He had put a leather thong around their necks and was gently pulling them along, now and then coaxing them onward when they stopped to nibble at a tuft of grass that looked particularly tasty. He thought of all the metaphors in the Holy Scriptures that depicted this very relationship between the good shepherd and his flock; right now he was truly no good shepherd.

When he reached the slaughterhouse with the lambs, they were at once taken in hand by a sullen lay brother, who without much ado hung them up on big hooks by one rear hoof and slit their throats. While the life ran out of the lambs and the whites of their eyes rolled up in terror, the lay brother took a reed broom and opened a wooden gate to a water channel so that the blood was flushed from the brick floor into an underground drain. When this was done another lay brother came in, and using a knife each man rapidly transformed the animals into something that more resembled meat and food.

Arn then had to take the still-warm skins to the tannery and the guts to the gut-cleaners. Then he went to the big stack of ice and dug out new ice blocks that he wheeled over to the cooling room, where the new, numbered carcasses already hung at the end of the row of calves, pigs, cows, ducks, and geese. The blocks of ice had to be placed by a flume in the middle of the cooling room so that the meltwater could run off into the drainage system. It was dark in there and cold. Arn shivered as he used something resembling holy-water sprinklers to splash the porous brick walls with cold water. The room had a high ceiling, and way at the top there were small holes that let in light and allowed all the unclean vapors from the animal carcasses to escape.

When Arn entered the big cookhouse the well-cured lamb carcasses had already been cut up and placed in basins to marinate with olive oil, garlic, mint, and various strong herbs from the home region of the Provençal cooks. The big baking ovens were being fired up. The roasts and ribs would be baked in the oven after they had soaked long enough in their marinade, but in the meantime the shoulders and the rest of the animals were cut into smaller pieces and placed in big iron pots. For supper there would be lamb soup with root vegetables and cabbage, and then some cherries with honey and roasted hazelnuts. The lamb would be served with white bread, olive oil, and fresh goat cheese.

It wasn't usual to drink wine every day at Vitae Schola. This had nothing to do with the cloister rules, but rather with the

difficulties of transporting wine in large enough quantities from
Burgundy all the way to the North. So it was Brother Rugiero
who decided when wine would be served with the meals, and
when water would suffice. He found that wine would go best
with the roast lamb, and Arn was sent out to the wine cellars
to fetch half a cask. He was admonished to take it from the far
end of the wine cellar, where the oldest wine was stored. They
always drank the wine in a specific order, and he was carefully
instructed how the cask would be marked. Yet Arn still returned
with the wrong wine cask on his wheelbarrow, and so he had to
go back and do the task properly.

When the midday meal was served and everyone else began
to eat, Arn went back out to the cookhouse and took a scoop
of water from the pure water stream that ran straight into the
cookhouse and was not to be confused with the drainage stream
that came from the lavatorium. He drank the cold water, savor-
ing it as a gift from God. Then he prayed an extra long grace
before he took some of the white bread.

He felt neither hunger nor envy for the brothers. They were
merely eating a normal meal, about the same as they always ate
at Vitae Schola. When he was done he began cleaning up and
tending to the big pots that contained the next meal.

After midnight mass the cookhouses had to be scoured carefully with water and all the waste had to be removed. It was put
either into the drainage channel to be transported further to the
stream and then down to the fjord, or it was taken out to the
big compost heap behind the cookhouses among all the stinging
nettles. Brother Lucien was very finicky about how the compost
heaps were tended, since it meant so much for his work to keep
making the earth more fruitful.

When Arn was done he was supposed to have two hours of
sleep before baking the bread. But tonight he had worked so

hard inside the hot cookhouses that he couldn't calm down; he still had the heat and the bustling pace in his body.

It was a cool summer night but he could smell the first scent of autumn in the air. The stars were out, the wind was still, and there was a half moon.

First he sat for a while on the stone steps of the big cookhouse and looked up at the stars without thinking about anything in particular. His thoughts flitted from the day's intense work to all the strong aromas in the cookhouses, and then to the morning's talk with Father Henri. He was sure that there was still something he didn't understand about love.

Then he went down to see Khamsiin and called him over. The powerful stallion snorted mightily as he recognized the boy and came trotting over at once, with legs lifted high and his tail in the air. Khamsiin was still a young stallion, but fully grown, and his color had now changed from the slightly childish white to a shimmering of gray and white. In the moonlight he looked like he was colored silver.

Without knowing why, Arn threw his arms around the stallion's strong neck and hugged him and caressed him. Then he began to cry. His chest shook with an emotion that he could not understand.

"I love you, Khamsiin, I truly do love you," he whispered, and his tears fell like a flowing stream. Inside he felt that he had thought something sinful and forbidden that he couldn't explain.

For the first time ever, he decided that there was something that he could not confess.

Chapter 6

Monasterio Beatae Mariae de Varnhemio became the name of
the cloister in Varnhem. Father Henri, who now sat in his old
scriptorium, felt a shiver of pleasure when he printed the name.
It was only right that the Blessed Virgin should have this monastery dedicated to her, since it was she who, by sending Fru Sigrid
a vision during the dedication of Skara Cathedral, was most responsible for the genesis of this cloister. And now at last there
would be better order here.

Father Henri in truth had much to rejoice about, and he was
now trying to express it all in his long letter. The Cistercians had
won a complicated and dangerous game against the emperor of
Germany, Frederick I Barbarossa himself. And Father Henri had
been allowed to attend in a corner, since his two good friends
Archbishop Eskil of Lund and Father Stéphan from Alvastra
were present too. Who could have imagined such a development
twenty years ago when he and Stéphan had come wandering the
long, cold, and gloomy road to the North?

Emperor Frederick Barbarossa had deposed Pope Alexander III and named his own more docile antipope in Rome. The Christian world thus had to choose sides, either the true pope, Alexander, or the usurper in Rome. The outcome of this strife was in no way certain.

Many kings feared the German emperor and thus wanted to stand with him; among them unfortunately was King Valdemar of Denmark and several of his more timorous bishops. But Archbishop Eskil of Lund, the friend of the Cistercians, had taken a stand against his king and for the true pope, Alexander III. Because of this, Eskil had been forced into exile.

The strife, of course, actually dealt with the old story about whether kings and emperors should have power over the Church, or whether the Church would remain exempt from worldly power.

The Cistercians' countermove had been Svealand and Götaland. King Karl Sverkersson, who did not know enough about Emperor Frederick Barbarossa to fear him, was persuaded to go along with the creation of a new archbishopric comprising Svealand and the two Goth lands. As the situation now stood, it did not make much difference in which city the archbishop's see was placed, as long as it was done. King Sverker had wisely avoided his own city of Linköping in favor of the Swedish city of Östra Aros. That was fine, the Cistercians had reasoned, because the main thing was to strike while the iron was hot.

And so it came to pass that Father Henri was allowed to attend the meeting in the cathedral in Sens when Eskil, in the presence of the pope himself, anointed Stéphan as archbishop over the new archdiocese of Svealand and the two Goth lands. Since the archdiocese of Norway was also faithful to the true pope, the struggle now turned to the disadvantage of Frederick Barbarossa and his antipope. Eskil had recently been able to return to Denmark in triumph, and Stéphan was already installed in Östra Aros. The battle was won.

A Cistercian brother holding the position of the third Nordic archbishop was truly no small thing. Varnhem, of course, had already been restored to favor by King Erik Jedvardsson, but now his successor Karl Sverkersson had assured the monastery new properties and new privileges. He had even donated some of his own land to establish a Cistercian nunnery up in Vreta in Eastern Götaland.

Now that the monastery was finally secure, it was time to make a new attempt to restore it to its former state. For Varnhem had long been languishing with only twelve brothers, whose task it was to repair and maintain the cloister and prevent the property from going to ruin.

During the years that had passed, Vitae Schola in Denmark had surpassed Varnhem in every respect. For that very reason it was also natural, now that Father Henri had taken on the management of the restoration work at Varnhem, to draw the first new monks from Vitae Schola itself.

Among those who were called to Varnhem were Brother Guilbert and Arn.

For Arn nowhere was home. Varnhem was not home, just as little as Vitae Schola by the Limfjord was home, or any other place. His home was wherever the brothers were, and, most important, where Brother Guilbert and Father Henri happened to be.

The difficult part about leaving Vitae Schola had been to leave Khamsiin. Brother Guilbert had decided that Khamsiin had to stay behind for breeding at Vitae Schola. He had explained this to Arn by drawing complicated patterns in the sand showing which horses had been sired by Khamsiin and which had been sired by Nasir, and why Nasir and a young stallion sired by Khamsiin and Aisha had to go with the caravan to Varnhem, while Khamsiin had to stay at Vitae Schola. Arn had not been able to question this decision.

The young stallion was dappled red and gray, and after the farewell mass at Vitae Schola Brother Guilbert had told Arn that the young stallion would be named Shimal, which in the secret language of horses meant the North. But when Brother Guilbert saw the sorrow in Arn's eyes he took him aside and explained that this was not a sin, nothing to be ashamed of, to miss his horse. Those who said that a horse was only a thing, a possession without a soul, and therefore not worthy of love, knew nothing. They were correct only in formal terms, but the world was full of men, also good men of God, who were formally right about one thing or another, and yet lacked true understanding. Before God and for many of God's men, it was entirely proper to love a horse such as Khamsiin. This Brother Guilbert swore.

On the other hand, Arn had to realize that his horses, like his neighbors and his brothers and kinsmen, would all eventually die. Even the simple fact that horses did not live as long as human beings meant that Arn would most likely have to mourn more than one horse. Grief was a part of life, such as God had ordered it.

Arn let himself be consoled somewhat, but only because it was not sinful to grieve when he was forced to leave Khamsiin behind.

Although he was now reckoned as a man and not a boy, he couldn't help shedding a tear as the column left Vitae Schola. No one saw it but Brother Guilbert. And no one but Brother Guilbert would have understood the reason. Like Arn, the other brothers and lay brothers had no home anywhere except where brothers resided in God's good world. And what did the others know about horses from Outremer?

Just before Bartelsmas in late August, the busiest harvesttime and also when the goats were slaughtered in Western Götaland, Arn saw Varnhem's church tower rising up in the distance, at first indistinct like some oddly scraggly or dried-up treetop or one that had been struck by lightning, in the midst of a luxuriant grove of oaks. Later it became very clear.

He recognized the church tower from his childhood, but that was not what moved him. He knew that buried inside the church lay his mother, whom he still talked to every evening in his prayers. He felt as though she might be found alive in there, although only her bones remained. From the recesses of his memory he retrieved a vague image of himself as a child standing alone among strange men, not yet his beloved brothers, at the funeral mass. Now, filled with solemnity, he rode in through the cloister gate, paying scant attention to whether he recognized the place, which he no doubt did, or to how dilapidated everything had become. When Arn greeted Father Henri coming to meet the newcomers just inside the cloister gate, he begged forgiveness and hurried into the church, falling to his knees at the entrance, and crossing himself before he continued up the aisle toward the altar.

At the front of the church knelt two lay brothers who were working with hammer and chisel on the stone block that covered his mother's grave. Previously it had been provided only with a small, almost unnoticeable symbol. Now that the Cistercians had won their great victory over the worldly power, and Monasterio Beatae Mariae de Varnhemio was a safe place for both the brothers and the bones of the dead, Father Henri had decided that the grave should be marked. The thought had been for the work to be completed before the caravan from Vitae Schola arrived, but the weather during their journey had been unexpectedly favorable.

Arn shyly greeted the lay brothers, first in Latin, which they didn't know very well; then in French, which they didn't understand at all; and finally in Norse, which was their language, although it was more lilting than he remembered. Then he fell to his knees and prayed in thanksgiving for arriving successfully.

When he read the text on the gravestone, both that which had already been carved and that which was only sketched in, he felt as if his mother were still alive. Not only her soul but also her flesh and blood self, as if she lay there beneath the limestone, smiling up at him. "Under this stone rests Sigrid, our most highly valued donor, in eternal peace, born in the year of the Lord 1127, died 1155, in blessed remembrance," he read. After the text there was a sketch of a lion and something else that he didn't recognize. He saw her hands before him and smelled her scent and thought he could hear her voice.

At the welcome mass when all were gathered, his mother was mentioned time after time in the prayers of thanksgiving. It filled him with feelings that he couldn't quite understand, which he at once decided to confess. He feared that he had been struck by pride.

✠

In the weeks before Father Henri's reinstallation as prior at Varnhem, which Archbishop Stéphan himself would attend on a visitation, Brother Guilbert and Arn worked feverishly along with a couple of local lay brothers to get the water supply fixed. The big millpond had silted up and had to be dredged; the aqueduct that was supposed to carry the water to the large and small drive wheels was in disrepair, so that the flow was diminished to a mere tenth of its potential power. The mill wheel and gear system also needed numerous repairs. The water stream was both the cloister's motor and its cleansing soul, just as important in the lavatorium and cookhouse as it was as a power source for the bellows, mills, and hammer-anvil. Because of the great importance of this repair work, the small group in charge of the water was relieved of attending all the day's masses and study hours. Arn fell into bed after vespers and slept dreamlessly until morning mass. One workday followed another until he began to have the feeling that time had stopped and the hours flowed together into one long work shift.

But on the day that the archbishop and his retinue came riding in through the cloister gates of Varnhem, new fresh water was purling through the lavatorium and cookhouse, and the guest rooms stood newly whitewashed and clean. In one of the smithies the clang of hammer on anvil was already heard.

After the installation mass the archbishop preached to the brothers about the victory of good over evil, and how the Cistercian order now held such a strong position that no outside threat was to be found in this corner of the world. What remained, however, was the constant threat that always existed inside each human being, that his own sins, pride or sloth or indifference, might bring down on him God's righteous wrath. And for this reason no one could take his rest or lean back in gorged contentment; each man had to continue his work in God's garden with the same assiduous perseverance as always.

After the thanksgiving meal, Archbishop Stéphan and Father Henri retired to the place out in the arcade where they always used to sit together in the past, near the garden plot that was now clearly overgrown. They had a long talk about something they didn't want the other brothers to hear, speaking so low that the brothers working in the garden could hear only an occasional word when one of the reverends flared up, briefly and intensely like a dry piece of tinder, and then quickly returned to more subdued tones.

After about an hour the two men seemed to have reached a

reconciliation, and then they summoned Arn, who was already hard at work in one of the smithies where the mechanisms that were supposed to drive the bellows had completely broken down.

Arn went to the lavatorium and washed his whole body clean, wondering whether he ought to shave his tonsure, which he had not done in recent weeks after he was relieved of all his duties except work on the water lines. When he ran his hand over his scalp he felt half an inch of stubble—no state in which to meet an archbishop. On the other hand, he could not be late now that they had summoned him.

Feeling a bit abashed, Arn went out to the arcade, knelt before the archbishop and kissed his hand, asking forgiveness for his unkempt appearance. Father Henri hastened to explain that Arn was one of those who had been assigned special work duties in recent weeks, but the archbishop simply waved off such a minor concern and asked Arn to sit down, which was an astonishing concession.

Arn sat on a stone bench facing the two venerable men but felt no peace with the situation. He could not understand why they wanted to speak with him in particular, since he was but a young lay brother. He would never have guessed what was now to become of him, since he no doubt believed that his life had already been given a fixed path, just as predictable as the stars' movement across the firmament.

"Do you happen to remember me, young man?" asked the archbishop kindly, surprisingly speaking in French instead of Latin.

"No, *monseigneur*, I cannot honestly say that I do," replied Arn with embarrassment, looking at the ground.

"The first time we met you tried to slap me, called me an old codger or something on that order, and said you didn't want to sit and read boring books. But I suppose you've forgotten that too?" the archbishop went on, with a sternness that was so clearly feigned that anyone on earth except Arn could have seen right through it.

"*Monseigneur*, I truly beg your pardon, I can only defend myself by saying that I was a child and knew no better," Arn replied, blushing with shame as he imagined himself laying a hand on an archbishop. But then both the archbishop and Father Henri burst out laughing.

"Now now, young man, I was trying to jest. I'm not actually here to demand vengeance for that tiny offense. I should be grateful, from what I've heard, that it's not today you choose to strike me. No, don't apologize again! Instead, you must listen to me. My dear old friend Henri and I have discussed your situation back and forth, as we also did when you came here as a child. You do know that it was a miracle that brought you to us, don't you, my son?"

"I've read the account," Arn said quietly. "But I don't remember any of it myself; I only recall what I read."

"But if Saint Bernard and the Lord did raise you up from the realm of the dead to bring you to us, what sort of conclusion would you draw from that? Have you contemplated that dilemma?" the archbishop asked in a new and more serious tone, as if he were now beginning the conversation in earnest.

"When I was a little boy and fell from a high wall, the Lord showed mercy toward me and perhaps toward my mother and father as well for their fervent prayers. That's what is true, that much we can consider certain," replied Arn, still not daring to raise his eyes.

"Certain, well, that's not saying too much, is it?" said Archbishop Stéphan with a scarcely perceptible hint of impatience in his voice. "But then don't we come immediately to the question of why?"

"Yes," said Arn. "We do come to the question of why, but I've never been able to find an answer. When it comes to the grace of the Lord, it is many times beyond what humans can conceive. I'm not exactly the only one who cannot understand everything about the grace of God."

"Aha! Now I'm starting to recognize the little rascal who tried to strike me and called me an old codger. That's good, young man! Just keep talking back, and I'm not being sarcastic; I like it when you talk back. So we haven't transformed you into some sort of passive vegetable in the garden; you have your free will and your mind intact, and we both think that is splendid. Henri has made a point of describing this characteristic of yours. By the way, I haven't spoken French in a long time, do you mind if we switch to Latin?"

"No, Your Grace."

"Good. Actually I had just intended to retaliate, because when we met the first time you chided me for not speaking very good Norse. Well, that jest fell flat, since your French is excellent. How can that be, since most of your studies are in Latin?"

"We've had an arrangement whereby I speak Latin about spiritual and academic matters, French when doing the other half of the work, and Norse with the lay brothers who don't speak much French," replied Arn, raising his head for the first time and looking the archbishop in the eye. By now he had conquered the worst of his embarrassment.

"An excellent arrangement. It's good that you retain your Norse language, even better if things turn out the way I think," muttered the archbishop pensively. "But let me now ask you something specific, and I really want an honest answer. Has the Lord God spoken to you? Has He revealed His intentions for you?"

"No, Your Grace. God has never spoken directly to me, and I know nothing of His intentions for me," Arn replied, once again feeling embarrassed and at a disadvantage. It was as if through sin he had made himself unworthy of God's original plan, what-ever it may have been.

The two older men pondered Arn's reply thoughtfully and in silence. They said nothing at all for a long time, but at last they exchanged a knowing look and nodded to each other. Father Henri made a great show of clearing his throat, the way he always did before launching into a long explanation.

"My beloved son, you must now listen to me and not be frightened," Father Henri began with visible emotion. "My good friend Stéphan and I have reached a decision which we believe is the only right one. We know as little as you do about what God has in mind for you; all we know is that it must be something special. But since none of us knows, it might be that His call has simply not been made as yet. Our task, and yours, could be to prepare you as well as possible for the call when it does come, don't you think?"

"Yes, of course, Father," Arn replied in a low voice. His throat was suddenly dry.

"Your education is remarkable and the work of your hands is of great joy to us here within these walls," Father Henri went on. "But you know nothing of the world outside. That is why you must now go out into that world; you must return to your father's estate at Arnäs, which lies a day's ride from here. Well, a Nordic day's ride, that is . . . you know what I mean, with horses from Outremer it would probably take half a day, I would guess. This is the *command* we now give you. You must return to the place that was once your home."

"I . . . I will naturally obey your command," said Arn, al-though the words stuck in his throat. He felt as though he'd been felled by an unexpected blow, as if he'd been excommunicated, cast out from the holy community.

"I see that you are not happy with our command," said the archbishop.

"No, Your Grace. I've tried to acquit myself well here at the cloister, and I don't mean to boast in any way when I say that, but I can honestly argue that I've done my best," said Arn, crushed.

"You are a Cistercian, my young friend," said Archbishop Stéphan. "Think on that. You will always be one of us, for what is done cannot be undone. Perhaps it is also intended that you shall remain one of us *intra muros* forever, that is what we do not know. Perhaps you will come back after finding that the world out there does not suit you, fully prepared to make your vows to the cloister. But first you must learn of the things about which you have no knowledge, and you can't learn about the outside world in here, no matter how hard you study. We want what is best for you. You should know that both Henri and I truly love you, and we will both pray for you while you are out there. But you must learn something about the other world, that is what is needed."

"When may I come back? How long do I have to stay out there?" asked Arn with a new spark of hope.

"When God wills it, you will come back to us. If God does not will it, He will give you another purpose out there. You must ask Him in your prayers. It's not something we can decide, since it's a matter between you and God," said the archbishop, starting to stand up as if the conversation were over. But then he thought of something to add and brightened up a little.

"Oh yes, one more thing, young man. When you are out there you must know that not only will your brothers within these walls be praying for you, but you also have the archbishop as your friend. You can always come to me with your troubles, remember that!"

With that Archbishop Stéphan stood up and held out his hand to Arn, who fell to his knees and with his head bowed as a sign of obedience, kissed the archbishop's hand.

✠

When Arn rode out from Varnhem it was at first with a very heavy heart. In spite of all Father Henri's explanations and exhortations he hadn't been able to shake the feeling that he was being punished, as if he had shown himself to be unworthy of the brothers' fellowship.

But in search of consolation he began to sing, and this soon eased his heart. When he discovered that it helped, his mood changed so that he sang even more and soon out of joy rather than seeking consolation. By now he sang like all the other brothers, a little better than some and a little worse than others, neither more nor less. But his singing was suddenly of more joy to him than in many years, almost like in the days when he sang soprano in the brothers' choir.

As his mood now shifted from dark to light just as rapidly and unpredictably as the spring weather, he also began to be filled with excitement and anticipation. It was certainly true that he knew nothing of the world outside the cloister walls. He could hardly remember what Arnäs looked like, the place that had once been his home. He remembered a very tall stone tower, a courtyard behind walls where he and other children had played a game with hoops and where his father had shown him how to shoot a bow and arrow. But he had a hard time summoning up any image in his memory about how they had actually lived. He thought he recalled that they all lived together somehow, that it was dark with a big fire, but he didn't trust his memories because they seemed so foreign. Now he was finally going to see everything with his own eyes. He should be there by tomorrow. With a better horse he could have been there by evening, but he was riding an old and slow Nordic horse, one of those that according to Brother Guilbert was no use for breeding and hardly good for anything else. But lay brother Erlend was now at Arnäs to teach new children to read, as he had once taught Arn and Eskil, and so Erlend would be given a compliant horse when he had to return to Varnhem. Father Henri was of the opinion that lay brother Erlend would be of little use at Arnäs, either for reading or anything else, after Arn came home.

A person had to learn to come to terms with the fate determined for him by God. It would do no good to grumble that one would rather be someone else or live somewhere else. Instead one had to try to make the best of the situation; that was the only way to fulfill God's plans. The last of the brothers to repeat these words to Arn before his departure was Brother Rugiero, who had also been called from Vitae Schola to Varnhem after Father Henri found the food up there wretched.

Brother Rugiero had secretly shed a few tears at their parting, but then foisted on Arn a gigantic package of traveling provisions that would have lasted a week or more. When Arn protested, Brother Rugiero quickly closed the boy's knapsack and mentioned that it certainly couldn't hurt to bring along a bit of food to provide for his welcome ale at home. Brother Rugiero, like the other brothers from Vitae Schola, knew little about Arn, surmising that he'd come to them because his parents were poor and were having a hard time with all the mouths to feed back home.

After a few hours Arn spied Skara in the distance; the double tower of the cathedral rose grandly over a conglomeration of low wooden houses. Soon he caught the scent of the town, since he was approaching from downwind. It smelled of smoke and putrefaction and rubbish and manure—a smell so strong that he would have had no trouble heading in the right direction for the last half hour even if it had been pitch dark.

When Arn came closer to the town his curiosity was aroused by a large building under construction, and he made a little

detour so he could watch the work at close hand. They were
erecting a fortress.

He reined in his horse and grew more and more astonished at
what he saw. A whole crowd was in motion; most of the people
were busy dragging stone blocks over rolling logs, but the work
looked to be proceeding sluggishly. Nowhere did he see any
block and tackle or hoisting mechanisms. Everything seemed to
be done by brute force. Many ill-clad men were toiling hard,
overseen by men with weapons who didn't seem at all kindly disposed toward the workers. And none of those who were doing
the dragging and laboring seemed happy about their work.

The walls were not very high, and they consisted mainly of
earthworks that an attacker could easily ride to the top; from
there a good horse could probably leap over in one jump. Khamsiin would be able to do it easily.

Arn didn't know very much about war and defensive works
except what he had read in books, which was mostly Roman
strategy and tactics. But it seemed to him that this fortress under
construction would be difficult to defend if the attackers built
their own covered wooden towers and rolled them up to the
walls. But perhaps the Roman methods were totally antiquated.

Some of the men supervising the work noticed Arn staring,
and they came over to him and let fall some harsh words which
Arn didn't fully understand, but he gathered that he should leave
because he wasn't welcome. He at once begged their pardon and
turned his slow horse back toward town.

The town of Skara was also surrounded by some sort of walls
that consisted of logs and piles of branches with dirt thrown on
top. Outside the town gate was an area with tents and people
singing foreign songs and playing instruments. When Arn drew
closer he saw that many men were sitting together in one of the
tents drinking ale, and they had no doubt been doing so for a
good while, since some had collapsed unconscious. He saw to

his surprise a woman with her clothing in disarray, staggering over to a smaller tent, and a man sitting utterly without embarrassment as he answered the call of nature.

Arn was completely bewildered by the behavior of his fellow human beings, and this was obvious from looking at him. Three small boys spotted him, pointed their fingers, and laughed, but he had no idea why. Yet he had to pass them to get through the opening in the wall, and then they whispered something amongst themselves before they approached to block his way.

"Here you have to pay toll to the poor to be allowed in, monk boy!" said the oldest and boldest of the three.

"I don't have much to give," replied Arn, truly sorry. "I just have a little bread and—"

"Bread would be good, because we have nothing at all. How much have you got, monk boy?"

"I have four pieces of bread baked this morning," said Arn truthfully.

"Fine, we'll take them. Give us the bread at once!" called all three. And it seemed to Arn that they suddenly looked happy.

Fortified by the thought that he could make his neighbor happy so easily, Arn opened his knapsack and handed over the pieces of bread. The three boys snatched them away and ran off, laughing wildly and without a word of thanks. Arn watched them go in amazement. He suspected that he'd been fooled in some way, but he didn't understand why anyone would want to do such a thing, so he felt guilty for thinking ill of his neighbor.

When he tried to go through the gate, two sleepy men with weapons in their hands prevented him from doing so. First they wanted to know his name and what business he had there. Arn replied that he was lay brother Arn from Varnhem and that he had come to visit the cathedral, but that he would be moving on soon. They let him in with a laugh and said something mysterious about how he should mind he didn't commit some act that he didn't understand either. And because his confusion was so obvious from his expression, the two men laughed even more.

When Arn entered through the gate he wasn't sure which way to go. The direction of the cathedral was clear from the two tall towers visible from anywhere in town. But there seemed to be nothing but compost amongst all the low and tightly packed wooden buildings. At first Arn thought he would have to find another way through all the garbage. But then he saw a man come riding down an alley that seemed to head straight for the cathedral. The hooves of his horse sank deeper with every step into sludge, manure, and rotting garbage. Very hesitantly and with the stench tickling his nostrils, Arn took the same alley in the opposite direction. It was still morning, or time that was reckoned as morning inside the town. Everywhere cocks were crowing, and at several spots along the alley he was almost struck by garbage thrown out from pots and cooking vessels. The people apparently shared living quarters with their livestock and poultry. He was filled with more astonishment than disgust.

But when Arn finally emerged from the alley and found himself in front of the cathedral itself, the crowded streets gave way to a large market square with long rows of tents where all sorts of trade was conducted. The ground was also cleaner out here.

Cautiously he dismounted from his horse, careful where he set his feet, and tied the reins to a post outside the cathedral where two other horses stood. He hesitated for a moment, wondering whether he should let his curiosity take over and go to see what was being sold in the tents, or whether he should go inside God's house first. As soon as he posed that question to himself he was ashamed that he'd had even the slightest doubt; he walked straight in through the church door, fell to his knees, and crossed himself.

It was almost deserted inside and so dark that he had to pause for a moment to let his eyes adjust. Up by the altar burned a score of small candles; he saw a woman just lighting a new one before kneeling down to pray.

Somewhere up ahead in the darkness a choir began singing hymns, but it didn't sound very good. He could clearly discern two voices singing off-key, and it filled him with wonder, as if they were mocking the Lord by singing like that in His house.

Arn went over to one of the side aisles and sat down on a little stone bench to meditate. He did not feel at home in this house of God. Up by the altar hung large tapestries woven in garish colors along with two pictures of saints and a Virgin Mary painted in blue, yellow, red, and green. Across from him, light shone through a glass window up along the side of the tower, breaking into all the colors of the rainbow. It made a presumptuous and false impression on Arn, as if the gaudiness were duplicitous. The image of Jesus Christ on one of the walls of the tower was spangled in gold and silver, as if the Lord had been an earthly prince. He knelt down and prayed first for the forgiveness of his sins and then asked God to forgive the people who had turned His house into a worldly manifestation of loathsome and idolatrous taste.

But from the limestone of the little bench he felt an odd warmth when he sat back down, as if the stone were talking to him. He had the notion that he had sat there before, although that was impossible. Then he saw his mother before him, as if she were coming toward him, smiling. But the vision vanished abruptly when the choir in front took up a new hymn.

This time the choir sang in only two-part harmony, but it still did no good, since the lead singer of the second voice kept leading the others astray. In the belief that he might now do a good deed, Arn went to stand next to the choir, taking up the second voice and singing it correctly. He had known the lyrics since he was a mere babe.

✠

Chaplain Inge felt at first as if God in jest, weary of all the false notes, had decided to correct them. But then he discovered that there was a young lay brother from Varnhem standing nearby, and he had shamelessly taken over the lead of the second voice. When they had finished the hymn the chaplain, who was leading the choir, went right over to Arn and put him in the middle of the choir, thus engaging his services for the rest of the mass.

Afterward several of the singers eagerly wanted to ask questions of Arn, but the chaplain quickly took him aside and led him into the sacristy, where light came in through two small windows so that they could see each other as they talked. Arn was asked to take a seat and was given a mug of water; the chaplain joked that it was poor compensation for such beautiful singing.

Arn, not realizing that this was said in jest, immediately refused the water, saying that he certainly wasn't demanding payment for singing in God's house. When asked his name he replied that he was called Arn of Varnhem, nothing more.

The chaplain now got excited because he thought he'd made a discovery. Here was clearly a young man who could not be admitted as a full brother by the Cistercians, who for some reason had been cast out and thus might be available as a blessed addition to the choir. No matter what anyone said about those foreign monks, they could certainly sing to delight God's angels; that much no one could deny.

Since no one had ever spoken to Arn with hidden intentions, he understood nothing of the import of all the questions that the anxious chaplain now showered upon him.

So he had left Varnhem to return home? And where was home exactly? And what did his father and mother do? Oh, his mother was dead, peace be with her memory and blessings on her soul. But his father, what did he do? Worked like everyone else in the sweat of his brow? Did the young man mean in agriculture? Was his father a peasant or a freedman then?

Arn answered as best he could without lying, except when it came to the difficult question of whether his father was rich, which he quickly denied. He considered the word "rich" to mean something shameful and didn't want to think such thoughts about his own father. And he wasn't sure what the words peasant or freedman signified exactly, even though he doubted either had anything to do with his father.

However, one thing was clear to the chaplain. Here was the son of a poor man who worked hard at farming, perhaps a freed thrall, who had too many mouths to feed and had tried to get rid of at least one of them at the cloister. And now the young man would come home, at the most ravenous age of all, and not be good for much more than saying grace. Here was a chance to do something beneficial for all parties; all he had to do was seize the opportunity.

"I believe, my young lay brother, that you and I might be able to help each other to our mutual advantage," said the chaplain.

"If I can help you with something, father, I shall not hesitate, but what in all the world might that be? I am only a poor lay brother," said Arn without lying, because he believed what he said.

"Well yes, many are the poor on this earth, but sometimes God gives even the poor great gifts. And you, Arn . . . wasn't that what you said your name is? Yes, you have truly received a great gift from God."

"Yes, that is true," said Arn, looking down in embarrassment because he was thinking of God's great gift when he got his life back.

"Then I have the pleasure of telling you, Arn, that now you may shed a great worry for both you and your father, and at the same time do a good deed that is pleasing to God. Are you ready to hear my proposal?" said the chaplain, leaning forward triumphantly and smiling so broadly that Arn could see his brownish-black teeth and smell his terrible breath.

"Yes, father," said Arn obediently, but shrank back in horror. "Although I have no idea what you're thinking of, father."

"We can offer you room and board, and new clothing too, if you stay here and sing in the cathedral choir. It's a great honor for a poor young man, you should know. But then you do have a rare gift from God, as you realize yourself."

Arn was so astonished that at first he could not reply. It finally dawned on him that the priest meant that his very ordinary singing was supposed to be the great gift, and not the fact that God had brought him back from the realm of the dead. He didn't know how to reply.

"Yes, I can understand that you would be dumbstruck," said the chaplain, pleased. "It's not every day one shoots so many birds with one arrow. Your father will be spared from having another mouth to feed; we can make souls, both living and dead, rejoice with more beautiful masses; and you will have clothing, meals, and lodging. That would be many blessings for a single day, don't you think?"

"No . . . I mean yes, of course, it might seem so," Arn said in confusion. For the life of him he didn't want to be taken captive by the ill-smelling priest, cathedral or not. But neither did he know how to get out of the situation. He had no idea know how to refuse someone he was supposed to obey.

The chaplain clearly considered the matter settled. "Come with me. We'll go over to the singers' quarters so you can meet the others and be given a bed that you need only share with one other boy."

"This is not . . . this won't work at all!" Arn stammered desperately. "I mean . . . of course I'm deeply grateful for your kindness, father . . . but it won't work . . ."

The chaplain cast a puzzled and astonished look at the young man with the tonsure that had just started to grow out and a thrall's knotty hands that revealed harsh manual labor. What in the name of all reason could make this poor awkward youth say no to such a generous offer? He even looked as though he was agonizing over his refusal.

"I have my horse outside. I'm responsible for the animal and must return it to another lay brother," Arn tried to explain.

"You have a horse, you say?" the chaplain muttered, confused. "You couldn't possibly—I want to see it with my own eyes!"

Arn obediently walked through the cathedral with the chaplain beside him. The father was busy calculating the value of a horse, deciding that it far exceeded what he had just offered the boy in the form of room and board.

Outside in the light stood Arn's borrowed horse, quite rightly, looking very tired with its head drooping heavily. Yet the chaplain decided at once that it was a splendid horse, and Arn discovered to his dismay that his knapsack with all of Brother Rugiero's lamb sausages and smoked hams was gone. He wondered who might be looking after them. But the chaplain was expounding loudly about his fine steed. Arn protested that there was nothing special about the horse, but that he couldn't understand what had become of his hams and sausages. Then the chaplain got angry and declared that surely he wasn't so stupid as to leave such things to thieves.

Arn was horrified at the thought that he might have been robbed, and in that way contributed directly to grievous sin. He asked innocently whether he couldn't go to the thieves and get his goods back, if he promised to forgive them. That made the chaplain even angrier and he strode off muttering angry words about horses and muttonheads. Arn at once said a brief prayer for forgiveness for the unfortunate souls who had given in to the temptation to steal. He added in his prayer that he took full blame for what had happened, because he had left his knapsack with the food to tempt those who were both weak in spirit and hungry.

On the way north from Skara the wedding of Gunnar of Rede-berga was being celebrated. He was a tenant farmer who worked for the cathedral dean, Torkel of Skara. The dean, who attended the wedding feast, was pleased with what he had arranged for his tenant, because this Gunnar was not handsome to look at and did not have much to offer as a morning gift. But the dean had taken pity on his tenant, and also out of concern for his own earnings he had arranged it so that Gunnar could take a wife.

A comfortably wealthy peasant named Tyrgils of Torbjörn-torp had received the cathedral dean's help in a difficult predica-ment, and then at his weakest moment had promised to return the favor. This favor now meant marrying off his youngest daughter Gunvor to Gunnar of Redeberga. It was a good ar-rangement in many respects because Tyrgils had not had to pay a large dowry as he would have if he'd made a better match for his daughter, and at least he'd finally gotten her married. Gunnar of Redeberga had equally low demands on him when it came to the morning gift he would have to present, so despite his lack of money and land and his ugly visage he did indeed marry a young and evidently fair maid.

The dean thought he had made a good bargain for all, but especially for his loyal and humble tenant Gunnar, who never could have won himself a fecund maid to marry on his own. Gunnar was diligent at handling his own affairs as a tenant farmer, and he returned to the dean sevenfold what he had spent. So it was wise of the dean to protect his own interest, ensuring that offspring were produced and the farm could be kept under the charge of the same family. That way he avoided the trouble of evicting Gunnar when he got old and had no children to support him or pay the rent.

So everyone was pleased with the arrangement. Except for Gunvor, who wept bitterly for a whole week before she was forced to say yes to the dean and utter the vows that would soon be honored so that the marriage could be consummated. She had importuned her father Tyrgils to let her be quit of this abominable man and instead be allowed to marry a different Gunnar who was the third son at the neighboring farm of Långavreten. She and the youth had spoken of the matter, and both were in agreement that their betrothal should take place.

But her father Tyrgils had flown into a rage and explained that he could ill afford such an arrangement. Långavreten was a farm as large as his own, and he would thus have to pay an exorbitant dowry if the neighbors were to unite their families in a wedding ale. Should he fail to provide a substantial dowry he would not appear to be a man of honor. There was no solution to this dilemma, and Gunvor's entreaties had not helped in the least. Her father had sought to console her only once, with assurances that the whims of young maidens were fleeting, and this one too would pass. As long as she got her first children to blow their noses, it would all be forgotten.

Now she sat there in her bridal gown while the men sitting at the wedding tables got drunker and drunker. She felt as if she were being stabbed with needles every time she heard a joke or laughter about the wedding night, which all wanted to witness. When she saw her slobbering and drunken husband being slapped on the back by men making gestures that meant a cock as big as a horse's, her blood ran both hot and cold. She prayed to the Holy Virgin to call her home at once. She sought the grace to fall dead on the spot without having to commit the sin of suicide. It was the only way to save her from this dreadful fate. But in her heart she understood quite well that the Mother of

God would never grant such a selfish request and that all hope was now gone. She would soon be irretrievably violated by that drooling old man and unable to do anything except obediently spread her legs the way the older women had taught her.

But as the afternoon sun was setting outside, inexorably heading toward evening, she suddenly heard the voice of the Mother of God strong and clear inside her. With a wild shriek Gunvor threw herself on top of the table and with one long, nimble bound she was over it and on her way out the door. She lifted her skirts and ran off as fast as she could.

Inside at the wedding ale it took a while before the drunken men realized what had happened; for various reasons most of them had not seen the bride run out. But then they collected themselves and on unsteady legs they initiated the chase for the runaway bride while someone—no one ever found out who it was—yelled, "Bride-robber, bride-robber, bride-robber!"

The drunken men then staggered back to grab their swords and spears. They saddled their horses with fumbling fingers, while worried women peered after the fleeing bride, who was still in sight, running toward the road to Skara.

✠

Arn came riding up in at a leisurely pace, his stomach churning. He was in no hurry because he knew that the night would be dark without stars or moon, and so he would have to seek a place to camp. He had no hope of reaching Arnäs before noon the next day.

Suddenly a young woman came rushing toward him with her clothes in disarray, a wild look on her face, and her arms flailing about. He stopped his horse, dumbfounded, and stared at her, incapable of either understanding what she was saying or uttering a friendly greeting.

"Save me, save me from the demons!" the woman cried, and abruptly fell exhausted to the ground before the hooves of his horse.

Arn got down from his horse, puzzled and frightened. He could clearly see that his neighbor was in trouble, but how was he to go about helping her?

He squatted down next to the small, gasping female body and cautiously reached out his hand to stroke her lovely brown hair, but he didn't dare. When she looked up at him, her face filled with happiness and she started talking in confusion about his kind eyes, about Our Lady who had sent an angel to save her, and other things that made him suspect she had lost her wits.

This was how the drunken, raging wedding guests found the runaway bride and her abductor. The first men to dismount instantly grabbed hold of the bride, who began screaming in such a heartrending fashion that they tied her hands and feet and put a gag in her mouth. Two men seized hold of Arn by grabbing both his hands behind his back and forcing his head forward. He offered no resistance.

At once the bridegroom himself, Gunnar of Redeberga, came riding up, and someone handed him a sword. According to the law he had the right to slay the bride-robber caught in the act. When Arn saw the sword being raised, he asked calmly to be allowed to say his prayers first, and the breathless mob considered this to be a Christian request that they could not honorably refuse.

Arn felt no fear when he fell to his knees, only astonishment. Was it only for this that God had spared his life? To be beheaded by a drunken mob who clearly believed that he had intended to do the woman harm? It was too ridiculous to be true, so he prayed not for his own life but for reason to return to these unfortunate people who were about to commit a mortal sin out of sheer confusion.

He must have looked pitiful as he knelt there praying. He was only half a man, with downy cheeks, dressed in a worn monk's cloak with obvious traces on his scalp of the monks' manner of shaving their tonsures. And then someone began to pray for Arn in the belief that he was helping the unfortunate in his prayers. Another said that it wasn't much of a manly deed to slay a defenseless young monk; at least they ought to give him a sword so he could defend himself and die like a man. Murmurs of agreement were heard, and suddenly Arn saw a short, ungainly Nordic sword drop down in front of him onto the grass.

Then he thanked God at great length before he took up the sword; it was clear that he would be allowed to live.

The cathedral dean, Torkel of Skara, had now come so close that he could see everything that was happening clearly, and what he saw, or thought he saw, would be very important.

Because when Gunnar of Redeberga attacked with his sword held high to put a quick end to the wretch who had ruined his wedding feast, he found himself striking at thin air. He had no idea what had happened, even though he didn't consider himself especially drunk.

He swung again without hitting Arn, and again and again.

Arn saw that the man facing him was defenseless, and he guessed that it might have something to do with liquor. All the better, he thought, since then he wouldn't risk doing harm to his neighbor.

But for Gunnar of Redeberga what happened was like a bad dream. His friends started laughing at him, and no matter how he swung the sword at that cursed demon, because a demon he must be, the wretch was somewhere else. He did not flee, yet he was always somewhere else.

Arn was circling calmly in the opposite direction with the sword in his left hand, since Brother Guilbert had always stressed that this would be the hardest for his opponent to defend against.

He didn't need to parry much with his own sword; it was enough just to keep moving. He reckoned that the old man would soon tire and give up, and that no one would be hurt, since God had interceded to save them all.

But humiliated and somewhat scared, Gunnar of Redeberga now asked the old warrior Joar to assist him in his lawful task. Joar was an experienced swordsman who had seen how the groom was fooled by simple tricks. So Joar now threw himself into the fight to make short work of the matter. The dean's desperate protests were of little avail.

Arn, who suddenly found himself in danger, grew frightened and tossed the sword to his right hand, spinning around to defend himself with two quick moves, for the first time fighting in earnest.

Gunnar of Redeberga at once fell to the ground with his throat slashed, and Joar sank down moaning after a lunge struck him in the middle of his soft belly.

The men stood as if turned to stone. The wedding guests had all seen with their own eyes something that could not possibly have occurred, something that had to be a miracle.

But Arn stood still in fright, because he realized full well, after taking part in so much fighting, that the man who first attacked him lay kicking out the last of his life's blood on the ground. And the other man, who knew how to wield a sword, was mortally wounded. Crushed by his evil deeds, Arn let his sword fall to the ground and bowed his head in prayer, ready in the next moment to suffer the beheading rightfully administered by any of the men present.

But the dean reached his arms in the air toward the sky and began singing a hymn, which at least for the moment made any renewed attacks on Arn unsuitable. And then the dean, filled with the spirit, spoke sternly about the miracle they had just witnessed, how an obviously innocent person had, because of

his innocence, received the highest protection. The dean himself
had clearly seen the archangel Gabriel standing behind the small
unprotected boy, guiding his arms in defense. Soon several of
the men declared that they too had witnessed the same thing, in
truth a miracle from God, how a defenseless young monk had
been able to vanquish two grown warriors.

Now they freed the bride from her bonds, and she too fell
into prayer, thanking God for sending someone to rescue her at
the last moment. They sang more hymns, but Arn was unable to
take part in the singing.

The cathedral dean then questioned Arn about where he
came from and decided to escort the poor monk personally back
to Varnhem. Gunnar of Redeberga would be carried home to be
buried and the gravely wounded Joar would be carried on a litter
to his home.

✠

It was a very oddly matched pair that came riding up to Varnhem
on that mild autumn morning when the rowan trees and oaks
and beeches around the monastery had begun to turn yellow and
red.

Cathedral Dean Torkel was in a radiant mood, for God had
granted him the opportunity to witness one of His miracles on
earth. It was a signal honor.

Arn, who had been fasting since his misdeed and refused to
spend the night anywhere but in the cathedral in prayer, was
ashen-gray in the face and weighted down by his grievous sin.
He was well aware that the dean's confused talk of a miracle was
untrue. God had shown him grace by giving him a sword, with
which he could have defended himself without injuring anyone.
But he had misused that grace and instead committed the worst
of sins. He knew that now he was lost, and it amazed him that

God had not smote him to the ground at once when he committed such an unforgivable deed.

When they were let in the cloister gate beneath the two tall ash trees that were the only visible remains of what Arn's mother had once donated, Arn began praying at once for forgiveness. He slunk into the cloister church to pray for the strength to be able to do honest penance soon.

Dean Torkel proudly asked for an audience with Father Henri, because he had such magnificent news to report.

The conversation between the two men was very strange, and not only because they had a hard time understanding each other. Dean Torkel spoke Latin as poorly as Father Henri spoke Norse, and besides, Dean Torkel was so excited that he couldn't tell the story sensibly. Father Henri had to ask him to calm down, drink a glass of wine, and then begin at the beginning.

And when it gradually dawned on Father Henri what a catastrophe had occurred, he was at a loss to understand the dean's giddy enthusiasm.

It was obvious that Arn was no bride-robber. How he could even be accused of something like that was at first very difficult for his uneducated Nordic colleague to explain.

When someone foolishly took it into his head to toss a sword to Arn, it was equally obvious that the result would be one dead and one dying man. But it was (blasphemous thought) as if God the Father were cruelly joking with the wedding guests in that case. Or, perhaps rather, He was punishing them for their ruthless thoughtlessness when a frightened woman ran off and they took the first man on the road to be a bride-robber. The latter displayed despicably barbaric behavior, especially as they then supposed they had the right to slay on the spot the man they had encountered. On the other hand, the laws were such in this part of the world that the poor misguided souls had to some measure acted in good faith.

But the hardest thing to swallow was the dean's self-righteous notions that he had been granted the opportunity to witness a miracle with the archangel Gabriel standing behind Arn, helping him to wield each stroke of the sword.

Father Henri muttered to himself that if the archangel Gabriel had really seen what was going on, he wouldn't have rushed to help Arn but instead come to the aid of the foolish drunkards. But he said none of this aloud.

The imagined miracle became a more delicate matter in that Dean Torkel was now asking the cloister's help to have his account written down properly, while he still had the images clear in his mind and also remembered the names of all the witnesses.

At first Father Henri gave an evasive reply to the request and asked instead to be informed of what the laws outside the walls said about lay brother Arn's behavior. For a long while Dean Torkel was distracted from his request for written assistance.

The laws said that bride-robbers could be struck down if caught in the act. But not an innocent person, because that would be concomitant to murder.

On the one hand, the law was such that if twelve men swore that Arn was innocent and that a miracle had occurred, then Arn would be acquitted at the *ting*, if the matter went that far. On the other hand, if the families of the dead man, or in the worst case the two dead men, wanted to bring a suit at the *ting*, then the question would arise as to whether Arn, as he clearly was named, had anyone who could serve as his oath-swearers and who were not foreigners. Did Arn have anyone who could be his oath-swearers, and did he possibly belong to any clan?

"Yes," sighed Father Henri in relief. "The young man does belong to a clan. His name is Arn Magnusson of Arnäs, his father is Magnus Folkesson, and his uncle is Birger Brosa of Bjälbo. Eskil the judge is his kinsman, et cetera, et cetera. The boy thus belongs to the Folkung clan, although I am unsure whether he entirely understands what that means. Of course there would be no problem getting oath-swearers."

"Well, is that so! Praise be to God!" exclaimed Dean Torkel. "I shall hurry to inform the kinsmen that they should not expect success at any *ting*. This is even better, now they won't have anything against testifying that the account of the miracle is true!"

Despite the fact that the two men of God now seemed to have found a simple solution to a legal problem, they were of much different minds. The dean was so happy he seemed to be hovering a bit above the ground, for his account of the miracle, which he would speak of at great length in the cathedral, had now been saved and would also be recorded in calligraphy on parchment by those who did such things best.

Father Henri, who knew that no miracle had taken place, was relieved that Arn would not be subjected to the harsh and blind justice of Western Götaland. But he grieved for Arn's sake, and he grieved for his own sin, for he now realized that he and Brother Guilbert must share the blame for what had happened.

"Could I receive at once the writing help that this great and important matter deserves?" asked the dean, full of bright enthusiasm.

"Yes, of course, brother," replied Father Henri in a surprisingly deliberate tone. "We shall see to it at once."

Father Henri summoned one of the scribes and explained in French, which he was sure that the uneducated dean did not speak, that he should keep a straight face and keep writing and make no objections, no matter how demented the whole thing might sound.

When the dean, with a youthful bounce to his step and praising the Lord vociferously, was led toward the scriptorium, Father Henri got up with a heavy heart to seek out the unhappy Arn. He knew quite well where he would find him.

Chapter 7

Dean Torkel was a practical man and scrupulous with money, especially his own. His tenant farmer Gunnar of Redeberga had now departed this life most inopportunely in the prime of his life, and without bringing any future farmers into the world. His wedding had also been interrupted in the most distressful way.

After Dean Torkel had recovered from the wondrous aspect of this event—the fact that he had been granted the opportunity to witness a miracle of the Lord with his own eyes—he soon began to ponder the more earthly results of what had happened. He needed a new, industrious tenant farmer for Redeberga; that was the most pressing problem.

Because he was the father confessor of Gunvor, the betrothed and very nearly married young bride, he hadn't been able to avoid forming certain basic notions from what he heard in her confession. She had most assuredly wished that life should leave both herself and her intended husband, for which he imposed only a week of mild penance. But she had also confessed that her sinful wishes were due to a strong liking for another young man whose name was also Gunnar.

This Gunnar of Långavreten, as Dean Torkel soon discovered, was his father's third son. Normally he would not be allowed to marry at all, since that would mean dividing up the Långavreten estate into three plots, each of which would be too small to work profitably. But Gunnar was a healthy young man whose heart was set on working the land rather than moving away to become a retainer for some lord.

Dean Torkel soon summoned the young Gunnar, heard his confession, and then quickly devised a way in which everything could be arranged. The young man was apparently pining for Gunvor as much as she was for him.

It could all work out for the best if the young couple became Dean Torkel's new tenant farmers at Redeberga. Tyrgils of Tor-björntorp, Gunvor's father, may have envisioned a better match for his daughter than as the wife of a third son. But as the situation now stood, she wouldn't be easy to marry off, even as fair as she was, because the story of her terrible bridal ale had quickly traveled throughout Western Götaland. The dean himself had played a significant part in spreading the story, since he was eager to have his account of the miracle mentioned in many sermons. So for the freeholder Tyrgils the safest bet was to marry off his Gunvor as soon as the first opportunity arose.

And for young Gunnar's father, Lars Kopper of Långavreten, it was not a bad idea at all to marry off his third son, and to someone the boy happened to prefer. Both fathers would benefit from the dowry and morning gift in that way. And besides, the young couple would probably not leave their fathers any peace when they realized the opportunity that had now come like manna from heaven.

Dean Torkel had planted the first seed in a sincerely restorative conversation with Gunvor; then he had done the same with Gunnar; and after that it was simple to call in the two fathers, and the matter was soon settled. The betrothal ale could be arranged at once.

At Michaelmas, when the harvest respite began and the fences around the fields no longer needed to be maintained, the betrothal ale was held at Redeberga with the dean himself attending to confirm the vows between Gunvor and Gunnar. He spoke to them at a moment in the festivities when the guests were still sober enough to listen to what a man of God might say, reminding them to honor the miracle of the Lord that had finally, against all earthly rhyme or reason, brought them together.

For Gunvor this was the happiest day of her life. What did it matter that she would live her life in somewhat lesser circumstances than those she was born to? Here she sat in the wicker betrothal chair with her true Gunnar, whom she thought she had lost forever. From the depths of despair she had risen like a lark to heavenly bliss.

After the betrothal ale had gone on for several hours they went out in the courtyard for a while to watch the sunset. They held hands, feeling both trepidation and happiness at the thought that they would now live together, to grow old and die on this farm. The somewhat difficult subject that Gunvor now wanted to discuss was met with no objections from her betrothed, and that eased her mind at once. For she was eternally grateful to the Holy Virgin for saving her from the jaws of misfortune at the last moment. Indeed, she would never forget to mention this in her prayers. So she wanted to give the two sorrel horses they had received as a betrothal gift to the cloister at Varnhem. They would make a journey there to convey their thanks to the young monk who had saved their happiness at the risk of his own life.

Gunnar thought that this was a very good idea, and he praised her for it, offering at once to accompany her to Varnhem to settle this matter.

Their decision would come as a delightful balm to the soul of the young man, who was in no way as small and pitiful as Gunvor remembered him.

✠

Brother Guilbert had been working in the smithy making a sword for six days, laboring as if in a fever or a rage or filled with divine inspiration. Naturally he had as good as ignored most of his other duties, yet Father Henri had not said a word about it. The hammer blows from the smithy resounded constantly at Varnhem, even during some of the prayer hours.

It had been a long time since Brother Guilbert had made a sword according to the new methods, although it would have been unreasonable to sell such things to the Nordic barbarians. They would never have dreamed of paying the full price for such work. Besides, they had no particular need for Damascene swords, since they could scarcely handle their own.

When he made Nordic swords Brother Guilbert began with three types of iron, which he combined by folding the billet over and over and hammering it out again. Through this layering he was able to achieve a certain flexibility, and yet he could polish the blade as shiny and patterned as Nordic men would have it. The better the decoration the finer they considered the sword. Most desirable was a pattern that appeared as a serpent when they breathed on the cold blade. And yet Brother Guilbert still gave the sword a strength that was greater than was usually found in this corner of the world.

But the sword he was working on now, toiling in holy desperation, had possessed from the beginning a single core of hardened steel. The art of transforming iron into steel was not known in the North. Brother Guilbert had used his very best iron for the purpose and fired it for three days and nights, packed in charcoal, leather, and brick, for the transformation to occur. The blessed steel core he then welded inside layers of softer iron. The edge would be sharp enough to shave a monk's head. With each blow of the hammer on the anvil and with each prayer he slowly but surely completed a masterpiece the likes of which could only be found in Damascus itself or in Outremer, where others like himself had taught themselves the Saracen art. Brother Guilbert had many divergent views when it came to Saracens, but it was one subject that he wisely refused to discuss. No matter how much he loved Father Henri as the wisest and kindest prior a sinner like himself could ever serve, he knew for certain that Saracens were not a suitable topic of discussion under any circumstances.

He had come far in his work by the sixth day, when a lay brother came to interrupt him. He had been sent by Father Henri, who had now summoned him to an urgent meeting, smithy or no smithy.

Brother Guilbert stopped his work at once and went to the lavatorium to make his appearance worthy of his prior.

Father Henri was waiting for him in the scriptorium, his second favorite place. It was still the beginning of autumn but the evenings had begun to grow chilly, and Father Henri had never learned to tolerate the Nordic cold. So he chose the scriptorium rather than the stone benches in the arcade by the herb garden.

"Good evening, my dear Vulcanus," Father Henri greeted the smith jocularly when the washed but still sweating Brother Guilbert bowed his head to enter the doorway intended for much smaller men.

"Good evening, my dear Father Jupiter, in that case," replied Brother Guilbert in the same tone of voice, sitting down unbidden before the writing desk where Father Henri stood sketching.

There was a moment of silence while Father Henri finished off a curlicue and then wiped the quill pen and put it aside. Then he cleared his throat in the way that Brother Guilbert and many others at Varnhem or Vitae Schola recognized as a signal that now a rather lengthy explication was to ensue.

"I'll be hearing our son Arn's confession in a while," Father Henri began with a deep sigh. "And I will give him absolution. At once. He won't be expecting it and he won't like it, because he is very remorseful and filled with thoughts of his sin and, well, everything you can imagine. But you must know, my much beloved brother, that I have truly ransacked my heart over this, and what I've arrived at is not exactly pleasant for you or me. What happened is not Arn's fault, but rather yours and mine. Naturally we have a conflict here. On the one hand there is the secular law, no matter how barbaric it may appear to us when it comes to this part of the world. And on the other hand is God's law. The secular law will not affect Arn, nor will the divine law. For your part and mine it is a more delicate matter, and by this time you must know what I'm getting at. Now be so good as not to say, I told you so!"

"I did tell you so, father, in all humility," Brother Guilbert was quick to reply. "We should have told him who he was. If he had known who he was when he met those drunken peasants . . ."

"I know. Then no one would have needed to be hurt!" Father Henri interrupted him with more despair than annoyance in his voice. "Regardless, we did what we did, and now we have to think about what comes next. For my part I have to start with the task of persuading Arn to understand that he is forgiven before God's law, and I don't think it will be easy. So help me God, I truly love that boy! When he rode away from us to set out for his father's estate he was that rare individual: a human being without sin . . ."

"A Parsifal," muttered Brother Guilbert pensively. "In truth a young Parsifal."

"A what? Oh yes, that. All right, let it go," muttered Father Henri in reply, his train of thought disturbed. He paused for a moment before he went on.

"Now, Brother Guilbert, I command you as prior to do this: When Arn comes to see you after I talk to him, you must tell him who he is in all the aspects that I could not explain. Do you know what I mean?"

"Certainly I know what you mean, father, and I shall obey your command to the letter," replied Brother Guilbert with great earnestness.

Father Henri nodded, silently thinking. Then he got up and left with a wave of goodbye. Brother Guilbert sat there for a long time, praying sincerely for the strength to shape his words well when he carried out the order he had just been given.

✠

Arn had spent ten days in one of the guest cells at Varnhem. But he had set aside all the things that were given only to guests: the well-packed straw mattress, the red quilts, and the sheepskin. He had taken a vow of silence and lived on bread and water.

Father Henri found him pale with dark rings under his eyes, and a look that was frozen with grief. It was impossible to tell how the young man was going to speak or behave, whether he was even in his right mind, and whether he would understand what would soon happen to him. Father Henri decided to act solely in accordance with his calling at first, and offer neither consolation nor reprimand.

"I am now prepared to hear your confession, my son," said Father Henri, sitting down on the hard wooden bed and motioning to Arn to sit beside him.

"Father, forgive me, for I have sinned," Arn began, but he had to break off to timidly clear his throat, since his ten days of silence had made his voice uncertain. "I have committed the most heinous of sins and have nothing to offer as excuse. I killed two men although I could have merely wounded them instead. I killed two men although I knew that it would be better for my soul if I myself died and met the Lord Jesus without this sin on my back. I am therefore prepared to submit to whatever penance and punishment you impose on me, father. And nothing would seem to me too harsh."

"Is that all? Nothing else, as long as we're at it?" asked Father Henri in a light tone, regretting at once that he no doubt sounded as if he were mocking the young man's anguish.

"No . . . that's all . . . I mean, I've had bad thoughts, ill-conceived thoughts, when I tried to place the blame on someone else, but all that is contained in what I have already confessed," said Arn, palpably embarrassed.

Father Henri felt relieved that Arn was still so lucid that he had control over his speech when responding to such a bewildering question. But now came the momentous part, the grace of God which so often passes human understanding. Father Henri took a deep breath and consulted God one last time before he spoke the two crucial words. Then he waited a moment until he felt that God within him was giving the support that was necessary.

"*Te absolvo*, I forgive you in the name of the Father, the Son, and the Holy Spirit, my son," he said, making the sign of the cross first over Arn and then over himself.

Arn stared at him as if under a spell, unable to understand what he had heard. Father Henri waited until the meaning of the words had sunk in deep. Then he cleared his throat at great length, this time quite conscious that it was a sign that he would now present his explication.

"The grace of the Lord is in truth great, but you are now truly free of sin, my son. I have forgiven you as your father confessor and as God's humble servant and with His consent. Let us rejoice over the great thing that has happened, but let us not take it lightly. You shall know that all this time you have spent in solitude consulting with God, I have done the same. And if God may have said something to you that He has not said to me, there may possibly be an intention behind that as well. For we have indeed had to deal with a very difficult matter, the most difficult I have ever encountered as a father confessor. The anguish you have suffered during these days as you offered genuine repentance has been a part of the testing of your soul."

"But . . . but it . . . it can't be possible . . . murder . . .?" Arn stammered.

"Stop interrupting me and listen," Father Henri continued firmly, yet he was relieved because Arn seemed to be much more capable of speech than he had feared. "God's good world is twofold in this case, and we have to try to look at the whole. There is a world out there, *extra muros*, with its sometimes very peculiar laws. According to those laws you are without guilt; so far it is very simple. But we have our own higher world *intra muros*, and it places considerably higher demands upon us. First, my own sin and that of Brother Guilbert is greater than yours, when it comes to these killings. I shall explain in more detail in a moment. Second, we have to try to see your deed from God's higher perspective, no matter how difficult this may appear to us poor sinful humans. And we must try to understand what God meant. It was not for this deed that He has kept watch over you, you can be assured of that. Your great task in life, whatever it is, still lies before you. But God used the most practical instrument He found available to punish men who had committed a dire sin. Because this is how it was: They had forced a young woman, Gunvor, whom you met for the first time there by the road, to marry a man for whom she felt disgust. And they forced her to do this for the sake of their own desire and their own profit.

When she in desperation tried to escape her adverse fate, they were filled with wrath and wanted to kill anyone who crossed their path. Then they lied loudly that the first man they met would be a bride-robber, and according to the laws out there, they would have the pleasure of killing him. When God saw this He grew angry and set you in the path of the sinners in order to punish them as severely as only He can. That cathedral Dean Torkel was thus not entirely wrong when he spoke of how he saw an angel guiding your hand, although all that nonsense about a miracle, et cetera, et cetera, is drivel, of course. You were God's instrument and carried out His judgment, which you might not have been able to do if Brother Guilbert and I had not deceived you. That is why you are now forgiven and without sin, my son. Your fast ends today, but be careful to eat cautiously this evening; it's not good to gulp down food after such a long fast. So. That's all."

Arn did not reply for a long time, and Father Henri left him to his thoughts. What he had said needed time to put down roots in Arn's mind before they spoke more about that matter or anything else.

Arn had no difficulties seeing the formal logic in what Father Henri had said. But the basic assumption behind such logic was that every building block rested on absolute truthfulness and humility before God. Otherwise it would be a mere twisting of words. He was ashamed over what he had first thought when he heard those two redemptive words. He thought that Father Henri had temporized in his conviction out of a corrupt love for his son, that he had constructed a special benevolence in this case that would not have applied in other cases. It was wrong to think such things about Father Henri, and Arn realized that it proved he couldn't keep himself free of sin for very many breaths after receiving forgiveness. But this was not the time to begin confessing all over again.

"So we have reached the question of my own and Brother Guilbert's sin and our share of the guilt for what happened," sighed Father Henri. "Out there in the other world people categorize others and evaluate them differently, as if they all did not have the same soul. It's not like it is with us, where we are worth no more nor less than our brother. People out there weigh a man not according to his soul; their neighbor is not what they see first. They see a thrall or a king, a jarl or a freed slave; they see a man or a woman who either has noble ancestry or does not, much the way you and Brother Guilbert judge horses. That's how it is out there in the other world, unfortunately."

"But everyone has ancestors, everyone comes from somewhere, all the way back to Adam and Eve, and we're all born equally naked," Arn objected with a hint of wonder in his voice.

"Yes, indeed we all have ancestors. But some, according to that method of judging, have ancestors who are superior to others, and others have wealthier ancestors, and they inherit property from each other out there."

"So if someone is born rich, then he remains rich; and if he has ancestors who are superior, then he doesn't have to do anything for his own sake, since he's naturally superior? So it doesn't matter if he's good or evil, intelligent or stupid—he remains superior?" Arn pondered this, at the same time looking oddly astute as he took this first stumbling step into an awareness of the other world.

"That's precisely how it is, and that's why some have thralls out there even today. You're aware of that, aren't you?" said Father Henri.

"Well, yes . . ." Arn said hesitantly. "My own father had thralls. It's something I haven't thought about in a long time, as if it were something my memory didn't like. I've mostly thought about my mother at evening prayers, but not so much about my father, and never about the fact that he had thralls. But so it was.

Now I recall that he beheaded a thrall once, I forget why, but I'll never forget that sight."

"You see. And I'm afraid that your father has thralls even today. He is from a superior clan, and that means, and pay close attention to this, that means that you are as well. On your mother's gravestone there are two marks, as you have surely seen although we've never talked about it. One is a dragon head and a sword; that is your mother's mark. The other is a lion rampant, and that is your father's mark. It is the mark of the Folkung clan, and you are therefore a Folkung. And you probably don't know what that entails."

"No . . ." said Arn hesitantly. He looked as though he couldn't even imagine the import of being somebody other than who he was.

"Specifically it means this," said Father Henri straight off. "You have the right to ride with a sword, you have the right to carry a shield with the mark of the Folkungs. And if those rough customers had seen you thus, they would have never dreamed of attacking you. If you did not have a sword and were not carrying a shield with the mark of the Folkungs, you would only have needed to tell them your name, which is Arn Magnusson of Arnäs, and their belligerence would have instantly melted away. This is what I never told you. I never told you who you are in the eyes of the other world, and that was very wrong. If I have any excuse to offer, it is that in here we do not view our neighbors as they do out there. And I didn't want to lead you into the temptation of ever believing that you were superior to other people. I think you can understand that, and perhaps even forgive me for it."

"But this can't make me into someone other than who I am, can it?" Arn protested, puzzled. "I am as God created me, just as everyone else is, just as you are or the thralls are out there. I bear no blame for that, nor do I benefit from it. And by the way, why would the unfortunate souls who wanted to kill me let themselves be checked by a name? I was still only a 'monk boy' who couldn't handle a sword in their eyes, so why would a name frighten them?"

"Because if they laid a hand on you, none of them would live to see the sun go down for more than a few days. Not one of them. Then they would bring down the whole Folkung clan, your clan, on their necks. And no peasants in all of this unfortunate land would ever dream of doing something that stupid. That's the way it is out there, and you're going to have to get used to it."

"But I don't want to get used to such an unreasonable and evil order of things, father. Nor do I want to live in a world like that."

"You must," said Father Henri curtly. "Because so it has been decided. You must soon go out into the other world again—that is my command."

"I will obey your command, but—"

"No buts!" interrupted Father Henri. "You no longer have to shave your head. You shall break your fast starting now; just remember to eat cautiously at first. Immediately after supper you shall go to Brother Guilbert, and he will explain the other part of the truth about you, the part you do not know."

Father Henri arose heavily from the small wooden bed. He suddenly felt old and stiff and thought for the first time that his life was turning to autumn, that time was running out of the hourglass, and that he might never find out what sort of task God had prepared for his beloved son.

"Pardon me, father, but one last question before you go?" ventured Arn with an expression of bewilderment on his face.

"Yes indeed, my son, ask as many last questions as you like, because the questions will never cease."

"What was the nature of the sin that you and Brother Guilbert committed? I still can't conceive of it."

"Very simple, my son. If you knew who you were, you wouldn't have had to kill. If we had told you who you were, you would have known. We kept silent about the truth because we believed we were protecting you with lies. And God enlightened us in a most brutal fashion, showing us that nothing good can come of something evil. It is that simple. But nothing evil can come of something good, either, and you had no evil intent. So, see you at vespers!"

Father Henri left Arn alone for the hours he now required for his prayers of thanksgiving, something Father Henri did not need to mention. Because as soon as Father Henri had closed the door behind him, Arn dropped to his knees and thanked God, the Holy Virgin, and Saint Bernard in turn for saving his soul through Their ineffable grace. During his prayers he felt as though God were answering him, since life returned to his body like a warm stream of hope and, finally, in the form of something as trivial as ordinary hunger.

✠

Gunvor felt as if intoxicated by her own goodness, and it made her happy. For certainly it was a great sacrifice that she and Gunnar were now about to make. The two sorrels were almost half of all that she and her betrothed owned, and giving away so much was no easy task. But it was the right thing to do, and she was proud and glad that neither she nor Gunnar had felt any doubts as they approached the cloister at Varnhem. As Gunvor saw it, the Holy Virgin had answered her sincere prayers, not by taking her into the liberating embrace of death but by sending a young monk who with two strokes of his sword transformed both her own life and Gunnar's forever. Now they would live together until the day that death parted them. On no day of that journey would they ever neglect to offer prayers of thanksgiving for the decision of Our Lady to save their lives and give them both what they held dearest in all the world.

Even though the monk boy had only been an instrument, as insignificant as a mucking shovel in comparison with the Blessed Virgin, he was still the only person to whom Gunvor and Gunnar could offer their thanks. And he belonged to the cloister which was the only place in this world where the grateful could present their offerings. Her father had always taken care to impress on her the importance of offerings, even though he also gave offerings to others besides God's saints.

Following close behind her betrothed Gunnar, with mother Birgite and Gunnar's sister Kristina behind her, she rode into the receptorium at Varnhem, where outsiders were always greeted. She felt a great reverence inside the walls, within the lovely vaulted stone where the hooves of the horses echoed like music, and before all the blazing colors of the flowers she saw in the little inner garden with the babbling fountain. She was filled with a sense of solemnity because as soon as the strangers entered the cloister, the place breathed with God's presence.

They dismounted and tied their horses. The brother who served as the receptarius came to greet them kindly, inquiring as to why they had come. When Gunnar explained, the monk asked them to take a seat on the stone benches by the fountain and sent for ale and bread, which he blessed and broke for them as he bade them welcome. Then he went to fetch the prior.

They had to wait a good while but did not speak much since all four of them were entranced by the quietness of the place. Finally a small oak door with iron fittings opened at the far end of the receptorium, and the venerable prior came to meet them. His hair was silver-gray, curling in a wreath around his bald head, but his friendly brown eyes were full of life, which made him look younger than he probably was. He blessed them all, sat down calmly, and for the sake of courtesy shared a piece of bread with them which he also blessed. Then he got straight to the point and wanted to hear why people who were not rich—they didn't know how he could see that at once even though they had all dressed in their finest clothes—wanted to give such a costly gift to the toilers in God's garden. His language was sometimes difficult to understand because he used many priestly words in church language.

Gunnar, who was the one who should have spoken for them, was too embarrassed. So Gunvor immediately took over the responsibility of explaining, and Gunnar gave no sign of objecting. She told Father Henri how she had so devoutly placed her last remaining hope in the hands of Our Lady, how she was saved when a little monk boy was sent to her, and how because of that she and the one she loved most in life would be able to live together for all their days on earth.

At first the prior listened very attentively, interjecting a question or two about things that Gunvor did not realize were important. Soon the face of the venerable old man shone as if with a joy that radiated from within. Then he summoned a gigantic monk who emerged covered in soot and sweat. He examined the horses with grunts, sometimes approving and sometimes cross, and then he explained something to the prior in a completely incomprehensible language.

"The Lord be praised for your wondrous gift," said Father Henri, and now they all listened tensely because the huge monk went over to the mare and took her by the halter, speaking kindly to her, while he didn't seem at all interested in the stately stallion.

"Your sacrifice is great, your willingness to give us the most costly of your possessions is worthy of much respect," Father Henri went on. "But we can accept only the mare, and that is because the stallion cannot do us any service. But you mustn't take it as any disrespect. The intent of your gift has already been received, and perhaps the Mother of God took mercy on you and thought that you had offered too much. And so I beg you to keep the stallion."

As they hesitated at how to reply, Father Henri gave a little sign to Brother Guilbert, who bowed like a gentleman to them all and then led the mare in through the wooden gate, closing it behind him. Gunnar was very pleased, because he had been most reluctant to part with the stallion. But since the mare had always been a bit tricky to handle he was also surprised that the foreign monk was able to take her by the bridle just like that and lead her away through a narrow gate without her protesting in the least. He assumed that monks wouldn't know very much about horses.

When Father Henri observed that the generous and grateful guests accepted his partial refusal of their gift, he settled in his chair with pleasure and asked out of courtesy whether there was any favor he might do for them, some form of intercession per-haps?

Then Gunvor, blushing, asked if she might be allowed to thank the young monk in person, and she immediately apologized for her bold request but added that her betrothed was agreed with her in this matter.

Perhaps she had expected that the old monk would scowl and find her question unseemly. But to her relief his face instantly lit up and he thought that it was an excellent suggestion. Then he jumped up as if he were a young man, turned to hurry off, but thought of something and stopped short.

"But you must meet him alone," he said to the couple, smil-ing very broadly so that they could see a big gap between his lower teeth. "The young man would be unnecessarily timid if his prior were hovering over his shoulder. He isn't used to receiving thanks. But don't worry, he is one of you and will understand everything you say."

Father Henri blessed his guests as he departed, humming softly as he strode quickly like quite a young man through the oaken door.

They sat for a moment, talking about how they should interpret this response, but could find no explanation. In any case it did not seem unfitting for a young monk to be alone with guests, not even female ones, though it would have seemed improper for Gunvor and Gunnar to travel alone to Varnhem.

When Arn, freshly washed and timid, came to meet them, Gunvor fell to her knees before him and took his hands, which she could do because her betrothed and mother Birgite and sister Kristina were standing nearby. With an outpouring of words she let her gratitude flow over Arn.

But as she spoke she realized that the hands she was holding were in truth not those of a little boy. His hands were rough and as hard as stone; it was like taking hold of her father's hands, or a smith's. But when she looked up at Arn's bright visage it was as though his childlike and kind face did not belong with such hands. It occurred to her that Our Lady had perhaps not sent her a young monk at all, for these hands did not belong to a weak boy.

Arn stood blushing and didn't know how to deal with the situation. On the one hand, he had to respect the young woman's genuine gratitude. On the other hand, he probably thought that she was directing her thanks in the wrong direction. He carefully pulled his hands free of hers as soon as he dared and asked her to get up. He blessed her words of thanks and reminded her that they should be directed instead higher up. Gunvor agreed at once, assuring him that this she would do for as long as she lived.

Then Arn took the others by the hand, and they all felt and understood the same thing as Gunvor had when they clasped his calloused hands. They all sat for a while in embarrassed silence.

Then Gunnar felt that he had to say something before it was too late, for if he did not say something now he would regret it for the rest of his life. It was also a man's way of showing courage and honor to speak bluntly of what he was thinking.

And Gunnar began to explain, at first in a somewhat abrupt and stumbling fashion, that he and Gunvor for many years had loved each other in secret. They had constantly prayed to God for a miracle that might bring them together, despite the fact that there was no indication of such a possibility and even though both their fathers brushed aside their dreams as childish whims. But Gunnar had felt that he couldn't live without his Gunvor. And she had felt the same. On the day she was led away to the wedding ale, he had not wanted to go on living. And she had not wanted to live either. It may have been Our Lady who finally took pity on them, but it was Arn who had acted in her service and carried out her will.

Hearing the words of this simple man who was sincerely trying to express the meaning of Grace in his coarse language, Arn felt both respect and gratitude. It was as though what he had already become reconciled with—his conviction that Father Henri's absolution was correct—had served as the scaffolding and the framework of a house but not a finished house. Yet with the gift of love that these simple peasants had received and for which they had now so fervently thanked him, God's humblest instrument, it felt as if the house suddenly stood there finished with the walls and the half-timbering and all the windows in place.

"Gunnar, my friend," he said, rejoicing inside, "what you have said to me will stay with me forever, of that you can be sure. But all I can give the two of you in thanks are words from the Holy Scriptures, and do not think ill of that before you have heard what words they are. For it was your love that conquered all, and the Mother of God saw your love and then showed you mercy.

So hear now the following words of the Lord and let these words forever live in your home and in your hearts:

> *Set me as a seal upon thine heart, as a seal upon thine arm:*
> *for love is strong as death; jealousy is cruel as the grave:*
> *the coals thereof are coals of fire, which hath a most*
> *vehement flame.*
> *Many waters cannot quench love, neither can the floods*
> *drown it: if a man would give all the substance of his*
> *house for love, it would utterly be contemned.*

He had read the text in their own language so that they would understand. He had to repeat it several times to impress it upon their memory, and he told them where in the Holy Scriptures these words of God were found: The Song of Songs 8:6–7.

When they parted, Gunvor took his hand again and then asked his name. Arn tried for the first time to use his name, the name that belonged to the other world, Arn Magnusson of Arnäs. But he could not do it; he felt arrogant. He told them merely that his name was Arn.

Gunnar rode off with his betrothed sitting in the saddle in front of him and with his arms around her waist, for as things now stood they still had the strong stallion and there was no reason to walk. He breathed in great gulps of autumn air and he thought it had never smelled freer or more lovely. He rode with his wife-to-be in his arms, feeling the warmth of her body and her pounding heart against his forearm. Together they repeated over and over God's own words about their victorious love.

✠

Darkness fell rapidly that day, and the weather changed to storm. It was impossible to have a conversation outdoors, and they had been told that they could have the parlatorium next to the chapter hall to themselves. As Arn, his cloak flapping in the wind, hurried along the arcade to the meeting, he prayed that Gunvor and Gunnar might be well protected on their way home in the first storm of autumn, protected by more than the love that warmed them. Although he also thought that their love was probably strong enough to protect them against all winds, the winds of life as well as the storm that was on its way.

Brother Guilbert was already waiting in the parlatorium, thoroughly scrubbed and with his hair still wet, when Arn came in. The three candles that were lit flickered a little as he quickly opened and closed the door. They first said Pater Noster together and then a silent prayer for themselves as they faced what now had to be told.

When Brother Guilbert finally looked up after his prayers, his gaze was filled with love for his disciple, but also with an unfamiliar sadness that Arn had glimpsed only a few times before.

"As a brother in this order, my name is Guilbert de Beaune, as you well know," Brother Guilbert slowly began. "But that was also my name in another order which is closely akin to ours; one could call it our armed sister order, which also has the same spiritual father as we do, and you know who that is."

"Holy Saint Bernard de Clairvaux," said Arn, clasping his hands in front of him on the heavy oak table and bowing his head to show that now he would listen without saying anything himself.

"True, he and none other," Brother Guilbert went on, taking a deep breath. "He was also the one who created the Holy Army of God, the Order of the Knights Templar, in which I fought for God's cause for twelve long years. I was a soldier in Outremer for twelve years, and I have faced more than a thousand men in battle—good men and bad, courageous and cowardly, skilled and untrained—and none has ever defeated me. As you quite well realize, there is a theological side to this matter too; it is not merely a matter of knowing how to use your hands and feet. But I'll skip over that aspect for now. The fact is that I never met my match with sword or lance, not even on horseback, and I say this not to boast, because you know that none of us in the cloister would do that. I say it because it's true, and so that you will understand from whom you have learned the art of using the sword, lance, shield, bow, and perhaps most important of all, the horse. Before I go on I have to ask you a question out of sheer curiosity. Did this really never occur to you?"

"No-o," said Arn uncertainly, at the same time bewildered that for all these years and as long as he could remember he had crossed swords with a divinely blessed master. "No, at least not at first, because it was just you and I. But afterwards when I thought about the men who tried to kill me, and the childish and clumsy way they handled their swords, then I began to wonder about things. There was all the difference in the world between them and you, dear Brother Guilbert."

"Well, let's stop there and talk a bit about that. It's not dangerous; in fact I think it's good for you," Brother Guilbert continued as if changing the subject, having said what he wanted to say. "If I understood all this correctly, a man came at you at an angle from behind and took aim at your head, is that right?"

"Yes, I think so," said Arn, squirming a bit. He didn't like the turn the conversation was taking.

"You ducked, of course, and changed your sword to your other hand at the same time. The man facing you dropped his guard because he wasn't looking at your sword but at your head,

which he thought would fall to the ground. You saw the opening and struck at once. But at the same time you instinctively
knew that you should turn around fast and step to the side so
you wouldn't have the second man on you again. And so you
did. The second man managed to raise his sword but now had to
shift his weight to the other foot, and you saw the opening at his
midriff between his elbow and his bent knee and struck again.
That's how it happened, all faster than you or anyone else could
imagine. Am I right?"

Brother Guilbert had spoken with his eyes closed, concentrat-
ing hard, as if he were picturing it all again in his mind's eye.

"Yes, that's exactly right," replied Arn, shamefaced. "But I—"

"Stop!" Brother Guilbert interrupted, holding up his hand.
"Don't apologize any more for what you did; you already have
been given absolution. But now, back to what Father Henri ordered me to explain to you. It wouldn't have made any difference
if there had been three or four of those peasant louts, you could
have killed them all. I honestly don't think that your equal with
a sword exists out there, at least not in this country. But imagine
if you and I were really to fight to the death. What do you think
would happen then?"

"Before I had a chance to blink twice you would strike me
down . . . or maybe before I could blink three times," replied Arn
in bewilderment. He couldn't imagine such an unlikely scenario.

"Not at all!" snorted Brother Guilbert. "Of course I don't
mean that we should practice, which is what we've always done
with me giving the commands and you obeying them. But what
if you could think for yourself and were forced to do it, how
would you attack me?"

"I can't think such sinful thoughts. I would never be able to
raise a weapon in malice against the one I love," said Arn in
shame, as if that thought had just occurred to him.

"I'm ordering you to think of this; we're dealing with theory, and that's nothing to balk at. So, how would you attack me in theory?"

"I probably wouldn't go straight for you," Arn began hesitantly, thinking a moment before he obediently continued wrestling with the problem. "If I went straight for you, your strength and reach would quickly prove decisive. I would have to keep my distance, circle around you, wait and wait until—"

"Yes?" said Brother Guilbert with a little smile. "Until what?"

"Until . . . an opportunity arose, until you moved so much that your weight and strength were no longer to your advantage. But I would never—"

"That's how it is when you're allowed to think for yourself!" Brother Guilbert interrupted him. "And moving on to more important matters; Father Henri's idea never to tell you who you were is easy to understand, from a logical standpoint, isn't it? We had to prevent at all costs a boy from becoming conceited, we had to protect him from all pride, especially when it concerned matters that here in the cloister are counted as base things, though that was hardly the case where I was before I came here. I trained many brothers during my life in Outremer; that's all we did when there was no war. But I've seen few men who possess your God-given gifts when it comes to dexterity with weapons, and you have two secrets that make you very strong. I believe you know what one of them is, don't you?"

"I can change from my right to my left hand," Arn answered in a low voice, looking down at the table before him. It was as if he were ashamed without understanding why.

"Precisely," said Brother Guilbert. "And now I'm going to tell you what your other secret is. You're not a tall man like myself. More than half the men you may encounter with a sword out there will look bigger and stronger. But all your life you have

trained to fight someone who is bigger, and that's what you
do best. So never fear the man who looks big, rather fear the
one who is your own size or smaller. There is one more important thing. The danger of pride, which worried Father Henri
so much, truly exists, although perhaps not in the way he had
imagined. I have seen many men die simply because they were
vain. In the midst of a battle with an inferior opponent, or perhaps someone who merely looked smaller, they came to admire
their own prowess too much. God knows I have seen men die
with a vain smile still on their lips. Remember this and remember it well! For although all your countrymen out there might
be inferior to you in practice, which I do believe, almost any
one of them could wound you or kill you the moment you are
struck by pride. It's as if God's punishment somehow strikes
more quickly the one who sins with weapon in hand. It is the
same with anger or greed. I tell you this, and you must never
forget it: the art you have been taught within these sacred walls
is a blessed art. If you raise your sword in sin, you will bring
down God's punishment upon you. For the third time, never
forget this. Amen."

When Brother Guilbert had finished his explanation they sat
in silence for a while. Arn fixed his gaze absently on one of the
three flickering candle flames, while Brother Guilbert surrepti-
tiously observed him. They seemed to be sitting there waiting
each other out; neither wanted to speak first, afraid that the
other might want to talk about something else.

"Perhaps you're wondering which sin it was that drove me
from the Knights Templar to the Cistercians?" Brother Guilbert
asked him at last.

"Yes, that's clearly what I'd like to know," said Arn. "But I
can't imagine you as a great sinner, dear Brother Guilbert. It
simply doesn't add up."

"No doubt that's because you can't imagine the world out

there, for the world is full of sin and temptations; it's a quag-
mire, it's a field with many pitfalls. My sin was simony, the worst
sin in the rules of the Templar knights. Do you even know what
that is?"

"No," replied Arn truthfully, though he was also astonished.
He had heard a thousand sins spoken of, large and small, but
never this "simony."

"It means to take money for carrying out services on behalf
of the Lord," said Brother Guilbert with a sigh. "In our order we
certainly did administer large sums of money back and forth,
and sometimes it could be difficult to see what was sin and what
was not. But I won't make excuses for myself; I confessed my sin
and I'm doing penance for it even today. It was not granted to
me to die blessed for God's cause with sword in hand. So it goes.
But if it weren't for my sin which led me to this peaceful order,
you never would have met me. Then you would have been a completely different man than you are today. You should also think
about this, since God has a plan for everything that happens."

"I promise not to fail you, not to disappoint you, my dear
brother," said Arn quickly and with feeling.

"Hmm," said Brother Guilbert, leaning forward to gaze with
amusement into Arn's childishly open face and his wide eyes.
"You should probably wait a bit before making promises, because you will be required to make more sooner than you think.
But for now our conversation is done. Tonight you must spend
the hours between midnight mass and morning mass in our
church. Seek God in your heart during this stormy night; this
command comes from Father Henri. Now hurry to sleep a few
hours, and perhaps we'll see each other at midnight mass."

"As you command so shall I obey," muttered Arn and stood
up, bowing to his teacher, and went to his sleeping cell, where
he set his mind to wake up for midnight mass and not oversleep.
Then he fell asleep at once.

Brother Guilbert remained sitting by the flickering candle flames for a while, lost in thought. Then he blew out the candles and strode off to the smithy, which two of the lay brothers had kept going during his talk with Arn. He was not quite finished; he would now use the last of the secret oils he had brought back from Outremer, and there were also details to plan for the ornamentation.

✠

After midnight mass Arn was left alone in the church at Varnhem, and he spent the first hours on his knees at his mother's grave before the altar. For such long prayer sessions he was allowed to kneel on soft cushions that could be brought from the sacristy.

He was in such a daze that he no longer felt that he knew himself. It was as though he were two persons. One was familiar: he was lay brother Arn who belonged more to Vitae Schola than to Varnhem. The other was Arn Magnusson of Arnäs, who was more of a cipher than a real person. On this stormy night he prayed for God's guidance to find what was good in these two, and he prayed to Saint Bernard to show him the way in life so that he would not stumble amid all the sin that seemed to fill the world out there. Finally he prayed for guidance to avoid the sin of pride above all others.

It was not his own belief that pride should be the foremost sin he must try to avoid—he honestly felt himself free of that particular sin. Yet he knew that this was the sin that Father Henri and Brother Guilbert feared so much that they had kept secrets from him.

In his prayers Arn made the storm outside cease and time come to a stop. Or rather, when he entered into prayer with his whole spirit, time no longer existed. So dawn came quickly, and with the dawn the storm abated.

To his surprise the whole choir came in and took up position behind the altar; some of the choir singers gave him kindly winks. He guessed that it was going to be a farewell mass of the type that was held whenever a brother who was much more important than himself was about to depart.

But then he heard from the creak of rope and tackle that the big baptismal font by the church door was being lowered, and when he turned around he saw them preparing the holy water for the baptismal font. Now he had absolutely no idea what was about to happen.

Then the choir suddenly began singing the mightiest of all praise-songs to the Lord, the hymn about the eternal kingdom and eternal power. He could feel at once that the singers were approaching their task with the utmost gravity, truly doing their best. He murmured along with certain passages, keeping his eyes closed, and feeling as if he were by turns freezing cold and very hot. His breast became filled with holy light, and he was lifted by the secret power of the song up toward the Lord.

But when Arn looked up during a slow passage he discovered that some of the singers were craning their necks to look toward the baptismal font, naturally without straying in the least from their song. When he turned around he saw a sight that was the strangest and most astonishing he had seen in all his life. There stood Father Henri, blessing a sword that Brother Guilbert was holding out to him. The sword was sprinkled with holy water as if being baptized. It was unheard of: a sword in the house of God!

After the choir had sung all the verses of the mighty hymn "Te Deum," Father Henri and Brother Guilbert walked up to the altar. Brother Guilbert carried the sword in his outstretched hands as if it were an offering or some other blessed object. The sword was carefully placed in the middle of the altar, and Father

Henri began saying the Pater Noster and everyone murmured along with the prayer. Then Father Henri turned to Arn and signaled for him to move close to his mother's grave, and when he obeyed, the choir took up a new hymn in French which Arn had never heard before. The singers had not mastered it as well as all the others. But Arn was now so filled with the ineffable that he did not hear the words of the song. His wide eyes instead devoured everything that was taking place before him.

Now the sword was taken from the altar and placed directly over his mother's grave in front of him with the hilt toward the altar and the point of the sword toward Arn. It was a wonderfully beautiful sword with a blade that shone of a white tempered steel that Arn had never seen. The hilt of the sword was shaped so that the gilt guard formed a cross, and on it was engraved a motto that could not be misunderstood: *IN HOC SIGNO VINCES*, "In this sign shalt thou conquer," that is, *only* in this sign can one conquer, Arn realized immediately.

The hilt of the sword was shaped perfectly to fit Arn's hands. He grasped the hilt and felt how it lay in his hand like a part of himself. The gilding shone from being newly applied. In strong sunlight he would have a more steady feel for his parrying blows from the brilliance of the gold; the gilding had nothing to do with wealth or ostentation.

Father Henri and Brother Guilbert then knelt down facing Arn on the other side of his mother's grave, and the church fell silent, as if they all were holding their breath. Father Henri whispered to Brother Guilbert that it was probably best if he handled what came next, since he was more familiar with it. Brother Guilbert gave him a quick, pale smile at this understatement, filled as he was by the strange moment. Then he turned to Arn and looked him in the eye.

"Arn, our beloved brother," he began in French, not in Latin, speaking in a loud voice that resounded beneath the vault of the church, "swear now the following oath which I will administer to you:

> I, Arn Magnusson, swear by Jesus Christ
> at the Holy Sepulchre and the Temple
> that the sword I now receive
> shall never be raised in anger
> or for the sake of my personal gain.
> This sword shall serve God's righteous cause,
> the truth, and the honor that is my brother's and my own.
> With this faith and in this sign
> I shall be victorious.
> But should I waver in my faith,
> God shall justly smite me to the ground.
> Amen.

Arn had to repeat the oath twice in French and then a third time in Latin, as he held the sword with both hands around the blade. Then Father Henri took the sword, kissed it, and held it out as he said a silent prayer with his eyes closed. Then he turned to Arn and said these words.

"Never forget your oath to God, my son. This sword which is now yours for as long as you shall live is a blessed sword which can be wielded only by you or by a Templar knight of the Lord. This sword and others like it are the only swords that are allowed inside the house of God, also remember that. And bear your sword without wavering in your love for God and without betraying the honor that accompanies this sword."

With hands that were slightly trembling, Father Henri then handed the sword to Arn, who seemed to hesitate before he finally accepted it. It looked as though he was afraid that the sword might burn him.

But when he held it in his hands, the choir took up a new and jubilant hymn which he did not know, and it too was in French.

✠

Arn set off that very day. But this time his departure from Varnhem was better prepared than his first journey, which had quickly ended in misfortune. The horse he now rode was the stallion Shimal, who had already served in breeding for the year and need not come back until it was time again. Arn had donned clothing made of gray and red fabric, like a man of the base world. He could not even remember the time as a child when he had worn attire other than that of a lay brother. And they had cut his hair so that it now was short but even around his head and there was no trace of the tonsure.

Brother Rugiero had prepared a heavy knapsack, and no one was going to trick him into losing it as soon as he left the walls, not this time. It also contained a good selection of plants that had to be kept moist in their leather sacks, along with seeds and fruit pits.

By his side hung the mighty sword in a simple leather scabbard, the sword that felt so light in his hand, as if it became a living part of himself when he swung it. The sword was so perfectly balanced that he could easily have stood upright and cleaned his toenails with it, not even holding it in both hands.

With a few words of thinly disguised pride Brother Guilbert had told him everything about such swords and what differentiated them from ordinary swords. Well, perhaps not everything, he added modestly. But the rest Arn would soon discover for himself.

Arn had taken a lengthy and emotional leave of them all. He was utterly filled with their love for him, which he had never really understood until that last mass when he saw and heard the great solemnity of the singers, offering him the most beautiful farewell they could give him.

Finally, out in the receptorium he was alone with Father Henri and Brother Guilbert. Father Henri nodded silently for him to mount his horse, and Arn swung up into the saddle of the impatiently prancing Shimal.

"There is one last thing you should think about now as you venture out into the other world better equipped than last time," said Father Henri, stopping because he seemed briefly overcome by his emotions. "You carry a mighty sword at your side, as you already know. But remember also the words of Saint Bernard: *'See, God's warriors, what are your weapons? Are they not foremost your shield of faith, your helmet of salvation, and your chain mail of gentleness?'* "

"Yes, father, I swear never to forget that," replied Arn, looking Father Henri in the eye without blinking.

"Au revoir, mon petit chevalier Perceval," Brother Guilbert then said, and gave the impatient stallion a hard slap so that he galloped off at once with thundering hooves, heading out through the narrow stone passage to the world outside.

"That was a bit incautious of you. What if he'd fallen off the horse?" muttered Father Henri sadly.

"Arn doesn't fall off horses, and that's hardly the thing that threatens him most just now," said Brother Guilbert, shaking his head with a smile at his prior's unfounded concern.

"By the way, I don't like that nonsense about Perceval and the Holy Grail and such vulgar songs," Father Henri snapped as he turned abruptly and took a few steps toward the oak gate. But as so often happened, he thought of something else he wanted to say and turned halfway around.

"Perceval this and that, all those things will soon be forgotten like all the other base stories, it's rubbish!"

"For something that is rubbish, you seem to know these vulgarities rather well yourself, father," Brother Guilbert said with a bold laugh, displaying a merriment he didn't usually show toward his prior.

Without a doubt both of them were moved by the farewell with Arn, although neither of them wanted to admit it. But Brother Guilbert, unlike Father Henri, was firmly convinced that he would see Arn again. Because unlike his prior, he was also entirely certain of what the task was that God had prepared for young Arn.

Chapter 8

Herr Magnus was in a bad mood as he sat in the longhouse in the middle of a sunny afternoon, drinking too much ale. He was regretting that he was unable to love his second son Arn, whom his wife Sigrid, blessed be her memory, had loved above all else in life.

Magnus had a hard time admitting, even though he was now forcing himself to do so with the aid of liquor, that he had two grown sons who did not bless his house with the honor that was due their clan. For what good did it do if they had royal blood in their veins, as long as people pointed their fingers and snickered at them both.

In Eskil's case Magnus had long since accepted how matters stood, because what people still had a hard time trusting was everything that belonged to the future. This included trade and new ways of using the soil and making the silver grow in the coffers; in all this Eskil was very talented and would probably leave an inheritance twice as large as what he would one day receive.

Those who reproached Eskil because he was not interested in the more manly virtues were ignorant wretches. They understood nothing of God's will behind human striving in earthly life. With regard to everything that had true meaning Eskil would become a wise and wealthy lord of Arnäs; about that there was no doubt.

The fact that his eldest son was certainly no man of swordplay was something that Magnus could live with, however, without great disgrace, since it was to the advantage of Arnäs that Eskil would live longer for not using sword and shield.

But the fact that his second son was also utterly lacking in the manly virtues was worse and made the disgrace much greater. Magnus had heard some of his retainers whispering scornfully about Arn as the *nun* from Varnhem. He had chosen to swallow the affront and pretend that he hadn't heard it rather than draw more attention to what was said. It was bad enough that his retainers seemed to be entirely right in this case, for it was not easy to understand what the monks had done with the little boy— whom Magnus remembered as a lively rascal who had learned to use a bow and arrow when he was very young. There had been lovely prayers said at table since Arn came home, but that added little to the honor of the house.

The boy had come riding up one beautiful autumn day on a skinny horse that provoked much laughter; even worse, he wore a sword at his side that seemed designed for women, if such a sword could be imagined. It was much too long and too light, with poor smithwork and too bright a sheen. Magnus had soon seen to it that the sword was put away in the tower's armory so as not to prompt malicious laughter toward the innocent boy.

A father had to love his lawful sons, that was God's inescapable commandment. But the question was how much disappointment and dishonor could gnaw at that love until in the end what he felt could no longer be called love.

Another question, of course, was whether they could even make a man of the boy; it seemed as though he had been with the monks so long that he had become like one of them. Magnus felt that in a way, which was not entirely to his pleasure, it was like having a priest in the house, as if at the evening meal they could no longer talk freely about what they happened to be thinking but had to watch their words so as not to sound ungodly.

Nor did Arn drink to any extent. This had been evident at their first meal to welcome him home, which was intended to be a joyful celebration. Just like the account in the Holy Scriptures, Magnus had slaughtered the fatted calf upon the prodigal son's return, although in this instance it was a fatted suckling pig, which was much finer. And they had all dressed up for the feast, Arn wearing some of Eskil's clothes that he had grown out of in recent years, for Eskil had almost degenerated to the state of his great-grandfather Folke the Fat.

But during the evening no one could fail to notice that this son Arn was not much of a man, since he drank only two tankards of ale the whole evening and picked at the excellent pork like a woman. Even though he did make an effort to seem amenable, he was a bit slow to follow everything that was said, he had a hard time understanding jokes, and he was not quick enough to toss words back to anyone who tried to draw him into the revelry. He seemed to have inherited none of his mother's quick wit or sly tongue.

Since ale loosened his thoughts the same way it loosened his tongue, Magnus reeled into the abhorrent idea that Arn had become like a woman among the monks. Such stories were told by the ungodly and those of little faith about the unnamable sins of certain monks.

With his acuity now somewhat muddied Magnus tried to judge whether the fact that Arn seemed more comfortable among women meant that he had succumbed to that particular abomination of the monks, or whether his proclivity for getting along better with women actually indicated the opposite.

It must mean the abomination, he thought at first. Since such fallen men were just like women and so perhaps felt more comfortable with women.

It must mean the opposite, he corrected himself. For if a man had fallen into an abomination of a similar type, such as fornicating with heifers, wouldn't he seek out heifers more or less in secret? There were plenty of young thrall boys at Arnäs, but considering how everyone was keeping an eye on the irresolute prodigal son, the slightest attempt to assault one of the thrall boys would have led to a storm of gossip. And that would not have escaped the attention of the lord's family.

No, he was definitely not a catamite. That would have been the worst shame he could have brought down upon his father's house and his clan. In that case he would have to be killed quickly to restore the honor of the house.

Magnus shouted angrily to his terrified house thralls to bring out more ale; they obeyed wordlessly and swift as the wind.

After reflecting on his latest conclusions, when after half a tankard he remembered where he was, Magnus began to weep, overwhelmed by emotion. In truth he had thought much too ill of Arn who was his true son, and who was the apple of his dear Sigrid's eye. What did the Lord God actually mean by all this? First Arn was to be given as a little boy to God; all the signs had spoken so clearly that there could be no doubt. And if Arn had remained a man of God for the rest of his life all would have been well, for Magnus certainly was not among those who denied all the good that the monks had accomplished in Western Götaland. On the contrary, he admitted to all and sundry that much of what had made Arnäs a better farm than others was due largely to the monks' knowledge.

But now Arn, instead of doing God's good work among the

monks, had been released to what had once been his home, and he came as half a man and half a monk. What could be the meaning of that? Those who said that the ways of the Lord were often inscrutable had indeed good reason for saying so.

But even worse perhaps was that the boy persisted in working like a thrall. Only a few days after Arn had returned to Arnäs, he began busily digging, building walls, and hammering everywhere. It hadn't helped matters when Magnus carefully explained to his son that he didn't need to toil that way, since he could use thralls to perform such tasks, and there were plenty of them idle this time of year. Then Arn had merely increased his activity as he ran from one job to the next. It was hard to know what would come of all this, but it would have been unwise for Magnus to stop it before he knew more.

One thing, however, had won the admiration of all the men, even the most scornful retainers. Arn had examined all the estate's horses, and he had forged a new type of horseshoe with a nail that stuck up from the forward edge of the hoof and prevented the shoe from falling off. These horseshoes were certainly an improvement over the old ones. Magnus had asked both his retainers and the smithy thralls, and they all agreed.

It was a good thing, because anything that was made better at Arnäs was considered a good thing, and that was the opinion of Magnus as well as Eskil. But what was embarrassing was that his lawful son should be working in the filth and smoke as if he were a thrall, and was not in the least ashamed of it. On the contrary, when Arn said grace at table, which he now did in normal language, he always thanked God for the day's blessed work.

Eskil had been less of two minds about all of this than his father, saying that knowledge must never be disdained. And the manual skills, which his brother Arn had learned so well from the monks, were something that could be taught to others. If Arn taught the thralls, they would eventually be able to take over the work themselves. But first they would have to be properly trained, and the only one who could do that was Arn. It was wrong to scorn such work if it moved the estate forward. Advances were to the advantage of everyone.

Perhaps it was so, Magnus consoled himself, that Arn had brought so many new techniques from the monks that Arnäs would be made stronger and richer. Although it was crucial to ensure that the thralls were taught quickly, so that Arn wouldn't have to go about disgracing his clan by continuing to sweat like a thrall.

Something even better, thought Magnus, now that the ale had made him sentimental, was that Arn had become reconciled with his stepmother Erika Joarsdotter. Magnus didn't know exactly what Arn and his wife Erika did out in the cookhouses, since he never set foot inside, but Erika seemed very pleased and happy about what had evidently taken place. Besides, it was good for Erika that someone in the family treated her well. Eskil had always had a hard time enduring his stepmother, and although Magnus had got her with child several times, since such was expected of him, it was not until the third pregnancy that she had given birth to a son. That son was not going to end up with any monks, by God. He would be taught by the retainers from childhood on, Magnus had decided.

Erika had a deformity that everyone noticed. She was lovely to look at, but as soon as she opened her mouth anyone could hear that she spoke with a cleft palate, and the sound of her words came more from her nose than her mouth. Less polite people might then burst out laughing, which had caused Erika never to speak when strange men were present. She was equally timid whenever there was a feast and she had to ensure that the guests' women enjoyed the celebration. Magnus had a hard time talking to his wife, and he often thought back to Sigrid, who was the person he had felt closest to of anyone. But he could say this only to himself or to God.

However, it was not to be ignored that Erika was the niece of a king, that she had royal blood, and that the two daughters and one son to whom she had given birth also had royal blood, and from two separate lineages at that.

⊣⊢

An angel had come to Arnäs. Everything he touched instantly became better or more beautiful, and he was the only man Erika Joarsdotter had ever met who spoke to her as if she had the wit of everyone else. He never let on that he found her speech muddled; instead he excused his confusion by saying that he had not yet re-gained his childhood language, since he had spoken mostly with Danes when he was growing up. And unlike his older brother Eskil, he never gave any sign that Erika was like a stranger who had replaced the boys' mother.

Quite early, right after dawn when all the other men were still asleep after the welcome feast held in his honor, Arn had come out, sober and freshly washed, to the cookhouses where Erika had just begun the day's long work with her house thralls. He had politely and with kind and considerate words asked her to show him the domains for which she was responsible as mistress of the manor, and they had taken a tour of the storehouses and cookhouses. From all the questions he asked, Erika soon grasped that he knew more than most men about the way meat had to be hung, smoked, and stored and how fish should be cooked. And he seemed not in the least embarrassed by his knowledge.

It did not take long before he began to change everything, al-though he was careful to let her accompany him and help make the decisions. He took her by the arm and walked around with her, explaining what could be done at once and what would take more time.

Arnäs was a village flanked by water on two sides. At the far end of the village close to Lake Vänern stood the castle and the defensive walls where the two arms of the water narrowed and formed a moat. But the drainage from the tanneries and latrines, from the slaughterhouse and brewery, went into both bodies of water, and according to Arn that uncleanliness was the reason that many of the thralls' children had red eyes and pustular lips as well as nasty rashes on their skin. Many of the youngest also died even after surviving the most dangerous period after birth.

The great transformation would be that in the future they would dump waste only in the eastern arm of water around Arnäs, while the western one would be kept free of refuse. By drawing pictures in the sand, pointing out and describing the whole process, Arn had shown her how they would be able to direct a water flow from the clean side in through the cookhouses and then discharge it into the unclean water. With a constant flow of water through the cookhouses they would save much time in their work, and the cookhouses could be kept clean so that all the food was more palatable. The cookhouses would also be improved by laying brick over the packed dirt floors, at a slight slope so that water would run off into the new drains.

The most difficult thing to change was the disposal of human waste. According to Arn it was fertilizer as good as livestock manure if it was used for that purpose, although it was a worse pollutant than livestock manure if it got into the food or water. Instead of letting each thrall follow the call of nature wherever it seemed suitable, now they would all be forced to use special latrine pits with crossbars, and anyone caught shitting anywhere else would be sharply reprimanded.

There was some grumbling among the thralls at these changes, but Erika Joarsdotter showed herself to be a stern mistress, because she soon came to trust Arn more than she did anyone else.

Since she had spent five years as a novice in a convent before she was suddenly fetched by her father to be married off, she was actually familiar with much of what Arn described to her. Perhaps she had thought that God had arranged things differently inside the cloister walls, that this better ordering of things belonged to the higher world, that everything *intra muros* was supposed to be much cleaner than on the outside, as though cleanliness had a spiritual significance. That was why, before Arn arrived and opened her eyes, she had not even imagined that they might have the same orderliness in ordinary life as they did inside the cloister.

With Arn's arrival Erika Joarsdotter's days at Arnäs had brightened, and her own responsibility as mistress of the manor had become easier to bear. She got up before dawn happier than she ever could have imagined. And when the men in the long-house soon discovered that some of the food put on the table was different and better than before, they began to give her words of praise, which they had never done before. They especially liked the wonderful smoked ham.

Arn had brought along some sausages and smoked ham when he came from Varnhem. Even though most of it was consumed during the welcome feast and no one remembered much about the monk food, Erika had asked him how such things were made. Arn was soon busy building a smokehouse out of tarred lumber. When the building was finished he tested it on some pieces of pork; then he showed her the whole process, and soon she and her house thralls could smoke ham so that it seemed to have come straight from a monastery.

But by then Arn was already working on a brickworks. There was clay suitable for the task on the riverbank above the tannery on the eastern arm of the water, and it took Arn about a week to make his team of thralls understand how they were to shape the clay in wooden forms so that each piece was exactly the same size. He showed them how to bake the clay just as they baked bread, but for a longer time and at a higher heat using a bellows. Soon a new storehouse of brick began to rise next to the cook-houses. Arn took Erika on many tours around the building and up in the scaffolding to describe how they would be able to store ice from Lake Vänern to cool the brick chamber even during the hottest days of summer.

In her evening prayers Erika constantly thanked God that He had sent them this prodigal son. Although he was not her son, he treated her like his mother, giving her days at Arnäs a light and a meaning that they had not had before. But to God she did not dare say what she thought every day, that Arn had come like an angel to Arnäs.

✠

Eskil was ambivalent about Arn. He didn't really know what to make of this younger brother who suddenly rode into the castle courtyard one day on an ugly horse as if he had returned from the living dead, as miraculously as he had once been sent away, because of some alleged miracle.

His first feeling had been strong brotherly love, for what Eskil remembered better than anything else in his life was the day when he and his younger brother were torn from each other out-side the door of the longhouse. How he had run after the wagon in which Arn was taken away, and how at last he had collapsed sobbing in the wagon tracks, watching Arn in a haze of tears and road dust disappear forever, abducted on the orders of an incomprehensible God.

When Eskil embraced Arn upon his return to the very place where they once had parted, his first impression was of a skinny, almost undernourished young man, until he felt the bearlike strength in Arn's arms when they were flung around his waist. Arn hugged Eskil so hard that he almost lost his breath. That had certainly been a moment of almost incomprehensible joy.

But during the big welcome ale on that first evening, Eskil had already begun to feel uncomfortable for his younger brother. Arn didn't seem able to join in the celebration; he almost rudely shoved away his food, he drank ale like a woman, and in other ways he seemed to be a bit slow.

An uneasiness seemed to settle in the air as father and elder brother drew back from Arn, and he in turn sensed their displeasure and sought instead the company of the thralls and the mistress of the estate. The retainers were the first to make faces, roll their eyes, and mockingly clasp their hands behind Arn's back. It made Eskil want to reprimand them, but he couldn't because he himself shared the feelings that the retainers displayed with their scorn.

For a time the mood between them was neither light nor dark, and each minded his own business. Neither Magnus nor Eskil bothered to find out what Arn was working on with the thralls and cookhouse at the far southern end of Arnäs, since they seldom went there themselves.

But some things were impossible to avoid noticing. For new sorts of meat were put on the table, and Eskil found most delicious a smoked ham that was not hard and dry and salty like the winter rations. This ham was so deliciously juicy that his mouth watered just thinking about it. And the other thing that was impossible not to notice was how Mistress Erika had changed, how she began speaking loudly and without embarrassment despite her ugly voice, and how she laughed and giggled at the table when she answered questions about the new things she could now present for both dinner and supper.

Eskil was a man in favor of changes, just as he came to understand that his mother Sigrid had been as well, more so than his father. Changes that were good created wealth; if they were not good, then a different change was made. That's how it was and would remain at Arnäs; that's why their farm was better and bigger and richer than other people's farms where nothing was ever changed.

For this reason Eskil could soon no longer tolerate remaining uninformed. He told Arn he would like to see what was happening, and Arn immediately expressed how pleased he was, almost elated, and he wanted to jump up in the middle of the meal to show everything to his older brother.

What Eskil saw when they made their rounds caused him to change his fundamental opinion. Arn was in truth not slow at all; he knew exactly what he was doing. Eskil quickly admitted to himself that he had been unwise to judge him so hastily.

When they went down to the thralls' quarters everything looked different because all the garbage had been mucked out, the way the cows' stalls were mucked out in the winter. They could walk around without worrying where they set their feet.

At first Eskil said something in jest that he soon had cause to regret. He remarked that of course things looked better, but perhaps it wasn't much use letting thralls live more like real people.

Then Arn explained quite seriously that the thralls were healthier now that all the uncleanliness was gone, that more of their children would survive, that healthy thralls were naturally much better than sick ones, just as living thralls were better than dead ones. He said that the contagion from sick thralls could also be spread to people, and thus cleanliness was of benefit to all. Then he explained his plans for the two waterways, how one would be kept clean, and how the latrine pits would replace using anywhere for a toilet, and how the shit could then be used as fertilizer and thereby do good instead of spreading disease.

The seriousness with which Arn could speak of such base things as the thralls' shit made a twofold impression on Eskil. On one hand his words seemed funny as if they were a joke; on the other Arn seemed so boldly convincing that it made his head spin. Imagine that such simple measures, which even the thralls themselves could maintain, might really result in great improvements. Much would be gained with little work, and without the expenditure of a single silver mark.

By the time Arn had finished leading him through the cookhouses and the new smokehouse, and explained the concept of the icehouse, Eskil was so taken by these inventions that he had tears in his eyes. For he no longer had any doubt. He was absolutely convinced that his brother, although not a man that dull retainers might respect, had brought a great and blessed knowledge with him from the cloister. And this knowledge would truly allow Arnäs to take great new steps forward. For it was indisputable that everything had actually stood still for many years. Things at Arnäs were better than at other farms, yet there had still been little progress.

Eskil threw his arms around Arn, asking at once for forgiveness for failing to understand that his own brother really was his brother and his equal. Arn then had to console both Eskil and himself, because they showed great emotion. The house thralls who stood nearby stared at them in astonishment.

When Eskil noticed this he straightened up and gave the house thralls a stern look; they immediately slunk off and then Eskil suggested that Arn accompany him to the accounting chamber in the tower and share a tankard or two of ale.

Arn was about to say something about having too much work awaiting him, and that only at the end of the workday should a man enjoy the fruits of what he had accomplished by the sweat of his brow. But he quickly changed his mind when he realized that he shouldn't impose rules from his former life on the time he spent together with his own brother. After all, it was this very acknowledgment that he had been waiting for, including it in so many of his prayers. He had sensed the coolness and apprehension from both his father and his brother, and he had grieved over it. But he had also hoped that they would soon understand what he was doing, and that what he did was good. So it wouldn't be a sin to drink ale with his own brother, even if it was the middle of the afternoon.

✠

Herr Magnus sought an excuse not to take Arn along when he had to travel north to negotiate an inheritance in the clan in Norway. Occasionally it could be difficult enough to take Eskil to visit the Norwegian kinfolk, since Norwegian feasts often devolved into all sorts of swordplay when their strong ale took effect. Anyone who was not quick or dexterous or old enough to say no to young men's games would risk coming to serious injury among the Norsemen.

Despite this danger he wanted to have Eskil with him, because the business deals they had to do were difficult and unusual. Even after a great deal of ale Eskil was quite able to calculate in his head the value of all sorts of goods and say what it corresponded to in silver. The two of them had discussed the matter at length, deciding that it would be wisest to sell the Norwegian inheritance.

While it was a man's honor to retain his inheritance and not let it pass to some other clan, the advantages of owning a farm next to the great fjord were small unless one intended to live there. If they sold the property they would acquire more silver, which could be spent on something better. As things now stood, since Arn had come home, they had to look toward the future when perhaps even he must have something to inherit. So it would be better to buy new property within a safe distance from Arnäs or in a province neighboring to the Erik clan south of Skara. Or why not buy from the Pål clan near Husaby? Each of these possibilities would be safer, at least for Arn's sake, than sending him to the Norsemen who were so quick to the sword.

In the meantime a simple solution had been found to the dilemma of how to tell Arn that he must cancel his journey to Norway without hurting his feelings. It was the time of autumn when Svarte and his thrall-son Kol went out to hunt deer and wild boars. They had already brought home a good amount of game. Arn and Erika had plenty to do in the new smokehouse, since Arn had said that he was sure the wild game would be better smoked than salted and dried. But just before the journey to Norway, and the difficult, imminent conversation between Magnus and Arn about how unwise it would be for an inexperienced son to visit the Norwegians, Arn himself made a request. He wanted to accompany Svarte and Kol on their hunting trips and learn something about hunting.

Magnus was doubly glad at this request, for now he could avoid the whole embarrassing explanation about the Norwegian kinsmen and their swords and halberds after the ale. Besides, this was the first time that Arn had shown any interest in learning something that was part of the chivalrous life. A good hunter enjoyed great respect, even if he was a thrall.

But Magnus had little hope that Arn, who for better or worse was still a half monk, would be able to learn anything about the challenging but manly art of the hunt.

Svarte shared this view, but he was obliged to obey. When he heard that he would have to take along the other half-man of a son, he knew at once how things would go. Once, two years before, he had been forced to do the same with the lord's eldest son, Eskil, who at least had not yet grown as round as a cask of ale. Yet he was intolerable trouble, and because of him the hunt brought in almost nothing. It was not easy to take along the master's son, who had to decide about everything but understood nothing.

But Svarte was less sure of this second son Arn than he was of Herr Eskil, who was at least very like his father. The other thralls had talked a lot about Arn, describing him in several ways as a competent man who could do all the things that the rest of the master's family could not do, and he had a kind nature besides. He had never raised his hand to anyone, had never ordered anyone whipped, and had not even spoken in harsh words.

Svarte sensed that this peculiarity had more to do with the odd religion of the master's family than with what the retainers and others gossiped about. For the family's belief in the gods was incomprehensible in many respects. Their gods were so numerous that no one could keep them straight, and they were always chastising people even when they hadn't done anything special; as though the punishments were mostly for what people thought. As if the gods could hear what a person was thinking!

As far as this Arn was concerned, Svarte remembered quite well the day the boy went up in the high tower after a jackdaw and fell. The boy lost his breath for a while before he revived, but by then the master's family had prayed and pleaded to their gods and promised everything possible or impossible. The whole episode ended with their sending away the boy as punishment for themselves, or was it punishment for the boy? It was hard to know which it was, since one solution was just as difficult to understand as the other.

But now the punishment was apparently over, and he had come home; although he was no longer like any of the others. Svarte, who was reckoned the best smith at Arnäs, had watched Arn in the smithy and he reluctantly had to admit that there wasn't much he could teach the boy about hammer and anvil. If he were to be quite truthful, the opposite was more likely, which was embarrassing enough and not easy to swallow.

When they were about to set off, several things happened that set Svarte to thinking. Since they had a master's son with them they were allowed to go to the tower chamber and select freely from the cache of weapons. When Svarte saw how Arn picked up the bows and tested drawing them, handling even the strongest of them with no visible sign of effort, he knew that this master's boy had surely held more than one bow. Arn also unerringly chose correctly from the arrows once he decided which bow he wanted to take with him. Svarte had very dubious notions about what white Christian people did in their cloisters. The fact that they obviously practiced archery did not jibe at all with the scornful jests that he and the other thralls made about the matter.

After they had loaded their packhorses and brought out their mounts for saddling, Kol cautiously tried to tell Arn that as the son of Arnäs he could take whatever horse he liked, and there were many better ones to choose from than that monk horse, which didn't look like much. Then Arn laughed, though not maliciously, and said that as soon as they had ridden a bit on the open field he would show them that this was no ordinary horse.

Svarte was no more of a horseman than anyone else, nor was he any worse. He shoed all the horses at Arnäs, nowadays with the new horseshoes that were indeed better than the ones they had used before. He rode like all the others who had anything to do with horses, free men or thralls, peasants or retainers. But he couldn't ride like Arn, he had to admit that at once. When they were some distance from Arnäs, Arn did things that no other rider could do on horseback; Svarte and his son Kol agreed on that. The horse may not have looked like much when it was standing still, but when it ran so hard and so fast with Arn at the reins it was just as they had imagined Odin's steed would look.

They didn't have an easy time making themselves understood and often had to ask questions that made them feel embarrassed, so little was said for the first few hours.

As soon as they got up into the oak forests on Kinnekulle above Husaby, Arn showed himself to be just as wretched a hunter as his brother. But what clearly differentiated him from Herr Eskil was that he realized when he had made a mistake, apologized, and then asked many questions about the correct way to proceed.

This happened when for the first time they got very close to some deer taking their rest in a clearing. There was a strong wind, so they approached from downwind. Since there had been little rain, the fall leaves rattled in the wind, disturbing the stags' hearing so that the men could probably get within range even though it was broad daylight. Svarte and Kol had seen the animals well before Arn suddenly noticed them, announcing eagerly that he saw several deer up ahead. Since the deer surely heard what Arn had to say as well as Svarte and Kol did, and immediately understood what was going on, they jumped up and bounded off.

Around the campfire that evening Arn asked many childish questions, which Svarte and Kol answered patiently without revealing what they thought of such questions. Yes, he always had to approach from downwind, otherwise deer and boars, and all other animals for that matter, would know that he was coming. Yes, game could hear a person at a distance of an arrow-shot if it was quiet with little wind, otherwise from half an arrow-shot. No, he shouldn't shoot the ones with horns, they tasted the worst and especially this time of year when they'd just been in rut. Yes, rut was the time when the stags mounted the does and then the stags' meat smelled strongly of their piss. It was the same thing with boars; you shouldn't shoot the big ones but rather those of medium size. It would be good if he could shoot a sow with many small piglets following her, because when she lay down to die all the little ones would gather around her. And if he had luck and the gods' support he could shoot all the piglets one by one, and they tasted the best.

As the thralls sat there by the campfire, politely answering the ignorant questions of their master's son, a loud bellow was heard from the oak forest nearby. Arn jumped up in terror and grabbed his bow and quiver. He peered quizzically at Svarte and Kol, who sat quite still by the fire, smiling. When Arn saw that the others were not afraid, he sat back down but looked quite bewildered.

Svarte explained that uninformed people called that sound everything from the battle cry of the mountain king to the roar of the troll taking revenge on human beings. Such evils did exist, of course, but this was an old stag that still had some of his rut left in his body. The sound scared many people out of their wits because it was the loudest sound in the forest, but for hunters it was good to hear. It meant that in a few hours, when the first light of dawn appeared, they could hope to find all the does and yearlings that the old stags were after. If they followed the old stags in rut, tracking their roars in the dark, especially a bit earlier in the autumn, it was the surest method of finding does and yearlings to bring home to the spit-turners and cookhouses, for salting and drying.

Early that morning, well before dawn, they ventured cautiously into the forest to listen for the old stag and his does. But it was difficult to walk quietly since the night had arrived with frost. The frozen oak leaves and beech leaves and acorns crunched and crackled with each step, even under the light tread of Svarte and Kol. When Arn walked it sounded to the others like a flock of retainers in full armor. When Svarte didn't dare go any closer they had reached a clearing in the oak forest next to a tarn. They had the light breeze in their faces, since Svarte never would have approached in any other way, nor would Kol. But the tarn lay straight ahead of them on the other side of the clearing, in the direction of the wind. From the tarn the mist rose so thick that they could hear the mighty roars of rut from the old stag quite close, but they couldn't see the does or year-lings except to glimpse them occasionally in the mist. After a while Arn asked, very quietly as he had now learned to do, why they didn't shoot. They whispered back that they were too far out of range; they couldn't hit a stag until they were at half that distance. Arn gave them a skeptical look and whispered back that he could shoot.

Svarte wanted to shake his head at such nonsense but wisely thought that it would be better for Arn to learn from his own mistakes than from his thrall. Curtly he repeated something he had said by the campfire the night before. Aim far behind the shoulder, through the lungs. Then the stag would stand still if the shot was true. Because low behind the shoulder was the heart. And the stag would take off in fright and spread his fear to the others. If the stag was hit well in the lungs and stood still, he could try to shoot another one.

Arn nocked an arrow onto his bowstring, held it fast with his left thumb, and crossed himself. Then they waited.

After a wait that surely seemed much longer to Arn than to the thralls, three stags stood still, listening into the mist. But they were clearly visible. Arn touched Svarte lightly on the shoulder so he could ask with his eyes rather than say anything. Svarte whispered quietly in Arn's ear that they were in good position, but too far away. Arn nodded that he understood.

But then he suddenly drew his bow all the way and seemed to take aim an arm's length above the yearling that was clos-est within range. He let the arrow fly without hesitating. They heard the arrow strike, but then saw the yearling stand still as if uncomprehending that it now harbored death within itself. Arn shot another arrow. And another in rapid succession. Now they could hear the stags running off.

Arn wanted to run out into the mist to see what had happened, but Kol grabbed him by the arm and then grew frightened at what he had done. Yet Arn wasn't the least bit angry about being held back; he nodded that he'd understood. They had to wait until the sun had burned away the elf dance, which the thralls believed could bring nothing but trouble and misfortune.

After they unpacked their cloaks bundled on their backs, Svarte and Kol wrapped themselves in them and lay down next to a log and fell asleep. Arn sat down but couldn't sleep. He had shot as well as he could and was sure that his first two shots had hit home, but he was uncertain about what had happened to the third shot, although he had a feeling that something was wrong. Maybe he had shot too quickly, maybe he had been too tense. His heart had pounded so loudly that he thought the deer might have heard it.

When the sun later burned off the mist and they could see clearly, Svarte woke up and then roused his son. They went out into the meadow to see what they would find.

The yearling that Arn had shot first lay dead where it was struck, and nothing else was to be expected, explained Svarte as he thoughtfully examined the kill. The arrow had gone through both of the deer's lungs and out the other side. That was why the yearling lay where it had been hit. It had felt no pain and so had not tried to run.

The doe wasn't lying where it should have been, but Svarte and Kol immediately found traces of blood. When they examined the blood they nodded to each other and then to Arn. Kol said that this doe had also been struck in the lungs and would be lying dead somewhere nearby; they would soon find it. He rammed an arrow into the ground where they found the blood, and then he and his father bent forward and slowly surveyed the place where they all thought the third deer had been standing when Arn took his shot. They found blood on a blade of grass that they rubbed between their fingertips and then sniffed, and with that they seemed once again to know everything.

Svarte explained that this deer had been mortally wounded but not killed, and that it lay in fever two or three arrow-shots away. They could now bring the horses, for it was no use coming on her too soon. The doe must be allowed to die in peace.

When they returned with the horses it turned out that everything Svarte and Kol had said was true. The doe which Arn had shot with his last arrow also lay dead, although farther away. Svarte showed how Arn's arrow had struck a bit too far back, but when Arn apologized in shame, Svarte couldn't help smiling, even though he tried not to show it. He explained gravely that even if a deer was standing in precisely the right spot when the arrow was loosed, it might well take a small step forward as the arrow was on its way. That was what had happened.

Toward dusk they hunted deer again but without success. Svarte said that it was because the breeze had subsided and was unreliable, so the deer easily got wind of the humans no matter how they moved.

They were still in a very good mood when darkness fell, and the three deer they had taken hung in a row from a strong oak bough. They had indeed had good hunting that day.

By the campfire Svarte and Kol offered the deer's hearts to their gods, possibly believing that their master's son did not understand what they were doing when they turned their backs and muttered over the fire in their own language. When they were about to eat supper, however, Svarte and his son found themselves in a quandary. Kol had gone and fetched fresh hazel branches which he placed over the fire after it had died down, and on the osiers they skewered small pieces of liver and kidneys with some onion that Svarte took from one of his leather bags. To the amazement of the two thralls, Arn immediately showed himself willing to share their meal, although they all knew that such food was only for thralls. But Arn ate with the same appetite as the others, and even wanted another helping, pushing aside his salt pork. This served to bring all of them closer together and they felt less strained.

When they lay down, sated and full, by the fire and wrapped their cloaks tighter around them for the night, Svarte ventured to ask whether it was in the cloister of the White Christ that Arn had learned to shoot with bow and arrow in that way. Arn, who had by now realized that he had shot well, explained that it was not at all normal for monks to shoot with a bow and arrow, but that he had been especially fortunate to have a very skilled teacher. Svarte and Kol laughed loudly at this, and Kol said that they would very much like to meet this teacher. But when Arn replied in a jesting tone that such might indeed be arranged as long as Kol and Svarte agreed to be baptized, their faces clouded over and they stared silently into the fire.

As if to gloss over his offensive joke, Arn said that whatever they thought about the cloister of the White Christ, it was still a world where there were no thralls, a world where each man had the same value as every other man. But he received only silence in reply. Yet he didn't want to drop the subject, so he asked in words as clear and simple as he could muster why Svarte and Kol were still thralls as they had been ever since Arn was a little boy. Many others had been given their freedom, so why not Svarte and his family?

Svarte, who now had to reply no matter how unwilling he felt, reluctantly explained that whether a thrall could be set free or not depended on what each person had accomplished. The thralls who worked the land were more often set free than those who worked in masonry or as hunters. Those who tilled the earth were put to work breaking new ground for Arnäs and were given their freedom in lieu of a leasehold. But hunting for pelts in the winter and for meat in the autumn provided game directly to the households of Arnäs. A thrall engaged in such activities could not become a free man, since he did not work for the main estate itself. And the same applied to all masonry work, and smithing too for that matter. Feeling that he may have gone too far and spoken too boldly, Svarte now added that he wasn't complaining; many of the carpenters were in the same situation.

Arn pondered a moment as the others waited quietly, and then he said that he found this system unfair since, if he understood it right, ermine and marten pelts brought in much silver, probably as much as barley, turnips, and wheat. Kol laughed almost scornfully at this, and when Arn asked him why, Kol said with mirth in his voice that it was probably hard to find a way to make thralldom fair. Svarte kicked him in the leg under the skin rug to make him shut his trap.

But Arn was not the least bit angry at Kol's boldness. On the contrary, he nodded to himself and then offered an apology for having such ill-conceived thoughts; Kol was absolutely right. But he himself would never, could never, own another man as a thrall.

Since Svarte and Kol had not a single word to say about this matter, their conversation died out. Arn said evening prayers for all of them, wrapped himself in his cloak and skins in a way that showed he had slept outside before, and lay down to sleep. He then pretended not to listen as the other two lay whispering to each other.

But Kol and Svarte had a hard time falling asleep. They lay close together for the sake of warmth as they were used to doing, but for a long time they wondered about this master's son and his peculiar gods.

✠

They got up early because of the night frost, well before dawn, and made a breakfast of the soup that Kol had begun to prepare the previous evening. It had been sitting on the fire all night. Svarte and Kol had taken turns putting on more wood and adding water to the pot. Along with the soup made from onions and the yearling's flanks, they ate coarse brown bread, and soon the warmth returned to their bodies.

It was a beautiful morning, and when they rode with their heavy loads down the slopes of Kinnekulle through the sparse oak forest, all the lands of Arnäs lay spread out at their feet. They rode into the rising sun that colored Lake Vänern first in silver and then in gold, and Arn took deep happy breaths of the bracing air. In the distance he saw a reflection from the steeple of Forshem church, and then he could search in the right direction for Arnäs, though he couldn't see it yet.

The slopes of the mountain were mostly covered with dense oak forest and beech woods, but below the mountain great plowed fields spread out, now lying black and silvered with frost. Arn had never thought the world could be this beautiful; God must have created these particular oak slopes and fields in a very propitious moment. He began to sing with joy but saw out of the corner of his eye that his singing seemed to scare Svarte and Kol, so he soon stopped. He pondered whether to ask them what they didn't like about his song, whether it was the White Christ's magic that frightened them or something else. But he changed his mind because he decided that he had to proceed very slowly in his talk with these two who were so much thralls in their minds that freedom seemed to alarm them more than it tempted them.

During their journey the sun climbing in the sky soon melted the frost on the ground and took away the hard sound of the horses' iron shoes. The vast inland sea of Lake Vänern had shifted to a blue color, but they had now come so far down the mountain that they soon would see no more of the sea until they reached home.

They arrived at Arnäs around noon and were greeted with glad shouts that after such a brief hunting trip they could ride in with three deer. The house thralls were happy that Arn was the one who had shot the deer, and they raised their tools or whatever they had in hand and beat them together over their heads, emitting trilling sounds with their tongues. That was the sound the thralls made in welcome and jubilation. Arn couldn't help feeling some pride at this reception, but he instantly said a prayer to Saint Bernard to keep watch over him and warn him of the terrible sin of pride.

They flayed and carved up the deer and carried the skins to the tannery. But now they were no longer out on the hunt, where Arn was a novice. Just as Svarte and Kol could teach him about blood traces and crackling footsteps in the frost, he could teach them how meat should be smoked or hung, and so he now found it natural to make all the decisions.

✠

Algot Pålsson at Husaby owned many farms and woods, but in his own estimation only two treasures. They were his two daughters Katarina and Cecilia, who had now left their childhood behind and were blossoming like two delightful flowers. They were both the light of his eyes, he often said aloud. But since they also displayed clear signs of untamed mind and flirtatious behavior, especially Katarina, who was the older of the two, they were also his greatest worry. But he said nothing of this out loud.

When Katarina was twelve years old he had almost married her off to Magnus Folkesson at Arnäs, and that would have been a great happiness, just as good as a royal marriage. Or even better than royalty, considering how his fields and farms were surrounded by property belonging to either the Folkung or the Erik clan. To be sure, he was King Karl Sverkersson's steward at Husaby itself, which was a royal farm. It was honorable to tend such a place, but being associated so closely with King Karl Sverkersson was not without risks in Western Götaland, for as strong as the Sverker clan was in Eastern Götaland, it was equally weak in Western Götaland. On the day that King Karl was killed by one of the others, as kings usually ended their days, it would not be easy to be living at Husaby as his man.

Which is why the best arrangement would have been if Katarina became the mistress of Arnäs. Then Algot would truly not have put all his eggs in one basket. No matter which clan won the contest for royal power, his clan would be properly allied, securing both their lives and their property.

But it had all come to naught because Magnus Folkesson in the end preferred to marry into the Erik clan instead. Algot could not blame Magnus for this wise move at the same time as he bemoaned his own misfortune. However, it was not too late to solidify a secure position, for Magnus did have a son who was the same age as Katarina and Cecilia, and Eskil would in time become the lord of Arnäs. With a little good will such a betrothal might actually be viewed as a better solution, since otherwise Katarina would have been forced to marry a man in his best years when she was but a child herself.

Still, there was a problem with his daughters' unsuitable behavior. In their associations with young men neither of them displayed the modesty that a father might desire, and since this behavior harmed their reputation and in the worst case risked making it impossible to marry them off, Algot had decided to separate his daughters. When Katarina was home, Cecilia was a novice at the convent in Gudhem. Now it would soon be

Katarina's turn to go to Gudhem, and she had not a good thing to say about the matter.

It cost a good deal of silver for the nuns to keep the daughters at Gudhem, and silver was the only payment they accepted. But it was worth it, according to Algot, for what he laid out for his daughters would come back sevenfold if they married well. And besides, it gave him a convenient reason to do business with Magnus Folkesson, who was thought to have a limitless amount of silver in his treasure chests. By selling oak forests to Arnäs, Algot obtained the silver he needed, as well as many opportunities, after the business was concluded, to speak of his daughters' good manners, for which the money would be used. In this way he was often able to remind Magnus about the halfway-broken promise of marriage and about the fact that Katarina and Cecilia might still prove a good bargain for both men.

Algot Pålsson had heard only vague rumors about Magnus Folkesson's second son, who was sent to the monastery at a very young age and had now returned to Arnäs. What was said about the boy, however, was not intended to give him great honor, since he was deemed half a monk.

And Arn, as he was called, was obvious to everyone when he came riding in one cold and misty autumn evening two weeks before the big Western Götaland *ting* at Axevalla. He had two thralls with him, and they were heavily loaded with deer and swine that they now wanted to offer as Husaby's share of their hunt. Magnus Folkesson and Algot had come to an agreement regarding hunting on Algot's land, which was sometimes a better hunting ground than the one down by Arnäs, since the swine in particular made for the acorn woods in the autumn. A fourth of the catch was to be sent to Algot at Husaby as reimbursement.

Their hunt must have been very successful since everything they had with them was to be unloaded at Husaby. When that was done, their intent was to ride home at once, since the older thrall said he could find the way even in the dark.

But Algot objected. Allowing someone to ride off into the night would be ill mannered to those who came with such excellent meat. Besides, he quickly realized that it might seem quite providential to introduce Katarina to a son of Arnäs in this God-given way, even though Arn was the poorer of the two. It might make her prefer the eldest son.

And so a little feast was now arranged at Husaby just before All Saints' Day, when winter was near. After the horses were unsaddled and settled in their stalls, the meat was taken off to be flayed and prepared by Husaby's spit-turners, and Arn's thrall companions sent off to the thrall house. Then Katarina came to her father and suggested with an innocent expression that they shouldn't let the guest sleep in the longhouse with all the others, for at Arnäs they had more refined customs. Instead she would arrange it so that Arn had his own bed in one of the guesthouses which they were just about to close up for the winter. Algot merely grunted curt approval of this arrangement without either understanding or wanting to understand what sort of intentions Katarina might have.

Arn felt great embarrassment because he had never been anyone's guest before, and he wasn't sure how to act. He knew enough from Arnäs that it was considered an insult if one ate and drank too little. So as he unsaddled and curried Shimal he decided with a deep sigh to try to eat and drink like a pig so that his father would not be ashamed of how he behaved away from Arnäs. Fortunately, they'd had no food for many hours, so he had no lack of hunger, at least.

He went out to wash himself at the spring in the courtyard, where he saw that thralls had gathered. He realized as soon as he started washing that he was not behaving as a guest should. The thralls, startled and snickering, moved away as they pointed at him behind his back. But he wasn't about to give up this habit of washing, he thought. For even though he had to eat like a pig he didn't want to smell like one.

He lay down to rest for a while on the low wooden bed they had assigned to him and stared up at the ceiling, where he pictured clear images of deer and wild boar in the flickering of the candle flame. He was glad that he had accomplished something that his father was bound to appreciate more than his masonry work. With this consoling thought and with the wild animals before his eyes he fell asleep.

When a house thrall came and cautiously woke him it was pitch-dark; several hours must have passed since he went to sleep. In shock he jumped up at once, worried that it might seem as if he was declining his host's invitation, which would not likely be taken well. But the house thrall calmed him and said that the feast was just now starting, and all he had to do was come along. It had taken a good long time to roast the meat.

When Arn stepped into the dark hall at Husaby he felt himself transported back to ancient times. The long dark room was supported by two rows of carved pillars; Arn guessed that the roof was heavy with turf and earth and needed this support. Along the roof ridge were three smoke vents with lids over them, but he still felt some scattered raindrops on his face as he walked past the long log fire placed in the middle of the hall. The square pillars were decorated on all sides up to the height of a man with red patterns of winding dragons and mythological beasts. Similar patterns were visible around the high seat and the sleeping places in the corners at the end of the hall. This seemed to Arn a heathen, dismal, and cold abode.

He discovered that Algot and his daughter Katarina had dressed in feast clothes, as had the four men sitting around the high seat who were strangers to him. This made him uneasy, since he was wearing hunting garb of rough wool and deerskin. But he wouldn't have been able to do much about that. And now they all looked at him as if they expected him to do something. He greeted them with God's peace and bowed to them all, first to the lord and his daughter Katarina. He saw that she smiled a bit scornfully at him and surmised that he probably should have done and said something more.

But Algot Pålsson found no reason to plunge his important but awkward guest into more embarrassment. He stepped down from the high seat at once and took Arn by the arm to offer him the chair at his right hand, which was the place of honor. Then he called for the huge drinking horn, which according to tradition had been at Husaby since the time of Olof Skötkonung, the first Swedish king to be baptized, in 1008, in the spring at Husaby. Algot solemnly handed the horn to Arn and thereby the feast commenced.

Arn couldn't help studying the drinking horn for a moment before he raised it to his lips. At first he didn't think about how heavy it was, instead noticing all the heathen images that adorned it. The Christian cross seemed to have been added much later, as if to gloss over the sin. Realizing that he was no doubt expected to swill down the ale like an animal, he took a deep breath and then did his best to drink until he choked, with the others watching him intently. Panting, he set down the horn, but more than a third of the ale remained. Algot took the horn from him and quickly emptied it out onto the floor. Then he turned the horn upside down, and the others pounded on the table with their palms as a sign that the guest had honored their house by drinking it to the bottom. Arn already sensed that this supper was not something he would remember with pleasure.

Then the roast meat and more ale in huge tankards were brought in and served to everyone. The meat proved to be a deer roasted on a spit and a young pig roasted the same way. As Arn

expected, the venison tasted tough and dry and unspiced except
for salt, which had been liberally applied. They had roasted an
animal that had been alive that very morning, something that
Brother Rugiero would have viewed as a sin almost as serious as
blasphemy. Arn vowed not to betray his thoughts or complain
about anything, so he praised the excellent meat, drank eagerly
of his ale, and smacked his lips in contentment, because that was
what people did. Yet he had a hard time finding anything to say,
and Algot had to help him along by asking about the hunt. Any
man given the chance to brag about his hunt would become as
voluble as a bard, even if he was otherwise taciturn.

But Arn didn't know what to do when offered an opportunity
to boast, and he replied briefly, instead praising his thralls as
skilled hunters. This was not received well by the host and host-
ess. So at the beginning of the feast the conversation dragged
along reluctantly, like a forest slug on a dry path. At last Algot
asked whether Arn himself had shot any of the animals, which
was a wickedly bold question even though the guest could always
exaggerate without anyone thinking ill of him. Arn replied in a
low voice and looking down at the table that he had shot six of
the deer and seven of the boars, but he was quick to add that his
thralls had shot almost as many. Silence fell over the table, and
Arn didn't understand that no one believed him. They were all
now thinking that he certainly was allowed to brag a little, but
not so much that it was obvious he had told a bald-faced lie.

A young man whose kinship with Algot had not been made
clear to Arn now asked with a sneer whether Arn may have
missed a shot or two, or if he'd had such luck that he felled all
the animals with the first shot. Arn, who didn't see the trap in
this question, replied honestly that he had killed all the animals
with the first shot. But then the young man laughed derisively
and asked to be allowed to raise his goblet in respect for such
a great archer. Arn drank the toast in all seriousness, but his

cheeks burned when he saw scorn and mockery in the other man's eyes. He was well aware that he hadn't answered the questions he was asked wisely. But he had merely spoken the truth; why would it have been wiser to tell a lie? That question bore thinking about, for just now he almost wished he had been able to tell some clever lie and evade the disdain and contempt he saw all around him.

Algot Pålsson attempted to come to Arn's rescue, hastening to change the subject, saying that he had heard about some new plants at the cloister, and he wondered whether Arn might describe them. But the young man who had mocked Arn didn't want to let him wriggle off the hook, and with a knowing glance toward Katarina he loudly declared that it would be a shame if braggarts should win good women whom they didn't deserve in their own right. He uttered other, similar surly remarks, which made Arn suspect that the hostile man was in love with Katarina, though that was absolutely none of Arn's business.

Algot made a new attempt to steer the conversation toward the peaceful subject of the cloister and away from archery, which could only bring more dissension to the table. But Tord Geirsson, as the scornful young man was named, wanted to vanquish Arn and thus show Katarina how strong he was himself. Now he proposed that they fetch a bow so they might compete for a few shots, since the hall was quite long. Arn agreed to this at once, since he noticed out of the corner of his eye that Algot Pålsson had taken in a breath and was about to avert the contest.

House thralls were sent immediately to fetch a bow and quiver, and a tied-up bale of hay was set up by the door at the other end of the hall, at a distance of twenty-five paces. Tord Geirsson took the bow and the arrows, proclaiming that this wasn't a very difficult distance from which to shoot wild boar. Perhaps Herr Arn, who was so skillful, would show them first how it was done, and then Tord would take the second round.

Arn felt coldly resolute and stood up at once. He did not like the position he had landed in by telling the truth, and he wanted to get out of this predicament right away; as far as he knew there was only one way to do that. With long strides he went over to Tord Geirsson and almost rudely snatched the bow from him. He strung it quickly and skillfully, and carefully selected three arrows, holding two in his bow hand and nocking the third onto the bowstring. He drew it back as far as the bow would tolerate, wanting to shoot with the bow's full power so that the arrow would drop as little as possible on the way. And then he loosed the arrow. It struck the center, a mere thumb's-breadth below the middle of the bale of hay. They all craned their necks to see and then began whispering to one another. Arn now knew how the bow shot, and he took careful aim with the two following shots, which he loosed without hurry, and striking somewhat better. Then without a word he handed the bow to Tord Geirsson and went to sit down.

Tord Geirsson was white in the face as he stared at the three arrows protruding from the target in a tight pattern. He realized that he had lost, but he didn't know how to handle the quandary he had landed himself in. Of all the methods he could imagine, he found every single one shameful. He did not choose wisely. He flung the bow to the floor in pique and left the hall without saying a word, but with the loud laughter of everyone in his ears.

Arn said a silent prayer for him, asking that his anger might abate and hoping that he had learned something from his pride. For his own part he prayed that Saint Bernard continue to remind him about pride and that he might not be seduced into exaggerating the importance of this simple incident.

When Algot Pålsson recovered from his astonishment over Arn's skill, he was very pleased and soon had everyone around the table drinking a *skål* to Arn in earnest, now that he had proven what a skillful archer he was. Much more ale was brought in, and Arn began to feel more at ease, soon even deciding that the tough, unhanged venison tasted quite good. And he tried to drink ale like a real man.

Katarina had taken the liberty of pouring ale for Arn herself, which was polite and something she should have done from the start, since she sat in the mistress's place and Arn in that of the guest of honor. At first she had found him much too uncertain and humble. Now she found his stature more than impressive.

Soon she had changed places with her father in the high seat so that she was sitting next to Arn, close enough that he was aware of her body when she spoke to him, which she did more and more eagerly, showing how clever she found everything that Arn said. Her hands touched his now and then, as if accidentally.

Arn was even more enlivened by this, and drank more ale every time it was set before him. He was pleased that Katarina, who had seemed to look at him with such cold and scornful eyes when he first entered the hall, now beamed and smiled at him with such warmth that he felt the heat touch his own skin and rise up inside himself.

If Algot Pålsson had handled his position as lord of the manor with greater chivalry, he would have rebuked his daughter for this flirtatious behavior. But he decided that there was a considerable difference when such unsuitable behavior for a young woman was directed toward a proud but poor clan kinsman such as Tord Geirsson, instead of toward a young nobleman from Arnäs. So he looked through his fingers at such things when he noticed what good fathers cannot avoid discovering and usually choose to reprove.

Arn's head was soon spinning from all the ale, and almost too late he noticed that he had to vomit. He made his way quickly out of the hall so as not to defile the place where people ate. When the cold air struck him in the face outside, he bent over to empty his stomach of what seemed like half a tough deer and a good cask of ale. He bitterly regretted his actions but could not think of praying before he was done.

Afterward he wiped his mouth carefully and took deep breaths of the cold air, admonishing himself about how foolish he looked no matter what he tried. Then he went inside to say good night without eating any more, wishing everyone God's peace, and thanking them for all the generous food. Then he staggered on stiff but resolute legs out of the hall, into the court-yard, and over to the spring which now lay shrouded in darkness and drizzling rain. He splashed cold water on his face, chastised himself loudly in a slurred voice, and fumbled his way over to the guesthouse. He found his bed in the dark and fell forward like a clubbed ox.

When night came to the longhouse and only snoring was heard, Katarina cautiously crept off into the night. Algot Påls-son, who usually slept poorly after big ale feasts, heard her sneak off and understood full well where she was heading. As a good father he should have prevented her from such antics and chas-tised her roundly.

As a good father, he consoled himself, he could also refrain from doing so; if nothing else, in hopes of having a daughter at Arnäs.

Chapter 9

For anyone who did not know, it might look as though the
Folkungs were now going to set off to war from Arnäs. Even for
those who knew everything, this was conceivable.

A great host of soldiers had crowded into the castle courtyard,
and between the stone walls there were echoes of the horses'
iron shoes and snorting, the rattling of weapons, and impatient
voices. The sun was on its way up and it was going to be a cold
day, but without snow and with good road conditions. Two
heavily loaded carts were dragged on ironclad oak wheels whining and creaking out through the gate to make room for all the
horsemen. They were waiting for the headmen of the clan who
were saying prayers in the high tower room, and some joked that
they could well be lengthy prayers up there if the young monk
was in charge. As if to keep warm or burn off some of their impatience, four of the Arnäs retainers began fighting one another
with sword and shield, while terrified thralls had to hold their

restless stallions and kinsmen outside shouted merrily and offered good advice.

It was indeed Arn who had led the prayers with his father and his uncle Birger Brosa and Eskil, for they truly needed the protection of God and the Saint before this journey, which might end well but also might end with the ravages of war sweeping across all of Western Götaland.

When Arn came out into the castle courtyard and saw the four retainers hacking away at one another with swords, he stopped short. He stood speechless in amazement when he discovered that these men, who were supposed to be his father's finest fighters and armed guard, didn't know how to handle a sword. He never would have imagined anything like this. Although they were full-grown men and heavily clad in knee-length chain mail and tunics bearing the colors of the Folkungs, they looked like little boys who barely knew a thing about using sword and shield.

Magnus, who saw his son's sheepish stare and thought that Arn might have been frightened by these wild games, placed his hand calmly on Arn's shoulder and consoled him by saying that he had no cause to be afraid of such men as long as they were in the family's pay. But they were huge giants, which was good for Arnäs.

Then for the first time in a long while Arn looked as if he were slow to comprehend. But then a light apparently went on for him, and he smiled uncertainly at his father's consoling words, assuring him that he hadn't been frightened of the fighting at all. He said he felt safe at seeing that they bore the colors of the Folkungs like himself. He didn't want to hurt his father by saying what he thought of the ability of these men to wield a sword. For by now he had learned that sometimes it was wise out in the base world not to speak the truth.

There was more trouble when Magnus discovered that Arn

had heedlessly fastened the sword he'd received from the monks at his side. That sword would only arouse ridicule, so he went straight to the armory and fetched a good, beautiful Norwegian sword to offer Arn instead. But then Arn turned stubborn, the same way he did about wanting to ride his skinny monk horse instead of a manly Nordic stallion.

Magnus tried to explain that the Folkungs now had to ride with a great force to put fear into the enemy and pacify them. Even Arn who was clad in the Folkung colors had to do his share so that he did not entice ridicule. And it would be ridiculous if a son so close to the headman of the clan carried a sword like a woman's and rode a horse that was good for nothing.

Arn restrained himself for a good long while before replying. But then he suggested politely that he might consider riding one of the sluggish black stallions, but that he would rather not carry a sword at all than relinquish his own. And faced with this dilemma Magnus relented, not entirely pleased yet relieved at being quit of the most mortifying spectacle of his son on a horse that would arouse ridicule.

Finally the mighty force could ride out from Arnäs on its way to the *ting* of all the Goths, the *ting* that was now called a *landsting* because King Karl Sverkersson himself would participate for the first time in two years. This time he would have to choose between war and peace.

In the vanguard the leader of the retainers rode alone with the banner of the Folkungs raised on a lance. Then followed Birger Brosa and Magnus Folkesson riding side by side, clad in silver and blue. They were wrapped in their wide blue mantles lined with marten fur, and they wore shiny pointed helmets on their heads. On the left side behind the saddle they had fastened their shields on which the rampant golden lion of the Folkungs stood defiantly posed for battle. After them rode Eskil and Arn, dressed and armed in the same manner as the headmen of the

clan, and then followed a double rank of retainers who all carried lances with the colors of the Folkungs fluttering in the wind
from the tips.

An equal number of Folkungs would meet up with them
from the southern and western parts of the country, and outside
Skara they would join with the Erik clan to demonstrate clearly,
when they rode into the *ting* as the strongest contingent, that
war would make both the Folkung and the Erik clans enemies of
King Karl, since they belonged together not merely through their
bond of blood but also through their shared determination never
to be subjugated. The *ting* of all Goths would be held outside the
royal manor at Axevalla.

If two young men other than Eskil and Arn had been forced
to ride side by side for such a long way, they would have talked
most about the struggle for power in which they themselves had
unavoidably become involved. But Arn was still as passive and
quiet as he had been ever since returning from Varnhem. The
morning after the night he spent at Husaby, he had ridden in
a wild dash to Varnhem to confess to Father Henri. When he
eventually returned home he had morosely reforged the two helmets that he understood they were going to compel him and his
brother to wear. What he changed was not visible so much on
the outside, but the helmets were padded and warm on the inside
so that they would not freeze their ears off in the cold.

But two brothers could not ride together in silence, Eskil
thought. He supposed it would be better if he broke the ice and
talked about what was preoccupying his mind; afterward they
could more easily tackle what was obviously bothering Arn.

And so Eskil talked about the Norwegian business transac-
tions, which had gone very well. They had succeeded in acquir-
ing an offer of first refusal, so that the farms in question might
be said to remain within the same clan, yet they had still brought
home so much Norwegian silver that it was good for Arnäs. The

best thing was that they had been able to sell without arousing discontent or dispute.

What concerned Eskil right now was something else: dried fish that was called clipfish in Norway—split dried cod. Up in northern Norway ocean fish were caught in huge numbers. Near a place called Lofoten they were caught in such quantities that it was more than they could eat and sell in all of Norway. This meant there was a surplus of clipfish that was cheap to buy, easy to ship, and almost like magic could last without spoiling until it was softened up in water. Eskil's idea was to buy up all such surplus Norwegian fish and sell it in the Gothic lands, because there were many periods of fasting, especially the forty days before Easter, when it was considered a sin to eat meat. The fish that people caught in lakes and seas in the Gothic lands was not sufficient, particularly for those who lived in large communities and far from fishing waters, such as in the cities of Skara and Linköping.

To Eskil's surprise, Arn knew at once what he was talking about, although his word was not clipfish but *cabalao*, which he said he had eaten often and not only during fasting. Such fish had been common in the cloister world for a long time. Arn thought that if they could convince the town dwellers of the benefits of dried fish, which he didn't think would be an easy matter because he had a low opinion of town dwellers, then the business would surely bring in a lot of silver for whoever was first to provide the fish. It was definitely true that such fish were excellent for storing, shipping, and eating, and that the need for good food could be great at fasting times and during winters that were much too long. If one did not live in a cloister, that is.

Eskil was very glad to hear this, and he was convinced that he had discovered a new business that would soon yield much silver. He imagined hordes of slovenly town dwellers gobbling down his fish in great quantities, and he decided at once to send a trading party to his Norwegian kinsmen to place a large order. Dried fish was definitely something that belonged to the future.

When the mighty Folkung column rode past Forshem church, the last of the riders could not be seen at the same time as the first. The bell of Forshem church tolled as if to proclaim misfortune or wishes for success, and the peasants stood lined up along the road to watch the spectacle. But they stood silent and scared, for it was impossible to know whether this force of warriors was riding off to plunge the country into adversity or to maintain the peace, since that could not be seen with the naked eye. For an ordinary peasant the Folkung retinue was a sight that instilled more fear than hope.

After taking their rest at the halfway point, they would soon meet up with their kinsmen, and the host would swell to almost twice its present size. Eskil began cautiously to question Arn about what was making him so taciturn that he seemed almost dejected. He also asked about the reason for Arn's visit to Varnhem cloister, where he had submitted to ten days of penance with the hair shirt, which Eskil had noticed though Arn had tried to hide it, and only bread and water to eat. He hurried to add that he wasn't trying to breach the holy secrecy of the confession, but he was Arn's brother, and a brother should be able to talk to his brother even about things that were difficult, and not merely about fish and silver.

Arn then told him without circumlocution about how he had disgraced himself by getting drunk and vomiting, and how that night up at Husaby he had done something with a woman that belonged to the sacrament of marriage. And for these stupidities he felt great remorse.

But Eskil was not at all disturbed to hear this. On the contrary, he laughed out loud so that their father turned around in his saddle up ahead and gave them both a stern look, for the Folkungs were not riding to the *ting* in order to spread merriment.

In a lower voice but still in a cheerful tone Eskil told Arn that now he understood everything, since it wasn't hard to guess what Arn meant. As for vomiting after consuming too much food and ale, that was nothing to worry about; it merely showed that he had enjoyed the entertainment, and it was good manners. But then there was the matter of Katarina, because she was the one, wasn't she? Well, even if nothing was decided yet, it could well be that he or Arn would end up married to either Katarina or Cecilia. But since Algot Pålsson of Husaby was in a bind because he lacked silver yet constantly had to pay out silver, and he had no understanding of such things, it could turn out that his lands would eventually end up within the confines of Arnäs, without having to resort to a wedding ale. All the waiting had no doubt caused impatience up there in Husaby, and what Katarina had seen fit to do was simply a way to hasten God's plans in that respect. But that was more worthy of a laugh than a worried frown.

Arn still had a hard time laughing about what had happened. No matter how he twisted and turned the matter, he couldn't escape the thought that he was responsible to God for what he did of his own free will. Even if this free will might be perilously jeopardized because of so much ale. Like Eskil, however, Father Henri had taken a lighter view of this sin than Arn had expected, and although Father Henri had asked many questions, he had come to the same conclusions as Eskil. A lustful and greedy woman had seduced Arn with both ale and such wiles as women use when they are being as sly as snakes. And Arn, who was innocent in more than one respect, had therefore had a difficult time defending himself against these ploys.

That was why Arn had gotten off so easily with ten days' penance, and before God he was absolved of his sin. Even so he had a hard time feeling happy about what should have been a great relief to him. It was as if for the second time he had committed a grave sin and yet had received scant punishment, which had not made him happy at all, though both Eskil and Father Henri had obviously expected it would. He had a disquieting thought that his sin, even though it was forgiven, was still lodged somewhere inside him. For as he recalled, he had not been especially reluctant after Katarina showed him what he was supposed to do.

✠

King Karl Sverkersson stood on the crest of Axevalla's wall together with his closest men and saw the Folkungs and the Erik clan riding together toward the site of the *ting*. It was like watching a big blue sea approaching, for the Folkung colors were blue and silver and the Erik clan's blue and gold. The lance points with the fluttering blue pennants were like a forest that stretched farther than the eye could see. They had definitely not come with only a few dozen representatives, known as oath-swearers, but as a well-equipped army, and the message they wanted to convey was not hard to grasp. And what was worse, among those riding in the vanguard were not only Joar Jedvardsson and his son-in-law Magnus Folkesson, as could be expected, but also Birger Brosa from Bjälbo. That message was also easy to read. Now the Bjälbo clan, the strongest branch of the Folkungs, had joined up with the enemy.

Fortunately the aspirant to the throne, the young Knut Eriksson, King Erik Jedvardsson's son, was not part of the blue army. If he were, peace at the *ting* would be hard to hold. But the fact that Knut Eriksson was not included was also a sign of the Erik clan's good will to maintain the peace.

After that one could still hope for a happy outcome of the dispute between Emund Ulvbane and Magnus Folkesson. Because there was a well-set trap and Magnus was in certain respects the weakest link in the Folkung chain. If they could make that link burst then much would be gained.

The *ting* would not begin until noon, when the sun stood at its zenith, so there was now plenty of time for discussion. Outside the largest tent in the blue camp the Folkung coat of arms was raised with the golden lion, along with the Erik clan's new emblem, three golden crowns against a blue sky. This emblem could be viewed as an affront to King Karl Sverkersson: the Erik clan seemed to be heralding King Erik Jedvardsson as their king, since everyone knew that the three crowns had been his mark and no one else's. And anyone who heralded King Erik Jedvardsson in the presence of King Karl Sverkersson was thereby taking a stand that could be interpreted as hostile. The enmity was even clearer since all now knew for certain that Karl Sverkersson was behind the murder of Erik Jedvardsson and that the Dane, poor Magnus Henriksen, had merely been Karl's tool. He was lost the moment that Erik Jedvardsson fell dead to the ground. For in that instant, when Magnus Henriksen believed himself to be a victor up north in Östra Aros with a dead king at his feet, all support ceased and all promises were broken by Karl Sverkersson down in Linköping, who now instead took the field against his own regicide henchman.

That was how Karl Sverkersson had won the king's crown. And rumor had it that the man he sent to aid Magnus Henriksen in the murder of Erik Jedvardsson was Emund Ulvbane, and that Emund was also the one who wielded the sword that severed Erik Jedvardsson's head from his body.

If this rumor spoke true, then Magnus Folkesson was embroiled in a dispute with a king-killer, so it was important for him to think carefully about how this dispute should be handled. It was easy to see that it involved more than some outlying farms in between the lands of Arnäs and the land that the king's half brother Boleslav had recently granted to Emund.

But if he remained calm and did not get carried away or allow himself to become agitated by those who surely wanted to inflame matters, then the game would be possible to win without much difficulty. For the judge himself, Karle Eskilsson, who was the grandson of the judge Karle of Edsvära, had also married into the Folkung clan. And now he came to join the council in the Folkung tent.

Also present were Joar Jedvardsson, Birger Brosa, Magnus and his two sons, and the two leaders of the Folkung and Erik clan retainers.

There were two things to discuss, and Judge Karle, who was the most distinguished man in the tent, presided over the discussion. He spoke gruffly and straight to the point so that no time would be wasted. If King Karl now attempted to proclaim himself king of Western Götaland as well, which might be his intention, and all the Folkungs and men of the Erik clan then rejected him, the matter would be clear. In that situation no judge and no bishop could approve the requested position of king. But if, as rumor also had it, King Karl chose instead to seek the *ting*'s approval of his son Sverker as jarl over Western Götaland, how would they then react?

Birger Brosa said that in his opinion this might be a very good solution. King Karl would avoid ridicule and it would make him less desirous of going to war. Western Götaland would remain free of his royal power, and if he chose to call a mere babe a jarl, it might assuage his pride but had no real meaning. Only many years from now would such a jarl be able to act as the king's sword, but for now it was only a title. In this way war could be avoided between parties of equal strength, which was the worst sort of war.

Joar Jedvardsson and Magnus Folkesson agreed at once. War between those of equal strength was something that ought to be avoided. Whoever won such a war would pay for his victory dearly, ending up surrounded by many widows and fatherless children, as well as devastated and burned fields.

Judge Karle found that everyone was unanimous regarding this matter, and no one contradicted him.

Then they turned to the next issue, the property dispute between Magnus and young Boleslav's man Emund Ulvbane. There was something fishy about this dispute. The matter was too minor to incite dissension, and it seemed even odder to bring it before a *landsting*, so the intention may have been to start a quarrel which like a wildfire could flare up into war. Behind Emund Ulvbane stood King Karl's half brother Boleslav. But Boleslav was a child, not yet even an adolescent, and incapable of forging warlike intrigues on his own. Behind Boleslav stood King Karl, so he must be the one who wanted a quarrel.

Judge Karle said that he was well aware that this dispute had to be resolved with a light hand if peace were to be preserved. But since both sides in the dispute could bring forward dozens of oath-swearers, endless numbers if needed, the dispute could not be resolved in the manner prescribed by law. So what other approach could they take? What was Magnus's own opinion in this matter?

Magnus now spoke, briefly and in a manly fashion, and explained that he had thought this was exactly what would happen, that with oath-swearers the dispute would remain in the same place when the *ting* ended as when it began. So he intended to propose a reconciliation by offering 30 marks in silver for the farms in dispute. That might be 10 marks more than the farms were actually worth, but the price was not too high if by this means the dispute could be settled. If peace could be bought for the land for only 10 marks, then the price was cheap.

Judge Karle nodded thoughtfully and approvingly and then explained how they should proceed: First they would take an oath in which all declared that the dispute had reached an impasse and could not be resolved. Then Magnus would carry in his 30 marks in silver to the *ting* and offer a compromise just as he had proposed. After that it would be a simple matter for the judge and his lay assessors to declare a reconciliation, and no one would be able to offer any objections.

Eskil and Arn went off by themselves to look at horses and weapons and say hello to members of their own clan that Eskil knew though Arn did not. They also greeted people from the Erik clan that neither of them knew, while Eskil explained to Arn how a *ting* functioned. Arn needed to know, for instance, that swords were not allowed inside the white chalk ring, which was the boundary of the *ting* site itself. And when he had to swear an oath he needed to know the words and say them loudly and clearly without unmanly hesitation or stammering, since such things would make him seem unreliable. The words were as follows:

> *As true by the grace of the gods do I speak truly.*

When Arn objected that such an oath was heathen, Eskil merely laughed and explained that even if the words in the oath were from their ancestors' time, they referred to none other than the Lord God. To convince Arn of this he pointed out that the very first words in the law of the Goths made this matter clear as water, since they were:

> *Christ is foremost in our law. After that our Christian teachings and all Christians: king, peasants, and all domi-ciled men, bishops and all book-learned men.*

Arn was satisfied with this and jested that Eskil was probably included in this law as a peasant, while he necessarily had to slink along as a book-learned man. In any case it was clear that they did indeed have the law on their side.

When it was time, Bishop Bengt came from Skara and blessed

the peace of the *ting*. Judge Karle announced in a loud voice that the *ting* was in session, and anyone who broke the peace of the *ting* was an outlaw. Then a murmur rose up from the thousand men who in suspense watched King Karl slowly make his way up to the highest mound of the *ting* site, where the judge stood. Soon they would see how the question of peace or war would be decided.

When the king had reached high enough ground that everyone could see him, they could also see that he was carrying in his arms a babe in swaddling clothes. Many who now understood what that meant could breathe a sigh of relief. The peace was preserved, since Karl Sverkersson did not intend to demand the crown of Western Götaland with sword in hand.

Then everything happened as Karle and Birger Brosa had predicted. Karl Sverkersson raised his infant son high over his head so that all could see him and asked the *ting* to greet the new jarl, Sverker of Western Götaland. A great roar came from the direction of the Sverker clan; from the men who had flocked around the king's half brothers Kol and Boleslav came a great shout of "yes." Then all eyes were turned tensely to the part of the *ting* site gleaming with blue, where Joar Jedvardsson, Magnus Folkesson, and Birger Brosa stood in front.

Birger Brosa whispered with a smile that they should wait a few moments, which they all did, standing quite still just like their men behind them. The murmur around the *ting* site died down, and then it was so quiet that only the wind was heard. But all at once the three men in front stretched their hands to the sky as one man, and then a forest of hands shot up behind them, and soon jubilant cries of relief and joy thundered across the whole *ting* site. Bishop Bengt could now bless the new jarl, who shrieked in his tiny voice so that it seemed more like a baptism than the blessing of the foremost man in Western Götaland.

Next in the deliberations were such cases that concerned only

a few individuals, such as cases of killings and injuries. Then
several church thieves were to be hanged to cheer up the many
who had traveled so far to the *ting*, now that the major issue had
been decided. It took until late afternoon before they came to
the showdown between Magnus Folkesson and the king-killer
Emund Ulvbane, and a cold wind of suspense seemed to pass
over the *ting* as men dressed in the colors of the Sverker clan
came streaming in from every direction.

At first everything went just as the Folkungs had predicted.
Two dozen good men from each side were called to swear the
oath, and all swore by the grace of the gods that the land which
had been disputed since ancient times belonged to the man for
whom they now swore their oath.

Everything that followed also went as planned, for now
Magnus Folkesson brought out his silver and declared that with
these coins he was prepared to enter into a reconciliation. He
bade his opponent approve this action, for the price was good
and peace between neighbors was worth more than silver.
Emund Ulvbane bullheadedly refused to agree, but Judge Karle
and his lay assessors approved the compromise at once, without
even having to step aside and confer. And with that, men muttering in disappointment began to disperse in all directions, for
now all could see that this matter was decided and would not
lead to anything further.

But then Emund Ulvbane stepped forward and contemptuously put his foot on the silver he had just been awarded in
compensation and raised his right hand as a sign that he had
something to say. Everyone fell silent and waited in tense anticipation, for Emund Ulvbane looked both angry and scornful.

"Since the *ting* has decided, I must like any other man acquiesce," he began in a thundering voice, for he was a very powerful man. "But it aggrieves me that silver should take precedence
over honor and right. It also aggrieves me to have to compromise

with a man without honor such as Magnus Folkesson. For you, Magnus, bear no semblance to a man, nor are you a man in your heart, and I deem your sons to be equally foul, for they are both bitch puppies, the one a nun and the other an ale cask."

With that Emund Ulvbane motioned to one of his retainers to come and fetch the silver while he remained standing there with his hands on his hips. With disdainful glances he sought his enemies' eyes. But the only person on the other side to meet his gaze was one of those he had called a bitch puppy, a young man with a sheeplike, innocent face who looked at him without the wit to feel fear. Instead his expression seemed to display astonishment and pity.

Then a great tumult and loud shouting erupted at the *ting* and much uneasiness. Many men hurried away, because the peace that had seemed so secure was now in grave peril.

In the Folkung tent the men soon gathered to deliberate, and the mood was sorrowful. Both Joar Jedvardsson and Birger Brosa, who had some knowledge of the law, said they had a bad feeling about what the law now prescribed about someone who had so openly used words of abuse at the *ting*, and what sort of response was allowed in such a case. They could not defend themselves with silver this time.

They would have to wait until Judge Karle came and recited the law, and it was a dismal wait during which not much was said. Eskil saw to it that a cask of ale was brought in and tankards for one and all, but they drank in silence, as if at the beginning of a funeral ale.

When Judge Karle entered the tent it was immediately apparent from his face that he was weighed down by sorrow and worry. He greeted the men briefly and then got straight to the point.

"Kinsmen, you want to know what the law says about the words of abuse that have now been spoken. I shall tell you the law, and then you will have to decide for yourselves the wisest course of action, for in this I have nothing to say. But regarding these insults we heard Emund utter, the law is so clear that I don't believe Emund himself could have spoken such sharp rebukes without having many consultations and much advice. For hear now the law, I shall recite it to you at once."

When he noticed that ale was being served, he paused and took a tankard, drinking several deep drafts as he looked as though he were reviewing the law in his mind. Then he set down the tankard, wiped his mouth with the back of his hand, and in a high, singing voice he recited the text of the law:

> If any man utters words of abuse to another: "You bear no semblance to a man nor are you a man in your heart." "I am a man like you." They shall meet where three roads converge. If the one who said the words comes, and the one who received them does not, then he must remain as he was called; he may not act as an oath-swearer, nor is he competent to witness, either in the case of a man or a woman. On the other hand, should the one who received the words come, while the one who said the words does not, then the one insulted must shout three times "outlaw" and make a mark for him on the ground. Then he would be worse than the one who now spoke it, since he did not dare step forth. Now they both meet, fully armed. If the one falls who received the words, to him is charged half the price of a man. If the one falls who gave the words and word felony is worst, the tongue is the bane of the head, then he shall be deemed an outlaw.

It was quiet for a long while in the tent as all pondered the law. Judge Karle sat down and again reached for his ale, and soon everyone's gaze was directed toward Birger Brosa, who sat with his head bowed in sadness. He noticed this and understood that now he would have to be the one to speak the evil that most of the men in the tent might already be thinking, for his brother Magnus was white in the face, as if paralyzed.

"To meet Emund Ulvbane in single combat is for many a good man, also better men than those of us who sit here, the same as certain death," he began with a deep sigh. "It is also what King Karl and his advisers have slyly plotted, and that was why Emund was granted land bordering Arnäs, for this very case. My brother Magnus now has to choose between meeting Emund with a sword or becoming a man without honor, and that is a choice I wouldn't wish on my worst enemy. But that is how the matter stands, and I have no good advice to give."

Magnus said nothing, nor did he look as if he wanted to say anything just now. Instead Joar Jedvardsson began to speak.

"With such offense has King Karl rewarded our striving to keep war at bay," he began heavily. "But the war will come sooner or later, as Karl Sverkersson now has shown, and all of us who sit here understand as much. The reason that my broth-er's son, the aspirant king Knut Eriksson, chose not to come to this *landsting* was that then the peace of the *ting* would be difficult to maintain. But Knut is the one who with falseness and murder on orders from Karl Sverkersson was robbed of his father and his crown, and soon the time will be ripe, as we all know, for us to demand honor again. So I ask you all, my kinsmen, of what use would it be now for Magnus to offer his life? Many a man would follow Magnus Folkesson into battle behind the emblem of the Folkungs, but forgive me if I now speak as frankly as the case demands. It is less certain that as many would follow Eskil Magnusson. If Magnus has to die for our case, if God so wills, then he would die better on the battlefield in the war that must come. Now all of us in the Erik

clan and the Folkung clan should at the same time break camp
and march away from here. Then we will all have shown together where we stand. That is my opinion."

"That was wisely spoken, my dear kinsman," said Birger
Brosa, but at the same time he squirmed with obvious discom-
fort, which to those who knew him showed that he probably
meant the opposite of what he'd said. "However, the situation
is clear. If Magnus does not come to the single combat he is an
outcast, a man without honor who is not even competent to bear
witness. Such a man cannot lead the Folkungs; it has never happened before and must not happen now. That much we know,
but Karl Sverkersson knows it too, just as do his sly advisers who
have put us in this predicament. Magnus can choose between
only two things. This is difficult for a brother to say, but I must
speak the truth. Either he marches off with his life intact but as a
man without honor. Or else he goes to a single combat in which
only a miracle of the saints can save his life. The latter choice is
the better one. For no combat is decided in advance. But he who
flees in cowardice has decided everything for the rest of his days.
So it is."

Judge Karle stood up heavily and explained that he had nothing to add to this matter since there was no ambiguity as to the
content of the law. And the difficult decision that the three clan
leaders now had to make would be no easier because there were
more men present. He was shaking his head sorrowfully as he
left the tent.

It was quiet after his departure. They all now turned to hear
what Magnus himself would say, for the biggest decision, if not
the only one, was his. It was not merely a matter of his life but
also the honor of the Folkungs.

"I have made my decision," he said when he could sit still no
longer facing the intolerable anticipation of what he would say.
"Tomorrow at dawn at the place we here at the *ting* call Three

THE ROAD TO JERUSALEM

Roads Meet, I shall go against Emund fully armed as the law
prescribes. May God be with me and may you all pray for me.
But there is no other way, for none in our clan would choose the
way of dishonor, and it is also true that none would follow a
dishonored man."

Eskil and Arn had been sitting at the back of the tent together,
and none of the older men had paid any attention to the two
half-men. Now that their father had spoken and in everyone's
view had condemned himself to death, Eskil took a deep breath,
looking as though he might burst into tears, but he composed
himself at once. An excruciating silence followed when no one
contradicted Magnus, which was the same as agreeing and
thereby deciding to end his life. Then Arn mustered the courage
that came of despair to say what was needed.

"Forgive us if we, the sons of Magnus, also join in this matter,"
he began uncertainly. "But this affects us as much as everyone
else . . . in my opinion at least. Isn't it true that we were also insulted along with our father Magnus when that Emund called us
bitch puppies or whatever it was he said?"

"Yes, that's true," replied Birger Brosa. "You and Eskil were
just as insulted as your father Magnus. But it is his obligation to
defend the honor of all of you."

"But according to the law don't we have the same right as our
father to defend our honor?" asked Arn with the simple innocence of a child, so that some of the older men had a hard time
keeping from laughing despite the gravity of the occasion.

"It would not be to Magnus's credit if instead of standing up
for his honor like a man, he sent one of his half-grown sons to
the slaughter," muttered Birger Brosa morosely and stood up
at once to go outside and piss, leaving the others wordless and
empty of all feeling.

But after briefly hesitating Arn slunk out to follow Birger
Brosa. He had to do some searching before he found him, since

301

the winter darkness had fallen rapidly while they sat inside. He walked resolutely over to his uncle, who was just pulling up his hose, and spoke to him without hesitation and with great conviction.

"I have to tell you something true and important, my dear uncle. And you must believe me, for now in this grave hour there is really no time for untrue words. The truth is that of the three of us who were insulted, I am the one who can best handle a sword. It's also true that I think I could easily vanquish that Emund, or you yourself, or any of our retainers. That's why you must arrange it so that I am the one who goes to combat and not my poor father."

Birger Brosa was so taken aback by these words that he stood there holding up his hose as if he were still about to piss. The little he knew about Arn was what everyone joked about who'd had anything to do with a monastery, which even Emund Ulvbane must have heard since he had called Arn a nun. Yet now this God-fearing and very serious young man stood here telling him something that could not possibly be true, but his face bore no trace of prevarication or madness. Birger Brosa didn't know what to think. His doubt must have been obvious, for Arn made an impatient motion with his hands before an idea seemed to occur to him.

"My dear uncle, you are a much larger man than I, almost the same as that Emund," Arn said eagerly, clearly filled with his idea. "Take my hand and stand foot to foot with me," he continued, reaching out his hand to Birger Brosa, who took it out of sheer astonishment and then was shocked by the strength of his grip. Arn adjusted their feet so that they stood at an angle to each other as in an ordinary arm-wrestling match.

"So!" said Arn, suddenly cheerful. "Now try to knock me over with your strength that is greater than mine!"

Birger Brosa made a halfhearted attempt that had no effect

other than to make Arn laugh at him. Then he took a better grip, and the next moment he found himself pulled down into the mud and slush. Birger Brosa got up in surprise and grabbed Arn's strong hand again; once more he was dragged to the ground as if the boy could play with him at will. After the third attempt Arn didn't want to continue, but held up his palms for his uncle to stop.

"Hear me now, my uncle," he said. "I can handle Emund or anyone else the same way, and now I will tell you why. During all my years at the monastery, I had practice every day, more than any man you know, in weapons games from a man who once was a Templar knight in the Holy Land. I swear on Our Lady and Saint Bernard, who are my two patron saints, that I am the one who best of all of us can defend myself with a sword. And you must know that such a man as I would not lie to anyone, especially to my kinsmen and least of all at such a grave moment."

Birger Brosa now seemed to see Arn's conviction and truthfulness flowing like light between them. All at once he was convinced that what Arn said was actually true. And when he pondered more closely what it might mean, his face lit up and he looked at Arn with an almost happy expression as he embraced him. As the wise man Birger Brosa was in everything that had to do with the struggle for power, he now realized that the blackest hour for the Folkungs could soon be turned to white, regardless of whether Arn or Emund Ulvbane won the combat at the next day's dawning. Either Arn would win, or he would lose with greater honor than what Magnus could have mustered. But then Emund's victory would be reckoned worthless.

Yet his decision aroused both doubt and discontent when Birger Brosa again entered the tent with the already grieving kinsmen and explained that Arn was the man who should fight Emund Ulvbane. This choice should be justified by proclaim-

ing that Arn was the one who had been most wronged, in that
Emund had not merely called him a bitch puppy but also directed
scorn at the house of God where Arn had been raised.

Magnus objected with the greatest anguish. For at the same
time he saw his life now saved, the life from which he had already begun to take his leave, he also saw that he would lose a
son. And he worried that to many it would look bad if a man did
not dare take up his own obligation but instead sent a less than
full-grown son to the slaughter. He had a hard time taking seriously Arn's modest protestations that it was still wisest to send
into single combat the one who could best handle a sword.

Puzzled, Joar Jedvardsson now left the Folkungs to themselves
for the night, along with the four retainers. They all looked quite
bewildered when with downcast eyes they said farewell and God
bless to young Arn, who still had down on his cheeks.

When the Folkungs were left alone, Magnus suggested that
they pray for as long as they could that night. Arn found this to
be a good idea, but he perplexed them all when he began to pray
for Emund Ulvbane's life, his sin, and his pride.

✠

At dawn on the morning that everyone in Western Götaland
would remember in times to come and about which many
sagas would be told, almost as many men gathered as were
at the *ting*. They gathered at the place that was called Three
Roads Meet. It was three arrow-shots from the *ting* site, and
that marked the boundary for the peace of the *ting*. Few had
gone home the night before, even though business had been concluded, because few men wanted to miss seeing with their own
eyes the fight that could be the cause of war.

No one among the Folkungs and none from the Erik clan had

left for home, for together they had to show the king's men that he who killed a kinsman directed a blow against them all. Also, it was even more important to stand by the man whose life would be ended for the sake of honor. A man must stand by his kinsmen from birth until death, and now was the hour of death.

From the west the Folkungs and the Erik clan approached, all of them silent and solemn. From the east came the king's men and kinsmen with cheerful laughter and scornful talk, since they knew that victory was theirs, no matter how things turned out. If Magnus Folkesson chose to save his life by not coming, the king's men would be victorious because the Folkungs would be disgraced. And if Magnus Folkesson met Emund Ulvbane in battle, victory was equally assured but would be more entertaining to watch.

Foremost among the Folkungs came Birger Brosa, Magnus Folkesson, and his two sons, all wrapped in their thick blue mantles lined with marten fur, all wearing helmets and carrying the lion shield of the Folkungs on their left arm. Now the four took up position in front of their silent kinsmen and waited. Emund and his retinue deliberately arrived late.

The weather was cold, and the sun about to rise, coloring the sky red as blood behind the king's men. It would be a good day to die, everyone thought, as with an impatient murmur they flocked around and waited for the sun's first rays to break forth. That was the hour when the battle would be joined.

And when the sun's glowing rim was first seen, an inciting war cry rose from the king's side, and Emund Ulvbane threw off his mantle, drew his heavy sword, and walked with long, mighty strides out to the middle of the battlefield.

But what happened next no one could have imagined. The smaller of Magnus Folkesson's sons, the one they called the monk boy or the nun, now cast off his mantle, took off his helmet and his scabbard, drew his long, fragile sword and kissed it as he uttered an oath that no one could hear. Then he crossed himself and walked slowly but without hesitation toward Emund.

At first there was a great silence among the thousand men gathered, then a growing murmur of displeasure. Now all could see that the monk boy was not even wearing chain mail, so that the slightest blow could smite him dead to the ground. His helmet he had also left behind.

For Emund Ulvbane this was a raw affront since now they were trying to force him to quit the fight or without much honor slay a defenseless monk boy. That was what everyone must have thought. All the Folkungs realized it as well, and they were just as surprised as the king's men to see young Arn walk into single combat to the death instead of his father. It was a foolish and risky undertaking, for no one thought that Emund Ulvbane was a man to show mercy or walk away from a fight when victory was certain. But there was courage in that boy who was risking his own life to save his father's and the honor of his clan, and so thought the king's men as well.

But Emund Ulvbane would not let himself be trapped. Instead he decided to put a quick and humiliating end to the battle which this insult from the Folkungs deserved, and he now ran with great determination toward Arn with his sword raised, ready to sever the boy's head at once.

But Emund Ulvbane promptly found himself on the ground; he must have struck too eagerly at his opponent's head and thus badly missed his target. Yet the boy did not have the wit to exploit the God-given opportunity. He stood quite still, waiting for the raging royal giant to get up and attack again.

Three times Emund now struck at his opponent, who effortlessly and always moving in a circle avoided his sword without even parrying it with his own. Those who were standing far off and could not see clearly thought at first that Emund was toying cruelly with him, as a cat does with a mouse. But those who stood close saw clearly that that was not at all what happened.

From the Folkungs and the Erik clan now rose scattered laughter, and soon the battlefield thundered with laughter which washed like scorn over Emund Ulvbane, who despite all his furious efforts could only slice big holes in the air.

Arn already felt confident, for even though his opponent was big and rough, he wasn't as big as Brother Guilbert and not a tenth as skilled with a sword. The most important thing now was to spare Emund's life, not to be affected by pride, and soon, when Emund's panting got heavier and closer, to go on the attack. Arn was pleased that despite all good advice and the attempts to talk him out of it he had stood by his decision not to wear chain mail or a helmet. If he were going to win without killing he had to be able to move quickly, and he had to have good vision at every instant, for the slightest mistake would mean his death.

When Arn suddenly began to defend himself, Emund had already grown so sluggish in his movements that everyone could see it. And Arn made him even wearier by beginning to meet his opponent's blows with his sword or his shield, although always at an angle so that he deflected Emund's blows to the ground. Time after time sparks flew from Emund's heavy sword as he struck stone. Arn pretended to parry these blows straight on, but each time turned his wrist so that Emund's blows slipped past, and he didn't need to test this method long before Emund once again fell to the ground from his own weight and strength. Then Arn rushed up and pointed the tip of his sword at Emund's throat and spoke to him for the first time. Emund was on his knees, panting mightily, and it looked as though it was his final moment.

The two combatants were out in the middle of the battlefield, too far from all the shouting men for anyone to hear what was said between them. But one thing could be surmised, that the man who some called monk boy had offered Emund a chance to save his own skin if he surrendered, handing over his sword. Instead Emund suddenly threw himself back, away from the threatening tip of the sword, and stood up. So the battle was on again.

But now even the king's men realized what was happening and what they at first could neither see nor understand. The Folkung that Emund had insulted as a bitch puppy and nun was utterly superior to him, and it was no miracle or sorcery or accident, for they watched for too long for their eyes to have been deceived. Experienced warriors who stood close to other skilled warrior combatants began to describe what they were seeing, as they tried to understand and follow along in their minds what Arn was doing with his sword. They were already agreed that Arn's skill was great and that Emund had met his match. From the Folkung side the taunts began to grow louder, hurled toward the defeated man, and from the king's side scattered shouts were heard for Emund to surrender and hand over his shield. All had seen that his life had been spared several times over.

But Emund Ulvbane valued his honor higher than yielding to some puppy, and he had been in battle so many times that he was well aware that even hopeless defeats could suddenly turn without any miracle involved. But as he continued to fight he grew more cautious and began to move so as to save his strength.

At first Arn was somewhat confused by this and realized that now he could not win by causing Emund to surrender. That would have been the sensible thing to do when Emund noticed that his blows never hit home, and he should have begun to realize that Arn could strike him whenever he pleased. Arn felt that he had to think very clearly and not be affected by pride, no matter how defenseless Emund seemed. With great resolve he laid his shield on the ground to tempt Emund into new wild attacks that would sap him of all his strength.

A murmur of dismay spread across the battlefield when everyone saw that Arn had laid down his shield and shifted his sword to the wrong hand, for now Emund's chance to strike with one of his mortal blows was twice as great as before. And Emund took the bait. Reinvigorated, he attacked in both desperation and rage. Arn, who was now circling constantly in the wrong direction to Emund, had more opportunities to strike at his adversary's head or neck. Many saw this, though no one understood why he held back.

But Arn had a special plan. He had his eyes fixed not on Emund's head or neck but on his right wrist, where the Nordic chain mail offered no protection. The longer he circled around Emund, the more often that weak spot appeared, but he waited until he saw it openly displayed. Then he struck for the first time with all his might.

A gasp of horror passed through the thousand men gathered there when they saw Emund's great sword fly through the air with his right hand still gripping the hilt.

Emund dropped silently to his knees, tossed away his shield, and grabbed his severed wrist with his left hand to stanch the spurting blood.

Arn went up to him and pointed his sword at his throat, and everyone waited in abrupt silence for the mortal blow that was Arn's legal right.

Instead Arn picked up Emund's red shield with the black griffin head, turned his back to Emund, and picked up his own shield. Then he walked over to his father and handed him Emund's shield.

Some of the men who served Boleslav, the king's brother, hurried to Emund and carried him quickly out of sight.

With tears of pride and relief Magnus Folkesson triumphantly raised the conquered red shield to the sky, and the Folkungs drew their swords and beat on their shields so that a great battle noise erupted.

No man who was there would ever forget that day. And those who were not there would hear so many tell about it that they might as well have been present too.

Chapter 10

Like a stormy wind in the fall, Knut Eriksson, the aspirant to be king, came back from Norway to Western Götaland. First he rode to see his father's brother, Joar Jedvardsson, and celebrated Advent in the church at Eriksberg, offering prayers of thanksgiving for his return. But after that he had many kinsmen to visit and could say if nothing else that he came for the hunt. It had turned into a bitterly cold wolf winter in Western Götaland, when the snow was not too high for horses or plodding thralls but hindered the fleeing wolves. In such a winter the custom was for daring young hunters to ride from one estate to another to hunt for wolves. But besides the hunt there was a good deal to talk about concerning the victory of the Folkungs and the Erik clan at the *landsting* in Axevalla. And Knut had much to say about this and many ideas that he now wanted to sow to make it easier to reap when the time was ripe.

Knut's first and most important destination on this wolf expedition around the country was Arnäs. By the time he and his men arrived they were expected, since he had sent outriders the day before. Magnus had already sent Svarte and Kol with all the thralls available up to the forests north of Arnäs to encircle wolves where there were good hunting grounds.

They were rollicking, strong young men, and half were Norwegians who now with thundering hooves rode into the castle courtyard to be met immediately by house thralls running out to take their horses. With an agile leap Knut Eriksson was first out of the saddle, and he walked toward his host Magnus with his arms outspread. But the second person he embraced was Arn. He took the young man by the shoulders and shook him like a faithful friend, saying that this was in truth an especially dear meeting, for it was with Arn, and Arn above all, that he shared one of his strongest memories from his childhood. Arn at first didn't understand what that might be, but then Knut with great merriment reminded him of the time when the two of them sneaked into the very longhouse where they now stood to hear the Norse bard that Knut's father, Holy Saint Erik, had brought along. Then both of them had been pissed on by no less than a king and a saint.

Now Arn remembered and said that this was indeed a vivid memory, but it was also an event that was considerably better to remember than it was at the time. They both laughed loudly at this, and it was as if two friends had found each other after many years. With his arm around Arn's shoulder, Knut went into the longhouse as the foremost guest. The two young men had begun talking loudly and both at once, which prompted great amusement since one sounded like a Norseman and the other like a Dane.

It then felt as though God's blessing shone down upon this visit, for things had never been better at Arnäs. Nor had there ever been as much joy in the same place at the same time.

Magnus was now the esteemed father to a son who had vanquished Emund Ulvbane himself in single combat and brought immeasurable honor to his father's house and clan. Eskil felt equally pleased that his once defamed brother had now become the most talked-about man, and that all shadows between father and sons had been thereby chased away. Arn felt as though he, the prodigal son, was only now returning. Erika Joarsdotter was met with deep respect and lovely words from every direction. The oven-roasted venison ribs with Welsh spices and the small wild pigs with honey that she now was able to set forth with the house's best ale and mead aroused such loud cries of admiration and amazement from all the guests that they said *"skål"* to Magnus time after time to praise his good fortune at having found such a wife. None of the guests gave the least sign that they thought Erika's speech was muddled.

Knut Eriksson could not have received a warmer welcome at this estate, which for the sake of his plans he regarded as the most important in all of Western Götaland at the moment. He too felt great joy and relief at this visit.

When no one could possibly eat any more, though the ale still flowed, the talk turned to what all knew would come under discussion sooner or later, namely the battle at Axevalla *landsting*.

Arn was embarrassed and laconic on this topic of conversation, saying that he had merely defeated a lout with a useless sword and worse training, and thus there was little to recount. But Knut then asked to see the sword, at least, and whatever the son of a king and the guest of honor requested was done immediately. House thralls quickly returned with the sword, holding it outstretched.

In astonishment Knut drew the blade from its scabbard, at first weighing it in his hand. Then he went out on the floor and gave it a few tentative swings through the air, and it was plain to see that he had held a sword in his hand before. But he found the sword too light and too fragile, just as he had heard from the rumors, and he asked Arn to explain.

Arn objected that swords had little place at a banquet table with tankards of ale. But then he noticed Erika Joarsdotter's rosy, flushed face as she insisted that he show them all and explain, and so he obeyed at once.

He went over to Knut standing in the middle of the floor and asked permission to draw his friend's sword from the scabbard. He then weighed it in his hand.

"You have a heavy and beautifully decorated Norwegian sword, my dearest childhood friend," he said, swinging the sword thoughtfully through the air. "If you strike well then someone's helmet might not withstand it, but look here!"

He raised the sword as if to slam the flat of the blade in the middle of the fireplace, which would have snapped the sword in two. Knut shouted in horror. Arn checked his swing as if surprised, but then he laughed and respectfully handed over Knut's sword with care, saying that he naturally would never have damaged the sword with which a kingdom might be conquered.

But then he took his own sword from Knut, raised it, and slammed the flat of the blade with full force down onto the stone, and nothing happened except everyone heard the resounding ring of steel in the room.

"There you see the difference, my friend Knut," he taunted as he bent his sword at the tip several times. "Our Nordic swords are made of hard iron and can break; they are also heavy to wield. The sword I have is pliable at the top third near the tip; it will not break, and it is easy to swing."

What he said aroused wonder but not suspicion. Knut asked to exchange a few blows with Arn and drew his sword. Arn obediently raised his. As if to make a proper show of it, Arn parried Knut's blows a few times in the air, diminishing the power of the heavy sword with the light sword's flexibility. This enabled Arn to stand still and apparently not exert himself in the least while Knut had to use a great deal of strength for each blow without any effect. Finally Arn abruptly turned his wrist as he parried so that Knut's blow slipped down to the floor and he tumbled after. The Norwegian kinsmen in particular found this highly amusing.

But Knut got up more amazed than angry and went over to Arn to embrace his friend. He said that all the saints must see to it that their swords were always on the same side, for he would never want Arn as his adversary.

To this eloquence, these good words, and the ability to hold one's ale they now all drank together and with great emotion. They all felt that they were kinsmen in more than blood.

A moment later Erika Joarsdotter got up to bid everyone good-night. Eskil came over to her and offered his praise and thanks as he wished that she might sleep well. He had never done that before, and she felt as if long-frozen ice had finally melted as it does in late spring.

When Arn came to bid her good night she giggled happily and said she doubted whether anyone had ever received so much praise for someone else's cooking. Arn brushed off her remark and said that it was the cooking of the house that the guests had enjoyed, and that both of them had worked hard together to accomplish this. He added with a wink that it ought to remain their secret, for otherwise the rams from the North might once again find him unmanly. With that they parted with great love between stepmother and son.

Eskil now found occasion to make changes in the feast arrangements. Those who still had room for ale and mead could come up to one of his tower rooms over the courtyard; it was cold but soon the house thralls would bring in braziers. Then those who wished to sleep without noise in their ears could do so, and those who wanted to make noise could do that without bothering the mistress.

All the young men chose the tower room. Magnus found it wise to bid them good night.

Up in the tower room it was cold at first before the braziers were brought in, but the cold outside in the courtyard may have contributed as well, for by the time the young men were ready to resume their carousing the mood had changed.

In his cups Knut began to talk disingenuously about how it was actually ill advised that Arn had spared the life of Emund the king-killer. Although in another way it was also good that Arn had acted as he did, Knut hastened to assure them, for Emund was now the butt of eternal ridicule and was called Emund One-Hand instead of Ulvbane. But a king-killer did not deserve to live, and as his father's son Knut would have to finish off what Arn had not completed.

Arn blanched at these words and had nothing to say. Nor did he need to, since Eskil jumped into the conversation, but in a way that no one expected.

First Eskil affirmed that he understood full well Knut's intent, and he personally had nothing against it. Yet there was a minor vexation with this plan that as good kinsmen they perhaps could resolve.

He went and fetched a parchment map, rolling it out on one of the tables. Then he brought candles over and asked everyone to come and look. They gathered round him in curiosity.

Eskil first put his finger on Arnäs and followed the river Tidan over to the *ting* site Askeberga to the east, and then he stopped at Forsvik on the bank of Lake Vättern, which was the main estate of Emund Ulvbane, or One-Hand, he corrected himself.

"Look now and consider this," he said, circling Emund's lands with his finger. "Here Emund now sits at Forsvik, alone in an enemy land and with one hand cut off. That can't give him much joy or feeling of security. From the puppy Boleslav he can expect no help, and it will probably be a long time before Karl Sverkersson shows his snout here in Western Götaland. Look now! If we at Arnäs can buy Emund's lands, then we will own all the land between the lakes of Vänern and Vättern. We will have all roads and all trade in our hands. It would be a great step forward."

Eskil looked as if he thought everyone had understood what he was talking about, but that was not true. Knut replied gloomily that the one matter really had nothing to do with the other.

Then Eskil cloaked his objections in well-chosen phrases, suggesting that perhaps they could take care of this matter first, before they gave the king-killer what was coming to him. Otherwise his property would be passed down within the same enemy clan. But as things now stood, Eskil almost whispered, Emund would probably not oppose the idea of moving to more secure ground, and they might offer him quite a low price for Forsvik. That shouldn't be an excessively difficult negotiation.

Now two of Knut's Norwegian retainers named Geir Erlendsen and Elling the Strong, which he was called not without reason, burst out in thunderous laughter because they had understood the entire plan. Soon everyone in the room was laughing so hard the tears came; all except Arn, who had no idea what was so amusing.

They all merrily drank a *skål* to Eskil for his brilliant idea and promised as good kinsmen to see to it that this matter was attended to at once in the best way possible.

"Seldom have you, kinsman Eskil, had such a simple proposal to put to anyone," snorted Geir Erlendsen into his ale. "I do believe that Emund One-Hand will find it hard to say no to your offer, even if it's a low price. Then you can confidently leave the rest to us and it may well be that you'll end up getting back a good portion of your silver besides!"

"As sure as I am your leader and your future king, I swear that so shall we honor good kinsmen!" Knut Eriksson declared, and once again they all laughed with boisterous glee. Arn still understood nothing of the business that had just been concluded.

Before the hour grew too late, and since it would be a hard

ride through the snow the next day, the Norwegian kinsman Eyvind Jonsson suggested that it was time to hear the bard tell of ancestors and kinsmen and such sagas that bolstered the spirit. The bard, whose name was Orm Rögnvaldsen, then stepped forward but waited until everyone had refilled their tankards of ale. Then he sat down and made himself comfortable before he began. The West Gothic kinsmen were surely expecting stories of expeditions to the west, since these sagas were the favorites of all men. But what the bard began to recount was an entirely new saga, and it went like this:

It was at Ascension Day and many portents had been seen in the clouds. When Holy Saint Erik on this day took part in the high mass in the Holy Trinity Church on what was called the Lord's Hill in Östra Aros, a message was delivered to him by one of his men. The enemy was approaching the town, according to the message, and preparations must be made without delay to meet the foe with an armed troop. It is said that he replied: "Let me hear this great holy day mass to the end in peace. I trust sincerely in the Lord, and that we in some other place shall solemnly be allowed to hear what remains of His worship service." After these words he commended himself to God, crossed himself, and went out of the church to arm himself and his men. Despite their small number he proceeded bravely with them to meet the enemy.

The enemy joined them in battle, directing most of their forces against the king. When the enemy succeeded in felling the Lord's anointed king to the ground, they gave him wound upon wound. Soon he lay there half dead, but then they did even crueler things and subjected him to scorn and derision. With mocking words Emund Ulvbane, who was Karl Sverkersson's hired man, stepped forward and hacked off his venerable head, without respect and from the front. Then Holy Saint Erik went victorious from war to peace, and blessedly exchanged his earthly realm for the kingdom of Heaven. But at the place where his head fell a clear spring burst forth, and it runs to this day and is called Saint Erik's spring. Its waters have brought about many miracles. So Holy Saint Erik lives today and for all time among us.

When the bard Orm Rögnvaldsen finished his saga there was utter silence, with not even the sound of tankards being pounded on the table to call for more of the same. Instead Knut asked Arn to say a prayer for his father's eternal salvation, and to lend it more power by saying it in church language. Arn did so, but he was still shaken by sorrow and a feeling that resembled anger at what he had heard.

This was what Knut Eriksson had hired the skald Orm to recite at each and every house that they visited. Knut's intention was that no man in the land would be able to escape knowing this story.

The next day they had great success with the wolf hunt at Arnäs and shot eight animals. There was nothing better than wolf pelts in the winter.

That year a great mass was to be held early on Christmas morning at Husaby Church, which was the king's church. But no king would show himself there, for the West Goths had defended themselves against all such. But Judge Karle would be coming to Husaby, as the most distinguished man in Western Götaland.

And that was why the Folkungs would be celebrating their early Christmas mass in Husaby and not at their own church in Forshem.

But some days in advance a message came to Arnäs with a pupil sent by the priest in Forshem. He in turn had received an inquiry from the royal priest in Husaby which he himself had provoked by bragging about how good the choir singers were at his masses. Now the question was whether Arn could come a few days early to Husaby to practice with the choir so that the Christmas mass would benefit from his skill. Arn found this to be a Christian proposal that he could not refuse; he put aside his trowel and at once prepared to ride to Husaby. Magnus wanted to send retainers with him since Arn was now a man whose death would secure great renown for anyone who managed to kill him; he was also a man whose death would gladden the followers of the Sverkers. But Arn refused all such protection, declaring that on horseback and in daylight no one would dare attack him, at least not if he was allowed to ride his own miserable monk horse, he added with a laugh.

These days Magnus could also laugh at this matter, since he had realized that he was as wrong about Arn's horse as about his sword. Arn set off at dawn the next day, well armed and well wrapped in wolfskins, with church clothing in his saddlebags. There was a biting cold, but he set a good pace so that both he and Shimal kept warm without sweating, and he reached Husaby church and presbytery by noon. As soon as he had stabled Shimal and drunk a little welcome ale and broken bread with the priest's wife as custom required, he went to the church, which was the largest in Western Götaland after the cathedral in Skara. It had a huge tower on the west side which was built further back in time than anyone could remember.

He was in a very good mood because he liked singing and because the Christmas hymns were those that he believed everyone knew by heart, and besides, Christmas was a happy holy day which made the notes easy to sing, even for those who had not had much practice.

But among the singers in the choir he was not the only one who had received his training from the Cistercians. There was also Cecilia Pålsdotter, who in recent years had taken turns with her sister Katarina in being trained at Gudhem convent near Hornborga Lake.

He heard her voice as soon as he stepped inside the cold church. Her voice hovered clear and pure above all the others, and Arn stopped in amazement to listen. He had never heard anything so beautiful. That was how a boy's soprano could soar forth from a choir, just as he may have sounded as a boy at Vitae Schola. But he probably thought this was even better. There was more fullness and more life in this female soprano.

He had stopped far away from the singers who were rehearsing, and he couldn't see whose heavenly voice it was. Nor did he much care, since he had his eyes fixed on the stone floor so as not to be disturbed by anything as his ears tried to catch every last nuance of the music.

After the choir at the front of the church had sung four of the sixteen verses that Arn knew the hymn contained, the priest leading the singers paused to make a correction and scold someone singing in the second voice. Then Arn went over to greet the priest and bowed a bit timidly to the group of singers.

It was now that he saw her for the first time. It was as though he had seen Birgite from the Limfjord again, but now as a grown woman. The Birgite for whose sake he'd had to do so much penance. She had also caused him to argue with Father Henri about the true nature of love. He saw the same thick red hair in a plait down her back, the same merry brown eyes, and the same pale and lovely face. He must have been gaping at the young woman, because she gave him a teasing smile, apparently used to having young men stare at her. But she didn't know who he was, for the priest hadn't said anything about the fact that he had asked for an extra singer; he had especially refrained from mentioning who the singer might be, since he couldn't be sure that a son of Arnäs would take the trouble to come there just to practice a few carols.

The priest at Husaby was glad, of course, for if Arn was only half as good a singer as the somewhat boorish priest at Forshem boasted, this was going to be an unusually beautiful early Christmas mass. He already had an especially lovely soprano for the first voice. And as he was a priest who was more merry than strict and who welcomed a good jest and surprises if the occasion presented itself, he at once arranged a little practical joke.

He said only that another singer would be joining them from the church at Forshem, which Arn found to be a rather odd introduction, and now they would try the same piece they had just sung but with only two singers in two-part harmony. Then he motioned for Cecilia, who stepped forward with obvious confidence, once again showing her amusement at the staring peasant boy from Forshem.

Arn realized now that she was the one with the beautiful heavenly voice, and this insight made his gaping expression even more sheeplike.

Cecilia now did as the priest had asked, starting to sing the first voice by herself. She sang even louder, mischievously trying to put the singer from Forshem in his place.

But suddenly she then heard . . . no, it was more than hearing, she felt it through her whole body, as the new singer placed his second voice so close to hers, following her as if in a dance. Their voices intertwined, moving into each other, out, and then back, with the same ease as if they had always sung together. And she couldn't help raising her eyes to his. He was already gazing at her, and when their eyes met they both felt as though the Lord's voice had spoken through the other's voice. Then she began to vary her song, making it much more difficult. And he followed her, still in second voice, with the same ease as before; they no longer saw the other singers or the priest standing nearby. Everyone had been struck dumb by the beauty that now streamed out like light beneath the vault of the church, but the two young people saw only each other and they did not stop until all sixteen verses were sung.

It was a lengthy practice session that day but a great deal was accomplished. The Husaby priest was good to them all and in a brighter mood than anyone had ever seen him before. He showed kindness to those he wanted to correct, and soon everyone began to gain in confidence, understanding how all the carols should be sung. They now had the opportunity to hear two singers alone, each taking a separate part, but they also sang as a choir with two lead singers, and as a choir with one soprano voice, one second voice, and even a lone third voice, for Arn would insert a third voice wherever he liked in these simple, happy carols.

So all were in a very good mood when they stopped for supper. Now that Arn and Cecilia had a chance to talk to each other, they fell into lively conversation about where they each had learned to sing. Soon they were both talking at once about Gudhem convent and Vitae Schola and Varnhem. With eyes only for each other they came out onto the church steps where Cecilia's two retainers waited with her cloak and horse. Without staying for the evening meal, they were to accompany her home to Husaby manor for the night, as her father Algot had strictly prescribed.

One of the retainers took a couple of angry steps toward the singer boy, who was walking much too close to the maiden whose virtue he'd been sent to protect. But the second retainer, who had been at Axevalla *landsting*, took the man by the arm in warning, then pushed past and courteously greeted Herr Arn of Arnäs.

That was when Cecilia Algotsdotter came to an abrupt halt in all her happy chatter about singing at the convent, for she thought she must have heard wrong. This fair youth with the kind eyes could simply not be the man that everyone was talking about over every tankard of ale throughout Western Götaland.

"What is your name, cloister singer?" she asked with doubt in her voice.

"I am Arn Magnusson of Arnäs," Arn replied quickly and realized in the same instant that for the first time in his life he had said his name as it was. "And who might you be?" he added, with his gaze lingering on hers.

"I am Cecilia Algotsdotter of Husaby," she replied shyly, thereby making the same impression upon Arn as he had done upon her when he said his name. Both now understood that it truly was the Lord who had brought them together, just as they both had felt so strongly during the hot, intertwining encounter of their singing voices inside the church.

The early Christmas mass at Husaby church in the year of Grace 1166 would live on in everyone's memory. More beautiful praisesongs to the Lord had never been heard there before, on that everyone could agree. And during this mass it was as though not a single person succumbed to the weariness that usually came over everyone sooner or later from standing so long on the stone floor.

It seemed as though God were speaking even through what they all saw. The young Folkung in his blue mantle and with his blond hair stood beside the red-haired Pålsdotter in her green clan color. And when they sang together with such great joy and power, everyone could see what the Lord intended with these two. If their fathers, who were both present, didn't see it, there would be many at the coming feast at Husaby willing to speak to them about it. They all knew that there was neither silver nor business standing in the way, just as everyone knew that Algot Pålsson was in dire straits. It was as though Christ the Lord were speaking to the assembled congregation when he allowed the heavenly voices of the two young people to spread the joyful message of Christmas: that love is what redeems, love is the power that stands against evil, and love as they now saw and heard it at this Christmas mass was strong and clear.

Certainly Algot Pålsson had seen just as clearly what all the others who stood further back in the church could see. As the king's steward at the royal manor, he stood among the foremost parishioners, next to Judge Karle Eskilsson and Herr Magnus. And what he saw and what everyone else saw certainly did kindle a hope within him. But he knew from much experience that it was not easy to do business with Herr Magnus and his son Eskil. As things now stood, people were talking a great deal about the second son Arn, who was a close friend of Knut Eriksson, about whom it was whispered that he would be the country's next king. So what now looked like a clearly burning hope could turn to ashes as soon as business needed to be transacted. Perhaps the residents of Arnäs had big plans for a much finer match, perhaps they wanted to bind the Erik clan and the Folkungs even closer, perhaps they had thoughts of yet another Norwegian king's daughter. The fact that Cecilia and Arn had dreams that flew high and sang like birds for all to see and hear might not mean a thing when it came to negotiating a proper betrothal.

Algot Pålsson was thus cast between hope and despair as he pondered these possibilities. He also feared the feast, because it would be like burning all his ships on the beach behind him as their forefathers had done in the sagas when no return was possible. For Algot there was now no turning back.

Algot's obligation as steward of the royal estate was to see to it that the king could arrive whenever he liked, with as large a retinue as he wished, to be regaled for as long as he desired. A royal manor had to be ready at any moment to handle a large feast.

If the king himself, Karl Sverkersson, had sent outriders and announced that he and his retinue would be coming to the early Christmas mass in Husaby, as he and other kings had done many times before, everything would have been as it should be. But it also would have been unwise, considering what had happened to the king's father Sverker the Old on the road to the Christmas festivities. And right now Western Götaland was not safe ground for the men of the Sverker clan.

Instead a message had arrived that the Folkungs, with the judge and the men of Arnäs in the vanguard and many retainers, would be celebrating Christmas at Husaby as if the rights of the king were their own. To refuse would have been difficult, especially if Algot gave the only true reason, that this royal estate belonged to Karl Sverkersson and not to the Folkungs. Saying what was true and right would have been a death sentence.

But to say yes, as Algot Pålsson had done, might also be the same as death. Now it was winter and there was much snow, so no royal army would be coming before spring, and perhaps not even then. But if a royal army did come and proved victorious, it would not be easy to explain that the conquered enemy had eaten the king out of house and home at his own royal manor. The only thing Algot Pålsson had left to hope for was that the Folkungs and their kinsmen would be victorious in the spring. Otherwise he probably did not have long to live. He hadn't said a word to his daughter Cecilia about this quandary, and he had no idea whether in that girl's head of hers she would even comprehend what had happened.

But it was a very good feast. Of course, Algot Pålsson did at first feel squeezed tight between the shields when he sat with Judge Karle next to him in the high seat and the three foremost Folkungs from Arnäs seated in the places that followed in rank. It was not that difficult to see what they all thought about boldly eating the king's food as if it were their own. They showed no compunction in joking about the matter, every so often drinking a *skål* to the king, and each time laughing louder.

Cecilia and Arn had no opportunity to be alone at this feast. They could speak to each other with their eyes, for they sat only a few paces from each other. But this method of talking was the least discreet, since what they said was as clear to the eyes of everyone as bells tolling in the great hall.

Magnus and Eskil soon realized that they had a thorny problem facing them, but they had also agreed briefly in whispers that now was definitely not the right time or place to discuss the matter, either with Arn or amongst themselves.

After the Christmas feast at Husaby the Folkungs and their retainers rode south to Eriksberg to visit Joar Jedvardsson, Knut Eriksson, and their kinsmen for several days.

After much entertainment they returned wearily to Arnäs. But it wasn't long before Knut Eriksson and his wild Norwegian retainers arrived at Arnäs. They came armed as if they intended to do more than go on a successful wolf hunt up toward Tiveden Forest, although the hunt was the excuse they gave.

The weather, however, was at the moment unfit for hunting, which seemed to suit Knut Eriksson even better, since he had many things to discuss with the Folkungs. With Eskil he wanted to talk about what sort of business he ought to conduct once he became the king of the Swedes and Goths, and Eskil had plenty to say on that subject. Above all, Eskil thought that whoever ruled both Svealand and Eastern Götaland should do much more business with Saxony and Lübeck than they had done before. They had not understood how to exploit the Eastern Sea, acting as if it ended at the boundary with Denmark south of the forests of Småland. Such a trade route by sea could be very profitable, if they were allowed to have it in peace, which would mean concluding an agreement with the Lübeckers above all. But then they would also have to see about minting new royal coins, for the time was undoubtedly past when they could merely trade marten pelts for foreign goods. And then they would have to establish a trade route between Norway and the eastern parts of the realm that would extend from Lödöse across Lake Vänern, traversing the lands of Arnäs and then Lake Vättern. Above all Eskil thought that this route would be able to do plenty of business in dried fish from Lofoten, which could be purchased for almost nothing and then sold at a tidy profit.

Knut Eriksson was very enthusiastic about these business ideas. He said that as soon as he had won the three royal crowns, Eskil would become his foremost adviser in everything that had to do with money and trade.

There was only one thing that could be done at once, however, and that was the negotiation with Emund One-Hand over Forsvik, since his land was the missing link in the route from Norway to Svealand and Eastern Götaland. But since it was an arrangement that could be very good for one party and less favorable for the other, Eskil thought that they would have to conclude it in the new way, with a written bill of sale. There was little parchment and few writing implements at Arnäs but surely enough to accomplish this. Arn was asked whether he could compose such a document, and he said he could. At both Vitae Schola and Varnhem he had repeatedly worked alongside the archivarius, and at both these monasteries they archived many letters of this type dealing with donations and purchases. If they told him who would be buying what from whom and at what price, Arn could draw up such a letter immediately.

Arn listened briefly to Eskil's descriptions and then went up to the accounting room in the tower. But he came to supper with a beautiful letter on parchment to which he had affixed Magnus Folkesson's wax seal. Since the letter was in Latin, as such documents ought to be to possess the proper authority, he had to read it aloud in the vernacular several times for the others:

> In the name of the Holy and Indivisible Trinity, I, Magnus, lord of Arnäs, and my two sons Eskil and Arn, declare both for those now living and for posterity that the shameful and lengthy dispute between Emund Ulvbane and us and our sons is now at an end. And we have with God's help and the consent of both parties concluded the dispute as follows: that Emund Ulvbane shall transfer to us the estate of Forsvik with all appurtenances, fields, forests, fishing grounds, and all necessities belonging to the estate so that it may freely and forever after be owned by us. To this agreement for all posterity is attached 50 marks in silver in the people's language.
>
> Also I, Knut Eriksson, who next according to God have been the instigator of this conveyance and reconciliation, have with many witnesses participated in this conveyance. And so that this may be confirmed and irrevocable, we have sealed this letter with the impressions of both seals of Magnus and Knut and, through the power invested in us by Our Lord Jesus Christ, his Mother the Eternal Virgin Mary, and all the saints, we consign anyone who breaks this contract and agreement to outlawry. Witnesses hereto are Eskil and Arn Magnusson, Eyvind Jonsson, Orm Rögnvaldsen, Ragnar the Dean of Forshem, and many others, whose names we found too extensive to append.

After Arn had read his text three times so that all understood what it said, a long and lively discussion ensued. The Norwegian kinsmen thought that he shouldn't give Emund the name of Ulvbane but should properly call him One-Hand instead. Magnus countered that it was more likely that Emund would set his seal to a document that called him Ulvbane. Grumbling, the rams from the North eventually acquiesced.

After this Knut did not want to be called only by his patronymic but also with the appended *rex sveorum et gothorum*, words which at first Arn alone understood. He immediately objected to this title, observing that it would be like selling the skin before the bear was shot.

None of the others could make head or tail of this until Arn told them that the words meant *King of the Swedes and Goths*. Magnus then rose to speak, saying that he thought everyone present hoped, clear as water, that this would become true within the not-too-distant future. It should undoubtedly have happened already, but far too many Swedes and Goths actually believed that the king of Svealand and Eastern Götaland was Karl Sverkersson. Yet this was a document that would lose value if it possessed the slightest hint of inaccuracy. If they simply affixed Knut Eriksson's seal to the letter, then for all posterity it would have the same true value without those four additional words.

When Knut didn't seem willing to acquiesce in this matter, Arn pointed out that he had actually written the document as if Knut were already king, but with words that could have a double meaning, and then he read aloud the words, slowly and clearly:

> *through the power invested in us by Our Lord Jesus Christ, his Mother the Eternal Virgin Mary, and all the saints, we consign anyone who breaks this contract and agreement to outlawry . . .*

Arn explained that if one read this "we" to mean Knut Eriksson alone, then Knut had his power from God and only a king could have such. Besides, only a king had the sole authority to condemn someone to outlawry. The intention was to suggest that Knut Eriksson was king by God's grace, yet without saying it directly.

Knut then agreed to this and gave Arn his seal with the three crowns, asking him to go to the writing chamber to affix the seal. Now only Emund's seal was lacking, but they all considered it a foregone conclusion that it would soon be attached next to the other seals, even though Emund himself had not the slightest knowledge of this impending business transaction.

The next day Eskil and Knut, all the Norwegian retainers, and half of those from Arnäs were to ride to Forsvik on this errand. Arn wondered why they were so heavily armed for a peaceful mission carrying a load of silver, but Eskil explained that the best way to avoid a quarrel was to ensure that the man with whom one was about to conduct a tricky negotiation had as little desire to argue as possible. In that respect, Norwegian retainers would have a strongly cooling effect. When Emund affixed his seal to the document he needed to be in good health and of sound mind, otherwise everything would come to naught. Arn then thought that he understood and settled down.

Now Knut took Arn aside, saying that in this situation it would be best if Arn were not in the retinue, because his presence might adversely affect Emund's peace of mind. Arn easily and quickly agreed, so quickly in fact that it surprised Knut, who had been dreading this conversation. But Arn had other plans and other desires, and he mentioned somewhat cautiously that while his kinsmen were away on business near the shores of Lake Vättern, he would be taking care of some matters at Husaby. Knut understood at once what he was referring to, for Eskil had already told him about Cecilia and the difficulties that might arise for her and Arn.

It was just after St. Gertrude's Day, and spring was clearly felt in the air. The snow was easy enough to ride through but the ice was still hard, as the heavily laden and armed contingent rode out from Arnäs. They had to carry everything on their backs or in saddlebags, because no wagons could make it through at this point in the spring. Emund and his men would not be expecting visitors at this time of year, which would make the negotiations easier.

They rode first to the north until they reached the River Tidan; the ice there was still exposed, making it easier to proceed all the way to the Askeberga *ting* site. There they camped overnight in the shelters. The next day they started off at dawn so as to reach Forsvik by evening, wanting to enter the courtyard before Emund's men discovered their approach.

In this they were successful. Emund and his men were taken by surprise and swiftly disarmed. His retainers and others who looked capable of fighting were locked into storehouses and smithies and guarded closely by grim Norsemen. Present in the longhouse were only Emund himself, his grown son Germund, his wife Ingeborg, and three small children, as well as the house thralls that were necessary, although the visitors saw to it that none of them carried any weapons.

It was a somber feast at which Eskil and Knut ate heartily, speaking in loud, carefree voices, while Emund and his family replied suspiciously, giving curt answers to everything that was said.

Eskil seemed in especially good humor, and from the start he explained that he had come on business, and that they would surely succeed in reaching an agreement. After he had feasted for a while he ordered a chest of silver to be brought in. It was placed on the table between him and Emund, who brightened up a bit. The silver on the table spoke of business and not of death. And yet the conversation was sluggish.

After they had been eating for a long time, Eskil proposed

quite courteously that when they began to discuss the matter at hand, such discussions were best conducted among men, so Mistress Ingeborg and her children had the guests' permission to retire. The host family obeyed this command at once.

When Eskil and Knut were alone with Emund, Eskil spoke simply and clearly. He said that as far as the price was concerned it might seem a bit low, for it was clear that Forsvik was worth more than fifty marks in silver; anyone could see that. Here he broke off to open his silver chest and take out the bill of sale, which he read aloud in the vernacular, but without mentioning all the names in the letter and especially not Knut Eriksson's. With this Emund was even more convinced that this matter really did concern striking a bargain, although an unfavorable one for him.

Eskil then pointed out that the thirty marks in silver that Emund had received at Axevalla *landsting*, and now those words were mentioned for the first time, should be reckoned into the sale price. Those thirty marks had been intended as reconciliation, and Emund had not agreed to reconcile then, but he would be wise to do so now.

Emund nodded that he could understand that way of thinking and replied somewhat cautiously that eighty marks in silver was still a good sum, especially as it offered reconciliation into the bargain. Eskil said that he was glad it had been easy to understand each other so far.

But Emund was not ready to affix his seal and accept the silver until he had received certain assurances, for it did not seem safe and secure to do business with his own retainers taken prisoner by Norwegian berserkers of the most belligerent type. He could not understand why the man sitting at the table with them, the man called Knut, had anything to do with this matter, because he knew no Knut.

Eskil now replied that he could well understand Emund's apprehensions. But they could ease his concerns in a simple way: the next morning they would load the sleighs with Emund's family and those retainers who wanted to go along. After the sleighs had departed they would wait long enough for those who had left to reach safety before concluding the bargain. In this way Emund would not have to fear for the lives and safety of his family.

Emund concurred but added that his own life would not be worth much the moment he was left alone at Forsvik surrounded by men who were not his friends.

Eskil nodded thoughtfully at this and agreed that the same was true at the moment. But if Emund's kinsmen were allowed to leave alive with such a big head start that they could not be caught, then that would be much different from killing them all immediately, because an agreement was proving difficult to reach.

Emund then said that he would agree. But he had one last thing to suggest. The silver that would pay for the purchase should travel in the same sleighs with his family.

Eskil found that proposal unacceptable since it was not customary to pay for something one had not yet received. If Emund refused, all the silver would be lost and of no use. They agreed to meet each other halfway after wrangling for a while. Half the purchase price would leave with the morning's sleighs, and Emund would get the other half after he had confirmed the purchase with his own seal. There they left the matter, and they all retired for the night, though many at Forsvik had trouble sleeping.

When the morning came, half of the locked-up retainers were released so that they could have breakfast and prepare the sleighs that would be needed. Then Emund said goodbye to his wife Ingeborg and his children, who as agreed would carry half of the silver which Eskil brought out to the lead sleigh and placed next to Emund's wife. The sleighs then set off across the ice of Lake Vättern.

They waited without saying much in the longhouse until the sleighs' head start was so great that they could not be caught. Now it was time to conclude the bargain. Emund was melancholy and pale, and his left hand shook when with Eskil's help he burned his seal onto the bill of sale. The stump of his right arm, suppurating through his linen bandages, smelled terrible.

When the bill of sale was in order, Eskil carefully rolled it up and stuffed it inside his shirt. He shoved the chest with the second half of the purchase price over toward Emund and said goodbye, explaining that for his part there was nothing more to do at Forsvik. Some of his men would stay and maintain the manor until spring, when replacements from Arnäs would come to take over.

Then he went outside and gathered his waiting retainers from Arnäs. He mounted his horse and rode off without haste.

But inside the longhouse no one gave any sign of allowing Emund to leave in his waiting sleigh. When such a long time passed that Eskil was no longer in sight and could no longer hear any noise from Forsvik, Elling the Strong and Egil Olafsen of Ulateig went out to the courtyard and immediately killed the retainers who were waiting for their lord and flung their bodies into the sleigh.

When that was done they came back into the longhouse and sat down without saying a word, since nothing needed to be said. Everyone inside had heard and understood.

Now Knut turned to Emund and spoke to him in a low voice but with cold hatred.

"You wondered, Emund One-Hand, who I was since you did not know any Knut. I will now tell you, because I'm not an ordinary Norseman. I am Knut Eriksson, Erik Jedvardsson's son, and although you have paid your debt to Eskil Magnusson, you also have a debt owing to me."

Emund understood which debt he was referring to and jumped up as if intending to flee, but was caught with happy shouts by the Norsemen. With much scorn they dragged him out to the courtyard kicking and flailing, and there they spread him out on the ground by pounding spikes into the ground frost and tying his arms and legs so that he lay on his back with a piece of wood as a pillow.

Geir Erlendsen thought that they should have bound him in the other direction so that Knut could witness the good Norwegian custom of carving the blood-eagle into wretches who deserved to die in torment. But it would be sufficient, after the king-killer's ribs were broken and folded out like wings on the ground, if Knut could then with his bare hands rip Emund's heart from his body.

But Knut Eriksson refused to hear of it, since he did not want to soil his hands with an outlaw's blood. Rather, as the Holy Scriptures prescribed, the king-murderer should die in the same manner as he had murdered, by decapitation from the front.

Emund Ulvbane behaved in a manly way and did not beg for his life. With a single blow Knut Eriksson severed his head from his body and had it raised on a lance in the middle of the courtyard to remind the thralls who were left that there was a new lord at Forsvik. Emund's body was flung into the sleigh among those of the retainers, and the sleigh was sent off to be burned out on the ice of the lake.

Knut Eriksson and most of his men stayed only another day at Forsvik to go through whatever might seem useful in the storehouses and lake houses. What they found was good, for in one of the lake houses there was enough sawn oak to build the ship they had planned. Eyvind Jonsson, Jon Mickelsen, and Egil Olafsen of Ulateig had to remain at Forsvik to finish building the ship before the ice on Lake Vättern thawed. It would be a mighty task that only Norwegian shipbuilders could manage.

With the rest of his Norwegian retainers and some of those from Arnäs, Knut Eriksson headed back to Western Götaland. He had taken his first long stride on the path that would lead him to the three royal crowns.

⚜

> Listen, there is my friend!
> Yes, there he comes,
> bounding along on the hills.
> Like a gazelle is my friend
> or like a young stag.
> See, now he stands there behind my wall,
> he looks in through the window,
> he peers through the grating.
> My friend begins to speak,
> he says to me:
> Stand up, my beloved, you my beauty,
> and come outside.
> For see, winter is gone, the rainy time
> is over and has gone its way.

Again and again Arn murmured the words of the Lord to express what filled him more than anything else. He was riding toward Husaby, making great clods of earth and frozen snow and ice spurt up around Shimal's hooves. The stallion was hot and sweaty, but Arn bore his own heat within and thought that the springtime wind of speed could cool him. He knew full well that this might not be the most suitable state of mind for appearing in the house of the Lord to sing the Lord's praises and His alone. And he was very sure that Father Henri would have had many stern views on the matter.

But he rode like a lunatic with the speed of a fool because he could do nothing else. So filled was he with Cecilia that all else had to stand aside except the Lord Himself. And it felt as though the Devil were tempting him with evil thoughts, asking if he had to choose between the Lord's love or Cecilia's, which would he choose? Evil thoughts seemed to force themselves on him no matter how much he tried to defend himself, as if the Devil had truly discovered a soul with a great weakness.

He had to stop, dismount from Shimal, and pray for forgiveness for the wicked thoughts that had seeped inside him. He prayed until he was freezing cold and then even more. After that he continued on at a more modest pace, for he had come so close to Husaby that people there would soon be able to see him.

He arrived at the church in good time and led Shimal to the priest's stable. He wiped the horse down, covering him with homespun so that he wouldn't cool off too fast after the sweaty ride. Shimal looked at him with his big, grateful eyes—as if the stallion had been wronged and had seen through him.

It was Annunciation Day, the time when the storks came to Western Götaland and when the plow was to be put to work in the fields at Vitae Schola in Denmark. This mass was suited to Arn's voice just as well as the mass at Christmas. The Virgin Mary was the patroness of the monastery at Varnhem, and all singers who came from Varnhem thus knew every mass by heart that belonged to the Holy Virgin.

But during the singing in the church he still felt himself led astray into sin even though he sang with Cecilia as ecstatically as at Christmas. In lines of text when the words spoke of love for Our Lady he looked Cecilia in the eyes and meant every word for her, and in her voice when she replied he felt that she was singing in the same way and meant the same as he did.

Without realizing that he was thereby trampling on Algot Pålsson's self-respect, he invited himself to stay a few days at the Husaby royal manor so that he and Cecilia could practice new songs before the next mass. Arn had sensed, without knowing the reason for it, that Algot Pålsson was not a man to refuse any request that came from a son of Arnäs. So little needed to be said about the matter, before everything was arranged as Arn had requested.

But after that a conflict broke out between the two young people on the one hand, and everyone who wanted to or was required to watch over them on the other. They tried to use all their cunning to find a chance to speak together in private. Algot and the older women in the house saw this and in turn used all their cunning to watch them at every moment. As long as they sat demurely in the hall with other people close by and sang the Lord's praises in one song more beautiful than the last, no one had any objections. Both Arn and Cecilia had a great tolerance for sitting together and singing, but it was no greater than other people's tenacity in watching them. And a careful vigil was kept that they did not sit too close. At supper the two young people sat in the high seat, but with Algot as a mighty breakwater between them, and they couldn't come near each other except when Cecilia politely poured more ale for Arn, which caused him some torment because he had vowed never again in his life to drink as much ale as he had at the first feast in Husaby.

Just before Annunciation Day, Priest Sune in Husaby had attended a collegium with Bishop Bengt in Skara. Despite the terrible condition of the roads at this time of year, many more clergymen from the diocese had gathered than expected, a sign of the great unrest that had spread on the winds of gossip in all of Western Götaland after the *landsting* at Axevalla. Everyone knew that King Karl Sverkersson would not be content after having lost all power in Western Götaland, just as everyone knew that Knut Eriksson was the foremost contender to oppose the king and take his crown from him. If the worst happened, King Karl would come with an army to Western Götaland, and it was not easy to say who would win that battle. The only certainty was that such a war would severely ravage the land.

The question that the collegium with Bishop Bengt had to resolve was whether the church should speak for one or the other in this struggle for earthly power. The clergymen were equally divided between those who supported King Karl, including the bishop himself, and those who preferred Knut Eriksson. But most thought that the only wise position for the church to take would be not to get involved in this struggle. For if the church interjected itself in such a game, much grief could come from it.

But there were also other matters to discuss when the clergymen of the diocese had gathered. The cathedral dean had recounted for those who wanted to listen, and also for those who no longer wished to hear, how he had been an eyewitness to a miracle when a little defenseless monk boy from Varnhem, with the help of the archangel Gabriel, smote two warriors to the ground.

Since Priest Sune now sat at the supper table in the Husaby royal manor and saw Arn seated there too, he was reminded of this story of the miracle and recounted the tale as he had heard it. Everyone listened with eager attention except Arn, who did not seem to like what he heard. The priest was then struck by a thought that Arn perhaps knew more about this event; he came from Varnhem, after all. Perhaps he even knew the monk boy involved. So the priest asked Arn if he was familiar with the story.

Everyone could see that Arn found the question awkward, but

they could not understand why. It was hard to believe that Arn might feel envy toward one of the other monk boys.

Arn was slow to reply since he felt himself trapped, but unlike other people, he could not resort to lies. So he told the truth, pointing out that the cathedral dean's version of the story was all wrong. There was no question of a miracle, nor was the little monk boy defenseless, since Arn himself was the person in question. What happened was that drunken peasants had come running from a wedding ale and absurdly accused him of being a bride-robber, despite the fact that he had been outside the cloister walls for only a few hours. They had sought to kill him, but so that the killing would seem more honorable, they had given him a sword to defend himself.

At this point in his explanation Arn had to pause and think about how to continue. He would have preferred to avoid it altogether, as he thought he had already said what needed to be said, and as he was not the least bit proud of what he had done, but instead felt great remorse. Yet he had learned enough about how people thought out in the base world that he assumed they might find him boastful. The one who was bragging was actually the cathedral dean, who in his pride thought he had witnessed a miracle of the Lord, when it was merely an accident, but that too was difficult to assert without speaking ill of the dean.

In the intolerable silence that followed, Cecilia asked that he continue. He looked up and met her gaze, and it was as if the Virgin Mary spoke to him and told him how to couch his words to fashion a good story.

He passed quickly over the painful part. Drunken peasants had by mistake set out to kill someone they thought was a defenseless monk boy, although it was Arn, who had been trained in the art of the sword by a Templar knight of the Lord. So the fight was brief. It was no miracle, just as it was no miracle at the Axevalla *ting*.

And yet there was a miracle in this story, a miracle of love.

For in the subsequent events that the dean had not witnessed or failed to understand—the union of Gunvor and Gunnar—one could truly see the Virgin Mary's ineffable goodness and Her care for those who set their trust in Her. Arn blushed a bit at his audacious words regarding the dean, but no one in the hall scolded him or frowned.

Having come this far in his account, Arn then recited the verses from the Holy Scriptures about victorious eternal love, which he knew so well that he could recall them at any time. With this he made a great impression on everyone at the table and especially on Cecilia, just as he had hoped.

The priest from Husaby had turned thoughtful and attested that the words Arn had recited were all truly God's word. He added that love truly could accomplish miracles; the Holy Scriptures had many examples of this. It was assuredly no simple matter to understand, since most people who lived in the society of Western Götaland were forced to celebrate the wedding ale for entirely different reasons than those granted to Gunvor and Gunnar. But Arn had told this story with good ecclesiastical understanding, and for that reason the priest of Husaby was in agreement with him. Our Lady had truly demonstrated a miracle of love and faith and not a miracle of the sword or violence. From this there was certainly something to be learned.

To all around the table it seemed rather unclear what was to be learned, although it was a lovely story. But the priest of Husaby did not choose to clarify further. On the other hand, he did take Algot aside after the conclusion of the meal and prayers and had a conversation with him that no one else heard.

It may have been this conversation that caused Algot to have a number of new ideas, for the next morning Algot asked Arn if he, who was good with horses, would take Cecilia with him on a ride in the beautiful spring weather. Arn did not have to be asked twice.

And so it was that Cecilia and Arn rode side by side up the southern slopes of Kinnekulle on this first warm day of spring with gentle breezes. There were catkins on the pussy willows, there was plenty of water in the streams, and the ground was only flecked with snow. At first they didn't dare speak to each other although they were finally alone, for the retainers who followed them kept a polite distance so they could keep watch but stay out of earshot. All that Arn had said to her in his feverish nighttime thoughts or when he galloped along on Shimal and yelled the words to the wind now remained unsaid. Instead he soon found himself entangled in childish descriptions of Shimal's superior qualities and why horses from the Holy Land were so much better than other steeds.

Cecilia seemed only moderately interested in the topic. But she smiled as if to encourage him to speak in any case. She had also had long nocturnal conversations with Arn in her dreams, although then she had always imagined that he would say the right words first and that she would then urge him on so that he said more of the same. Faced with talk of horses' qualities and the best way to breed horses, she had little to say.

When Arn was near despair at his own shyness and the betrayal of all he had promised to say to her as soon as he had a chance, he prayed silently to the Holy Mother of God to give him just a little of the power that Gunvor had received. And at once the words came to him as if Our Lady were showing him the way with a gentle smile. He slowed Shimal, glanced nervously back at the retainers who were still out of earshot, and recited the words to Cecilia with his gaze fixed on her eyes and jubilation in his heart:

> *You have taken my heart,*
> *you my sister, my bride,*
> *you have taken my heart*

with a single glance
with a single link of the chain
around your neck.
How beautiful is your love,
you my sister, my bride!
Yes, sweeter than wine, and the scent
of your salves surpasses all spices.
Your lips drip with sweetness
my bride
your tongue hides honey and milk
and the scent of your clothing
is like the scent of Lebanon.

When Cecilia heard the words of the Lord, which were also Arn's words to her, she reined in her horse and gave him a long look, speaking to him with her eyes, just as they had been forced to say everything until now. She sat quite still in the saddle but was breathing hard.

"You can never understand, Arn Magnusson, how much I have longed for these words from you," she said at last without lowering her gaze. "Ever since our eyes met as our voices merged in our first song. I want to be yours more than I want anything else on this earth."

"I am also yours, Cecilia Pålsdotter, more than anything else on earth and for all time," replied Arn, filled with a solemnity that made the words sound like a prayer. "It's true that you took my heart with a single glance, as the word of God says. From you I never want to part."

They rode a bit in silence until they came to an ancient and half-dead oak leaning over a small stream. There they got down from their horses and sat on the ground, leaning against the oak tree. The retainers from Husaby hesitantly stopped a short distance away and seemed to disagree whether they should come closer. The sound from the stream meant that they couldn't hear anything unless they came very close. They chose to sit where they were so that they could see but not hear.

Cecilia and Arn took each other's hands and looked at each other without saying a thing for a long time, since they both felt the miracle within them.

Finally Arn said that now he had to ride back to Arnäs, no matter how hard it was to part, and explain to his father Magnus how things now stood. Perhaps, he said, they could hold the betrothal ale this summer.

At first his words made her so happy that she clutched at her heart almost in pain, but then a cloud seemed to come over her face.

"Perhaps we may need as much support from the Holy Virgin Mary as Gunvor and Gunnar did in that beautiful story you told," she said gravely. "For our love has difficult tests and great obstacles ahead, as you probably know, don't you?"

"No, I know no such things," said Arn. "There are no great obstacles, not a mountain that is too high, not a forest that is too deep, or a sea that is too wide to sail across. With God's help nothing shall stand in our way."

"We will have to pray mightily for God's help," she replied, with her eyes lowered. "For my father is Karl Sverkersson's man, and your father is Knut Eriksson's man; everyone knows that. My father fears for his life because of this, and as long as Karl is alive my father will probably not dare bind himself to the Folkungs. That's how it is, my dear beloved Arn. Oh, what a joy to say those words! Nevertheless, our love has more than a great sea to cross as long as Karl Sverkersson is king and my father is the king's man."

But Arn refused to be cast down by this. Not only was his

confidence great, but he believed that the Virgin Mary was on their side. And no matter how much he knew about Aristotle and Holy Saint Bernard de Clairvaux, about Plato's high and base worlds, and about the Cistercian rules for living—matters that people in Western Götaland knew nothing about—he still knew very little about the rules that applied in the struggle for power. And that is what people in Western Götaland knew everything about.

He relied entirely on his belief that the greatest of all things was love.

Chapter 11

Magnus and Eskil were sitting by themselves in the accounting room in the tower, and the topic they were discussing was not an easy one. It suited them that Arn was busy these days. He spent most of his time a short distance out on Lake Vänern, where he sawed blocks of ice shaped the same as building stones for walls. The ice blocks were pulled on a sledge back to Arnäs and stored in his ice cellar between layers of shavings from the carpentry shops. He had firmly announced that it had to be done now before the ice was too thin. It was just as well that he had this urgent task to do; it would have been hard to have this conversation if he were with them.

Both Magnus and Eskil knew from their own experience that young men, and apparently also young women according to what they'd heard, were struck by temptations that could be rather difficult. This was part of life, and there was not much to be done about it other than wait for it to pass, like a head cold in the spring. Magnus recalled such things from his early

347

youth, and as he thought back he also turned sentimental and confessed to Eskil that the woman who had been the first mistress of Arnäs, and mother to Eskil and Arn, at first had meant no more to him than a pair of beautiful chestnut horses or other fine acquisitions for the estate. But over time Sigrid had become more dear to him than anyone else. What Arn called love could grow with prudence if a couple lived well and sensibly together. When Magnus thought about it more closely, he'd noticed that Erika Joarsdotter had recently become fairer and easier to deal with too, and sometimes downright pleasant. At least it had never been as easy to have her in the house as now. That's how things went with what Arn called love.

But this was the wisdom of an elder, which could not be transmitted in words to the younger man. It was meaningless to try and talk sense in such situations, because sense was beside the point. It was the same as telling someone who had just lost a kinsman and laid him in the ground that time heals all wounds. It was true but meaningless at a time when grief was at its worst.

So what should they do with Arn and his talk about wanting to rush off to Husaby tomorrow and celebrate his betrothal ale?

Eskil thought that cooler heads ought to prevail, which would be much easier when Arn was not present, since he was like a red-hot iron. There were certain things that spoke for the betrothal and other things that spoke against it. These things and nothing else had to be weighed like silver to ascertain in the end which weighed the most.

Against Arn's proposal, more than anything else, was the fact that right now no one knew who would hold the power of king during the next two years. Nevertheless, as long as Karl Sverkersson was king, Algot Pålsson would have to be wary of binding his clan to the king's enemies, at least if he was a wise man. And for their own part it was also ill advised to unite by marriage with a clan that was an enemy of Knut Eriksson, who might well become king.

On the positive side, Forsvik on the shore of Lake Vättern belonged to Arnäs, and they controlled the entire northern part of Western Götaland—the section south of Tiveden Forest where the trade route between four countries would be established. The weakest part was the stretch near Kinnekulle, where Algot's land began. If Magnus could acquire Kinnekulle and the shore of Lake Vänern south of there, it would be worth a great deal. And if an opportunity arose to make such a deal, Algot would be hard-pressed to say no and might even be persuaded to give these lands as dowry, though the value was twice as much as was customary.

It was inconceivable that this could be accomplished as long as Karl Sverkersson was alive. But Algot would be all the more amenable to doing business if Karl Sverkersson left this earthly life as swiftly as Knut Eriksson intended.

That was the situation. As long as King Karl Sverkersson sat safely in his castle in the middle of Lake Vättern, there was nothing to be done. But if he departed this life, an important deal for Arnäs could be concluded at once.

Eskil could see only one weakness in his calculation. It was the question of whether Birger Brosa and the clan *ting* might have other plans. That's what had happened when his own father Magnus had considered celebrating a wedding ale with either Cecilia or Katarina, for precisely the same reasons that they had just discussed. Instead, Erika Joarsdotter had been chosen, because the clan *ting* found that marriage more beneficial.

But Magnus said that he hadn't heard mention of any plans of that sort. As things now stood, they had formed a good alliance with the Erik clan through Erika Joarsdotter. Knut did have a sister, whose name was Margareta, but she was already married to King Sverre of Norway.

Since Magnus's own brother Birger Brosa was married to Brigida, who was the daughter of King Harald Gille of Norway, the Norwegian bond was very strong. No, right now Magnus could see no marriage that would be considered more important for Arnäs or for the clan than with either Katarina or Cecilia, it didn't matter which.

It remained to decide who would convey their decision to Arn. The message was simple. As long as King Karl was alive there would be no betrothal ale.

But though the words might be easy to formulate, it would be no easy task to say them to a young son or brother living in the fever or madness called love.

Magnus ought to tell him, since he was Arn's father and the power over all wedding ales was rightfully his. Or perhaps Eskil should do it instead, since he was Arn's brother but had no power; he could not be talked out of it, but merely explain. For a while they twisted and turned this matter, like a tender joint of meat, and then decided that Eskil would be the one to tell Arn how matters stood.

A week before St. Tiburtius's Day, April 14th, when the ice still covered the lake but was beginning to soften, Knut Eriksson arrived at Arnäs without announcing himself in advance. He had traveled fast, accompanied only by Geir Erlendsen, the bard Orm Rögnvaldsen, and Berse the Strong. They had traveled far and wide in Western Götaland, where the bard had a chance to justify the good wages he was paid, and they had just come from Skara, where Knut had many eyes and ears. There they had purchased particularly good information from a man who had just left Karl Sverkersson's service at his castle out on Visingö in the middle of Lake Vättern.

Knut didn't reveal the purpose of his visit other than to say that he was looking for Arn, whom he found moping about among house thralls in the cookhouses, a place and a situation hardly worthy of a man like Arn, in Knut Eriksson's opinion.

To Arn's perplexity Knut immediately wanted to challenge him to an archery contest, so a target was made of straw bound together and set up in the castle courtyard. Arn didn't want to refuse, but he found no joy in this exercise. They set the target at a distance of forty paces, which Arn thought seemed too difficult for Knut, but that was what he ordered. They selected the best and strongest bows, and everyone at the estate gathered to watch, for they all knew that this might be the country's next king who was about to shoot arrows with one of the sons of Arnäs. And no one wanted to say afterward that he had failed to witness the contest.

When they stood next to each other with their bows ready, Arn still didn't seem to have any desire for the game. So Knut took him by the shoulders, embraced him, and said the following words, which he had thought out carefully:

"Now, my dearest childhood friend, you shall shoot to win against your king and nothing less, as if everything depended on these arrows. Imagine that it's about Cecilia; yes, I know all about you and her. Imagine that I am your king and can give her to you but only if you defeat me. Look, now I'll shoot first. Don't answer me now, just shoot well."

While Arn, shaken by these words, composed himself so he might do his best, Knut shot his ten arrows and aroused great admiration, for no one knew that he was such a good shot.

Then Arn shot, with a cold expression and a great silence inside, as if everything really did depend on these arrows. Afterward all could see that there was a great difference between the two, and that Arn was the better archer.

Now Knut grabbed Arn again and embraced him, saying that it

might well be that Arn had just shot his way to making Cecilia Algotsdotter his wife. Then they left the courtyard and went alone to the tower. There Knut asked to have ale brought up to them.

When they were alone, Knut did not wait for the ale before he began to explain the entire situation to Arn. The time had now arrived. For himself it was a matter of the crown, and for Arn it was Cecilia. Knut Eriksson had many informants around the country, which is how he knew everything that was important to know, and also some things that to many might seem less important, such as this matter with Arn and Cecilia.

Arn replied morosely that he could well understand that many sorts of skills were required for someone who strove to win a king's crown, but he didn't understand the intention behind this game with bow and arrow that they had just played. Why stage this contest when a prospective king took a great risk of losing and thus being talked about as the loser?

Just then the house thralls arrived with ale, and Knut smiled broadly at this interruption, because he seemed to understand Arn's impatience and puzzlement. They politely drank a *skål* to each other first, as custom demanded, and Knut saw in Arn's eyes the burning impatience that insisted on an immediate response. And yet he gave no answer, but began speaking of his father, Holy Saint Erik, who had been good to everyone, who had demanded nothing for himself, who had preferred his hair shirt and longs hours of prayer to courtly life, who had helped the weak and stood up to the strong, and who had died like a saint at the hands of an outlaw. Perhaps Arn had heard much of this story before, but there was one more thing to add.

Erik Jedvardsson's father was Jedvard of Orkney, who had sailed with Sigurd Jorsalafar to the Holy Land and there performed great services for the Norwegian king. In gratitude for this Christian help, King Sigurd had granted Jedvard of Orkney two small splinters of the Holy Cross on which Our Savior was tortured and died. King Sigurd had been given a piece of the holy wood from King Baldwin of Outremer, or the Kingdom of Jerusalem.

Here Knut paused in his story and asked Arn whether he had heard of Outremer, and Arn's happy laugh and eager nod made him quickly understand that he had.

Well, these two splinters from the Holy Cross had been inherited by Knut's father, Erik Jedvardsson, and he'd had them cast inside a gold cross that he always wore around his neck. When Emund One-Hand chopped off his head, the holy relic fell to the ground and was conveyed by a wily man to the one who stood behind the murder, the man now called King Karl Sverkersson. So he was not only a king-killer but also an outlaw who had violated a holy relic of God. The gold cross containing the wooden splinters from Our Savior's Cross inside was now worn by Karl Sverkersson himself around his neck, and this had to be a constant abomination in God's eyes. Surely there could be no doubt about that.

Arn at once agreed that this must be abominable in God's eyes, and he added that everything must be done to right this' wrong.

Then Knut Eriksson smiled at Arn and repeated quietly that now the hour was upon them. But to reach the place where God's holy relic might now be found, they would need a select few men who could tolerate cold and were able to sail well, who were skilled with a bow and could defend themselves better with a sword than any other men.

That was why they had staged this contest, Knut went on. There were men who could shoot well in a contest but could not do the same in battle, when their heads were full of anger and fear. Such had been the case for Arn when asked to shoot and simultaneously think about Cecilia, but Arn had acquitted himself well.

Now, not later, was when they must do what had to be done, Knut continued. Then a bit hesitantly and with an assurance that when he became king he would be the first to bless a wedding ale between Arn and Cecilia, Knut asked whether Arn wished to join this expedition as one of only eight men.

This was the third time that someone had told Arn he would never have Cecilia as long as Karl Sverkersson was alive. If he had hesitated the first two times, he did not do so now.

✠

When they arrived at Forsvik by the shore of Lake Vättern, they found that Eyvind Jonsson, Jon Mickelsen, and Egil Olafsen of Ulateig had built a small but elegant ship that was broad in the beam, had a shallow draft, and could be rowed with three pairs of oars. The Norwegian retainers apologized for not adorning the ship with the runes required to finish it completely, but seaworthiness had been foremost on their minds because the ice would soon begin to thaw. This small ship, which was built like a Norse longship, could be sailed faster than other ships of the day, especially in Western Götaland; it could be rowed faster than any other, especially with Norwegian oarsmen; and it could be dragged easily over ice. Knut was very pleased with what he saw and explained everything to Arn, who hadn't had as much to do with Norway as others in his clan.

After three days of waiting it was time to set out. They first celebrated a mass, which Arn, to lend the words greater power, held in church language. After the mass Knut Eriksson spoke to them and spurred them on. Their strength lay in the fact that they were eight good men who would cross Lake Vättern when no one believed it was possible. Out there on the southern tip of the island of Visingö sat the king-killer Karl Sverkersson with his retainers, assuming he was safe. But God would not stand by the man who had murdered a saint for his own gain. When they had won what now had to be won, each and every one of them would be rewarded according to his merits.

More was not said. The ship was pulled by horses up from the hole in the ice by the shore where it had lain so that the water would make the planking swell and grow tight. The horses were stabled, and then they finished loading the ship. Each of the men grabbed the end of a rope for the hard task of dragging the ship out to open water. But the broad-beamed vessel was easy to drag on the ice, and eight men were not too few.

After half a day's toil they came to a channel leading toward the open water in the middle of Lake Vättern, and from there they could already see Visingö. The wind was westerly as usual at this time of year, and they were soon able to set sail. The farther south they sailed, the more the channel widened. In the dusk they saw that the southern tip of Visingö lay surrounded by open water, and they understood then that God was with them. Had they come a day earlier they would have been forced to leave their ship out on the ice, fully visible as soon as day broke. A day later and the ice on Lake Vättern would have dispersed, and a guard would have been posted on the walls of the royal fortress of Näs to watch for dangers approaching from the sea.

They lowered their sail and rowed slowly toward Näs, reaching the shore only after it had long been dark. There they pulled in to wait in a little cove with dense alder thickets. They pulled the sail over their ship and lighted fires in two iron braziers, sending scouts ashore to make sure the fires weren't visible. For they did need heat, since the spring nights in the North were still bitterly cold.

Knut was in a good mood, as if all the difficult things had already been accomplished. He sat close to Arn and said that this was either their last night together or their first on a long journey.

Then he talked about the man who had murdered his own father, and who had tried to murder Arn's father with trickery and unfair single combat, but Arn interrupted him at once, saying that these words were unnecessary. He knew all this already and had given it much thought.

And yet he felt doubt, he admitted to Knut. He had sworn a holy oath not to raise his sword in anger or for his own benefit, and now it seemed that he was on his way to doing just that. He would gain much from Karl Sverkersson's death. He said that he understood that it was not merely a question of taking back the holy relic that rightfully belonged to his good friend Knut, and which hung unjustly around Karl Sverkersson's neck. He understood that this neck should be severed when the cross was freed.

Knut said nothing to release Arn from his anguish, because what Arn had said was entirely true. Instead Knut spoke in a low, warm tone about Cecilia and what a joy it would be as their king to bring them together in any church they liked, even before the archbishop in Östra Aros if they so desired. Arn then grew warm with tenderness despite the raw, damp late winter night, and replied that any church at all would be fine as far as he was concerned, as long as it was close by. And then they laughed together. As their laughter died away, Knut said that if he liked, Arn could borrow one of several good Norwegian swords that were not bound by a holy oath.

Then Knut lowered his voice and explained what was going to happen. In Skara they had bought much information, but most importantly from a man who a short time ago had left Karl Sverkersson's service at Näs. They had found out that when there was no danger at Näs, such as now when the ice could neither bear nor break, Karl Sverkersson took a short walk down to the beach each morning, to be by himself. Why he did this no one quite knew, but he always followed the same route in the early morning, just at dawn, when the first light allowed him to see where he set his foot.

For this important information, Karl Sverkersson's traitor had received the wages he so justly deserved.

If God was now with them, all this would happen by the time the night was over. All that remained now was to pray and then try to get some sleep.

A watch was set out. The ship was well hidden in the darkness behind the alders near the beach.

Arn did not sleep much on that cold night, and perhaps the other men didn't either, even though they were Norsemen and did not seem frightened that the next day might be their last.

But everything went as though God were standing by them. Arn stood ready with bow and arrow when it was still pitch-dark. With the very first light he moved to a somewhat better position. Next to him stood Knut himself and Jon Mickelsen and Egil Olafsen of Ulateig, and they all were wearing thick wolfskins and double leggings against the cold. They stood so near the royal fortress that they could have easily reached the top of the wall with an arrow-shot. Arn wore a Norwegian sword at his side. They didn't say much to one another.

When the heavy oak gate in the wall of Näs opened, however, it was as if all the cold in their limbs vanished, and they seemed to glow with excitement. They saw a man come out with two men by his side. They watched the three come walking toward the strand quite near to the place where they were standing. Arn made a move to draw his bow, but the other three stopped him at once.

In the faint light of dawn it was hard to distinguish colors. But when the three men from the castle walked past at a distance of a couple of paces, it seemed that the one in front was wearing a red mantle and a golden cross that gleamed at his neck. Knut Eriksson held up his hand in warning so that no one would act before he did, although they all knew it was the king walking past.

King Karl Sverkersson went all the way down to the shore of Lake Vättern. There he stopped and bent down to the water, cupping some it in his hand. He drank the water before he fell to his knees, and for the last time he offered a prayer of thanksgiving because this water had saved his life for another night.

There was no frost on the ground, so Knut Eriksson was able to stride forward as soon as the three men by the water had knelt down, and they could not hear him coming. He chopped off the head of the king at once and then did the same to one of the retainers. But he did not kill the other man. Instead he held his sword to his throat and waved for Egil and Jon to come forward at once, which they did swiftly after whispering to Arn to stay where he was.

Arn now saw how his dearest childhood friend leaned down to pick up the golden chain and rinsed it clean of blood in the water of Lake Vättern. He then walked quickly toward Arn after whispering something to his Norwegian retainers, and they dragged the survivor off with them, holding a hand over his mouth.

They pulled the ship into the water and got on board. The Norsemen sat down at the oars and Knut stood at the tiller in the stern holding the captive with one hand and the golden chain with God's holy relic in the other. When they were ready to cast off he released his prisoner and spoke to him in a loud voice.

"Now I say to you, captive, that you are free. You have been given your life, but you shall also know who, other than God, has given you life. I am Knut Eriksson and I am now your king. Go to the mass of St. Tiburtius tomorrow and thank God for your life, for just as He saved your life, it was He who led us here. But make haste so that no one thinks you were the one who killed Karl Sverkersson!"

Then Knut signaled with his hand for the rowers to pull away, and with powerful strokes of the oars they moved swiftly out into clear water farther than an arrow-shot could reach. The captive, who had been released like a kitten into the water by King Knut Eriksson, now ran as fast as he could toward the half-open oak gate in the walls of the royal fortress, the fortress that was built so securely that no one could ever have succeeded in killing the king inside.

The oarsmen rested on their oars to await Karl Sverkersson's retainers, who came running down to the shore with crossbows and longbows in hand. They shot their arrows in vain, and King Knut held the holy relic of God over his head in triumph.

Then they set a course for Forsvik, which lay against the wind. No pursuers in Western Götaland would be able to row against the wind like King Knut's Norwegian kinsmen.

✠

The week after the martyrs Filippus and Jacob were remembered on the first of May, when all the livestock were let out to pasture and the inspection of the fences was complete, the late spring all at once changed to summer. The mild south wind continued for a long time, all the tender greenery appeared at once, and among the oaks on the slopes of Kinnekulle lay a thick white carpet of wood anemones. The cuckoo was heard first in the west.

This time Arn came riding alone and at a leisurely pace toward Husaby. He seemed to want to draw out the sweet torment now that he knew that Cecilia would be his. He also had much to think about because recent days had been full of tasks in the service of Knut Eriksson. Much had happened, and he wasn't sure whether he understood Knut's intentions behind all of it.

When they returned to Forsvik after their successful journey to Visingö, they were able to sail right into the harbor, such was the difference in the ice after only one day. Knut immediately dispatched a messenger relay to Arnäs and Magnus Folkesson, who would send word on to Joar Jedvardsson at Eriksberg. First their own kinsmen had to be informed about what had happened, for soon armies would be assembling for war.

Arn had been prepared to ride with the news, thinking that it would arrive sooner that way. But Knut had said that there were important tasks that required Arn's assistance on behalf of his king; he could ride to Cecilia after everything that had to be done was done.

First Knut and Arn had to sail across Vättern again with both horses and retainers, and then ride together to Bjälbo and let Birger Brosa know what had happened. There was not a single day to lose, for ignorance could be the same as death; all their kinsmen had to be rallied in time before the enemy attacked. Besides, it was only right that Birger Brosa be informed about what had happened by one of his own who had also been involved in the outlaw's demise on Visingö. Likewise it was important to meet with the next most important man, Archbishop Stéphan in Östra Aros. Knut had to win over both Birger Brosa and the archbishop to his cause, and both these men were close to Arn. Arn had nothing to say against this.

When they came riding into Bjälbo, Birger Brosa had received them at first as if they were only young men arriving for a visit with kinsmen, and he apologized that he would have to leave the next day because he had important business in Linköping. But when they were left alone at Knut's request and Birger Brosa learned what had transpired, he no longer spoke of taking a business trip. No one from Bjälbo would set foot in Linköping for a long time, since it had been Karl Sverkersson's town and would now become Boleslav's or Kol's.

Birger Brosa sat in dull silence, pondering, without revealing with the slightest expression what his thoughts might be. Suddenly he sprang up and said that there was only one choice. Now the entire Folkung clan must stand as one man behind Knut Eriksson in his effort to take back his father's crown. It was the

only way. They had to stand united against the Sverker clan and
their Danish hangers-on. They had to show strength and resolve,
just as they had to make the most intelligent use of the advantage
they now held in terms of time and knowledge.

Considering the condition the ice had been in the day before
when Karl Sverkersson met his doom out in Lake Vättern, it
would take another day before the news spread to the main-
land. Birger Brosa took it upon himself to use that information
in Eastern Götaland, but he proposed that Knut also had to act
swiftly and set off for Östra Aros immediately. He needed to win
over Archbishop Stéphan to his side if possible, and then try to
rally the Swedes to a *ting* at Mora Stones in order to elect a new
king. All this had to be done quickly, so there was no more time
for a visit or a rest. Everything was to be done as Birger Brosa
had said.

Knut Eriksson agreed at once with Birger Brosa's plan, since
he knew full well that Birger Brosa was the wisest of men in
regard to everything having to do with the struggle for power.
But when they were getting ready to depart, Knut made one request that Arn found hard to understand. He wanted them to
fetch from the Bjälbo armory Folkung shields, blue mantles, and
pennants to fly from the lances, as well as a large group of retainers. Birger Brosa had nodded his assent immediately, as if he
understood precisely what Knut Eriksson was thinking with this
request. But Arn had also come to realize that the thoughts of
men like Knut and Birger often traveled along entirely different
paths than his own.

In Östra Aros, Archbishop Stéphan at first refused to receive
Knut Eriksson when he asked for admittance to the archbishop's
residence. According to a rumor, the archbishop had been angry
and said something to the effect that this man came only for the
sake of intrigue.

But when Archbishop Stéphan learned that Knut was ac-

companied by Arn Magnusson, he changed his mind and immediately received the two. When they met in the archbishop's
dim writing chamber Arn fell at once to his knees and kissed his
hand, while Knut at first was hesitant to do the same. To Knut's
chagrin the conversation was then conducted in church language
so that he was now the least important of the three; several times
he was tempted to be vexed at Arn for words that were not Arn's
but the archbishop's.

What Archbishop Stéphan had to say to Knut Eriksson was
clear and easy to understand, however, even if it was unpleasant.
The church neither could nor would take sides in this dispute
that now approached. As archbishop, Stéphan was concerned
with God's kingdom, and not with the disputes of earthly contenders for the crown, so there could be no question of support-
ing either Knut or Karl Sverkersson's brothers, or whoever else
might come running from the south. Earthly power was one
thing, and God's power was another.

Knut Eriksson controlled himself well when he understood
that there was nothing more to gain in this matter, but he asked
Arn to request that they might both receive Holy Communion
from the archbishop himself at the next day's mass. Even though
Archbishop Stéphan sensed that Knut had other motives beyond
receiving communion, he agreed. Perhaps he also perceived this
as a good and friendly way to disentangle himself from this dispute with a man who could well become the next king of the
realm. Even if the church could not get involved in the struggle
for the power of the king, the church at least ought to be on a
good footing with earthly authority.

As soon as they had respectfully taken their leave of the archbishop, however, Knut showed himself full of energy and eagerness. He said that there was yet much to be gained, and when
they went back to join their waiting men, still dressed in their

THE ROAD TO JERUSALEM

traveling attire and without the blue colors, he told them to go into town to spread certain rumors.

Knut and Arn rode at the head of the column of retainers to mass the next day, and now they showed the blue colors from their lance tips and mantles. Knut and Arn were also fully armed, with shields displaying the Folkung lion and the three crowns.

So many people had been lured by the rumors to this mass that most could not get into the church but had to stand outside. At the church steps Knut and Arn dismounted while their retainers stayed to hold their horses.

They entered side by side, and everyone respectfully made room for them. In the vestibule, Knut unbuckled his sword as was customary and set it aside. But when they proceeded up the aisle Knut was astonished to see that Arn had not removed his sword, and leaned over to whisper to him. But Arn gave him a secretive smile and shook his head. And what occurred when they reached the archbishop to receive communion served to benefit Knut Eriksson as much as it surprised him. For when they stopped, Arn drew his sword so that a startled gasp went through the whole congregation. In the next instant he handed over the sword to the archbishop himself, who accepted it reverently, kissed it, and sprinkled holy water on it before he handed it back. Arn then bowed, sheathed the sword in its scabbard, and fell to his knees, whispering to Knut to do the same at once.

All the others had moved away, and they knelt there alone to take communion from the archbishop himself. The two did not stay for the rest of the mass but walked slowly side by side out of the church as soon as they had taken God's holy sacrament.

When they came out onto the church steps there was already a great commotion, for the rumor of the sword that the archbishop had blessed had already reached the crowd, but no one there knew which sword it was.

Now, however, Knut drew his sword and declared in a loud voice that the sword he held in his hand was blessed by God and with this sword he had slain the man who was an outlaw and who had murdered King Erik on this very spot. Then he removed the golden chain that he wore around his neck and held it up in the sunshine so that the cross flashed. He announced that this was the holy relic of God which he had taken from the outlaw Karl Sverkersson, and since he, Knut, had equally great respect for the Swedes and their *ting* as his father Erik had always had, he now called a *ting* in five days and asked them to ride to the judges and chieftains in Svealand to tell them.

When he finished speaking a tumult broke out anew, instigated first by their own retainers, but soon enough involving everyone assembled. No one could now dispute that the archbishop himself had taken a position on the question of who should be elected king of Svealand. And so this rumor also spread with the speed of the wind.

Later the same day, when they were back in their camp, where Knut had ordered water fetched from Saint Erik's spring so that he could personally bless all of those who came to him for this reason, Arn was released from his duties to the king.

Knut took him aside and said that now they faced some boring days of waiting and conversations with one man arriving after the other. Knut suspected that Arn might not have much patience for this. What could be finer than to ride for all he was worth to see Cecilia? For Knut did not want to be so hard on his friend that he would stand in the way of such happiness any longer.

Then Arn embraced his best friend and they soon parted. Arn rode for the sake of his dreams, and Knut stayed for the sake of power.

It had taken Arn a week to reach the slopes of Husaby, yet that was faster than any man in the North could have managed it, at least on a Nordic horse. He had also stopped at home in Arnäs to tell them everything that had happened and to scour himself and change his clothes.

Now he was finally riding along with Husaby in sight, moving so slowly and with such short reins that Shimal pranced impatiently. The closer he came to Husaby the less he cared about all the strange things he had witnessed in the struggle for power.

Algot Pålsson had been called to Arnäs to settle the dowry, and they had found it just as well that such discussions be handled between Eskil and Magnus on the one hand and Algot on the other; Arn did not need to attend.

This proposal had suited him doubly. First, he was not in the least interested in whether he and Cecilia were a good bargain, or even a bad one, for either of their fathers. Second, he would rather meet Cecilia with all the fine things he had to say to her without being watched over by her father or his suspicious retainers.

Now everything seemed too good to be true. Soon he would be with her. Soon he would hold her in his arms and tell her that it was likely that the betrothal ale would be celebrated at Husaby as early as Eskilsmas.

Magnus and Eskil had arranged it, apparently without first asking Algot, so that the betrothal ale would be held at Husaby and the wedding ale at Arnäs. Cecilia would be given Forsvik as a morning gift. It would be up to Eskil and Magnus to squeeze the dowry out of Algot.

But Arn had no worry about such matters on his conscience. A few forests or beaches, what were they compared to the greatest thing of all that God had granted humanity?

And even if Algot did not care particularly about his daughter's feelings, just as Magnus would not take the wishes of his second son seriously in such matters, Algot was still going to secure the life and property of his own clan through this marriage. That much Arn did understand now.

A short time ago, when he'd last seen Cecilia, everything had looked dark and hopeless, but it was now suffused with light. Like Gunvor and Gunnar, Arn and Cecilia would never neglect to thank the Virgin Mary for her power, manifested once again, and for her teaching that greatest of all was love.

When Arn approached the Husaby royal estate, the thralls at work sowing turnips noticed him, and some of them ran up to the manor to announce his arrival. So a great commotion arose at once, and by the time Arn reached the house, all the thralls, retainers, and other people at the estate were lined up in a double row leading up to the door of the longhouse. When Arn rode in between them the thralls' warbling shouts of jubilation rang out, and the retainers banged on their weapons while the thralls did the same on whatever lay to hand.

Cecilia came out on the porch of the longhouse and at first took a few steps forward, as if she had thought to run and meet Arn. But then she restrained herself, clasped her hands, and stood erect as she waited for him. Her grandmother Ulrika came out on the porch looking as if she wanted to say something stern, but when she discovered Arn approaching between the ranks of thralls and retainers she stopped herself and stood waiting in the same manner as her granddaughter.

Inside Arn a battle was raging as he dismounted from Shimal and handed the reins to a thrall who came running. Arn's face was hot and he knew he was blushing. His heart was pounding so wildly that he thought he might lose his wits, and he had to exert all his self-restraint to go to meet Cecilia respectfully and courteously before all these eyes, just as she waited for him so calmly with her gaze lowered demurely.

But then she raised her eyes and they looked at each other

briefly, and all polite control burst, and they ran to each other. When they met they threw their arms around each other in a way that was not at all proper for young people who had not yet drunk their betrothal ale. Then the thralls' jubilant ululations rose again, and such a great noise commenced that none could make himself heard for a good long while.

The thralls of Husaby already knew everything about what had happened and what was to be expected, and many of them hoped to follow along with Cecilia after the wedding ale. They believed that anyone who went with Cecilia and young Herr Arn would be better treated than anywhere else. Among the thralls only good things were said of Arn, things that had nothing to do with swords and bows and other topics that free men discussed over their ale tankards. Instead they talked of how young Herr Arn treated thralls like men.

Cecilia and Arn did not want to let each other go, but forced themselves to do so when Grandmother Ulrika coughed for the third time. The two women and Arn then went into the longhouse so that Arn might be welcomed with some ale and break a piece of bread. Once inside the longhouse, Grandmother Ulrika spoke before the young people could say a word. She began to interrogate them about the morning gift, the dowry, and where the betrothal ale was to be celebrated. Arn had to make an effort to answer all these inquiries as if he really cared, and he had to describe the property at Forsvik, the number of outbuildings and the size of the main house, the number of thralls in the house, and other details of which he had no knowledge. Only then did Ulrika ask about things that seemed more important, about what stand the Folkungs in Eastern Götaland had taken and whether the Swedes had held a *ting* yet. Arn was able to reassure her that the Folkungs in both Eastern and Western Götaland stood united with the Erik clan, and that he did believe that Knut Eriksson had already been elected king at the *ting* of

the Swedes. Judging by all he had heard from everybody as he
rode south from Östra Aros through Svealand, there seemed to
be no doubt in this matter. King Erik Jedvardsson had been a
much loved king in Svealand, and as Arn understood it, Karl
Sverkersson was not at all liked in the same way. Up there among
the Swedes, they hardly knew who the king's brothers Kol and
Boleslav were, nor did they care. So presumably Knut Eriksson
was already the king of the Swedes, and he would come to the
landsting in Western Götaland in the summer to be elected king
here as well.

Mistress Ulrika let herself be satisfied with all these glad tid-
ings and also recognized that she had interrupted the young
people by forcing Arn to talk of such concerns that of course
were more important than their giddy and heated feelings and
yet concerned them little right now. So she surprised them by
remarking in a knowing tone that the weather was beautiful
and that there was no harm in taking a horseback ride up Kinnekulle. At these words Cecilia jumped up and embraced her
grandmother, who was otherwise so somber and strict.

Soon Cecilia had a good-natured mare saddled and bridled
and was dressed for a ride in a loose and warm green cloak that
reached from her throat to her feet. With a practiced hand she
swept her cloak over one arm and was in the saddle before Arn
or the thralls had time to help her. Arn accepted a leather bag
containing bread and bacon and wooden cups which a house
thrall kindly brought in case the ride should be a long one, as she
added with a shameless laugh. In the meantime Cecilia urged
on her mare and went galloping off. Some distance away she
turned in the saddle and shouted to Arn to try and catch her. He
cast his head back and laughed with heartfelt joy, patted Shimal
lovingly on the neck, and joked that now they both had a hunt
before them that must not fail. Then he leaped into the saddle
with a single bound that made those who were standing around

murmur in astonishment, and set off. At first he held Shimal back to a canter so that he wouldn't catch up too soon with the fluttering green cloak and the red hair far ahead of him, and yet only a few breaths away.

When they were out of sight of the Husaby royal manor he set Shimal into a full gallop. Like the wind he caught up with and passed Cecilia, wheeled Shimal around and stormed back toward her, veering off at the last second. Then he rode circles around her, enjoying her bright laughter that made him bold and soon reckless. He stood up in the saddle and balanced with his arms in the air as he again rode past her at full speed so that she had to rein in her horse. When he turned to her with a laugh, holding his hands arrogantly on his hips, he didn't see the thick oak limb that swept him like a glove to the ground.

It looked like a nasty fall, and he lay completely still. Beside herself with worry, Cecilia pulled up her horse, jumped off, and dashed over to Arn. She began caressing his lifeless face in despair. But then he opened first one eye and then the other, and laughing, took her in his arms, rolling around with her among the wood anemones as she feigned anger and chided him for scaring her so.

All at once they fell silent. They sat up and held each other for a long time without saying a word, as if there were no words possible just now, only the singing of the birds.

They sat there until their limbs began to ache from the uncomfortable position. She pulled away first and leaned back in the grass. He lay down next to her and caressed her face, struggling briefly with his shyness. He kissed her cautiously on the forehead first and then her cheeks and lips. Soon she returned his kisses and their shyness was as if blown away by the wind.

They came back late to the Husaby royal manor.

Chapter 12

It was Cecilia's goodness that plunged them both into the deepest unhappiness. As Arn so bitterly explained their misfortune, one had only to compare her for a moment with her sister Katarina to see it at once. Besides, it was between the two sisters that everything had been determined from the very beginning.

For Katarina, Cecilia's happiness meant her own unhappiness. Since Cecilia was no longer going to return to Gudhem for any further studies in either the progress of the spirit or the hand, it meant as Katarina saw it that she would be trapped like a rat behind the odious cloister walls. That feeling was even stronger when she found out what a large dowry her father Algot had been forced to part with to marry one of his daughters into the Folkung clan. It was now no longer plausible that Algot would allow Katarina to marry too, and she feared that she would be confined to the convent forever and would dry up like an old maid.

Cecilia and Arn had not yet celebrated their betrothal ale, though this was not of their doing but because of the ongoing power struggle. It had been somewhat more difficult for Knut Eriksson to persuade the Swedes to elect him king at Mora Stones than he had first imagined. And when that matter was finally settled, his plan to come to the *landsting* in Western Götaland was delayed still further by the fact that Boleslav sent an army against him. He had to convince the Swedes that the first thing they needed to do for their new king was to march off to war.

But Boleslav had not assembled a sufficiently large force and was defeated at once by Knut Eriksson and his Swedes, along with Birger Brosa and the Folkungs of Eastern Götaland. All was now well, but it had taken time, and the summer was more than half gone.

Magnus Folkesson at Arnäs, however, was bullheadedly determined to have a king at table when the wedding ale was drunk, so he wanted to wait until Knut managed to conclude his *landsting* in Western Götaland, where he no doubt would be elected with great unanimity.

As a consequence Arn and Cecilia might well have been man and wife before God as they now rode toward Gudhem, but they were merely betrothed. Yet it would soon be evident that Cecilia was carrying Arn's child under her heart.

With great concern Arn had inquired about this from Eskil, who was well acquainted with the worldly laws of the land. But Eskil had only laughed and said that what the law prescribed in this situation, if Cecilia's father really wanted to make a case out of it and drag their shame all the way to the *ting*, was that Arn would be obligated to pay six marks in silver for damages. Eskil thus waved this matter aside by saying that Algot Pålsson was hardly in a position to begin arguing over such paltry sums. Nothing worse than that would come of it.

Out of sisterly affection Cecilia wanted to meet with Katarina in order to offer her some solace if possible. For Cecilia it was not hard to imagine what torments Katarina must be suffering within the walls of Gudhem, since she believed she knew her sister well.

But she did not, as it turned out. If she had, she would never have set foot in Gudhem to try and console Katarina.

When the two sisters met in the cloister garden at Gudhem, Cecilia did her best to keep from bubbling over the whole time about her own happiness. She made an effort to console Katarina by saying that as soon as the wedding was over she would have a talk with their father, who would probably take her words more seriously after she had been accepted into the Folkung clan. They would find a way to make Algot listen to reason; perhaps something as simple as the fact that he was miserly and it cost much silver as well as oak forests to keep daughters locked up in a convent. Even more silver would be squandered, if it was a daughter who did not appreciate in the least this special form of fatherly love. At this truth they had a good giggle together.

Once again Cecilia was enticed to talk about her own happiness, about how they would first live at Arnäs as long as there were times of strife, how they then would move to Forsvik by Lake Vättern, how they would travel with Eskil to meet the Norwegian kinsmen, and anything else she could think of to talk about concerning all that Katarina regarded as the free, happy life outside the cloister walls. Cecilia was much too full of her own happiness to see how Katarina's eyes narrowed with hatred and envy. When Katarina almost furtively asked whether it was too much visiting recently that had made Cecilia's waist thicker than before, Cecilia could no longer hold back her joy. And she revealed the secret that was certainly no more than a small sin to be absolved for the price of six marks in silver and some Pater Nosters and Ave Marias, perhaps a hair shirt and a week on bread and water and whatever other penance there might be. But it was true that she was already with child. And since she had come to that topic of conversation she couldn't check herself for long, since she felt both so much dread and such great happiness at the prospect of bearing a child.

Katarina was no longer listening to her younger sister's childish prattle. For she was already thinking of how this matter could turn out to be her own salvation.

When it was finally time to part, she embraced Cecilia tenderly and told her to take good care of her unborn child and to give her warmest congratulations to Arn.

But as soon as the cloister gate closed behind Cecilia, who angered Katarina further by heaving a sigh of relief as she stepped outside, Katarina hurried to her prioress full of cold resolve. She sought to bring about a dramatic change, the sooner the better.

Gudhem was a young convent that had recently been established with donations from King Karl Sverkersson, just as he had donated the land for Vreta convent in Eastern Götaland. It was impossible to know for sure what the Erik clan thought of cloisters that had originated with Karl Sverkersson and his clan. But the prioress of Gudhem, Mother Rikissa, who was of the Sverker clan and close kin with the now murdered King Karl, had expressed her strong concern that Gudhem might either have to move or close. If Knut Eriksson became king, as everyone believed, it wouldn't be worth much to belong to the Sverker clan in Western Götaland, nor would it be wise to stay in a convent with Sverker origins. It was generally known how Erik Jedvardsson in his day had extended his greedy hands toward Varnhem.

Mother Rikissa was a grasping woman; some called her downright vicious, and it was sometimes difficult for young novices to deal with her. But as a close relation to the king, she also had a firm understanding of worldly power.

Katarina now came and unexpectedly confessed to an old sin that she had kept silent about in her earlier confession, recounting the carnal relations that she'd had with young Arn Magnusson. Mother Rikissa should have been very strict with Katarina because of her long silence. But as Katarina explained with her eyes lowered as she seemed to wipe away a tear, her sin had now become even worse. That same Arn had seduced not only her, as he with a smooth tongue promised her a betrothal ale, but also her sister Cecilia, who was now with child.

Mother Rikissa saw at once a great possibility opening up. Katarina had clearly also seen it, since she demurely pointed out that the seducer Arn was Knut Eriksson's close friend, and that much trouble could be stirred up for the enemy if Arn Magnusson were to be excommunicated.

Mother Rikissa prescribed a very mild punishment for Katarina's inadequate confession and belated admission, and sent her away for a week of solitude, silence, bread and water, and the usual list of prayers. Katarina humbled herself and kissed Mother Rikissa's hand in gratitude, thanking aloud the Holy Virgin for the kindness that had been vouchsafed her. Then she left with a little satisfied smile, which sharp-eyed Mother Rikissa did not fail to notice.

The prioress strode resolutely toward the scriptorum, ramming her heels hard on the floor, a sound that the novices at Gudhem feared more than anything else. There she wrote to Boleslav, insisting that he must appeal to the archbishop in Östra Aros regarding this matter. She also wrote to Bishop Bengt in Skara, telling him that he must deal with this excommunication as soon as possible, before the crime was compounded by being blessed by any servant of the Lord in the diocese who married the two sinners. She harbored a great hope of winning Bishop Bengt to her side, since she knew that he shared her uneasiness that the time of generosity toward the church and its foremost servants might now be at an end. For Bishop Bengt owed a great debt of gratitude to the Sverker clan as well.

Katarina and Mother Rikissa soon got what they both wanted, although they had very different reasons for wishing it to be so. Two weeks later Bishop Bengt announced at the mass in Skara cathedral that Cecilia Algotsdotter and Arn Magnusson had been excommunicated. No clergyman in all of Western Götaland could have anything to do with either of them. The only sanctuary they would be able to seek was within a cloister.

✠

For the second time Arn and Cecilia traveled together to Gudhem cloister, but this time their journey was lamentable. Magnus had sent an escort to accompany them on the road, and all the retainers were strictly enjoined to bear the Folkung colors and pennants. Magnus did not want his son to ride in shame and neglect to his penance and sanctuary.

They had not much to say to each other on the way, since everything had already been said before. Cecilia had found it difficult to forgive Arn, no matter how many times he explained that he was so drunk on ale when Katarina came to him that he hardly knew what was happening. But Cecilia objected to the fact that he had kept it from her anyway, so that she was unknowingly dragged into a sin that could have been avoided. He feebly tried to defend himself by saying that he hadn't found it easy to tell the one person in the world he loved above all others that he had sinned with her sister. And he hadn't known of the law that declared it an abomination. She believed him on the latter point, although she found it odd that he of all people wouldn't know the Christian law. After they had hashed this over again and again until it was more than enough, they started to think about the road ahead. As Arn understood the situation, it might take a long time before the sin was confessed to Rome and absolved, perhaps a year or even longer. She had a gloomier view of the future.

When they parted outside the walls of Gudhem he swore before God that he would come back one day to take her out of there. He swore on his sword to convince her even further, though she merely found that childish. But he stubbornly repeated that she had to believe him, and never waiver in that belief. For as long as he breathed he would always look forward to the day when they could be reunited, and he beseeched her not to take the three cloister vows, because such vows could not be taken back. Better to live as a novice, although novices, like lay brothers, had a worse time of it in the cloister than those who took the vows. She nodded silently at his words, tore herself away from him, and ran toward the gate where Mother Rikissa, scornful and stern, awaited her. When the iron-mounted oak gate slammed shut behind Cecilia, Arn felt such great sorrow that he thought he would breathe no more. He fell to his knees and prayed for a long time. In silence the retainers waited patiently some distance away. They too were filled with sorrow for his sake, for the sake of the Folkungs, and for all the joy that had been stolen from them and their Erik kinsmen. They felt hatred toward the Sverker clan because everyone knew that they were behind what had happened.

Arn rode only a short way together with his men from Arnäs. Then he stopped and changed into the Folkung battle garb, the simple gray homespun garment with a red border that he had worn as his first worldly clothing on that day less than a year ago when he had ridden out from Varnhem. At that time it was expected that he would learn something about the base world. He had indeed learned much in the past year, but right now he found that most of it was evil.

He decided abruptly that he would ride alone toward Varnhem along the eastern shore of Hornborga Lake and through the forest of the mountain Billingen. The retainers certainly tried to dissuade him from this, for the times were uncertain and no one could know for sure what lurked in the forests. Arn replied coldly that in truth he had no intention of relinquishing his sword and may the Lord preserve any highwaymen or other rabble who attacked him in his present state of mind. With that he wheeled Shimal around and rode off without another word. All the retainers in his escort knew that none of them would be able to follow his stallion at the pace it had set, and they could do nothing but begin the dismal return to Arnäs without the one whose life they had sworn to protect, with their own if necessary.

Arn rode a long time across fens and bogs where there was no human dwelling. It had already grown dark by the time he reached the slopes of Billingen. He knew that he needed only to continue north and he would soon come upon the fields of Varnhem, where he would either recognize the way or be able to ask directions. But it was risky to ride in the hills at night, and the sky was overcast, with neither moon nor stars lighting his way. He continued on listlessly for as long as he could see where he was steering Shimal, but he soon had to prepare to stop for the night. It was going to be cold, since he had no sheepskins with him and only a thin cloak, but he took this as only the beginning of the tests and the penance that he knew lay before him. He wanted to suffer much, if only it shortened the time of punishment, so that with God's help he would be able to fulfill his holy vow to fetch Cecilia from Gudhem.

In the dusk he found a little hut where a fire was glowing, and next to it stood a tumbledown stable where a cow lowed restlessly when he approached. He surmised that freed or escaped thralls lived here, but he would rather sleep in their hut than out in the cold woods.

He boldly entered the hut to ask for shelter for the night. He now feared nothing, since he could imagine nothing worse than what had already befallen him, and he had silver to offer as payment, which was the honorable and Christian thing to do instead of showing his sword as reason enough for his visit.

Yet he was somewhat shocked by the stooped old woman who sat by the fire stirring a kettle. She spoke in a croaking voice and greeted him not at all politely but with scorn and words that he didn't understand, saying that such as he should fear the dark, while such as she was a friend of the dark.

Arn answered her calmly and explained that he simply sought shelter for the night so that his horse might not be injured by continuing over the mountain in the dark. He added that he would pay her well for this service. When she didn't answer he went outside and removed the saddle from Shimal and put him in the stable with the lone skinny cow. When he came back to the hut he unbuckled his sword and tossed it on an empty bunk as a sign that this was where he intended to sleep. Then he pulled a little three-legged stool up to the fire and sat down to warm his hands.

The old woman peered at him suspiciously for a long while before she finally asked if he was someone who had a right to bear a sword, or one who bore a sword anyway. Arn replied that there were various opinions on that matter, but that she in any case had nothing to fear from his sword. As if to calm her he took out the little leather purse Eskil had given him when he left and fished out two silver coins, which he put down next to the fireplace so that they were lit by the glow. She picked up a coin and bit it, which Arn found incomprehensible, as he could not understand how anyone could doubt his word or good intentions. But she seemed satisfied with what her few teeth told her and asked if like all the others he had come here to find out what awaited him in the future. Arn replied that the future lay

in God's hands, and no one else could predict it. She laughed so
loud at this that she revealed her gaping mouth with only a few
blackened teeth. She stirred her pot in silence for a while and
then asked whether he would like some of the soup. Arn politely
declined. He was already resigned to a long penance on bread
and water.

"In what lies ahead for you in life I see three things, boy,"
she said suddenly, as if her alleged vision was pushing forward
despite Arn's lack of interest. "I see two shields; would you like
to know what I see?" she went on, squeezing both eyes shut as if
to look inside herself. Arn's curiosity was already aroused, and
maybe she saw that too behind her closed eyelids.

"What shields do you see?" he asked, sure that she would now
say something foolish.

"One shield has three golden crowns against the sky and the
other shield has a lion," she replied in a new singsong tone, her
eyes still shut.

Arn was dumbstruck. He couldn't conceive of how a solitary
old woman far out in the wilderness could have the slightest idea
of such things, and even less that she could know who he was,
or had been able to guess anything by looking at his clothes. He
remembered a story to which he had given little credence, a story
told to him by Knut, who said that his father Erik Jedvardsson, out on a crusade, had received a prophecy about the three
crowns. But that had happened far away, on the other side of the
Eastern Sea.

"What is the third thing you see?" he asked cautiously.

"I see a cross and I hear words with the cross, and what I hear
are the words 'In this sign shalt thou conquer,'" she continued in
her singsong way, without any expression on her face or opening
her eyes.

Arn thought first that she must have been more sharp-eyed

than he realized and read the Latin inscription on the hilt of his
sword.

"You mean, '*In hoc signo vinces*'?" he asked to test her. But
she merely shook her head as if the Latin words meant nothing
to her.

"Do you see a woman in my future?" he asked with some
trepidation, which could probably be heard in his voice.

"You will get your woman!" she shrieked in a shrill voice and
opened her eyes, staring wildly at him. "But nothing will be as
you think, nothing!"

She laughed at him in her hoarse, cackling voice, but it was
as if her mood had been broken and he could no longer get a
sensible word out of her. Soon he gave up and lay down to sleep
on the bunk where he'd tossed his sword. He wrapped his mantle
around him, turned to the wall, and closed his eyes, but he
couldn't fall asleep. He tossed and turned for a while, thinking
of what the old woman had said, and found that it was both true
and meager. The fact that she could see the Folkung and Erik
clans inside him was strange, he had to admit. But she hadn't
said anything that he didn't know for himself. That he would
have Cecilia back was reassuring, and that was what he believed.
At last he must have fallen asleep.

When he awoke at dawn she was gone, but Shimal was in his
place out in the little stable and neighed a welcome as if nothing
had happened.

It was after midday when he rode in through the gate of
Varnhem cloister, and all the familiar smells washed over him
from the gardens and Brother Rugiero's cookhouse. His arrival
was expected but it also aroused some commotion, and two
brothers ran to meet him; one led Shimal away and the other
escorted him in silence to the lavatorium and then pointed to
his clothes. When Arn did not understand, the brother said pee-

vishly that since he was excommunicated he could not be spoken to before he at least washed up a bit. After that he would be given a lay brother's clothing.

Arn washed himself long and thoroughly and trimmed his long hair as he said the appropriate prayers. In his lay brother's attire, which felt oddly familiar, he then reported to Father Henri at his favorite place in the arcade. Father Henri looked at him with much sternness but also love. Then he sighed heavily and took out his prayer stole and motioned for Arn to prepare himself for his confession. Arn fell to his knees and prayed to Holy Saint Bernard to give him the strength and honesty to perform this confession, which would not be easy to make.

King Knut Eriksson arrived at Arnäs with a royal retinue and Birger Brosa. They were many men and it would take some time to see to it that they were all properly quartered. But they were expected, and it was said in the nearest village that the many hungry and weary men would be received well.

Birger Brosa was impatient for them to hold a council as soon as possible instead of pouring ale into themselves first. Even with King Knut present, arrangements were made immediately as Birger Brosa desired, and those involved with the matter gathered in the hall of the longhouse with only a little ale in their bodies.

They prayed first for the Lord to bless this meeting, and that wise words would be spoken here and not foolish ones. Those phrases sounded so awkward and almost simpleminded that Arn's absence was felt like a gust of wind passing through the entire hall. But the question of Arn was only one of the many topics they had to discuss.

Birger Brosa was the one who took the floor when they had

settled down to begin the council, and he believed that the first concern had to be the *landsting* in Western Götaland, since much depended on Knut obtaining his second crown, and the sooner the better. No one was opposed.

They then spent a good while deliberating what messages should be sent and how knowledge of the *ting* should be disseminated best and as rapidly as possible. Since nothing that was said on this matter was either new or unfamiliar, this question was also swiftly resolved.

According to Birger Brosa, the next item involved the best way for Knut, once he was elected king, to proceed in order to lift the shame that had befallen the Folkungs with an excommunicated member of the clan. This, said Birger Brosa, was a matter that Knut himself must address.

Knut Eriksson began by assuring them that Arn, as they all knew, was his dearest friend, and that Arn had also done him very great services that had to be reciprocated. In addition, all the good that the Eriks and the Folkungs could do each other had to take precedence above all else. After saying this and more in the same vein, he got to the heart of the matter.

As far as he understood it, an archbishop could without difficulty annul the excommunication ordered by Bishop Bengt in Skara. The problem was that the archbishop had left his see and no one knew where he was. At least he was not in Linköping, and it would be unfortunate if he had been seized by the Sverker clan, but he was not in Svealand either. Knut's informants would have heard of this, because an archbishop was not that easy to hide.

Now, these men of God could sometimes prove obstinate. So even if they got hold of the missing archbishop, it was not easy to predict how things would turn out if his king required a decision on matters over which the church claimed authority. Priests could always be threatened, that was clear. The clergy were covetous and jealous of their lands, and they strove to gain new gifts of property, which could sometimes make them soft in negotiations. Yet it was impossible to say anything more about this before two things had occurred. First, Knut had to be elected king in Western Götaland as well, just as his dear kinsman and wise adviser Birger Brosa had said. Then he could negotiate from a position of strength with the archbishop. Besides, the prelate must be fished out from his hiding place before they would have a sense of what stand he might take.

Magnus sadly agreed and confirmed that in this matter they could go no further just now. But he wanted to move on to the next most important concern. With such cases undertaken by the church that had to be documented and sent to Rome, much was unclear for ordinary Christian folk. What they knew was that such complicated negotiations could take time. So they had to think about Arn and Cecilia's child. According to what the womenfolk said, Cecilia would give birth to Arn's son sometime after midwinter. And the Sverker hag at Gudhem would see to it that the child was cast out as soon as possible; they could certainly count on that. So what should be done?

Knut Eriksson spoke first, saying that if he was quickly elected king in Western Götaland, he would not without a certain satisfaction engage in a tussle with the Sverker hag at Gudhem. She would be made to understand that she no longer inhabited a safe vessel, which should make her vulnerable in negotiations.

Birger Brosa frowned. First, he pointed out, Knut should think carefully before he inflamed the church as his father had done. It would be better to take another tack, trying to persuade by hook or by crook, rather than using threats. Second, no child born of an unlawful bed could be held in a cloister. That would be too much to ask, and no one would be served by the malicious gossip that would result from such an eventuality. With that, the question seemed quite straightforward: Who would take care of Arn Magnusson's son? And for that matter, did unlawful sons become lawful when a marriage was later entered into?

Eskil had the answers to both these questions. To make arrangements so that Arn and Cecilia's child—whether it was a son or not, and he didn't understand how they all could be so certain of that—ended up with Algot Pålsson was not a good idea. Algot was already reported to have muttered that instead of a son-in-law he was going to have a bastard in his house. Such words did not testify to a good attitude. So the child would have to be cared for by the Folkung clan.

And as far as the other matter was concerned, whether unlawful children could become lawful, the answer was simple. If the excommunication could be lifted and the wedding ale that was envisioned between Arn and Cecilia celebrated, then all would be in its proper order once again.

Birger Brosa then said thoughtfully that since he too had infant children and a mother and two extra wet nurses to take care of them, it seemed best if the boy was allowed to come to Bjälbo. No one objected to that.

The last question they had to contend with was of lesser importance but still as vexing as a chafed foot. Algot Pålsson had not only grumbled about a bastard in the house, he had also complained out loud and bitterly that a son of Arnäs had so mucked up a good business deal that it was obvious it would come to naught. Algot of course was no dangerous foe, and he would think twice before drawing a sword against the Folkungs. Still, it was ill advised for him to be grumbling publicly like that.

Magnus replied with some melancholy that this was merely a matter of the priests' written report to Rome, and all the associated complications could take a great deal of time. If things moved quickly, then all would be arranged as it was intended from the start. But if the matter dragged on for several years, which such things had been known to do, then the situation would be much worse. In that case, Magnus thought, they ought to make the same bargain as originally intended, although with Katarina as bride and Eskil as bridegroom. For Katarina had just been released from the convent in Gudhem.

A sense of gloom settled over the table. Everyone knew that it was Katarina who was the actual cause of this trouble that had now befallen not only Arn and Cecilia but the whole Folkung clan. It seemed wrong, Eskil said with a sigh, to reward Katarina so highly for her malicious deed.

Birger Brosa responded coldly that it sounded like a wise thing to do, and that young Eskil ought to realize that they were speaking only of business, and not of emotions. So if Arn was not released, Eskil must be prepared to go to the bridal bed with a woman to whom he might not care to turn his back, for fear of inviting a dagger.

There the matter was left. At this table the issues were business and the struggle for power, and love by no means had the final word.

✠

Father Henri had not made the slightest move to give Arn absolution for his sins as he listened to his confession. Nor had Arn expected that he would, because he was excommunicated, and not even a prior like Father Henri could annul an excommunication. In brief Father Henri had explained the nature of Arn's sin and then sent him to a cell for meditation on bread and water and all the other acts of penance he might expect.

During his time in the base world Arn had managed to commit three grave sins. First, he had killed two drunken peasants;

second, drunk himself, he'd had carnal relations with Katarina; and third, he'd had carnal relations with Cecilia.

Of these three sins the first two had been forgiven so easily and simply that Arn himself had wondered about it. But the third sin, which arose because he had carnal relations with Cecilia as well, the woman he loved and wanted to live with as man and wife forever, had been such a grave sin that he had been excommunicated, dragging her to her own ruin. It was incomprehensible. Killing two men was nothing, and having carnal relations with a woman he didn't love was nothing. But doing the same thing with a woman he loved above all else on earth, as the Holy Scriptures described love—that was the gravest of sins.

They had sent him the text of the law from the archive at Varnhem, and in the text everything stood clear and inexorable. In the archive were kept only such law texts as the church itself had pushed through, of course; everything else, such as single combat, defamation, and monetary fines if one slew someone else's thralls or stole someone else's livestock, were of minor interest to the church.

But the law that Arn had broken was something that the church had fought for and ultimately pushed through. In the text of the marriage act for Western Götaland it said:

> If a man lies with his daughter, the case shall be reported in writing and sent to Rome. If father and son own the same woman, if two brothers own the same woman, if two brothers' sons own the same woman, if mother and daughter own the same man, if two sisters own the same man, if two sisters' daughters own the same man, it is an abomination.

So it was written. The passage was beautifully printed in Latin while the subsequent translation into the vernacular was written in cursive. Arn had no difficulty recognizing the prohibition, for he knew it had been taken from the Pentateuch of Moses in the Holy Scriptures.

But there were all sorts of senseless and peculiar prohibitions to be found in the Holy Scriptures, and everything that Arn thought he knew about how to interpret such things now fell flat on the ground. That it was abomination if someone lay with his daughter was easy to understand. But it was impossible to comprehend how lying with Katarina once when he was drunk could be considered the same as what he and Cecilia had done together out of love—while physically there might be a resemblance, there was none in spirit.

Arn brooded for a long time over God's law. He tested his theological reasoning on the regulations from the Old Testament, comparing his crime to similar prohibitions such as wearing clothing of a certain color during the month of mourning or having one's hair cut in a certain way. But it made no difference and all such ruminations were useless because the same prohibition had been written into the laws of Western Götaland. He remembered well the respect that his kinsmen had displayed when Judge Karle recited the law regarding slander. There was so little room for interpretation that his own father had been prepared to die as prescribed by law.

But according to this law, he had committed a crime that was equivalent to the abomination of lying with his own daughter.

Yet it was God's holy church that would judge. And among men of God the thoughts and intentions behind a crime were given different consideration than among the West Goths.

No matter how Arn twisted and turned this question, everything finally came down to what Father Henri would decide. For it was clear that Arn would not be judged by any *ting*; he snorted at the thought of how easily he would be able to defend himself either with a sword or a countless number of Folkung oath-swearers.

He would be judged by God's holy church, and that meant there was at least a reasonable chance of weighing good against evil. So he hovered between hope and despair.

His hope grew even greater when a brother came to fetch him to a meeting with Archbishop Stéphan. Arn had no idea that the archbishop was at Varnhem, and at first he thought that it might have something to do with his own case, since the archbishop had once told Arn that he would always have a friend out there in the other world, a friend who would stand by him, and who was none other than the archbishop himself.

Arn hurried to the arcade where he found Father Henri in his usual place, and to his joy also Archbishop Stéphan. He fell to his knees at once to kiss the archbishop's hand and did not take a seat until he was told to do so.

Yet it was not kindness that Arn saw in the archbishop's eyes as the prelate studied him for a while in silence. And with that, Arn felt the warmth of his hope swiftly cool.

"These are no small lapses that you have managed during your brief time out there in the base world," the archbishop began at last. He sounded very stern, and Father Henri sitting next to him did not look at Arn but seemed to be examining his own sandals.

"You know very well," continued the archbishop in the same stern tone, "that the power of the church must not be intermingled with earthly power. And yet that is just what you have done, and you have now placed me in quite a quandary. With open eyes you did this, and even with some cunning."

The archbishop paused as if to hear what excuses or explanations the young man might offer. But Arn, who had been completely prepared to take part in a discussion of his carnal sins,

now felt utterly bewildered. He didn't understand what the archbishop was talking about, and he said so, apologizing for his stupidity. The archbishop then heaved a great sigh, but Arn caught
the trace of a smile on the face of the venerable man, as if he did
indeed believe Arn's plea of ignorance.

"You can't have such a short memory that you've forgotten
that we saw each other not so long ago up in Östra Aros, can
you?" asked the archbishop in a voice that was both agreeable
and harsh.

"No, Your Excellency, but I don't understand how I then
should have sinned," replied Arn uncertainly.

"That's remarkable!" snorted the archbishop. "You show
up with a man in tow who was one of those contenders for the
crown who are unfortunately so numerous in this part of the
world. You join in his request that I in some way should make
haste and practically crown him on the spot. When I then refuse
this request, for reasons which you surely knew in advance, what
do you do then? You fairly fool the robe off me and leave me
standing with my bare rump showing, that's what you do. And
since you are one of us, and will remain so forever, both Father
Henri and I have conducted lengthy and sincere deliberations,
trying to decide what you were thinking when you acted as you
did."

"I wasn't thinking about much at all," Arn replied, since it
now began to dawn on him what they were talking about. "As
Your Excellency so truly says, I did know that there could be no
talk of the church immediately announcing its support of Knut
Eriksson. But I found no fault in the fact that Your Excellency
himself should present this view of the matter to my friend. And
that was what happened."

"Well, but then, what were you thinking later when you staged
the spectacle that caused the stupid crowd outside to believe that
I had anointed and crowned the cunning devil?"

"I didn't understand much of what went on out there," Arn replied in shame. "We hadn't talked about what would happen if Your Excellency should refuse to approve Knut Eriksson's wishes. He thought he was presenting a simple request, and I couldn't persuade him otherwise, since he felt that he was already king. So I thought that Your Excellency would have to explain the whole matter, just as you did."

"Yes, yes, yes!" snapped the archbishop, waving his hand impatiently. "You already said that. But now I'm wondering about what happened after I put the scamp in his place!"

"Then he wanted me to ask Your Excellency whether the two of us might have the honor of receiving Holy Communion from Your Excellency in person at the next day's mass. I found nothing un-Christian in such a request. But I didn't know that—"

"So the two of you hadn't talked about that beforehand? You didn't know a thing about what trickery would follow?" the archbishop interrupted him sternly.

"No, Your Excellency, I didn't know," replied Arn, shamefaced. "My friend had not expected that his first request would be refused at once. But the request to receive Holy Communion was not something we had spoken about at all."

The two older men now looked intently at Arn, who did not avert his eyes or show the least hesitation, since what he'd said was entirely true, as surely as if he were under the oath of confession.

Father Henri cleared his throat lightly and looked up at the archbishop, who met his gaze and nodded in agreement. They had drawn definite conclusions about something they had discussed in advance, that much Arn could see.

"Well, well, my young friend, sometimes you are more than a little childish, I must say," said the archbishop in a different and much friendlier tone of voice. "You took your sword with you and handed it to me, and you knew that I could do nothing but bless it, and you were both dressed for battle. What was your intention?"

"My sword is sanctified, and I have never broken its oath. I felt pride when I could bear such a sacred sword to Your Excellency. I also thought that you, Your Excellency, would feel the same way, since the sanctification of the sword occurred right here with the Cistercians," replied Arn.

"And you had no idea how your friend, Knut Eriksson, was going to exploit the occasion?" asked the archbishop with a weary smile, shaking his head at the same time.

"No, Your Excellency, but afterward I did understand—"

"Afterward there was a great commotion all over Svealand!" snapped the archbishop. "The rumors made it look as though I, from my see, had blessed the sword that was supposed to have murdered King Karl Sverkersson, as if I furthermore had blessed Knut Eriksson and practically anointed and crowned him. Since then I haven't had a peaceful moment, for now all the petty kings and half kings and king pretenders are after me! I'm going to be leaving the country for a while; that's why I'm here and not for your sake, as you may have thought. However, I believe what you've said about everything that happened up in Östra Aros, and you have my forgiveness."

Arn fell to his knees before the archbishop and kissed his hand again. He thanked him for showing such forgiving kindness, no matter how undeserved, since ignorance was not a sufficient defense. In a brief moment of happiness Arn imagined that everything was now over, that his sin was not having lain with Cecilia in love but rather that he had sinned by helping Knut Eriksson, who for dishonest purposes had made a fool of the archbishop himself.

But it was not over. When Arn stood up at the archbishop's kind exhortation and sat down in his place facing the two old friends, he received his judgment.

"Listen to me carefully," said the archbishop. "Your sins are forgiven with regard to the trick you played on your own archbishop. But you have broken God's law by having lain with two women who are sisters, and for such a sin, which is abomination, there is no easy grace. It would be normal for us to sentence you to penance for the rest of your life. But we shall show you mercy because we believe that it is the intention of the Lord. Your penance you shall serve for half a lifetime, twenty years, and the same applies to your mistress. You shall serve your penance as a Knight Templar of the Lord, and your name henceforth shall be Arn de Gothia and nothing else. Go now to your penance, and may the Lord guide your steps and your sword, and may His Grace shine upon you. Brother Guilbert will explain everything to you in more detail. I will be leaving now, but we will see each other on the road to Rome, which is where you must go first."

Arn's head was spinning. He realized that he had been shown mercy, and yet not. For half a lifetime was longer than he had been alive, and he could not even imagine himself as an old man, at the age of thirty-seven, when his sins would be absolved. He gave Father Henri a look of entreaty though without saying a word, and it seemed as though he could not bring himself to leave before Father Henri had said something to him.

"The road to Jerusalem took many turns in the beginning, my dear, dear Arn," Father Henri said quietly. "But this was God's will, of that we are both convinced. Go now in peace!"

When Arn with head bowed and almost staggering had left them, the two men sat there for a long time, becoming entangled in an ever deeper conversation about God's will. Because it was clear to them both that God's intention was to send yet another great warrior to His Holy Army.

But what if Knut Eriksson had become king somewhat earlier, and Arn and Cecilia had already been blessed as man and wife? What if Cecilia, who seemed to be as equally good-hearted and childish as Arn, had not visited her sister Katarina? What if Prioress Rikissa had not been of the Sverker clan and had not used her power and great determination to instigate this whole disturbance?

If all this and much else had not happened, God's Holy Army would have been missing one warrior. On the other hand, the philosopher had already shown that this type of reasoning was never tenable. If this were not so, the archbishop would have been a horse. But God had clearly shown His will, and before His will they must bow.

✠

Brother Guilbert proceeded cautiously with Arn over the next few days as he set about the task of making him understand what now and for a long time to come would be his fate. He did not allow Arn to start talking about his punishment or all that he would have to leave behind; he kept to the practical matters.

Arn would ride with Archbishop Stéphan to Rome, but there their ways would part, since the archbishop had things to work out with Pope Alexander III, while Arn would report to the castle of the Knights Templar in Rome, which was the largest such castle in the world. That was because it was in Rome that all who sought admittance to the order would be either approved or rejected. Naturally there were many who felt themselves called to fight in God's Holy Army, not least since they would thereby do penance for all their sins and gain entry to Heaven if they died with sword in hand. Consequently it was only one out of ten aspirants who were accepted after testing.

But this testing would hardly present difficulties for Arn. Acceptance into the order required that one came from a clan with a coat of arms, a rule that Brother Guilbert did not favor because he had seen many warriors in battle who would have been good

brothers of the order if not for that very rule. But it was no problem for Arn, who bore the lion of the Folkung clan on his coat
of arms. Nor would the other two requirements present any difficulties. Brother Guilbert smiled when he dryly explained that
those requirements involved knowing about one-fourth as much
as Arn already knew about the Holy Scriptures, logic, and philosophy. And even a fourth of Arn's skill with weapons should
be enough. In addition, of course, he needed letters from the
Nordic archbishop and Father Henri. But that was not the important thing; such letters of recommendation were something
that many hopeful Frankish sons of counts brought with them.
They did not arrive with Arn's skills. And no one could dispute
the clearly expressed will of God.

Arn complained a bit about God's will, which seemed to
have been meted out rather harshly. Why did he first have to
be plunged into misfortune and then leave his beloved Cecilia
behind in order to fulfill God's will on the battlefield in Outremer?

Brother Guilbert admitted that he had no answer to that question, but suggested that the answers might reveal themselves with
time. However, he said that he had known for many years that
this was how things would turn out. Brother Guilbert believed
that he had met few if any men with Arn's abilities, and since
God had given him these rare gifts, then there must be a definite
reason behind it. And it was probably for the same reason that
God had sent Arn to Varnhem at the age of five to be educated in
all that would now make him an acceptable Templar knight.

Arn could easily see the logic in this reasoning, but it didn't
assuage his sorrow or his longing.

Brother Guilbert showed Arn some new equipment on which
he had worked a long time, using Arn's measurements. Most important was the chain mail with more than forty thousand rings
in two layers and with homespun felt in between and a soft fabric

lining on the inside. The chain mail went up over the head, down along the arms to the wrists and far below the knees, yet it was lighter to wear than Nordic chain mail. He had also made pantaloons, which protected the legs and went down around the feet. Anyone dressed in this mail would be protected from top to toe, and this was what the new type of warfare demanded. Finally, Brother Guilbert took out a black mantle with a white cross that covered the entire chest. These were the church colors that Arn had to wear when he accompanied the archbishop, riding as part of his escort to Rome. But it was also the squire's attire in the order of the Knights Templar, so this meant that Arn would arrive prepared at their castle in Rome. He had the archbishop's permission to wear the raiment during the entire journey.

Arn felt respect and pride when he tried on these things, but there was no joy in his eyes. Nor had Brother Guilbert reckoned that there would be. But for Arn's departure two days later he had saved a special surprise which he believed might have the intended effect on the mind of his young apprentice.

Brother Guilbert put his arm around Arn to console him and walked with him down to the farthest horse enclosure as if only for a moment's conversation. When they reached the stable he didn't say a word, but only pointed. There stood Arn's beloved stallion Khamsiin.

Arn was silent at first. Then he called and Khamsiin instantly pricked up his ears and turned his head toward him. The next moment the huge stallion thundered toward him at his fastest gallop and reared before the gate where Arn and Brother Guilbert stood. The horse whirled about a few times, reared again, and whinnied as if shrieking either a complaint or a welcome to a dear friend.

Arn jumped over the gate, threw his arms around Khamsiin's neck, and showered him with kisses.

"He's yours now," said Brother Guilbert. "He is our parting gift to you, Arn de Gothia. For I have learned as a Templar knight that in the Holy War, trust in God is certainly most important. Next comes practice and humility. But after that come good weapons and a horse like Khamsiin."

When Arn, wearing his black mantle with the white cross, mounted Khamsiin to begin his long journey, his expression was determined but still clearly sorrowful, as it had been since he received his judgment.

All masses had been sung. All words of farewell had been said. But still Father Henri and Brother Guilbert stood there alone with Arn as if to say something more. They had a hard time behaving with Christian dignity, for Arn's sorrow no doubt pained them even though their conviction was strong that the will of God was to be carried out at last.

"For God and death to all Saracens!" said Father Henri with forced bravado.

"For God and death to all Saracens!" replied Arn, drawing his blessed sword which he held pointed straight to Heaven as he swore this new oath. Then he nudged Khamsiin in the flanks and set off at a leisurely pace.

Father Henri wanted to go back inside the cloister at once, but Brother Guilbert held up a finger as a sign that they should wait a bit, and then he pointed toward Arn.

They remained standing like this, although Father Henri did not understand the purpose of it, but Brother Guilbert was still holding up his index finger as if waiting for something.

Suddenly they saw Arn take a few galloping steps to the right, then to the left, and then he urged his powerful stallion to switch galloping steps to the right and left with each leap, a difficult art as far as Father Henri understood. But Arn's joy at being able to perform such tricks was unmistakable.

"You see what I see, dear Father Henri," whispered Brother Guilbert almost reverently. "God preserve Arn, but may God also preserve the Saracens who will encounter him."

This last seemed incomprehensible to Father Henri, and bordering on blasphemy. But now was not the time to voice reproach, not as they stood and watched Varnhem's most beloved son ride away forever.

Besides, Father Henri knew full well that Brother Guilbert in certain respects had a peculiar view of Saracens. But he assumed that Arn, who once had been as pure in spirit as Percival, would never be struck by any such scruples. God would surely hold His sheltering hand over a warrior like Arn.

Read on for an excerpt from

THE
TEMPLAR KNIGHT

JAN GUILLOU

Available in hardcover in
May 2010 from

HARPER

An Imprint of HarperCollins*Publishers*
www.harpercollins.com

Chapter 1

During Muharram, the holy month of mourning, which occurred when the summer was at its hottest in the year 575 after Hijra, called Anno Domini 1177 by the infidels, God sent His most remarkable deliverance to those of His faithful He loved best.

Yussuf and his brother Fahkr were riding for their lives and right behind, shielding them from the enemies' arrows, came the Emir, Moussa. Their pursuers, who were six in number, were steadily gaining on them, and Yussuf cursed his arrogance, which had made him believe that something like this would never happen since he and his companions possessed the swiftest of horses. But the landscape here in the valley of death and drought due west of the Dead Sea was just as inhospitably arid as it was rocky. This made it dangerous to ride too fast, although their pursuers seemed completely unhampered by this. But if one of them happened to take a spill, it would be no less fateful than if any of the men being chased should fall.

Yussuf suddenly decided to cut across to the west and head up

1

toward the mountains, where he hoped to find cover. Before long the three pursued horsemen were following a *wadi*, a dry river-bed, up a steep slope. But the *wadi* began to narrow and deepen so that they were soon riding in a long ravine, as if God had caught them in flight and was now steering them in a specific direction. Now there was only one road, and it led upward, growing steeper and steeper, making it harder and harder to keep up their speed. And their pursuers were coming steadily closer; they would soon be within shooting range. The men being chased had already fastened their round iron-clad shields to their backs.

Yussuf was not in the habit of praying for his life. But now, as he was forced to decrease his speed more and more among all the treacherous boulders at the bottom of the *wadi*, a verse came to him from God's Word, which he breathlessly rattled off with parched lips:

He who has created life and death in order to test you and allow you to prove who among you, by his actions, is the best. He is the Almighty. The One who always forgives.

And God did indeed test His beloved Yussuf and showed him, first as a mirage against the light of the setting sun, and then with terrible clarity the most horrific sight that any of the faithful in such a hunted and difficult situation could see.

From the opposite direction in the *wadi* came a Templar knight with lowered lance, and behind him rode his sergeant. Both of these foes were riding at such speed that their cloaks billowed behind them like great dragon wings; they came like *jinni* out of the desert.

Yussuf abruptly reined in his horse and fumbled with his shield, which he now had to pull around to the front to face the infidel's lance. He felt no fear, only a cold excitement at the nearness of death, and he steered his horse over to the steep wall of the *wadi* to present a narrower target and increase the angle of the enemy's lance.

But then the Templar knight, who was only a few breaths away, raised his lance and waved his shield, as a signal to Yussuf and his brother to move aside and get out of their way. They complied at once, and the next moment the two Templar knights thundered past as they let their cloaks fall, which fluttered to the dust behind them.

Yussuf quickly issued an order to his companions. With difficulty, their horses' hooves slipping, they clambered up the steep slope of the *wadi* until they reached a spot from which they had a good view. There Yussuf turned his horse around and stopped, for he wished to understand what God meant by all of this.

The two others wanted to take advantage of the opportunity and escape while the Templar knights and bandits settled matters as they saw fit. But Yussuf rejected all such arguments with a curt gesture of annoyance because he truly wanted to see what would happen next. He had never in all his life been this close to a Templar knight, those demons of evil, and he felt strongly, as if God's voice were advising him, that he had to see what was going to happen; mere common sense would not stop him. Common sense dictated that they should continue their ride toward Al Arish for as long as the light permitted. But what he now saw he would never forget.

The six bandits had few choices once they discovered that instead of chasing three wealthy men they were now facing two Templar knights, lance to lance. The *wadi* was much too narrow for them to be able to stop, turn around, and affect a retreat before the Franks were upon them. After a brief hesitation they did the only thing they could do: They grouped themselves so they were riding two by two and spurred their horses so as not to be killed by standing still.

The white-clad Templar knight who rode in front of his sergeant first feigned an attack to the right of the first two bandits, and when they held up their shields to counter the dreaded blow of his lance—Yussuf wondered whether the bandits understood what now awaited them—the Templar knight spun his horse around with a swift movement that shouldn't have been possible in such tight quarters. This gave him a whole new vantage point, and he thrust his lance right between the shield and body of the bandit on the left. At the same time, he released his lance so as not to be wrenched out of his saddle. Just at that moment the sergeant came in contact with the astonished bandit on the right, who was huddled behind his shield, waiting for the blow that never came, and who now looked up only to see the other foe's lance coming towards his face from the wrong direction.

The white-clad man with the loathsome red cross now faced the next two enemies in a passageway so narrow that there was barely room for three horses abreast. He had drawn his sword, and at first it looked as if he intended to attack head-on, which would have been unwise with a weapon on only one side. But suddenly he turned his handsome steed sideways, a roan at the height of its powers, and lashed out behind him, striking one of the bandits and toppling him out of the saddle.

The second bandit then saw a good opportunity since the enemy was approaching him sideways, almost backwards, with his sword in the wrong hand and out of reach. What he did not notice was that the Templar knight had dropped his shield and switched his sword to his left hand. When the bandit leaned forward in the saddle to strike with his saber, he exposed his whole neck and head to the blow, which now came from the opposite direction.

"If the head can retain a thought at the moment of death, if only for a brief breath, then that was a very surprised head that fell to the ground," said Fahkr in amazement. He too was now captivated by the drama and wanted to see more.

The last two bandits had exploited the moment of decreased speed that had befallen the white-clad Templar knight as he dispatched the other bandit. They had turned their horses around and were now fleeing down the *wadi*.

At that moment the black-clad sergeant reached the godless dog who had been knocked to the ground by the Templar knight's horse. The sergeant dismounted, calmly grabbed the reins of the bandit's horse with one hand and with the other used his sword to stab the dazed, reeling, and no doubt bruised bandit in the throat at the spot where his steel-plated leather coat of mail ended. But then the sergeant no longer made any attempt to follow his master, who had now put on speed to chase down the last two fleeing bandits. Instead, the sergeant hobbled the horse he had just caught with the reins and then cautiously began rounding up the other loose horses, seeming to talk to them reassuringly. He did not appear at all worried about his master, whom he had been following so closely to offer protection. Instead, he seemed to think it more important to gather up the enemies' horses. It was truly a strange sight.

"That man," said Emir Moussa, pointing toward the white-clad Templar knight who was far down the *wadi* and about to disappear from the sight of the three faithful, "that man there, sire, is Al Ghouti."

"Al Ghouti?" said Yussuf, puzzled. "You say his name as if I should know him. But I do not. Who is Al Ghouti?"

"Al Ghouti is a man you should know, sire," replied Emir Moussa resolutely. "He is the man God sent to us for our sins, he is the one among the devils of the red cross who sometimes ride with the Turcopoles and sometimes with their heavy horsemen. Now, as you can see, he is riding an Arabian stallion as a Turcopole does, but carrying a lance and sword as if he were seated on one of the slow and heavy Frankish horses. He is also the emir of the Knights Templar in Gaza."

"Al Ghouti, Al Ghouti," muttered Yussuf thoughtfully. "I would like to meet him. We will wait here!"

The two others looked at him in horror but realized at once that he had made up his mind, so it would do no good to offer any objections, no matter how wise.

While the three Saracen horsemen waited at the top of the *wadi*'s slope, they watched the Templar knight's sergeant. Seemingly unperturbed and as though carrying out the most ordinary daily task, he had rounded up the horses of the four dead men. He then tied them together and started lugging and dragging the corpses of the bandits. With great effort, although he appeared to be a very powerful man, he hoisted them up and bound them hand and foot, each dead man slung over his own horse.

The Templar knight and the two remaining bandits, who had been the pursuers but were now the pursued, could no longer be seen.

"Very clever," muttered Fahkr as if to himself. "That is clever. He ties the right man to the right horse to keep the animals calm in spite of the blood. He is obviously thinking of taking the horses along with them."

"Yes, they are truly fine horses," agreed Yussuf. "What I do not understand is how such criminals could have horses that are fit for a king. Their horses kept pace with our own."

"Worse than that. They were closing on us at the end," objected Emir Moussa, who never hesitated to speak his mind to his lord. "But haven't we seen enough? Wouldn't it be wise to ride off now into the darkness before Al Ghouti comes back?"

"Are you certain that he will come back?" asked Yussuf, amused.

"Yes, sire, he will come back," replied Emir Moussa morosely. "I am just as certain of that as the sergeant is down there; he hasn't even troubled to follow his master when there are only two enemies to fight. Didn't you notice that Al Ghouti had thrust his sword into its sheath and had pulled out his bow and stretched it taut just as he came around the bend down there?"

"He pulled out a bow? A Templar knight?" asked Yussuf in surprise, raising his slender eyebrows.

"Yes he did, sire," replied Emir Moussa. "He is a Turcopole, as I said; sometimes he travels light and shoots from the saddle like a Turk, except his bow is bigger. Far too many of the faithful have died from his arrows. I would still dare to suggest, sire, that—"

"No!" Yussuf cut him off. "We will wait here. I want to meet him. We have a truce with the Knights Templar right now, and I want to thank him. I owe him my gratitude, and I refuse even to consider being indebted to a Templar knight!"

The two others could see it would do no good to argue any further. But they were uneasy, and all conversation ceased.

They sat there in silence for a while, leaning forward with one hand resting on the pommel of their saddles as they watched the sergeant, who was now done with the bodies and horses. He had started gathering the weapons and the cloaks that both he and his master had flung off right before the attack. After a while he picked up the severed head in one hand, and for a moment it looked as if he were wondering how to pack it up. At last he pulled the headdress off one of the bandits, wrapped it around the head, and made a parcel which he tied onto the pommel of the saddle over which the body with the missing head was slung.

Finally the sergeant was finished with all his tasks. He made sure all of the packs were fastened securely and then mounted his horse and began slowly leading his caravan of linked horses past the three Saracens.

Yussuf then greeted the sergeant politely in Frankish, with a wave of his arm. The sergeant gave him an uncertain smile in return, but they could not hear what he said.

Dusk began to fall, the sun had dropped behind the high mountains to the west, and the salt water of the sea far below no longer gleamed blue. The horses seemed to sense their masters' impatience; they tossed their heads and snorted now and then, as if they too wanted to get moving before it grew too late.

But then they saw the white-clad Templar knight returning along the *wadi*. In tow behind him came two horses with two dead men draped over the saddles. He was in no hurry and rode with his head lowered, making him look as if he were lost in prayer even though he was probably just keeping an eye on the rocky, uneven ground. He did not appear to have seen the three waiting horsemen, although from his vantage point they must have been visible, silhouetted against the light part of the evening sky.

But when he reached them, he looked up and reined in his horse without saying a word.

Yussuf felt at a loss, as if he had been struck dumb because what he now saw did not coincide with what he had witnessed only a short time ago. This spawn of the Devil, who was openly called Al Ghouti, radiated peace. He had hung his helmet by a chain over his shoulder. His short fair hair and his thick, unkempt beard of the same color framed a demon's face with eyes that were as blue as you might expect. But here was a man who had just killed three or four other men; in the excitement Yussuf had not been able to keep track of how many, even though he usually could recall everything he saw in battle. Yussuf had seen many men after a victory, just after they had killed and won, but he had never seen anyone who looked as if he had come from a day's work, as if he had been harvesting grain in the fields or sugarcane in the marshes, with the clear conscience that only good work can provide. His blue eyes were not the eyes of a demon.

"We were waiting for you . . . we wish to thank you . . ." said Yussuf in a semblance of Frankish that he hoped the other man would understand.

The man who was called Al Ghouti in the language of the faithful gazed at Yussuf steadily as his face slowly lit up with a smile, as if he were searching his memory and had found what he sought. This made Emir Moussa and Fahkr, but not Yussuf, cautiously, almost unconsciously, drop their hands to their weapons beside their saddles. The Templar knight quite clearly saw their hands, which now seemed to be moving of their own accord toward their sabers. Then he raised his glance to the three on the slope, looked Yussuf straight in the eyes, and replied in God's own language:

"In the name of God the Merciful, we are not enemies at this time, and I seek no strife with you. Consider these words from your own scripture, the words which the Prophet himself, may peace be with him, spoke: *Take not another man's life—God has declared it holy—except in a righteous cause.* You and I have no righteous cause, for there is now a truce between us."

The Templar knight smiled even wider, as if he wanted to entice them to laugh; he was fully aware of the impression he must have made on the three foes when he addressed them in the language of the Holy Koran. But Yussuf, who now realized that he had to be quick-witted and swift to take command of the situation, answered the Templar knight after only a slight hesitation.

"The ways of God the Almighty are truly unfathomable," and to that the Templar knight nodded, as if these words were particularly familiar to him. "And only He can know why He sent an enemy to save us. But I owe you my thanks, knight of the red cross, and I will give you some of the riches that these infidels wanted. In this place where I now sit, I will leave a hundred dinars in gold, and they belong by rights to you for saving our lives."

Yussuf now thought that he had spoken like a king, and a very generous king, as kings should be. But to his surprise and that of his brother and Emir Moussa, the Templar knight replied at first with a laugh that was completely genuine and without scorn.

"In the name of God the Merciful, you speak to me out of both goodness and ignorance," said the Templar knight. "From you I can accept nothing. What I did here I had to do, whether you were present or not. And I own no worldly possessions and cannot accept any; that is one reason. Another reason is that the way around my vow is for you to donate the hundred dinars to the Knights Templar. But if you will permit me to say so, my unknown foe and friend, I think you would have difficulty explaining that gift to your Prophet!"

With these words, the Templar knight gathered up his reins, cast a glance back at the two horses and the two bodies he had in tow, and urged his Arabian horse on, as he raised his right hand with clenched fist toward the men in the salute of the Templar knights. He looked as if he found the situation quite amusing.

"Wait!" said Yussuf, so quickly that his words came faster than his thoughts. "Then I invite you and your sergeant instead to share our evening meal!"

The Templar knight reined in his horse and looked at Yussuf with a thoughtful expression.

"I accept your invitation, my unknown foe and friend," the Templar knight replied, "but only on the condition that I have your word none of you intends to draw a weapon against me or my sergeant as long as we are in one another's company."

"You have my word on the name of the true God and His Prophet," replied Yussuf quickly. "Do I have yours?"

"Yes, you have my word on the name of the true God, His Son, and the Holy Virgin," replied the Templar knight just as quickly. "If you ride two fingers south of the spot where the sun went down behind the mountains, you will reach a stream. Follow it to the northwest and you will find several low trees near some water. Stay there for the night. We will be farther west, up on the slope near the same water that flows toward you. But we will not sully the water. It will soon be night and you have your hour for prayers, as do we. But afterwards, when we come in the darkness to you, we will make enough noise so you hear us, and not come quietly, like someone with evil intentions."

The Templar knight spurred his horse, again saluted in farewell, got his little caravan moving, and rode off into the twilight without looking back.

The three faithful watched him for a long time without moving or saying a word. Their horses snorted impatiently, but Yussuf was lost in thought.

"You are my brother, and nothing you do or say should surprise me anymore after all these years," said Fahkr. "But what you just did really surprised me. A Templar knight! And the one they call Al Ghouti at that!"

"Fahkr, my beloved brother," replied Yussuf as he turned his horse with an easy movement to head in the direction described by his foe. "You must know your enemy; we have talked a great deal about that, haven't we? And among your enemies, isn't it best to learn from the one who is most monstrous of all? God has given us this golden opportunity; let us not refuse His gift."

"But can we trust the word of such a man?" objected Fahkr after they had been riding for a time in silence.

"Yes, we can, as a matter of fact," muttered Emir Moussa. "The enemy has many faces, known and unknown. But that man's word we can trust, just as he can trust your brother's."

They followed their foe's instructions and soon found the little stream with fresh cold water, where they stopped to let their horses drink. Then they continued along the stream and, exactly as the Templar knight had said, came to a level area. There the stream spread out to a small pond where low trees and bushes grew, with a sparse pasture area for the horses. They unsaddled the animals and took off the packs, hobbling the horses' forelegs so that they would stay close to the water and not go in search of grazing land farther away, where none existed. Then the men washed themselves, as prescribed by law, before prayers.

At the first appearance of the bright crescent moon in the blue summer night sky, they said their prayers of mourning for the dead and of gratitude to God for sending them, in His unfathomable mercy, the worst of their foes to rescue them.

They talked a bit about this very subject after prayers. Yussuf then said that he thought God, in an almost humorous way, had shown His omnipotence: revealing that nothing was impossible for Him, not even sending Templar knights to rescue the very ones who in the end would conquer all Templar knights.

Yussuf tried to convince himself and everyone else of this. Year after year new warlords arrived from the Frankish lands; if they won, they soon returned home with their heavy loads.

But some Franks never went back home, and they were both the best and the worst of the lot. Best because they did not pillage for pleasure and because it was possible to reason with them, making trade contracts and peace agreements. But they were also the worst because some of them were fierce adversaries in war. The worst of them all were the two cursed devout orders of competing monks, the Templars and the Hospitallers of St John. Whoever wanted to cleanse the land of the enemy, whoever wanted to take back Al Aksa and the Temple of the Rock in God's Holy City, would have to conquer both the Knights Templar and the Hospitallers. Nothing else was possible.

Yet they seemed impossible to conquer. They fought without fear, convinced that they would enter paradise if they died in battle. They never surrendered since their laws forbade the rescue of captured brothers from imprisonment. A captured Hospitaller knight or Templar knight was a worthless prisoner that they might just as soon release or kill. Thus they always died.

It was a rule of thumb that if fifteen of the faithful met five Templar knights out on a plain, it meant that either all or none of them would live. If the fifteen faithful attacked the five infidels, none of the faithful would escape with his life. To ensure victory of such an attack, they had to be four times as many and still be prepared to pay a very high price in casualties. With ordinary Franks this was not the case; ordinary Franks could be defeated even if there were fewer men on the side of the faithful.

While Fahkr and Emir Moussa gathered wood to make a fire, Yussuf lay on his back with his hands behind his head, staring up at the sky where more and more stars were appearing. He was pondering these men who were his worst enemies. He thought about what he had seen right before sundown. The man called Al Ghouti had a horse worthy of a king, a horse that seemed to think the same thoughts as his master, that obeyed instinctively.

It was not sorcery; Yussuf was a man who ultimately rejected such explanations. The simple truth was that the man and the horse had fought and trained together for many years, in the most serious fashion, not just as a pastime to be taken up when there was nothing else to do. Among the Egyptian Mamelukes there were similar men and horses, and the Mamelukes, of course, did nothing but train until they were successful enough to obtain commissions and land, their freedom and gold granted in gratitude for many good years of service in war. This was no miracle or magic; it was man alone and not God who created these kinds of men. The only question was: What was the most crucial characteristic for attaining that goal?

Yussuf's answer to this question was always that it was pure faith, that the one who wholeheartedly and absolutely followed the words of the Prophet, may peace be with Him, regarding the *Jihad*, the holy war, would become an unconquerable warrior. But the problem was that among the Mamelukes in Egypt it was impossible to find the most faithful of Muslims; usually they were Turks and more or less superstitious, believing in spirits and holy stones and giving only lip service to the pure and true faith.

In this case it was worse that even the infidels could create men like Al Ghouti. Could it be that God was demonstrating that man uses his own free will to determine his purpose in life, in this life on earth, and that only when the holy fire separates the wheat from the chaff will it be apparent who are the faithful and who are the infidels?

It was a disheartening thought. For if it was God's intention that the faithful, if they could unite in a *Jihad* against the infidels, should be rewarded with victory, why then had He created enemies who were impossible to defeat, man to man? Perhaps to show that the faithful truly had to unite against the enemy? The faithful had to stop fighting among themselves because those who joined forces would be ten to a hundred times more numerous than the Franks, who would then be doomed, even if they were all Templar knights.

Yussuf again recalled the image of Al Ghouti: his stallion; his black, well-oiled, and undamaged harness; his equipment, none of which was merely for the pleasure of the eye but for the joy of the hand. Something could be learned from this. Many men had died on the battlefield because they couldn't resist wearing their stiff, new, glittery-gold brocade over their amour, which hindered their movements at the crucial moment, and thus they died more from vanity than anything else. Everything they had seen should be remembered and learned from, otherwise how were they going to conquer the devilish enemy that now occupied God's Holy City?

The fire had already begun to crackle. Fahkr and Emir Moussa had spread out the muslin coverlet and were starting to set out provisions and drinking vessels of water. Emir Moussa squatted down and ground up his mocha beans to prepare his black Bedouin drink. With the descending darkness a cool breeze came racing down the mountainside from Al Kahlil, the city of Abraham. But the cool air after a hot day would soon give way to cold.

The westerly direction of the wind brought Yussuf the scent of the two Franks at the same time as he heard them out in the darkness. It was the smell of slaves and battlefields; no doubt they would come unwashed to the evening meal, like the barbarians they were.

When the Templar knight stepped into the light of the fire, the faithful saw that he was carrying his white shield with the red cross before him, as no guest ever should. Emir Moussa took several hesitant steps toward his saddle where he had stacked up their weapons with the harnesses. But Yussuf quickly caught his nervous eye and quietly shook his head.

The Templar knight bowed before each of his hosts in turn, and his sergeant followed his master's lead. Then he surprised the three faithful by lifting up his white shield with the loathsome cross and setting it as high up as he could in one of the low trees. When he then stepped forward to unfasten his sword and sit down, as Yussuf invited him to do with a gesture of his hand, the Templar knight explained that as far as he knew, there were no malicious men in the area, but you could never be certain. For that reason the shield of a Templar knight would probably have a chilling effect on their fighting spirit. He generously offered to let his shield hang there overnight and come back to get it at dawn when it would be time for all of them to move on.

When the Templar knight and his sergeant sat down near the muslin coverlet and began setting out their own bundles—dates, mutton, bread, and something unclean were visible—Yussuf could no longer hold back the laughter he had tried so hard to suppress. All the others looked up at him in surprise, since none of them had noticed anything amusing. The two Templar knights frowned, suspecting that they might be the objects of Yussuf's merriment.

He had to explain, saying that if there was one thing in the world he had never expected to have as night-time protection, it was in truth a shield with the worst emblem of the enemy. Although on the other hand this confirmed what he had always believed, that God in His omnipotence truly was not averse to joking with His children. And at this he thought they could all laugh.

Just then the Templar knight discovered a piece of smoked meat among the items his sergeant was setting out, and he said something harsh in Frankish and pointed with his long, sharp dagger. Red-faced, the sergeant removed the meat while the Templar knight apologized, shrugging his shoulders and saying that what was impure meat for one person in this world was good meat for another.

The three faithful now understood that a piece of pork had been lying in the middle of the food, and thus the entire meal was unclean. But Yussuf quickly whispered a reminder about God's word in those cases when a man finds himself in need, when laws are not laws in the same way as when a man is in his own house, and they all had to be content with that.

Yussuf blessed the food in the name of God the Merciful and Gracious, and the Templar knight blessed the food in the name of the Lord Jesus Christ and the Mother of God, and none of the five men showed any disdain for the beliefs of the others.

They began offering each other food, and finally, at Yussuf's invitation, the Templar knight accepted a piece of lamb baked in bread, slicing it in two with his grey, unadorned, extremely sharp dagger. He then handed half of it on the tip of his knife to his sergeant, who stuffed it into his mouth, hiding his distaste.

They ate in silence for a while. The faithful had placed the lamb baked in bread along with chopped green pistachios baked in spun sugar and honey on their side of the muslin coverlet. On their own side, the infidels had dried mutton, dates, and dry white bread.

"There is something I would like to ask you, Templar knight," said Yussuf after a while. He spoke in a low, intent voice, the way his closest friends knew he always talked when he had been thinking for a long time and wanted to understand something important.

"You are our host, we have accepted your invitation, and we will gladly answer your questions, but remember that our faith is the true faith, not yours," replied the Templar knight with an expression as if he were daring to joke about his own faith.

"Doubtless you know what I think about that matter, Templar knight, but here is my question. You rescued us, we who are your foes. I have already acknowledged that this is true, and I have thanked you. But now I want to know why you did it."

"We did not rescue our foes," said the Templar knight thoughtfully. "We have been after those six bandits for a long time. We've been following them at a distance for a week, waiting for the right moment. Our mission was to kill them, not to rescue you. But at the same time God happened to hold a protective hand over you, and neither you nor I can explain why."

"But you are the real Al Ghouti himself?" Yussuf persisted.

"Yes, that is so," said the Templar knight. "I am the one the nonbelievers in their own language now call Al Ghouti, but my name is *Arn de Gothia*, and my mission was to free the world of those six unworthy men, and I completed my mission. That is the whole of it."

"But why should someone like you do such a thing? Aren't you also the emir of the Knights Templar in your fortress in Gaza? A man of rank? Why should such a man take on such a lowly mission, and a dangerous one at that, setting out for these inhospitable regions just to kill bandits?"

"Because that was how our order came into being long before I was even born," replied the Templar knight. "From the beginning, when our troops had liberated God's Sepulcher, our people had no protection when they went on a pilgrimage down to the River Jordan and the site where Yahia, as you call him, once baptized the Lord Jesus Christ. And back then pilgrims carried all their possessions with them, instead of leaving them in safekeeping with us, as they do now. They were easy prey for bandits. Our order was created to protect them. Even today it is considered a mission of honor to offer protection to pilgrims and kill bandits. So it is not as you think, that this is a lowly mission we give to just anyone; on the contrary, it is the heart and soul of our order, a mission of honor, as I said. And God granted our prayers."

"You are right," Yussuf concluded with a sigh. "We should always protect pilgrims. How much easier life would be here in Palestine if we all did so. By the way, in which Frankish country is this Gothia located?"

"Not exactly in any *Frankish* country," replied the Templar knight with an amused glint in his eye, as if all his solemnity had suddenly vanished. "Gothia lies far north of the land of the Franks, at the ends of the earth. But what country do you come from? You don't speak Arabic as if you came from Mecca."

"I was born in Baalbek, but all three of us are Kurds," replied Yussuf in surprise. "This is my brother Fahkr, and this is my . . . friend Moussa. Where did you learn to speak the language of the faithful? Men like you do not usually end up in long captivity, do they?"

"No, that is true," replied the Templar knight. "Men like me don't end up in prison at all, and I'm sure that you know why. But I have lived in Palestine for ten years; I am not here to steal goods and then go home after half a year. Most of the men who work for the Knights Templar speak Arabic. My sergeant's name, by the way, is Armand de Gascogne; he's quite new here and doesn't understand much of what we're saying. That's why he is so silent, not like your men, who don't dare speak until you give them permission."

"Your eyes are sharp," murmured Yussuf, red-faced. "I am the eldest, you can already see grey hairs in my beard; I am the one who administers the family's money. We are merchants on our way to an important meeting in Cairo, and . . . I don't know what my brother and my friend would want to ask one of the enemy's knights. We are all peaceful men."

The Templar knight gave Yussuf a searching glance but said nothing for a while. He took his time eating some of the honey-drenched almonds. He paused and held up a piece of the delicacy to the firelight to examine it, concluding that these baked goods must have come from Aleppo. Then he pulled out his wine-skin and took a drink without asking permission or offering an apology, and handed the skin to his sergeant. Afterwards he leaned back comfortably and drew his big, thick white cloak around him with its terrifying red cross, looking at Yussuf as if he were assessing his opponent in a game of backgammon, not as a foe but as someone who must be evaluated.

"My unknown friend and foe, what use do any of us have for falsehoods when we eat together in peace and both have given our word not to harm each other?" he said at last. He spoke very easily, with no rancor in his voice. "You are a warrior, as I am. If God wills, we shall meet next time on the battlefield. Your clothes betray you; your horses betray you, just as your harnesses do, and your swords, which are leaning against the saddles over there. They are swords made in Damascus; none of them costs less than five hundred dinars in gold. Your peace and mine will soon be over; the truce is about to be ended, and if you don't know this now, you will know it soon. Let us therefore enjoy this strange hour. It's not often that a man gets to know his enemy. But let us not lie to each other."

Yussuf was struck by an almost irresistible urge to tell the Templar knight honestly who he was. But it was true that the truce would soon be ended, although it had not yet been felt on any battlefield. And their mutual oath not to harm each other, the reason they could sit and eat together at all, was valid only for this evening.

"You're right, Templar knight," he said at last. "*Insh'Allah*, if God wills, we will someday meet on the battlefield. But I also think, as you do, that a man should get to know his enemies, and you seem to know many more of the faithful than we know of the infidels. I now give my men permission to speak to you."

Yussuf leaned back, also drawing his cloak closer around him, and signaled to his brother and emir that they were allowed to speak. But they both hesitated, accustomed as they were to sitting an entire evening and just listening. Since none of them made any attempt to speak, the Templar knight leaned toward his sergeant and carried on a brief whispered conversation in Frankish.

"My sergeant wonders about one thing," he then explained. "Your weapons, your horses, and your clothes alone are worth more than those unfortunate bandits could ever have dreamed of. How did it happen that you chose this perilous road west of the Dead Sea without sufficient escort?"

"Because it is the quickest route, because an escort arouses a great deal of attention . . ." replied Yussuf slowly. He did not want to embarrass himself by again saying something that wasn't true, so he had to weigh his words. Any escort of his would certainly have attracted attention because it would have consisted of at least three thousand horsemen if it was to be considered safe.

"And because we trusted our horses. We didn't think a few worthless bandits or Franks would be able to catch us," he added swiftly.

"Wise but not wise enough," the Templar knight nodded. "But those six bandits have been plundering these regions for almost half a year. They knew the area like the backs of their hands, they could ride faster on these stretches than any of us could. That was what made them rich. Until God punished them."

"I would like to know one thing," said Fahkr, who now spoke for the first time and had to clear his throat because he was stumbling over his own words. "It is said that you Templar knights who reside in Al Aksa had a *minbar* there, a place of prayer for the faithful. And people have also told me that you Templar knights once struck a Frank who tried to prevent one of the faithful from praying. Is this really true?"

All three of the faithful now gave their full attention to the enemy. But the Templar knight smiled and first translated the question into Frankish for the sergeant, who at once nodded and burst out laughing.

"Yes, there is more truth to that than you know," said the Templar knight after thinking for a moment, or pretending to think in order to spur his listeners' interest. "We do have a *minbar* in *Templum Salomonis*, as we call *Al Aksa*, *"the most remote of prayer sites."* But that is not so unusual. In our fortress in Gaza we have a *majlis* every Thursday, the only day possible, and the witnesses then swear on God's Holy Scriptures, on the Torah, or on the Koran, and in some cases on something else entirely that they regard as holy. If the three of you were Egyptian merchants as you claimed, you would also know that our order conducts a great deal of business with the Egyptians, and none of them share our beliefs. *Al Aksa*, if you wish to use that name, is where we Templar knights have our headquarters, and where many people come as our guests. The problem is that every September new vessels arrive from Pisa or Genoa or the southern lands of the Franks with new men filled with the spirit and the zeal, perhaps not to enter paradise at once, but to kill unbelievers or at least lay hands on them. These newcomers create great difficulties for the rest of us, and each year, shortly after September, we always have disturbances in our own quarters because the newcomers turn against people of your faith, and then of course we have to deal with them harshly."

"You would kill your own kind for the sake of our people?" gasped Fahkr.

"Of course not!" replied the Templar knight with sudden vehemence. "For us it is a grave sin, just as it is in your faith, to kill any man who is a true believer. That can never come into question."

He went on after a brief pause, his good humor restored, "But nothing prevents us from giving rogues like that a good thrashing if they refuse to be persuaded. I myself have had the pleasure on several occasions . . ."

Quickly he leaned toward his sergeant and translated. When the sergeant began nodding and laughing in agreement, a great sense of relief seemed to come over everyone, and they all joined in with hearty laughter—perhaps a bit too hearty.

A gust of air, like the last sigh of the evening wind from the mountains near Al Khalil, suddenly carried the stench of the Templar knights toward the three faithful, and they shrank back, unable to hide their feelings.

The Templar knight noticed their embarrassment and rose to his feet immediately, suggesting that they change sides and wind direction around the muslin coverlet, where Emir Moussa was now setting out small cups of mocha. The three hosts complied with his suggestion at once, without saying anything offensive.

"We have our rules," explained the Templar knight apologetically as he settled into his new place. "You have rules about washing yourselves at all times of the day, and we have rules that forbid doing so. It is no worse than the fact that you have rules permitting hunting while we have ones forbidding it, except for lions; or that we drink wine and you do not."

"Wine is a different matter," objected Yussuf. "The prohibition against wine is a strict one, and it is God's word to the Prophet, may peace be with Him. But we are not like our enemies; just consider God's words in the seventh *Sura*: '*Who has forbidden the beautiful things that God has granted His servants and all the good He has given them for their sustenance?*' "

"Well yes," said the Templar knight. "Your scriptures say

many things. But if, for the sake of vanity, you want me to expose my modesty and make myself fair-smelling like worldly men, I might just as well ask you to stop calling me your enemy. For just listen to the words of your own scriptures, from the sixty-first *Sura*, words of your own Prophet, may peace be with Him: *'Faithful! Be God's disciples. Just as Jesus, the son of Mary, said to the white-clad: "Who will be my disciple for the sake of God?" And they answered: "We will be God's disciples!" Among the children of Israel, some came to believe in Jesus while others rejected him. But we supported those who believed in him against their enemies, and the faithful departed with victory.'* I particularly like the part about the white-clad . . ."

At these words Emir Moussa sprang to his feet as if he were about to reach for his sword, but halfway there he restrained himself and stopped. His face was red with anger when he stretched out his arm and pointed an accusatory finger at the Templar knight.

"Infidel!" he cried. "You speak the language of the Koran; that is one thing. But twisting God's words with blasphemy and ridicule is another matter that you would not be allowed to survive if it weren't for His Majes . . . because my friend Yussuf has given you his word!"

"Sit down and behave yourself, Moussa!" shouted Yussuf harshly, regaining his composure as Moussa obeyed his command. "What you heard were indeed the words of God, and they were from the sixty-first *Sura*, and they are words you ought to consider. And don't think, by the way, that the phrase "the white-robed" refers to what our guest spoke of in jest."

"No, of course it does not," the Templar knight hurried to smooth things over. "It refers to those who wore white robes long before my order existed; my clothing has nothing to do with it."

"How do you happen to be so familiar with the Koran?" asked Yussuf in his customary and quite calm tone of voice, as if no disruption had occurred, and his high rank had not been almost revealed.

"It is a wise thing to study your enemy; if you like, I can help you to understand the Bible," replied the Templar knight, as if trying to joke his way out of the topic, seeming to regret his clumsy invasion of the faithfuls' territory.

Yussuf was about to utter a stern reply to his lighthearted talk of entering into blasphemous studies, when he was interrupted by a long drawn-out, horrifying scream. The scream turned into something that sounded like scornful laughter, rolling down toward them and echoing off the mountainsides above. All five men froze and listened; Emir Moussa immediately began rattling off the words the faithful use to conjure up the *jinni* of the desert. Then the scream came again, but now it sounded as if it came from several spirits of the abyss, as if they were talking to each other, as if they had discovered the little fire below and the only people in the area.

The Templar knight leaned forward and whispered a few words in Frankish to his sergeant, who nodded at once, stood up, and buckled on his sword. He drew his black cloak tighter, bowed to his unbeliever hosts, and then, without saying a word, turned on his heel and disappeared into the darkness.

"You must excuse this rudeness," said the Templar knight. "But the fact is that we have the scent of blood and fresh meat up in our camp, and horses that must be tended to."

He didn't seem to think he needed to offer any further explanation, and with a bow he stretched out his mocha cup for Emir Moussa to refill it. The emir's hand shook slightly as he poured.

"You send your sergeant into the darkness and he obeys without blinking?" said Fahkr in a voice that sounded slightly hoarse.

"Yes," said the Templar knight. "A man must obey even if he feels fear. But I don't think that Armand does. The darkness is more of a friend for the man who wears a black cloak than the one who wears white, and Armand's sword is sharp and his hand steady. Wild dogs, those spotted beasts with their horrid barking, are also known for their cowardice, are they not?"

"But are you certain it was only wild dogs we heard?" asked Fahkr doubtfully.

"No," replied the Templar knight. "There is much we do not know between heaven and hell; no one can ever be certain. But the Lord is our shepherd, and we shall not want, even though we wander through the valley of the shadow of death. That is doubtless what Armand is praying as he walks along in the dark right now. That is what I would pray, at any rate. If God has measured out our time and wishes to call us home, there is nothing we can do, of course. But until then we cleave the skulls of wild dogs as we do those of our enemies, and in that respect I know that you who believe in the Prophet, may peace be with Him, and deny the Son of God, think exactly as we do. Am I not right, Yussuf?"

"You are right, Templar knight," Yussuf confirmed. "But then where is the borderline between reason and belief, between fear of and trust in God? If a man must obey, as your sergeant must obey, does that make his fear any less?"

"When I was young . . . well, I am not yet a particularly old man," said the Templar knight, seeming to think deeply, "I was still preoccupied with that sort of question. It is good for your mind; your thoughts grow nimble from exercising your mind. But nowadays I am afraid I grow sluggish. You obey. You conquer evil. Afterwards you thank God—that is all."

"And if you do not conquer your enemy?" asked Yussuf in a gentle voice, which those who knew him did not recognize as his normal voice.

"Then you die, at least in the case of Armand and myself," replied the Templar knight. "And on Judgment Day you and I will be measured and weighed, and where you will then end up,

I cannot say, even though I know what you yourself believe. But if I die here in Palestine, my place will be in paradise."

"You truly believe that?" asked Yussuf in his strange, gentle voice.

"Yes, I believe that," replied the Templar knight.

"Then tell me one thing: Is that promise actually in your Bible?"

"No, not exactly; it does not say that exactly."

"But you are still quite certain?"

"Yes, the Holy Father in Rome has promised . . ."

"But he is only a man! What man can promise you a place in paradise, Templar knight?"

"But Muhammed too was merely a man! And *you* believe in his promise, forgive me, may peace be to his name."

"Muhammed, may peace be with him, was God's messenger, and God said: *'But the messenger and those who follow him in faith and strive for the sake of God, offering up their property and lives, shall be rewarded with goodness in this life and in the next, and everything they touch will prosper.'* Those words are very clear, are they not? And it goes on . . ."

"Yes! In the next verse of the ninth *Sura*," the Templar knight interjected brusquely. " *'God has prepared for them gardens of pleasure, watered by streams, where they shall remain for all eternity. This is the great and glorious victory!'* So, we understand each other, I presume? None of this is foreign to you, Yussuf. And by the way, the difference between us is that I have no possessions, I have put myself in God's hands, and when He decides, I will die for His sake. Your own beliefs do not contradict what I say."

"Your knowledge of God's word is truly great, Templar knight," said Yussuf, but at the same time he was pleased that he had caught his enemy in a trap, and his companions could see this.

"Yes, as I said, you should know your enemy," said the Templar knight, for the first time a little uncertain, as if he too realized that Yussuf had backed him into a corner.

"But if you speak in this way, you are not my enemy," said Yussuf. "You quote from the Holy Koran, which is God's Word. What you say does apply to me, but not to you for the time being. For the faithful, all of this is as clear as water, but what is it for you? In truth, I know as much about Jesus as you know about the Prophet, may peace be with him. But what did Jesus say about the Holy War? Did Jesus speak a single word about you entering paradise if you killed me?"

"Let us not quarrel about this," said the Templar knight with a confident wave of his hand, as if everything had suddenly become petty, although they could all see his uncertainty. "Our beliefs are not the same, even though they have many similarities. But we have to live in the same land, fighting each other in the worse case, making treaties and conducting business in the best case. Now let us speak of other matters. It is my wish, as your guest."

They were all aware how Yussuf had driven his opponent into a corner where he had no more defenses. Jesus had clearly never said anything about it being pleasing to God to kill Saracens. But when pressed harder, the Templar knight had still managed to wriggle out of the difficult situation by referring to the faithfuls' own unwritten laws of hospitality. And so his wish had to be granted; he was the guest, after all.

"In truth, you do know a great deal about your enemy, Templar knight," said Yussuf. Both his voice and expression showed that he was very pleased at having won the discussion.

"As we agreed, it is necessary to know your enemy," replied the Templar knight in a low voice, his eyes downcast.

They sat in silence for a while, gazing into their mocha cups, since it seemed difficult to start up the conversation in a natural way after Yussuf's victory. But then the silence was again shattered by the sound of beasts. This time they all knew it was animals and not some devilish creature, and it sounded as if they were attacking someone or something, and then as if they were fleeing, with howls of pain and death.

"Armand's sword is sharp, as I said," murmured the Templar knight.

"Why in the name of peace did you take your corpses with you?" asked Fahkr, who was thinking the same thing as his brothers of the faith.

"Of course it would have been better to take them alive. Then they would not have smelled so foul on the way home, and they could have traveled with ease. But tomorrow it will be a hot day; we must start our journey early to get them to Jerusalem before they begin to stink too much," replied the Templar knight.

"But if you had taken them prisoner, if you had taken them alive to Al Quds, what would have happened to them then?" persisted Fahkr.

"We would have turned them over to our emir in Jerusalem, who is one of the highest ranking in our order. He would have turned them over to the worldly powers, and they would have been disrobed, except for that which covers their modesty, and hung up on the wall by the rock," replied the Templar knight, as if it were quite obvious.

"But you have already killed them. Why not disrobe them here and leave them to the fate they deserve? Why do you defend their bodies against the wild animals?" asked Fahkr, as if he did not want to give up or did not understand.

"We will still hang them there," replied the Templar knight. "Everyone must see that whoever robs pilgrims will end up hanging there. That is a holy promise from our order, and it must always be kept, as long as God helps us."

"But what will you do with their weapons and clothes?" wondered Emir Moussa, speaking as if he wanted to bring the conversation down to a more practical level. "Surely they must have had quite a few valuables on them."

"Yes, but they are all stolen goods," replied the Templar knight, some of his old self-assurance back. "Except for their weapons and amour, for which we have no use. But their thieves' cache is in a grotto up where Armand and I have our camp. We will take heavily laden horses home with us tomorrow; keep in mind that those beasts have been plundering here for more than half a year."

"But you are not allowed to own anything," objected Yussuf mildly, raising his right eyebrow, as if he thought that he had once again won the argument.

"No, I am not allowed to own anything!" exclaimed the Templar knight in surprise. "If you think we would take the thieves' treasures for our own, you are greatly mistaken. We will place all the stolen goods outside the Church of the Holy Sepulcher next Sunday, and if those who have been robbed can find their possessions, they can have them back."

"But surely most of those who were robbed are now dead," said Yussuf quietly.

"They may have heirs who are alive, but whatever is not claimed will be donated to our order," replied the Templar knight.

"That is a most interesting explanation for what I have heard, that you consider yourselves too good to plunder a battlefield," said Yussuf with a smile, seeming to think he had won another exchange of words.

"No, we do not take plunder from battlefields," replied the Templar knight coldly. "But that should not present a problem, since there are so many others who do. If we have taken part in a victory, we turn at once toward God. If you would like to hear what your own Koran has to say about plundering a battlefield . . ."

"Thank you, no!" Yussuf interrupted him, holding up a hand

in warning. "We would prefer not to return to a topic of conversation since it would seem that you, an infidel, know more than we do about the Word of the Prophet, may peace be with him. Let me instead ask you a very candid question."

"Yes. Ask me a candid question, and it shall be given the answer it deserves," replied the Templar knight, holding up his hands, palm out, to show, in the manner of the faithful, that he agreed to change the topic of conversation.

"You said that the truce between us would soon be over. Is it Brins Arnat you are referring to?"

"You know a great deal, Yussuf. Brins Arnat, whom we call Reynald de Châtillon, has begun plundering again. And by the way he is no "prince" but an evil man who is unfortunately allied with the Knights Templar. This I know, and I regret it. I would rather not be his ally, but I obey orders. But no, he is not the major problem."

"Then it must be something about that new *prince*, who came from the land of the Franks with a great army. What is it he is called: *Filus* something or other?"

"No," said the Templar knight with a smile. "He is indeed *Filus*, meaning the son of someone. His name is Philip of Flanders, he is a duke, and yes, he came with a great army. But now I must warn you before we continue this conversation."

"Why is that?" asked Yussuf, feigning nonchalance. "I have your word. Have you ever broken a vow you have sworn?"

"I once made a vow that I have not yet been able to fulfill; it will take ten years before I can do so, if it is God's will. But I have never broken a promise and, may God help me, I never will."

"Well then. Why should our truce be broken because of the arrival of someone named *Filus* from some Flamsen? Surely such things happen all the time."

The Templar knight gave Yussuf a long, searching look, but

Yussuf did not avert his eyes. This went on for some time; both refused to give in.

"You wish to keep secret your identity," said the Templar knight at last, without taking his eyes off Yussuf. "But few men could know so much about what goes on in the world of war; certainly not someone who claims to be a merchant on his way to Cairo. If you insist on speaking more about this, I can no longer pretend that I do not know who you are; a man who has spies, a man who knows. There are not many such men."

"You have my word also; remember that, Templar knight."

"Of all the unbelievers, your word is no doubt the one most of us would trust most."

"You honor me with your words. So, why will our truce be broken?"

"Ask your men to leave us if you will continue this conversation, Yussuf."

Yussuf pondered this for a moment as he pensively tugged on his beard. If the Templar knight truly understood who he was talking to, would it then be easier for him to kill and at the same time break his word? No, that was unlikely. Considering how this man had behaved when he killed earlier in the evening, he had no need to make it easier to betray his vow; he would have drawn his sword long ago.

Yet it was difficult to understand his demand, which seemed unreasonable. At the same time, no one would particularly benefit if it were met. In the end Yussuf's curiosity won out over his caution.

"Leave us," he commanded curtly. "Go to sleep close by; you can clean up here in the morning. Remember that we are in the field, under camp rules."

Fahkr and Emir Moussa hesitated. They started to get to their feet as they looked at Yussuf, but his stern glance made them obey. They bowed to the Templar knight and withdrew. Yussuf waited in silence until his brother and his closest bodyguard had moved far enough away and could be heard arranging their bedding.

"I don't think my brother and Moussa will have an easy time falling asleep."

"No," said the Templar knight. "But neither will they be able to hear what we say."

"Why is it so important for them not to hear what we say?"

"It is not important," said the Templar knight, smiling. "What *is* important is that you know they won't hear what *you* say. Then our conversation will be more candid."

"For a man who lives in a monastery, you know a great deal about human nature."

"In the monastery we learn much about human nature; more than you imagine. Now to what is more important. I will speak only of things that I am positive you already know, since anything else would be treason. But let us examine the situation. As you know, a new Frankish prince is coming. He will remain here for some time; he has everyone's blessing back home for his holy mandate in God's service, and so on. He has brought a great army along with him. So what will he do?"

"Acquire riches as fast as possible since he has had great expenses."

"Precisely, Yussuf, precisely. But will he go against Saladin himself, and Damascus?"

"No. Then he would risk losing everything."

"Precisely, Yussuf. We understand each other completely, and we can speak freely, now that your subordinates are out of earshot. So where will the new plunderer and his army go?"

"Towards a city that is sufficiently strong and sufficiently wealthy, but I do not know which one."

"Precisely. Nor do I know which one. Homs? Hama? Perhaps. Aleppo? No, too far away and too strong a city. Let us say Homs or Hama, as the most obvious. What will our worldly Christian king in Jerusalem and the royal army do then?"

"They do not have much choice. They will join in with the plundering even though they would rather use the new forces to attack Saladin."

"Precisely, Yussuf. You know everything, you understand everything. So now we both know what the situation is. What do we do about it?"

"To begin with, you and I will both keep our word."

"Of course, that goes without saying. But what else do we do?"

"We use this time of peace between us to understand each other better. I may never have the chance to talk to a Templar knight again. You may never have the chance to talk to . . . an enemy such as myself."

"No, you and I will probably meet only on this one occasion in our lives."

"The singular whim of God . . . But then let me ask you, Templar knight, what is needed more than God if we, the faithful, are to vanquish you?"

"Two things. What Saladin is now doing: uniting all Saracens against us. That is already taking place. But the other thing is treason among those of us on the side of Jesus Christ, betrayal or grave sins, for which God will punish us."

"But if not betrayal or these grave sins?"

"Then neither of us will ever win, Yussuf. The difference between us is that you Saracens can lose one battle after another. You mourn your dead and you soon have a new army on the march. We Christians can lose only a great battle, and we are not that foolish. If we have the advantage, we attack. If we are at a disadvantage, we seek refuge in our fortresses. It can go on in this fashion forever."

"So our war will last forever?"

"Perhaps, perhaps not. Some of us . . . Do you know who Count Raymond de Tripoli is?"

"Yes, I know . . . know of him. And?"

"If Christians like him should win power in the kingdom of Jerusalem, and you have on your side a leader like Saladin, then there can be peace, a just peace, in any case something better than eternal war. Many of us Templar knights think as Count Raymond does. But to return to our previous topic concerning what is going to happen right now. The Hospitallers followed the royal army and the "prince" up to Syria. We Templar knights did not."

"I already know that."

"Yes, doubtless you know this; because your name is Yussuf ibn Ayyub Salah al-Din, the one we call Saladin in our language."

"May God be merciful to us, now that you know this."

"God is merciful to us by granting us this strange conversation during the last hours of peace between us."

"And we will both keep our word."

"You surprise me with your uneasiness about that point. You are the only one of our enemies who is known for always keeping his word. I am a Templar knight. We always keep our word. Enough said about that matter."

"Yes, enough about that matter. But now, my dear enemy, at this late hour before a dawn when we both have urgent errands, you with your foul-smelling corpses and I with something else that I will not discuss but which you certainly can imagine, what do we do now?"

"We take advantage of this only opportunity that God may give us in life to speak sensibly with the worst of all enemies. There is one thing that you and I can agree on . . . forgive me if I address you so plainly now that I know you are the Sultan of both Cairo and Damascus."

"No one but God hears us, as you so wisely arranged. I wish for you to use the informal means of address on this one night."

"We agreed on one thing, I think. We are risking eternal war because neither side can win."

"True. But I will win, I have sworn to win."

"As have I. Eternal war then?"

"That does not sound promising for the future."

"Then we will continue, even though I am merely a simple emir among the Knights Templar, and you are the only one of our foes in a long time that we have had reason to fear. Where should we begin now?"

They began with the question of the pilgrims' safety. That was the most obvious. That was the reason they had met in the first place, if they sought a human explanation for it and did not look solely to God's will in all things. But even though they both firmly believed, at least when they spoke aloud, that God's will guided everything, neither of them was a stranger to the idea that man, with his free will, could also bring about great calamities as well as great happiness. This was a cornerstone in both of their faiths.

They talked for a long time that night. At dawn, when Fahkr found his older brother—the glorious prince, the light of religion, the commander of the faithful in the Holy War, the water in the desert, the Sultan of Egypt and Syria, the hope of the faithful, the man whom the infidels for all time would call by the simple name Saladin—he was sitting with his chin resting on his knees, huddled under his cloak which was wrapped around him, and staring into the dying embers.

The white shield with the evil red cross was gone, as was the Templar knight. Saladin wearily looked up at his brother, almost as if he had awakened from a dream.

"If all our foes were like Al Ghouti, we would never win," he said thoughtfully. "On the other hand, if all our foes were like him, victory would no longer be necessary."

Fahkr did not understand what his brother and prince meant but supposed it was mostly meaningless weary mutterings, as had happened so many times before when Yussuf stayed up too long and brooded.

"We must head out; we have a hard ride to Al Arish," said Saladin, getting stiffly to his feet. "War awaits, we will soon be victorious."

It was true that war awaited; that was as written. But it was also written that Saladin and Arn Magnusson de Gothia would soon meet again on the battlefield, and that only one of them would come away victorious.